The Actor

The Actor

CHRIS MACDONALD

MICHAEL  JOSEPH

MICHAEL JOSEPH

UK | USA | Canada | Ireland | Australia
India | New Zealand | South Africa

Michael Joseph is part of the Penguin Random House group of companies
whose addresses can be found at global.penguinrandomhouse.com.

First published 2024
001

Copyright © Chris MacDonald, 2024

The moral right of the author has been asserted

Set in 13.5/16pt Garamond MT Std
Typeset by Jouve (UK), Milton Keynes
Printed and bound in Great Britain by Clays Ltd, Elcograf S.p.A.

The authorized representative in the EEA is Penguin Random House Ireland,
Morrison Chambers, 32 Nassau Street, Dublin D02 YH68

A CIP catalogue record for this book is available from the British Library

HARDBACK ISBN: 978–0–241–65822–2
TRADE PAPERBACK ISBN: 978–0–241–65823–9

www.greenpenguin.co.uk

For Sadie and Otis.

Never be afraid of throwing yourself
into what you love, but never
let it define you.

Act 1

I.i

I didn't know until much later but it was me, the night I saw Louanne's body hanging above our bed, I awoke the ghost. I had sprinted through the forest, oblivious to everything around me, knowing if I got there in time I could save her. I tripped on mangled roots, stumbled through dead leaves, chest heaving from what felt like a lifetime sprinting. But as I burst open the cabin door, the air thumped out of my lungs. I was too late. I barrelled across the floor anyway, took out my knife and cut her down, held on to her for too long, wheeling her round, squeezing the life back in, face buried in her skirts. But Louanne was dead. I laid her down, gazed through a hole in the roof at the stars over the Wasatch Mountains and groaned for a God I didn't believe in. I collapsed onto my knees and even though waves of tears overwhelmed me, I knew it was hopeless. After a short time shaking at the foot of the bed, I looked up at my teacher, Jonathan Dors. His face was set in a death mask.

I sank back on my haunches and as if a lens had been

twisted, reality came into focus. The camera rig loomed over us. Tower lights arrowed at me like siege weapons. Near twenty black-clad crew squeezed into the cabin behind them. We'd been shooting the climactic scene of *Woodsman* since ten o'clock that morning. It was midnight. Jonathan murmured something to my manager, Vanessa, and she asked for the room. The figures emptied out, leaving only Jonathan, Van and me.

Jonathan took slow steps towards the bed, every creak of the floorboards making me wince, dragged a chair from the desk and sat, his domed head just above the lifeless eyes of the mannequin of Louanne.

'That night at The Conservatoire,' he said.

'I know.'

'It is a gift for this scene.'

I looked up into his crab-eyes.

'So. Use. It.' He separated the words with a scalpel. 'Take yourself back.'

I closed my eyes, breath held at the thought of what he was asking me to do, and took myself back twenty years to the dark halls of my old drama school, The Conservatoire. Invisible hands led me along the corridor, beckoning me through the open doors of Room 1.

'The smell,' Jonathan said. Dust, dripping wax. My forearm started to tremor, none of the manufactured waterworks I'd just been trying to fool the camera with. Good, it was good. 'The music.' I heard the choir, a requiem playing through speakers on the concrete pillars of the school's main rehearsal space.

4

'Now look,' he said.

I shook my head.

'You know you must.'

I could barely hear his voice as I pictured the Room 1 stage in semi-darkness and found myself, eyes closed still in the real world, turning towards the severed rope from where I had cut down the mannequin of Louanne.

'This is too much for him, Jonathan,' Vanessa said.

'Quit meddling!' I said, in my character Harrison's Midwestern growl.

'Fuck sake,' my manager said as she left, arctic parka rustling as she stormed out of the cabin.

'See it here,' Jonathan said. 'It's essential, for the scene.'

My eyes sprang open and there it was, a different body, the body from that night twenty years ago, swinging above the bed. Tears pricked, I was desperate to look away, but Jonathan was right, I had to see it.

'Think about what you did,' he hissed in a whisper.

I bit down on my top lip, wrung the fake-blood-soaked sheets in my fingers, pain in my stomach like an organ bursting at the thought. Jonathan scraped back the chair. A voice barked an order somewhere in the distance. The crew flooded in.

'First positions,' someone said. In seconds the cabin was full, my make-up checked, Louanne hung back up again. But I was still at The Conservatoire, biting my lip so hard it bled, struggling to hold the pain inside, waiting for the moment. Someone moved me to the doorway. I had to do everything in my power not to throw my arms around the girl, Van's assistant it must have been, and beg her to take me away. But then the machine, my lover and torturer for the past two decades, cranked up its gears.

'Sound.'

'Speed.'

'Camera.'

'Rolling.'

'And action.'

Hours later I was still in the cabin. Production had given me the night to do some rituals to help say goodbye to my character. I mopped the fake blood from the floor and built a fire to burn the mannequin. As I stood at the blistered mirror in the corner of the room paring back Harrison's frontier fuzz, Adam's face, my face, emerged, unfamiliar. A boy I might once have known.

Jonathan said nothing after that final take so I knew I'd given him what he wanted. The crew burst into spontaneous applause when they called cut. It was my last scene on the film. Bryce, the director, grabbed me by the shoulder and gave a speech. There were whoops. There were whistles. It felt like standing in front of a firing squad. They all expected me to give them something in return, to thank them, clap back, smile even. But cracking a grin after having been back to that night in Room 1 would have felt like walking on a broken bone. I always send crewmembers something afterwards, try to make it personal, to let them know how much the work we did together meant to me. It didn't make up for refusing to break character, ignoring them, but I needed them to know that whatever I was doing to prepare, however weird or uncomfortable it might have been for them, we were all there for the same thing, to create great work.

When I'd taken off the beard and hair, I thought of sinking into the metal tub they'd left filled, but instead wrapped myself in a floor rug and went outside, sat by the fire and drank in the forest a final time until all I could taste was sap. I could already feel the curdling sense of loss for my character Harrison, for the space his life had filled in me. The mannequin squealed a high, reluctant firework sound. I looked through the smoke at its Disney princess eyes and extraterrestrial cheekbones, the perfect facsimile of my co-star Emmy Reed's face, and realised how much I would miss her too.

Although fifteen years younger than me, Emmy was a fellow Conservatoire alumnus, and getting to work like we had during our training bonded us in a way you rarely find in the industry. We spent most of the shoot in character, working on exercises, hunting, shovelling snow, two nights repairing our cabin's roof in the lashing rain after shooting all day. As the weeks passed, we fell into that closeness actors sometimes talk about in interviews but can never really describe, somewhere between siblings and amicable former lovers. But the shoot was over. I had to return to myself and although Emmy and I would rekindle our friendship for the press junkets, we both knew, by then, it would be another performance.

The air seemed to become thicker, as if fog had

descended, though it was a clear night. A cold breeze swirled around my neck and although I was alone, I had the sense someone was watching me. My body felt weighed down with rocks and I began to drift towards sleep.

Something doggish growled inside the cabin. I went back in. There was no animal but the sound continued, insistent. It was my phone vibrating against the desk drawer where it lived – a bigger surprise than if it had been a coyote. Vanessa was the only person who had the number, and she would never call when I was trying to leave a character behind.

I yanked the stuck drawer open and watched the phone trembling. A gust of something moved the cabin's wooden slats. I answered and for a moment there was nothing. A click on the end of the line. Static silence.

Then a voice I hadn't heard for two decades. A voice that couldn't be on the end of a phone because dead people can't speak.

'How could you?' it said.

I looked at the rope above the bed. It seemed to sway, feathered by invisible fingers. I garbled something like 'What?', trying to clear my throat of a basement full of dust. Static on the end of the line. The click.

'How could you?' The same words, the same unmistakable, impossible voice.

'I—' I tried to find words, to answer a question I never asked. The line went dead.

I dropped the phone, senses overrun like I'd been swallowed by a wave. The world went black.

The next thing I remember, I was being hauled out of the cabin's nineteenth-century bathtub by Vanessa's assistant, Amber.

'Please,' she was saying. 'Adam, please.' She had a hand under my armpit, pounding on my chest with the other. I was fully clothed, water pouring down my front. Amber was flooded with relief as she felt my body becoming conscious in her arms. She sat back, looked around, no idea what to do. 'I'll call Vanessa,' she said.

'Don't,' I said, 'don't tell her, please.'

Amber stared at me, green eyes near vibrating with the adrenalin, before nodding. It would remain our secret.

'What happened, Adam?' she said, some moments later, voice cracking. I thought of the phone call. What could I tell the person who brought me bottles of water, this young woman I barely knew?

'I must have fallen asleep,' I said. 'In the bath.' She looked at the floor, took a breath, trying to believe me. The water was cold, the dawn breaking above us. I glanced at the desk where my phone had been. The drawer was shut. 'Did you close that?' I asked.

'What?'

'Have you got my phone?' Amber's brow furrowed. She finessed wisps of auburn hair behind her ears as she walked over to the desk. I'd slept in the cabin for the last six weeks in character and didn't want any contact with modern technology, but Vanessa insisted she have a way to contact me. Amber tried to open the drawer, but it was locked. She took a key out of a box and opened it.

'It's here,' she said.

'What?'

'The phone's in here, where it's always been.'

I blinked, listened to the silence, trying to conjure the voice, the voice that felt so real. But I couldn't hear it. I opened my eyes and saw the rope hanging stock still above the bed.

No body, no voice, just a thread above an old bed.

I was at Ganymede, a rehabilitation centre in the hills near Fresno when Vanessa brought me the script of *Woodsman*. I was in exile, a method actor who'd taken things too far, an embarrassment to the industry. I wasn't sure I'd act again.

In my twenties, dirt blond hair cut short, pale skin that journalists called 'translucent', they couldn't get enough of me as the broken boy. From a scene-stealing role playing a child killer to a troubled poet in a period thing, before my breakout playing Picasso's impotent best friend in *Casagemas* and, the following year, a vain soldier who broke into Auschwitz to save women and children in *Coward*. There were innumerable articles about the way I prepared for my roles, the mind-boggling commitment to become the characters I was playing. I became an effervescent spring of fascination. I was nominated for an Oscar for *Casagemas* and *Coward* and was expected to win for the latter. I won neither. I was crushed for some time, but at The Conservatoire we were taught the only way to overcome obstacles and get what we wanted, both for ourselves and our characters, was to work harder, to go further.

Jonathan and I had continued working together after I left The Conservatoire.

He would read scripts and help decide what movies to choose, then set out how I should go about preparing each character. It was a fruitful collaboration but after the second Oscar loss, I started choosing ever more traumatised protagonists, thinking that pushing myself to the limit in my preparation, reaching for extremity in performance, would be my route back to the Academy Awards. An Arctic researcher who gets shut-in for two years, the cracked cellist Bjorn Sveltedt, the serial killer Paul Dettins. With hindsight, the scripts weren't strong enough, but I was convinced I could single-handedly elevate them, so desperate was I to win an Oscar and write my name indelibly in the pantheon of the greats.

When the films faltered, as they were always bound to, my reputation made me an easy scapegoat. Directors called me too intense, too uncompromising, as if my taking my job seriously had kiboshed their projects rather than the sub-par scripts and myriad mistakes they had made. But people liked the narrative. The media, who had lauded my dedication, began to enjoy painting me as pretentious, ridiculous even. So, ten years after my second Oscar defeat, having become more curiosity than movie star, it was an enormous risk when they hired me for *The Bends*, a big-money love story set amongst professional divers. It was a beautiful screenplay, ripe for awards, and had a marketing budget big enough to get us amongst them. Vanessa and I had very high hopes.

My dad had died six or seven months before the shoot and even though I felt fine as we'd never had a great relationship, Van suggested I take a more measured approach to my preparation for the movie. She told me to toe the line, everyone else's line, to 'keep things sane'. I spent a month training for the dives with Paulo the divemaster, but that aside, stuck to learning my lines and not thinking too much about the character. It seemed to work. The execs, production, Van, everyone was very, very pleased with me.

But when the shoot began, my acting felt so general, vague, the sort of work anyone could do. I expected the director to take me aside and ask for more, for someone – Vanessa – to tell me I was phoning it in. But no one said a thing. They were all so delighted I was turning up and standing in the right place, so they could tick the box on their shot list and move on to whatever was scheduled next. I was dumbfounded. I could feel myself acting badly and no one seemed to notice.

I found myself standing on sound stages, staring at the machinery around me, at the hundreds of skilled professionals who'd dedicated their lives to the movies, the thousands of dollars spent every second, the cinematographer crafting shots like fine art that wouldn't matter because I was giving an empty performance the audience would forget in moments. And not a single person around me seemed to care. I was just about managing to keep my head above water, telling myself I was doing my job and if the producers were happy, my reservations, my standards, didn't matter, but at the hotel one night the director asked me what it was like training under Jonathan and I realised that one day he would see me giving this milksop performance. It pushed me over the ledge into a deep pit of depression.

Finding myself almost unable to leave my trailer to go to set, I resolved to try and channel my old drama-school teacher – what would Jonathan do? So when we were filming one of the final scenes in the movie, in which my character Andrew nearly drowns trying to save his daughter from a wrecked biplane, I detached my safety harness before I was due to dive down. I knew I couldn't fake the panic and terror of a man seconds away from a slow, certain death, it had to be real.

I don't know how long I was under before they realised, but I'd started to see a disco ball of spinning lights behind my eyelids and was only semi-aware of someone plunging in and dragging me up to safety. It must have been the cortisol coursing through me – I don't think I'm a violent person – but once I was conscious, I got up and went for Paulo, the divemaster who'd rescued me. I was so out of it I could barely land a punch, which was lucky because I was unlikely to win a fight against Paulo. I was kicked off the film and the story – my nearly drowning myself for the sake of the scene – got out. The reputation I had as being obsessive, intense, a little too committed, changed to a much simpler label – crazy.

For a few months, it was open season on me. Fight directors shared anecdotes about my asking them to kick me in the throat; co-stars leaked stories of overnight exercises in waterlogged trenches; Anais, a former co-star I'd been convinced to date, told the press I'd 'fucked like a jaguar' while playing a mercenary in *North of Bamako* but couldn't get it up while doing *Casagemas*.

It was the fallout from *The Bends* that led me to Ganymede. I'd been there for four months when Vanessa arrived with *Woodsman*. She was waiting for me in the recalibration area next to the pool, surrounded by yuccas and the smell of watered grass. She wore a coral suit, arrow-straight dark hair pulled over into a cord on one side of her neck, the manuscript held by her hip like a sheathed sword. I had told her I didn't want to act again, convinced myself even, but the electric charge of anticipation I felt when I saw the screenplay, a child on Christmas Eve, exposed my proclamations about retirement as bullshit. Which, of course, Van had known.

But she didn't hand it to me straight away.

'The curious incident of the harness in the fucking water tank,' she said with uncharacteristic earnestness. 'You promise you weren't— It was for the character, wasn't it?'

'What do you mean?'

She cleared her throat. 'You weren't trying to hurt yourself?'

'No, I told you. Not at all.'

She took a deep breath and sat opposite, smoothing out the creases in her trousers. She looked at the script's cover for a moment longer before sliding it across the table. For the next two hours, she sat tapping matching coral nails on her phone, drinking earth-coloured liquid the staff brought, pretending she wasn't scrutinising my every twitch as I read the script.

Van and I were in the same year at The Conservatoire: Group 28. But after we finished, she pivoted into the family business. Her father was Alasdair Nixon, a founding partner of GNM, one of the most illustrious acting agencies at the time I joined them, and Van had looked after me as my de facto manager almost ever since. We weren't close while we were training, not until the last year, but she had been the most consistent presence in my life since we left. The transactional nature of our relationship continually relaminated the thread that bound us twenty years before, which would have frayed and severed had we merely been friends.

As I turned the final page of the screenplay my hands were shaking.

'Oh shit, you've got that face,' she said when I looked up. 'Like a fucking matador.'

'This is . . . perfect,' I said.

'Jesus, don't be all—I thought you'd say no.'

'You don't think I can do it?'

'I know you can do it, whole-fucking-heartedly. But I'm not sure you should.'

'Why bring it then?'

'You're an actor, Adam, there's really nothing else you can do.' She plucked goji berries out of a bowl of dried fruit. 'I wanted you to have some time to get better, but we won't ever get sent another script that lines up so well,' she said. I edged forward on my lounger, chest thrumming as

15

I realised what she might be about to say. 'Timing, optics, the meta-narrative. This is the sort of phoenix-from-the-ashes circle-jerk the Academy gets all juiced about.'

'They wouldn't give me an Oscar now,' I said. 'After what I did?'

'Come on, Ad, monumental fuck-ups mean you can do the whole hero's journey thing and, with the right film, the right circumstances—'

I saw her right eye twitch at the thought of what happened that night at The Conservatoire.

'I think it could happen. But, only if you're in the right frame of mind.'

I knew. As I read, I'd felt it in my stomach, a physical yearning to play Harrison. The enforced break, my first without either shooting a film or preparing for one in more than twenty years, had felt far too real for me. They sent me to Ganymede to get 'better', but the best I ever felt was when I was being someone else. Jonathan said therapists were poisonous for the actor, so I'd spent my months there sitting silently in group sessions, collecting the other participants' stories for future roles while drinking my body weight in cucumber water. I did at least leave the place well-hydrated.

'I have to do it,' I said, wafting the screenplay in front of me like a burning knot of thyme. Van put her head back and looked at the palm trees above, as staff in beige uniforms primped cushions on nearby benches.

'If you have to go back to that night, Ad, I'm not sure whether you'd come back.'

I hummed out a laugh and took one of the berries Van had piled up on a paper serviette for me.

'We have to do it,' I said.

She nodded, head still turned to the sky, unable to look at me. 'It's a gift.' Which turned out to be prescient, because nine months after we shot the final scene of *Woodsman*, Van called to say I'd been nominated for an Oscar.

Two hours after she'd delivered the news, I was doing a roundtable for *The Hollywood Reporter* with my fellow nominees. The ceremony was just over a month away.

'When you find her hanging there—' said Carl Dillane, two-time Oscar-winner, six-times nominated, the so-called nicest man in Hollywood and foundation-stone of the movie-making establishment. 'Camera tight in. I swear to God I saw your soul collapsing. Extra-ordinary, truly. I never really understood that method stuff but when I saw that? Whoo!'

I took a sip of water and glanced at the other actors around the table in the TV-set conference room. This sort of thing seemed to come so naturally to them. They had thought-through, crafted personas, but I had never felt comfortable playing myself and, despite the universal acclaim I'd received for *Woodsman*, I still felt like a pariah.

I cleared my throat and took a moment to hear my real accent before I spoke. I'd been developing a voice for my next role as a Soviet defector, and even so many months after wrapping on *Woodsman*, Van still had to point out to me when I'd fallen back into Harrison's Midwestern vowels.

'Laurence Olivier, there are two stories about him,' I said, pulling up the sleeves of a black corduroy jacket. They'd put us all in different textures of black, as if actors talking about their craft wasn't pretentious enough. 'The first one you'll know, him and Dustin Hoffman doing *Marathon Man*. Olivier's on set and Hoffman turns up a wreck, no sleep for three days, having run himself ragged all night around the city, in agony for this torture scene he has to do. Olivier asks him what the hell he's doing and Hoffman says, "I'm getting into the character." Olivier stares at this broken man in front of him and says, "My dear boy, why don't you just try acting?" You've all heard it?' I said.

'Sure,' Carl said, eyes glistening as the others nodded along.

'In the other story, Olivier's doing *Othello* in the West End. Maybe it was *Macbeth*. Anyway, one night he gives the most unbelievable performance. An "everyone in the audience will remember it for the rest of their lives" kind of performance. He can feel it on stage, the other actors can, he's gone to another level. The show ends — ten-minute standing ovation. But Olivier storms backstage and locks himself up in his dressing room. He's livid. The rest of the cast is baffled. One of his co-stars comes backstage and bangs on the dressing-room door. "Larry, what's wrong?" she says. "That was magnificent, even for you." Olivier bursts out of the door, grabs the woman by the wrists, full of anguish. "I know," he says. "But I have no idea how I did it."'

My fellow nominees gave identical half-smiles, underwhelmed there wasn't a better punchline.

'The work I do,' I said, 'I know it can seem out there' – Carl gave a laughing sigh – 'but I'm so lucky to do what I do. I feel such a responsibility, not just to the audience but to every other actor who'd kill to have the opportunities I've had.' Something got stuck in my throat as I thought of the ghost at the end of the phone line in the cabin that night, which having found the phone locked in the drawer, I knew couldn't have been real. The nominees' faces softened at my seeming to have become overcome with emotion. 'I'm just doing everything I can,' I said, 'to make sure that when it comes to the moment the camera's on me, I'm leaving as little as possible to chance.'

It must have been Carl talking about my soul that caused me to get choked up because this wasn't the first time I'd wheeled out the Olivier anecdotes. It was part of our campaign. The master craftsman, the man-of-the-world perfectionist, working-class boy done good, making his big, earthy comeback. I'd told other journalists about growing up in the industrial terraces of Kippax outside Leeds, wrapping Quality Street at the Nestlé factory as a seventeen-year-old. Van and Delilah Queiroz, our PR supremo, had crafted it all, throwing the kitchen-sink drama at it.

'Those stories,' Carl Dillane took on the role of moderator, 'they come from Jonathan Dors?' I took a deep breath and gave a rueful laugh.

'That and everything else I know.'

Vanessa, stood left of camera, gave me an almost imperceptible nod at my perfectly pitched humility.

'He's become very in demand since the two of you

reunited,' Carl said with a twinkle that seemed a little venomous. 'How important was that, working with your old teacher again?'

I smiled, looked down. In *Woodsman*, when Louanne comes to my character Harrison, pregnant by his brother and fleeing her abusive family, she doesn't know how to live in the world until he teaches her. When the nomination came through that morning, I told the team I wanted the master craftsman's reunion with his mentor to become part of the story of our campaign too.

'Honestly,' I said, the base of my throat filling like a drain full of leaves, 'I wouldn't be sitting here with you today if it wasn't for Jonathan Dors.'

I.ii

I first encountered Jonathan in nineteen ninety-four. He walked into my audition for The Conservatoire as I was halfway through my speech: Hamlet's first monologue. I peered outside to see if it had clouded over because the air in the room felt different with him in it.

'Your mother's dead?' he asked after I'd finished the speech. His voice was so uncanny I almost couldn't understand what he'd said. It had the tonal quality of a singing bell and he leant into the ends of words like a drill going through masonry. When his question landed, I looked at the other teachers on the audition panel for help, expecting them to be as shocked as I was. But the two of them, Aggie Claire the school principal and Daniel Vasquez the head of voice, stared back at me with android smiles.

'She's dead,' I said. 'Cancer.'

'*Hamlet*. Bit on the nose, isn't it,' Jonathan said, moving over to stand in front of me. He was unfathomably tall, limbs so thin you could make out their outlines through his clothes, his whole appearance Dickensian. 'Picture your mother at her most perfect,' he said.

I saw her lying on the sofa, a black-and-white film playing.

Jonathan noticed the impulse. 'Now, imagine her doing the one unspeakable act that would damage you – you, Adam – further than any other. Throttling a baby sister, drowning your new kitten, making love with the neighbour you've watched leering at her from afar. Picture it.' I didn't have to imagine. I felt faint, put my hand out to steady myself.

'Can I just—'

'Speak the speech,' he said. 'Now, speak it now.'

I plummeted into the 'too, too solid flesh' speech and barely remember a thing about it. When I finished it felt like I'd emptied my guts onto the sprung floor. Jonathan turned to look at his colleagues and blinked. Less than a week later, I had a letter inviting me to attend the school.

I fought hard to take up the place. The admin staff helped me get a grant, but it wasn't enough. My dad Martin could have lent me a little – he didn't have much – but he dismissed my acting as attention-seeking, which, considering how distant he was during my childhood, was probably insightful. I didn't want him holding any stake in my future.

That summer, I ruined myself working double shifts at the Nestlé chocolate factory in Wakefield I'd worked at since I was sixteen, which, aside from the exploitative working conditions, had very little in common with Willy Wonka's place. I saved every penny, cut myself off from my mates who blew their earnings at raves, because I had the sliver of an opportunity to become someone, and I was certain Jonathan was the prophet who would lead me there.

On my first day, my train from the bedsit I'd found near Wimbledon got stuck in a tunnel, so I had to run from Kentish Town station into the square of Georgian terraces surrounding The Conservatoire. The school was in an old Methodist church, only ever referred to as The Church, and it might have been the early autumn sun but, as I took it in that morning, the place seemed to almost glow. The grand stone steps down to the gate, the columns on each side of the large metal-studded wooden doors, made it more akin to a Greek temple, reinforcing my belief I'd find the oracle inside, replete with answers about myself to questions I didn't know how to ask.

I rushed up the steps, through the doors and was assaulted by a chaos of bodies. Lithe figures in tight dance clothes draped over each other on battered sofas; topless men comparing sculpted torsos by a row of lockers. Despite the competing Lynx deodorants and shea body butters of the incumbent second- and third-year students, the smell of decades-old sweat seemed to breathe from the walls. I stood inside the entrance, scanning doors I'd learn led to two small studios and various teaching rooms, trying to find some clue as to where I was meant to be. But, aside from the noticeboard I'd seen in the vestibule, the hallway that served as the school's communal space was utilitarian. No soft furnishings, murals or pictures on the faded magnolia walls; it could have been a military barracks. I would discover this wasn't accidental. Nothing with Jonathan ever was.

I caught three of the most eye-catching women I'd ever seen laughing at me as I stood there gawping. One of them, a Middle-Eastern-looking third year, came and pointed me towards the huge double doors into what was the old nave of The Church, the final-year students' rehearsal and performance space: Room 1.

I peered into the vaulted room, painted black from the beams on the ceiling down to the stone pillars holding it up, and was relieved to see my new classmates down by the stage where an altar should have been, waiting for the introductory session to start. I filtered in, hoping no one noticed me while wishing someone would.

Staff were perched on the edge of the stage, peering at us with different shades of disinterest, but Jonathan wasn't amongst them. The school principal Aggie, a plum-shaped middle-aged woman who tied her hair up with marbled scarfs, stood fawning over a tall Indian woman with smoky eye make-up she called Vanessa who, although she was in her early twenties, seemed too comfortable in herself to have been starting the training that day.

The rest of my peers were easier to decipher from the staff and seemed to have bonded quickly, chatting together in clusters of three or four. As I moved down to them, I heard southern accents talking about the plays they'd seen, the bits of North London they were staying in, favourite films, the home counties they'd grown up in. It's odd to recount now, but their clipped consonants made my tongue feel thick at the back of my throat as I heard my accent in my head. It sounded lazy, uneducated, and I started worrying what to do with my vowels if someone were to ask me anything.

There was one group of three men whose deep guffaws and shoulder-slapping echoed around the cavernous space. They were all past six foot, heavily stubbled with the build of sportsmen. They made me, just eighteen, shoulders narrow, with facial hair that grew in enigmatic tufts, feel about eight years old. One of them was Irish, his lilt singing through the humming chatter. When he turned and half-acknowledged me with a raised eyebrow, I was struck, almost frightened, at how good-looking he was. Bottle-green eyes under a wave of hair so dark it was almost blue, jawline from a Mills & Boon and the sort of easy smile that made me wonder whether I'd ever felt so delighted. From the stolen glances of the girls and some of the boys around, you could feel there was a universal attraction towards him.

'Patrick Moran,' he said like a celebrity who assumed I already knew who he was, presenting a beefy paw for me to shake when he saw me still staring at him. I mumbled my own introduction. Patrick put an arm on my shoulder, an acre-wide smile.

'Adam,' he said, a little unsure of me. 'Great to meet you. Next three years are going to be fucking insane!' He let go of my shoulder and turned back to his people.

I retreated into a pocket of space and was scanning the

others, trying to find one amongst them who felt anything but right at home in this place where, with my grown-out buzz cut, pale skin and blackheads, I stood out like a gloveful of sore thumbs, when Jonathan strode in bang on nine o'clock and everyone, students and staff alike, stood up straighter. When he stopped at the side of the stage, Aggie clapped her hands and began her introductory monologue.

'You are part of a lineage,' she began, owl-face beaming. 'Dander, Mikkelsen—' The names of the school's founders. 'Grotowski, Strasberg, all the way back to the great Stanislavski.' Classmates nodded. 'Oscars, BAFTAs, Oliviers, every "gong" the industry dangles before us has been held aloft by someone who's performed on the stage behind me.'

Jonathan put a thumb to his temple and looked at the ceiling. He had heard the speech before and didn't care for it. Although Aggie was the principal and he the head of acting, Jonathan *was* The Conservatoire to the outside world, the teacher students came to the school for, not someone of whom you could demand deference.

'But we don't want accolades,' Aggie continued. 'We want truth. Truthful acting, free of artifice, is the purest form of artistic expression. We don't care about who you are, what you know, how talented people have thought you to be. You have been chosen because we believe, if you give all of yourself to the school's methodology, the truth is something you could achieve.' She let her words settle before turning to Jonathan, who was still fixed on the ceiling. 'Anything to add?'

Jonathan lowered his face. Since he'd walked in, I'd spent every moment desperate for him to look at me, but he kept his eyes fixed in front of him. He took a breath in, all of us leaning in to hear his pronouncement, before he closed his eyes and gave a barely perceptible shake of the head, no. Aggie clapped again and proceeded to go through some housekeeping as Jonathan slunk back out the way he came.

I turned, almost right around, bereft. I thought he'd seen something in me at my audition, that he might light up when he saw me, put an arm around me and bring me into The Church to begin working on my bright future. But I wasn't special. One of twenty, from what I could infer; the least impressive, least welcome of Group 28.

Someone beside me swallowed a giggle. I looked up and saw a familiar face, a nest of chestnut curls, grinning at me – Nina. I wanted to speak to her, but she pursed her lips, indicating Aggie was still talking. Nina hated getting in trouble. We stood side-by-side as the principal rattled through logistics none of us would take in, the two of us swaying with excitement at seeing each other again.

Nina and I met at the audition. I was taken to a horse-shoe of plastic chairs in one of the corridors off The Church's main thoroughfare and she was sat alone, eyes closed, taking audible breaths through her nose. I sat op-posite and couldn't help watching her. She looked my age, a heart-shaped face, plum-round cheekbones dotted with freckles. Her small frame heaved up a little with each breath, a tremor in her wrists, but that aside she was perfectly still.

Which is why I laughed out loud when she suddenly

stuck out her tongue as far as it would go and made a sound like a dragon breathing fire. Her eyes sprung open on hearing me.

'Oh bollocks,' she said, blushing beetroot-pink. 'I'm so sorry!'

'No, I am, shouldn't have laughed.'

She cocked her head and seemed to notice something about me I didn't know was there. I looked down, then did her dragon breath back to her. She squawked out a laugh.

'OK,' she said. 'Objectively, it is pretty funny.'

'Thought I should even it up,' I said. She was auditioning after me but had got there an hour early. She could see I was nervous so, in the ten minutes before I was due in, she led me through the rest of her warm-up. We sang scales pinching our noses, chewed an imaginary toffee, stretched our tongues around our mouths like we had something stuck in every tooth.

Nina knew all that stuff because she'd wanted to be an actor since before she could remember. Her parents Tommy and Liv told the story about her setting up sofa-cushion stages with a duvet curtain to do theatrical versions of *Brookside* and *Coronation Street*, and that after they took her to a drama group age four, she begged them to take her to something like it every day. Nina's parents spent the entirety of her childhood outside various sports halls and community centres reading novels in the car as she did every dance, singing and acting class the suburbs of South East London could offer.

When I was called in for my audition, Nina took my hands

in hers, looked into my eyes and said, 'Break a leg, mate.' I bounced in to face the panel, feeling more motivated to get in and be with people like Nina while, conversely, caring less about acting than I ever had. But afterwards, I was so floored by my run-in with Jonathan, head like a black hole trying to understand how I'd just done the best acting of my life, I didn't go back to the horseshoe to say goodbye to Nina, to say good luck. But she hadn't needed it, she'd got in.

Back on that first day, Aggie finished by stressing the importance of the ensemble, how in the following three years our group would become the closest friends we'd ever have, closer than family. Nina grabbed my elbow and squeezed.

'Look after one another,' Aggie said. Nina and I looked at each other and she raised her eyebrows like we were about to jump out of a plane together.

For the next two and a bit years, that was the most excited the two of us would be about being at The Conservatoire. Aggie and Jonathan made all decisions on the casting of the internal plays, projects and exercises we did and, within a few weeks, a hierarchy emerged.

Patrick became the golden boy and he and the two others I'd seen him with that first morning, Ben and Victor, 'The Boys' as they came to be known, set the social timbre for our whole time at the school. They had us linking arms, belting out Oasis at the parties they hosted; goaded us into one-handed push-up competitions in the halls; quoting *Goodfellas*, *Scarface*, *Full Metal Jacket*; snorting coke; wearing vests; downing Stella. It could be the three of them were overcompensating – acting's not the most macho of professions – but, although the other years weren't quite as overt as ours, The Conservatoire's whole methodology promoted masculine values. 'Get in the ring' we were always told when going in to play a scene – The Boys took the ball and ran with it.

But it wasn't just the teachers, we were all a little in love with Patrick. His family were so impressive I thought it was a joke when I first heard about them. He was one of four, the youngest son. His dad was a big property mogul, eldest brother Rory the youngest minister in the Irish cabinet and the middle brother, Cillian, was pushing to be outside centre for the national rugby team. The daughter was a bit younger but was no doubt on her way to being Ireland's premier brain surgeon. All of which made it even more surprising that Patrick made everyone he talked to, even me, feel like they were the extraordinary one.

Vanessa was also one of the chosen ones. Although we soon found out who her father was, and the teachers were aware long before we started, the Lady Macbeth she gave us in the first week when we reworked our audition speeches blew the other girls out of the water, putting paid to any accusations of nepotism.

But then, at the other end of the spectrum, you found me and Nina. The man who I'd thought would be my champion, turned out to be entirely ambivalent to me.

Jonathan didn't direct students until final year, so our only contact with him was his classes, where I struggled from the start. We spent first year going over the theory behind the school's methodology – Jung, Aristotle, Nietzsche, Stanislavski – names my university-educated classmates bandied around like they were talking about their pets, but that to me, having left a bang-average comprehensive before sixth form, felt like things he'd made up to test my spelling. There were times I wished Jonathan would call me out for my silence in class, but it seemed I wasn't even worth that.

As the months passed and we began showing our projects and plays to the wider faculty and receiving their often coruscating feedback, I began to feel more and more invisible. Patrick was told he fell back on his charisma, which made his acting 'tricksy'. Vanessa was praised for her understanding of characters, but told she needed to give more of her emotional life to the audience. Nina, who like me had been playing servants in Ibsen and drunk commoners in Bernard Shaw, had her work branded superficial and shiny, her teenage summers with the prestigious National Youth Music Theatre held against her as if she'd been part of a genocidal regime. My exercises however would end with a sigh, a shrug, and once something mumbled that sounded like 'essentially a non-starter'. I became desperate for the teachers' attention, however harsh. Anything would have been better than the thunderous void I spent every night lying awake filling with my own neuroses.

I should have been careful what I wished for. Midway through the last term of first year, I was called into Aggie's office and told the staff were considering asking me to leave.

I didn't know enough. My understanding of the repertoire, of the theory of the school's methodology was entirely lacking and, more disturbingly, she said they didn't know how to place me, either in casting terms or as a person.

'They can't throw you out,' Nina said when I told her later at Ankos, the Greek café opposite Kentish Town station.

'They pretty much said they are.'

'But then they'd all realise how shit I am!' she said, laughing.

I didn't laugh. 'OK, no, no, fuck, I'm not going to let them.'

She called the waiter over, ordered us beers, two ouzos, chips and a shedload of dips. She opened her bag, which was always overstuffed with books, and we got to work. For the next four weeks, we'd go back to her parents' house in Bexleyheath every night and she'd drill me through the history of theatre and acting theory from Medieval mystery plays all the way to Sarah Kane. From the Ancient Greeks to French clowning; Japanese symbolism to Brando, De Niro and the American method. She spent time pinning down my casting. I was skinny, pale, eyes were too big in my face, I didn't have a haircut so to speak, just hair that grew from my head.

'Theatre has a hell of a lot of Kings, lots of Gods, heroes basically, which isn't you. No offence,' she said to me one night in her childhood bedroom with its green frog coverlet, TLC playing on her HiFi. If anyone else had said it, I would have been offended. 'You're the outsider, the invalid, the bastard.'

'Is that how you see me?'

'As it stands, I'm the fucking milkmaid, mate!' She jumped to her bookshelves and grabbed something, walking over with it held behind her back.

'Film, however, is full of losers.' She dropped a coffee-table-sized book in my lap: *The Greatest Speeches in Cinema*. Nina bumped down next to me and we flicked through the pages, a glossy shot from the film on one side, the speech printed on the other. *Scent of a Woman, To Kill a Mockingbird, Network*. I turned the page and my breath caught: Marlon Brando in his plaid jacket in *On the Waterfront*.

'This one?' Nina said.

'I don't know.'

'Could work,' she said. I stood up, squeezed at my eyes with my fingers and moved across to her make-up table. I had watched the movie with my mum when I was seven; we watched all those classics. I did the speech for her for weeks after we watched it. Used to make her howl with laughter, a six-year-old saying: 'I could have had class, I could have been a contender. I could have been somebody. Instead of a bum, which is what I am,' in a twangy, exaggerated American accent.

'You have seen it, right?' Nina asked, bringing me back into the room with her.

'Yeh.' I saw myself in the mirror, the child I was. I had told Nina my mum died of cancer when I was eight and she never pressed me on it, despite being desperate to know more. 'Let's try it,' I said.

Nina worked with me on the speech, helped me apply

the methodology from Jonathan's classes. I gave it to the teachers in an open showing session of our work in the penultimate week of the year. Bolstered by Nina's faith in me and the work we'd done, for the first time since my audition I didn't feel like a newborn giraffe in front of the teachers and I thought it had gone OK. Nina gave me a Cheshire-cat grin, Van arched eyebrows in surprise and Patrick gave me a sideways thumbs-up, a pout of encouragement as I sat back down after I'd finished.

Jonathan said nothing, Aggie only that I should go to our speech teacher about my American accent as soon as I could. So I spent the last week mired in dread, flinching every time I felt someone close to me, assuming it would be the tap on the shoulder asking me into the office. But it never came. News filtered through to us in the summer break that three of us had been asked to leave but I wasn't one of them. I'd been reprieved and it was all down to Nina.

That summer I was renewed. Bathed in Britpop, the royal parks baked dusty brown from a six-week heatwave, London felt like the centre of the world. I moved into a squat in Limehouse to save money and to align with The Conservatoire's generalised anti-establishment pose and exchanged the weekend job I'd had at a tea-room off Wimbledon Common for a few shifts at a pub-club in Hoxton, giving myself more time to work on plays, more time with Nina.

I tried to make our cramming more mutual, seeking to help Nina with her so-called 'acting problem'. I challenged her to work on darker characters, got her to watch violent films, dragged her to challenging gallery openings my squat-mates invited me to. If she could expose me to what I should have learnt at school, perhaps I could expose her to things they'd never teach there. I took her to warehouse parties and because I'd seen dark rooms baked in sweat and ill-looking kids with drug-wild eyes before at raves back home in Manchester and Leeds, I became Nina's protector, her guide. If I saw a flinch of disquiet, I'd put my arm around her waist as we danced in front of speakers twice our height in Shoreditch car parks and decrepit buildings with blacked-out windows. She'd smile at me for making her feel safe.

We'd get night buses back to her house and collapse onto her bed after these nights. She would fall asleep and I'd lay awake, breathing in the smell of oranges from her shampoo, feeling an unfamiliar sense of peace. It was embarrassingly chaste. I wanted to hold her, draw her close to me. I used to look down at her, hands pinned to my sides, imagine touching her cheek, how her lips would feel against mine, but I didn't dare make any kind of move. I'd never had a relationship with someone who gave me such a surge of energy, of warmth. She sought me out before anyone else, saw my neuroses as a puzzle to solve, seemed to embrace the very basic facts of me. Having Nina in my life became sacred. I knew I couldn't do anything that would endanger that. We had two more years living in each other's pockets and, most pertinently, it was enough for me. At that time, having what we had was enough.

I started the second year telling myself the same about

the training. They had let me stay. If I worked hard and did what the teachers demanded, I'd get into third year, maybe get an agent, one day get paid to be an actual actor. If you'd asked the sixteen-year-old Adam staring at fifty years on the line at Nestlé, he would have bitten your hand off. But second year was where things got serious.

The school was famous for providing the only training that combined psychologically demanding American method-acting concepts with the rigorously physical Russian Conservatoire tradition. In the middle year, we found out quite how hardcore that was. We had two-hour movement sessions every day with Varda, a Ukrainian ex-ballerina, whose job it was to hone our bodies into the perfect specimens of strength and flexibility. She believed in fairies and encouraged farting and burping as a sign we were shuffling off our Western reserve, but also pushed us so hard we often had to dash out of her studio to be sick. With Aggie and an Austrian acting teacher Max Webern, we worked on scenes and various plays, having six or seven different characters' lines and thoughts in our head at any one time. And with Jonathan we began exploring certain method approaches to our characters. He'd have us sprint around the school before doing a speech, plunge ourselves into freezing showers. We'd hit ourselves, pinch, give ourselves Chinese burns. He told us students had touched themselves in exercises to incite arousal, though none of us went that far, not in front of each other at least. This was the first part of the training that clicked for me. It didn't require me to have read a book, seen some play ten years before or know obscure Russian theory. The physical extremity shifted you out of yourself, gave an insight into character I never seemed to be able to find from merely thinking about it. Not that Jonathan noticed my new enthusiasm.

I didn't expect praise, Jonathan didn't seem to believe in it, but I couldn't cope with his ambivalence and would listen enviously at the way he'd critique the work of my classmates. He was the most brutal to Patrick.

'Homo erectus dances the Sugarplum Fairy,' Jonathan said to him after a Romeo speech. 'The body of a rower and the mind of . . . a rower,' in response to something from *The Life of Galileo*. Most punishingly, Jonathan once told him 'Your desire to be adored will forever block you from being a truthful actor.' He was much harsher, crueller even, to Patrick than the rest of us, but implicit in it was a sense it was because he was worthy, that Jonathan cared enough about his work to prod and provoke him because it would make him better. Patrick took it all with a smile in his eyes, like it was dressing-room banter. Where Nina and I would spend hours going over how we'd failed Jonathan, Patrick would be in the pub afterwards handing out pints, buoyant as if Jonathan had awarded him a medal.

Vanessa and Jonathan's relationship was more nuanced. It emerged he and her father Alasdair had known each other for years, after they'd done a play together in Bristol when both had just graduated from drama school: Alasdair RADA and Jonathan The Conservatoire. He knew Vanessa's family, had been to garden parties at their house,

West End press nights, the agency's Christmas shindigs. He had known Vanessa since she was a little girl and though he was as forensic with her as he was with all of us, there was a tension, something withdrawn about him with her. Jonathan's method needed the teacher–student roles to be starkly defined. Vanessa blurred them, introduced a sense of past and future, where Jonathan required us to be tightly in the moment.

Nina went a different way that year. Max did an art project with us in which we had to do a tableau of famous paintings and gave Nina *The Birth of Venus*. Nina threw herself into it, dyed her hair, got extensions, spent hours working on the emotions in the face, the shape of the pose. But at the showing, as soon as she took her position, Jonathan stood up and walked out.

'We give you the most world-famous archetype of lust,' Max berated her afterwards. 'And you give us your little-girl underwear.' She'd done the exercise in bra and pants, whereas in the painting Venus is naked. Nina was distraught; it hadn't even occurred to us she should strip naked. After that, she decided the die was cast with Jonathan. He would always see her as too young, too callow, unable to 'go there' – a favourite phrase at the school – so she threw herself into what she knew: dance, singing, the other teachers' classes.

By this point, I was living with Nina, staying in the attic room of her parents' house in Bexleyheath. At a New Year's rave at my squat, a dozen or so people had climbed up on the central girder supporting the ceiling and it came crashing to the ground. No one was badly injured but, even if we weren't all evicted, the space was uninhabitable. Nina insisted I move in with them, which I was unsure of, but Tommy and Liv wouldn't hear of me finding another squat. I became part of Nina's family, which was wonderful if a little alienating. Their home radiated love and bonhomie which were things I'd never known to be part of day-to-day family life. In a way it made things simpler between the two of us, living under one roof, we became almost sibling-like. But there were moments, hazy nights after too many ciders, her cracking jokes over Liv's beef stroganoff, I found myself overwhelmed by the desire to put my arms around her. But I never did.

As our second year went on and the two of us continued to be cast as characters for Vanessa's Lady of the Manor to talk down to, for Patrick's bounding hero to lean on, once literally, Nina and I started referring to ourselves as 'the chaff'. We made up songs about how to upstage the favourites in our third-year shows without anyone noticing, talked about how we'd have to get the agents' attention using elaborate eyebrow work because we wouldn't have any lines.

But our in-jokes, gallows humour, the badly acted insouciance were just a veil we used to cover the slowly suffocating sense of despair we both felt at Jonathan's apathy towards us. He was the sun The Conservatoire spun around. We were either shining in his orbit or drifting aimlessly in the infinite darkness of space.

I.iii

MOVIEBITCH.NET

MADMAN SEALEY'S ACTING COACH IMPLICATED IN GIRL'S DISAPPEARANCE

Following wins at the SAG awards and the Golden Globes, Adam Sealey looks to be in a promising position to pick up the Oscar at his third time of trying. But could a controversy involving his celebrated acting coach, Jonathan Dors, turn out to be the reason Adam continues to be the bridesmaid and not the bride?

A comment below the line of a *Hollywood Reporter* interview hints that Dors left the world-famous Conservatoire of the Dramatic Arts, where he'd taught for forty years, under suspicious circumstances.

'Adam Sealey's teacher Jonathan Dors retired in the middle of term, less than a week after the disappearance of a female student.'

Sealey, now better known for his extreme acting process and fighting with stuntmen than many of his movies, left The Conservatoire more than twenty years ago and has made no secret of his working with Dors again on his Oscar-tipped comeback film *Woodsman*.

'It's not fucking great, is it?' Van said to the iPhone on the table in the rental above Mulholland Drive we'd lived at for the previous four years. It was the day after the nominations. I stood braced against the doors to the garden, rain spattering behind me.

'This is standard whisper campaign tactics, Vanessa,' Delilah Queiroz said, Queens accent twanging through the speaker.

Delilah was in her early thirties but had the world-weariness of a war doctor. 'The Balenciaga Midas when it comes to the Academies' Van had assured me when she was recruiting her as our publicist a few months before.

'Happens every year. Soon as a frontrunner emerges, the other studios dig for dirt to try get their guy back on top.'

'This is—' I crossed my arms in front of me, uncrossed them. 'I can't believe they'd actually do that?'

'This is good news, Adam,' Delilah said. 'Means they think you might win. And if this is all they can find on you' – Van and I locked eyes – 'then we're cruising through absolutely very calm water. Lake Geneva in the spring.'

Van twisted her hair onto her shoulder, measuring my expression.

'We have to distance ourselves from Jonathan,' she said.

'Because of this?' I laughed but it came out strained.

'A powerful man in his seventies quits after a female student goes AWOL?'

'What are you thinking Jonathan's done?' I said.

'It's the optics.'

'He never did anything like that, you know he didn't. There was never a sniff.'

Vanessa twisted her macchiato in its cardboard holder. 'Be that as it may.'

'This is a blatant smear, trying to stop me getting the Oscar. And if it is a studio doing it, wanting to steal this away from us, we need to find out who it is and hold them to account.'

'Hey, hey, *tranquilo, tranquilo*, guys,' Delilah said through the phone. 'The less we react the better. We go after it, it looks like we've got something to hide, if we row back on the Jonathan-mentor stuff, it piles all sorts of attention on a story buried away on a gossip site no one reads. Now, have you reached out to him yet?'

'We've left messages,' Van said. She meant on his answering machine. No one ever asked why Jonathan didn't have a mobile. It seemed too fitting to question. 'Reached out to a number of people on the ground in London, but no one seems to know about anyone who's disappeared.' I hadn't

42

realised the cogs were already rolling on this story. Van had come back to the house from the office with a sheaf of still-warm printer pages and presented me with the blog twenty minutes before the call.

'That's been the response my side has had too,' Delilah said.

Amber, who was still working for Van, dropped a can of something as she unpacked groceries in the kitchen, and held up a hand in apology.

In the weeks after I finished *Woodsman*, the LA heat and overbearing civilisation left me feeling desiccated, so I stayed indoors for some time and it was Amber's job to check in on me. She was in her mid-twenties, from Edinburgh, Oxbridge but didn't wear the education too loudly. She lived in Doc Martens, combat pants and spaghetti tops, bobbed hair clipped back but never that effectively, very un-LA. Although the nineties look was in, there was something of the throwback to Amber, so it felt less of a pose on her. She always wore retro headphones round her neck and used a MiniDisc player she didn't let Van see for fear she'd get labelled a hipster. She'd play old indie disco stuff through the kitchen speakers – Blur, Radiohead, their later imitators – never music I liked when it came out, but so ubiquitous in my youth I couldn't help finding it a comfort. The two of us spent that time watching movies she hadn't seen and eating average pasta sauces I made for actual gluten-filled pasta. Finding me in the bath in the cabin like that had given us a quiet intimacy with each other. If I knew she was in the house, it somehow kept the image of the hanging body away when I shut my eyes. I could finally sleep.

'We should find the girl,' I said, turning away from Amber to look at the raindrops sprinkling gyroscope patterns on the surface of the pool.

'What?' Van said.

'No one knows who the girl is who's disappeared. If we find her, it puts it to bed.'

Van took her forehead between her fingers and massaged her temples.

'I love the hustle, Adam, but we don't engage,' Delilah said. 'You go to London Thursday, the pictures for the *Times* profile with Jonathan and wonderful Emmy Friday, the BAFTAs Sunday, so you leave all this to me. It's my jam, it's what I'm very good at, it's my pleasure.' I walked over to the table and knelt in front of the phone.

'What if we go there?' I said.

'Go where?' Van said, concern etching on her face.

'The Conservatoire.'

Vanessa's eyes went owl wide.

'I could meet the current students, give a masterclass or something.'

'Adam, I'm really not sure—' Van scoffed.

'If this story gets traction, we're the good guys who've gone to help the students.'

Van was shaking her head, mouth pinched into a snarl, trying to get me to stop talking.

'Look, Delilah and I will work out—'

'I like it.' Delilah's disembodied voice down the phone.

'It aligns us the right way. In the movie, Harrison teaches Louanne how to stand on her own two feet, so it fits beautifully.'

Van stared at me with the severity of a horse trainer.

'But, talk it over between the two of you. Say the word and I can make arrangements.'

Amber was looking over, arms around a huge clump of kale. I'd found her one afternoon in the cinema room watching *Coward*, mascara pooled under her eyes. She told me she snuck in to see it when she was thirteen. She'd cried during the famous train scene then, and every time she'd seen it since. That was Jonathan, what I did in that scene was all because of Jonathan. I should have won an Oscar for it, for him as much as me. They should have written that moment of ours into history.

'Let's do it,' I said. 'Let's make it happen.'

Van pushed her chair in with a clatter and walked past me into the garden as Delilah ended the call, telling me she loved it, loved working with me, how she couldn't wait to make me a celebratory margarita at Elton John's party in a month's time.

Van was on the far side of the pool, eyes closed, doing one of her breathing exercises. When she went on the three-month breathing course after *The Bends*, she said she was going to take the twelve thousand dollars out of my next fee. I assumed she was joking. The California sun broke through the clouds as I went to join her, making the paving stones in the garden steam around us.

'What if this is the first snowflake of the avalanche?'

she said as I arrived next to her, voice pitching at serene as she pushed her breath down with a tai chi-like movement.

'What does that mean?'

Her eyes sprung open. 'You know what it means. There's no Oscar, no career, no walking around a free person possibly, if it gets out what we did.'

'Jonathan saved us that night,' I said. 'You think we'd be near an Oscar, think I'd have ever made a movie, your career too, you think we'd have anything if it wasn't for him?'

She looked me up and down, sighed and let her hands fall by her side.

'You're right, Adam,' she said. 'Everything's down to Jonathan.' Vanessa wrapped her arms around herself, walked out the side-gate and left me alone. Her Tesla purred away and she was gone.

I went back in and picked up the wad of papers on the table to read the comment again. Jonathan told me he'd retired because The Conservatoire's methodology had become irreparably diluted after it was subsumed by a university a few years before. But he'd always been so dedicated to his work, to his students, it was unthinkable he'd leave them in the middle of their training. Amber slammed the door of the fridge. She must have found space for the kale.

I flicked through the papers, the whole comment thread from the video of the Oscars roundtable. On the third page, someone had highlighted the comment featured in the blog. I continued scanning down, faceless names, diffuse opinions. Carl Dillane's jowls, how much they wished

Al Groban would split with his wife Gina and, inevitably, my accent being compared to an international school brat and the policeman from *'Allo 'Allo!* Four pages later, there was another highlighted section. It was a reply to someone from the same moniker – @measuredbella.

@joelfalorun – This teacher has a reputation. Why is Adam working with him?

@Measuredbella – Adam, how could you?

'You OK?' Amber was on the opposite side of the table.

'Fine,' I said through tremors in my stomach. Measured-bella had asked me the same question I thought I heard the impossible voice ask that night in the cabin.

'Are you sure?' Amber said, waggling a cup of smoothie.

I looked past her at an inflatable swan drifting across the pool.

'Looks like you've seen a ghost.'

I.iv

In my final year at The Conservatoire, a few weeks in, something shifted. I was working on a speech for our showcase to agents later in the year in the studio we used for Varda's movement classes, a ripe stench coming from the floorboards, more sweat than wood after so many years.

I ran my speech, Giovanni in *'Tis Pity She's a Whore* grappling with his desire for his sister Annabella, but my voice was thin and the words didn't seem to mean anything. So, I began sprinting around the studio, trying to rattle myself into the mind of someone considering incest. It must have been when I hit my hip on a pillar that Jonathan ghosted into the studio because, when I looked up, he was perched on an armchair regarding his thumbnail as if he were about to paint it.

'Do you think of me as a conversationalist?' he said as I stood breathing heavily. He leant forward, eyes growing wider in disbelief at me until the penny dropped that he wanted me to do my speech.

'Lost! I am lost!' I began. 'My fates have doom'd my death.

The more I strive, I love; the more I love' – Jonathan looked disgusted as I continued the speech – 'Oh, that it were not in religion sin to make our love a god, and worship it!'

'What do you love?' Jonathan said, stopping me.

'Sorry?'

'The character is willing to endure everlasting hell for his love. So, what do you love?'

'What do I love?'

'God? Sex? Poodles? Hare Krishna?' He paused. 'What do you love?'

'I . . . I love this. Acting.'

'Why act?'

'Er, I' – Jonathan stood and seemed to grow several feet wider – 'I'm not sure what you mean?'

'Giovanni wants to sleep with his sister because, what could it be, big blue eyes, she understands him like no one else, his burning desire to transcend morality and bring about the ultimate self-destruction? There is a reason he wants what he wants. So, why act?'

I cleared my throat, had to steady myself. This felt like the most he had ever talked to me – even better, Jonathan was directing me. I was paralysed, desperate for the correct answer.

'I suppose—' I thought back to the feeling of my first school play aged thirteen. One of the brothers in *A View from the Bridge*. The applause at the end felt good but it was while I was up there, the audience watching me, seeing me, holding all of them as time seemed to beat to its own rhythm. 'I just like it more than anything else I've done.'

'That's not enough. Giovanni feels incomplete without Annabella. What does acting give you?'

He and I said nothing for some moments. 'Feelings, I suppose,' I said.

'Feelings?'

'I used to watch old films with my mum,' I said. 'One day, we watched *A Streetcar Named Desire*. I thought it was boring but then Marlon Brando came on and, I felt something. I wanted to do that.'

'Make people feel?'

'Yeh.'

'Mark yourself upon them.'

I shrugged.

'You want immortality, that's relatable. Again,' he said, rolling up his sleeves to reveal arms that rarely saw the sun. 'Incest, the most colossal crime a human being can commit. Giovanni chooses eternal damnation. It has to cost you everything. So, if I don't believe you this time, I will write to every theatre director in the country and tell them you're a thumb-sucking Northern simpleton whom they should never employ. Eternal damnation.'

'Sorry?'

'The speech.' He wheeled away and looked out towards the window. I stared ahead, trying to work out if he was serious. Jonathan was always serious. I thought about it, the chasm after graduation, every opportunity, every champion who could take me on and help me take steps towards making my passion a career, told I was a no-hoper from the start. Despair. I took a few deep breaths, turned and gave the words straight to Jonathan. I had the sensation of fighting for my life, an absolute necessity to win him over. I pressed my nails into my skull and realised I had to tell my sister I loved her, just as I had to make acting my life, because fate had decreed it and, even though it might destroy me, if I didn't, I would wither and die.

I felt like I'd run over a cliff when I finished. That was it, it was something. I looked up and saw the double door of Studio 1 swinging shut. I scanned the studio for him, as if it must have been a joke, someone else coming in by accident, but I was all alone. Jonathan had gone.

'Who knows what it means,' Nina said after I told her what happened later that evening in my room at the top of her house. 'Try not to read too much into it.'

I looked at her for a moment before we both burst into laughter at the preposterousness of not reading into something as gargantuan as Jonathan dropping in unannounced. After she went to bed, I spent that night going over my speech trying to work out whether it was an aimless arm movement or sloppy intonation that drove Jonathan away. At about four, I felt so alone with my exhaustion that I found myself stood outside Nina's bedroom. I wanted to smell her shampoo, have her feet, gnarly from childhood ballet, digging into my ribs. Jonathan walking out on me had shaken something in me. I reached to open the door but stopped myself. Chose to lean on the floorboard I knew would give a loud squeak, waiting to see if I'd woken her and she'd come to let me in. Her room was still. I returned upstairs.

I felt different the next morning and, despite the lack of sleep, I bounced into The Church with an electrical charge and went to change for our stage combat class with The Boys instead of at my locker as I usually did. Patrick greeted me with a squeeze of the shoulder; Ben watched Victor doing pull-ups on the pipe above the shower. They were all in their pants and, where most of us had got wiry from Varda's classes, the three of them had seemed to swell. As I got undressed with them, it was like statues from the British Museum had wandered up to NW1.

Patrick told us about the townhouse of the first year he'd gone home with after the Saturday-night party, the insane sound system, the drinks cabinet stuffed with ancient single malts. He always had some kind of romantic involvement but was never seen as a womaniser or lothario. Things would always fizzle out between him and whichever girl he'd taken an interest in after a few weeks or months, but the miracle was that it would always end amicably, without jealousy, the girls somehow liking him more as a friend than they ever had before.

'Will we partner up in there, buddy?' Patrick said to me as we walked towards the studio.

I shrugged, nodded, acting like I wasn't over the moon to be asked as Ben and Victor pretended they weren't crestfallen to be left to each other.

We were the last ones into class and our stage combat tutor Ricky bounced up from where he was doing capoeira in the corner as we took our places.

'Grab your pieces,' he said, pointing to a selection of

swords so shiny he must have spent all his time outside class polishing them. He saw himself as a Steven Seagal-like sensei and had the struggling ponytail to match. We took our positions, Nina giving me a mock offended look at my going with Patrick instead of her, and began running our sword-fighting choreography. Ricky walked up and down the line checking the tension in our wrists before moving to his conga drum in the corner, increasing the tempo like we were galley slaves. I was counting the routine in my head, where Patrick could have done it looking the other way. So it was difficult when he started speaking.

'Was Dorsy in your rehearsal yesterday?'

'What?' I parried a cut to finish the sequence. The drumming stopped; we swapped sides.

'Gay James' – there was only one James – 'said he saw him walking out of Studio 1 yesterday while you were in there. Did you ask him for help?'

'No,' I said, quickly, as a guilty man would. The drums began again.

'Performance speed! You're at war.' Ricky yelled like it was Agincourt. I caught Nina rolling her eyes at James and felt a pang of jealousy at the fun she was having without me. Patrick steamed in with the first move despite it being my turn to start.

'Fine if you did, buddy,' he said. It wasn't. Asking for private help from the teachers was seen as a huge betrayal to the harmony of our group.

'He just came in, honestly. And he walked out before I finished.'

'He walked out? Fuck! That's brutal!' Patrick said. I felt myself hit harder. Patrick responded, a smirk of competition in his eyes. The room sensed something happening between us. Ricky brought his drum over.

'Circle back and go again,' Ricky said when we got to the end, the rest of the class stopping to watch. I loped to the far side of the room, blinking sweat from my eyes. When my vision cleared, I noticed a shadow by the window in the studio door, a tall figure hunched down. Jonathan.

Patrick emerged from the other corner and I charged at him, swinging the sword over my wrist. He could feel how much force I was putting into every blow and an esteem for me I'd never seen swam into his eyes.

It made something in me snap. I blocked his sword with my arm, its full force pounding my wrist, and cut between his neck and shoulder, once, twice, a third time, before Ben intervened and wrestled the sword away. As Victor pulled me away, I glanced over to the door. Jonathan wasn't there.

Ricky got us to shake hands, buzzing at the conflict, but Patrick gave me a bear hug instead and told me it'd been 'fucking insane'. With the weight difference between the two of us, my arm was far worse off than his shoulder but I felt amazing, every nerve alive like I'd walked in from a hurricane.

Nina took me outside for a cigarette afterwards.

'What was that, Ad?' she said.

'I don't know,' I said. 'Red mist came down.'

'You don't have a red mist.' She took my cigarette and smoked it. I couldn't tell her I'd been trying to impress

Jonathan, I didn't know whether he'd even been there, nor that it was Patrick bestowing his respect like I was a peasant impressing the baron that drove me to go for him. I wanted to tell her how powerful it had felt, the whole year in shock, frightened even, as I went for Patrick. But I shrugged, took back the cigarette. 'Be you, Adam,' Nina said, ruffling the back of my head. 'Don't try and become what you think they want you to be.'

No one talked about the incident afterwards. The Conservatoire was meant to be a sandpit, a safe environment to find out how far we could push ourselves as actors. Months of watching exercises in which two people spent half an hour kissing or simulating smothering the other with a pillow made what I did to Patrick unremarkable. But in the following weeks, Group 28 began paying me more attention, their backs straighter as they watched my exercises. The Boys brought me closer to them. Patrick's pylon arms would grab me in the corridor, or he'd grip the back of my neck like I was a treasured younger sibling. The tectonic plates had moved. The favourites had qualities the teachers, and therefore the industry, could identify. Patrick's looks, Vanessa's sharp mind and, for the first time, I realised I might have something too – the fearlessness of having nothing to lose.

It was a trait that emerged a couple of weeks later when I confronted Jonathan over how he treated Nina in one of his classes.

We were working on emotional memory, where the actor goes back to significant moments from their own past to unearth the extreme emotional states the character is going through. Jonathan had us practise this discipline by reliving a traumatic moment from our childhood in front of the rest of the class. We were watching Nina's exercise with her imagined parents sat in rows behind Jonathan at his desk. In the scene, her parents had just confessed that their cat Shosti wasn't staying with her aunt and had, in fact, been hit by a lorry.

'What do you mean she's dead?' Nina said. 'She—She can't be—Mum?' She looked from her dad to her mum, before tumbling into tears; words strangled by snot. 'You lied,' she said, 'how could you lie?' I wanted to get up and go to her. I could see Tommy and Liv there, shuffling guiltily in their sitting room, but around me the class fidgeted. Vanessa gave a baggy sigh.

'Who's next?' Jonathan said, looking at his notebook.

Nina snapped back to herself, staring at us as if she were an animal thrown into captivity. 'Let me start again,' she said.

'Who is due next?'

Nina stumbled up from her seat, dumbstruck. We'd talked about this exercise at home relentlessly. I'd heard her running through it as she brushed her teeth. She couldn't eat that morning, didn't talk to me on the train in anticipation.

'I can go again.' She tugged on her tangled hair, trying to make sense of where she'd gone wrong.

'Tell her why, Vanessa?' Jonathan said.

Van half-turned so the class saw her calculating where to plant her allegiance. 'You always cry, Nina,' she said.

Jonathan put an index finger into the air confirming she was right. Nina swayed in the draft of our collective focus, before moving back towards her seat. Jonathan extended a long arm to block her.

'You show me this side of you because you're scared. And a scared actor,' he spoke in a stage whisper, 'isn't an actor.' He withdrew his arm and Nina sat down next to me. I went to put an arm round her, but she didn't want to be touched, and leant forward, letting my hand fall onto the back of her seat. I felt furious at the way he'd gutted her but even worse when a boy called Oban went up straight after, burst into tears and Jonathan commended him for eliciting the same emotion he'd humiliated Nina for. The cruelty singed the pit of my stomach.

At the end of the class, Jonathan rose from his desk and I bolted from my seat with him.

'What are you doing?' Nina tried to grab at my wrist but I got past her and through a barricade of chairs. The Boys whooped with laughter; Vanessa gave a theatrical yawn. In the corridor, Jonathan hovered along the wall that skirts Room 1 towards the staffroom. I followed, side-stepping second years carrying a wardrobe and dropping a shoulder to avoid a never-brief chat with our eighty-year-old music teacher.

As Jonathan turned, I arrived from the other side of the corridor and stopped the staffroom door as he opened it. He stared at me, brows arched, neither of us expecting something so abrupt. I swallowed air.

'You can't do that,' I said.

Jonathan blinked, eyelids taking forever to close and open again. 'I'm going to smoke,' he said, disappearing into the staffroom. I waited, with no idea whether he'd meant me to, and had the feeling of clanking up the incline of a rollercoaster as I realised quite how far I'd transgressed. Jonathan stalked The Church like a wraith, venturing into the corridor only moments before his classes, timing metronomic. You did not stop him outside class.

I stared at the first years getting changed for ballet, exhausted joy in their eyes, their pride at getting into such a prestigious school intact, bodies still soft and febrile. I looked at my hand gripping the door, veins popping through taut skin.

Jonathan emerged in a black puffa-jacket.

'It's raining,' he said, sweeping past.

I grabbed Nina's flowery cagoule from the top of her locker and went to join him, steps on the flagstones marshmallow-light at the preposterousness of going to smoke with Jonathan Dors.

He was sheltering under the rhododendron in the courtyard outside his room we called The Rose Garden when I joined him, overlong cigarette in his mouth.

'You were telling me what I can and cannot do?'

'Nina worked so hard.'

'Hard work is rather a low bar.'

'She'll go over it again and again after that, torturing herself.'

Jonathan blew a puff of smoke. Clumps of rain darkened the shoulders of our coats.

'Do you never think about that?'

He offered me a cigarette without looking at me. I took one, which felt like a surrender.

'Familiar with Icarus?' he asked. I nodded as he lit my cigarette with a corner-shop lighter. 'What's often forgotten is that his father warned him about flying too close to the sun and melting the wax binding his wings, but also of getting too close to the sea, water-logging the feathers and being dragged to his death. If you add mere survival to the two, it could be said Icarus chose the best fate for himself, because who remembers the name of the father who survived him?'

'That a long way of saying you don't care?'

Jonathan let out a strained hum. 'If a friend tells you how wonderful you were in a play, would that improve your performance the following night?' He nodded. It wasn't a rhetorical question.

'Maybe not.'

'But if I watch and tell you the truth, unvarnished by any consideration about how it may make you feel, you have something on which to work. And the next night, the audience should get something better. Ingram used to have a saying' – Ingram Dander was, along with San Mikkelsen, The Conservatoire's founder, the man who entrusted Jonathan as the guardian of his methodology. Jonathan mentioned him often in class as the benchmark, explaining how he was like a cuddly chinchilla next to his mentor – '"Your friends are your enemies, and your enemies are your friends." The other day you told me acting was the love of your life, not Nina.' I blushed, swallowed a lump in my throat. Everything he said felt like a test I wasn't sure how to pass.

Jonathan extinguished his cigarette on the heel of his shoe and dipped his hand under the foliage to check the rain had abated. As he left, he turned back and stretched a flat palm a foot from my chest.

'Your final show might not be Henry,' he said.

'Really?'

He gave a Gallic shrug. 'I'm not sure it's the best use of our . . . munitions.' He nodded to me and strode back into the building.

This was a huge shock. Over the summer, whispers went round that our final show would be *Henry V*, a star vehicle for Patrick, which made so much sense it had petrified into being all but confirmed. A change in repertoire at this stage wasn't unprecedented, what was strange was that Jonathan had chosen to reveal it to me.

'He already thinks I'm some pathetic little girl; you being the big man doesn't help.' Nina was angry with me on our journey home.

'He was such a dick to you.'

'He's a dick to everyone.'

'I don't know what happened, I just—I couldn't help it.'

'If you were hoping to get noticed, I hope it worked.' I hated her inferring it had all been some stunt to get Jonathan's attention but I couldn't argue. I hadn't thought about what I was doing at all. If I had, there was no way I would ever have confronted Jonathan. But whether I had done it out of chivalry or some unconscious opportunism, Jonathan and I had had an actual conversation. He'd chosen to give me the most valuable inside information and ever since he left me in The Rose Garden, the only question whirring around my head was why. On the walk from the station, my thoughts landed on the Shakespeare showing we were due to give the following day.

I went up to my room, took my shirt off and did my speech, Edmund from *King Lear*, in the mirror. I watched myself trip through the words but knew it wasn't right. Knowing what I knew about the final year show, the stakes now felt stratospheric. I needed something arresting, something unexpected. I tore through my Complete Works but nothing seemed right. I couldn't ask Nina because I'd have had to tell her about *Henry V* and, it seems mean-spirited to admit, but having been on the outside for so long, I didn't want to share my secret, even with her.

At about one, after I'd started learning a God-awful bit of *Timon of Athens*, I hit upon the answer. After a few more hours working on my new speech, I had another brainwave. I snuck downstairs and crept into Liv and Tommy's ensuite bathroom and found something I knew would get Jonathan's attention.

I felt giddy the next day as I watched the rest of my year give their speeches from the back row of chairs in Room 1. The head of voice Daniel Vasquez, who was in charge of the project, was dressed up even more than usual for the occasion. A violet oversized-collar shirt, high-waisted trousers and a golden belt so chunky it could have come from an Inca temple. He only wore Giorgio Armani, his mellifluous voice riding around the vowels of 'Giorgio' like he was tasting the thickest yoghurt. Daniel was The Conservatoire's self-appointed aesthete and felt it his place to comment on how the industry would perceive our looks. For me, my teeth, for Nina, her skin, which was based on a few spotty weeks in first year. Even Patrick was once told in class his face would be perfect if not for his 'Celtic splodge of a nose'. No one took it to heart because Daniel also thought huge choirs built the pyramids with their voices.

Patrick went before me and though I tried to remain focused, it was hard not to get pulled in as his Prince Hal warmed the cavernous room with his boundless magnanimity. Everything about it was effortless. I loved him for it and despised him. Every time he performed, it felt like a coronation.

The room swelled with applause when he finished, Aggie's enthusiasm, as always with Patrick, inappropriately over-the-top. I rose from my seat, fist clenched, and looped around the back of the audience, not daring to look at Jonathan as I passed. I leaped up the stairs and stood in the centre of the stage, back to the audience. Beneath the black paint of the back wall, I saw the ghostly lines and letters of past productions and thought about those who'd stood on the stage before me, the magical lineage I was part of, before turning to face my audience.

I lifted the razor blade I'd taken from Tommy's shaving

kit high into the air, so it glinted in the lights, and felt the room suck in towards me as they realised what I was holding. As if it was nothing, I scored a line down from the top of my palm to just above the cluster of veins on my wrist and watched as the blood plumed out.

Aggie cleared her throat, ready to stop it; Nina stood from her seat. At the edge of my vision, I felt Jonathan stilling them with a look.

'Oh that this too, too solid flesh would melt, thaw and resolve itself into a dew,' I began the *Hamlet* speech Jonathan saw something in at my audition. I stared at the blood as it dripped, clenching my fist to get it to pool and splash onto the stage. I brought the blade up to my other wrist at one point and the room's collective gasp felt like a hit of hard drugs. Holding them in my spell was so intoxicating I thought I might pass out.

When I came to the end, there was no applause. I looked to Jonathan but he was making notes, expression devoid of feeling. Daniel hurried the next person up. On stage, I had felt the room fizzing with the danger of what I did, but as I walked down, everyone looked pissed off. There were lines you didn't cross with the method. Not drinking real alcohol was one, and it seemed my self-harm, however mild, was another. I had probably known. Aggie gave me a distorted grin and, looking at the room of disappointed faces, I realised it wasn't cutting myself, nor the blood, that made my performance so distasteful to them, it was the desperation.

But I hadn't done it for them, I told myself as I walked

back to my seat, I did it for Jonathan. But he wouldn't, would not, look at me.

I sat next to Nina. She turned my hand over and began dressing the cut with a bandage from the first-aid kit.

'What did you think?' I whispered.

She glanced at me before looking away, shook her head repeatedly, a depth of sadness in her eyes. She balled my hands together and held them tightly in hers as Anna T began giving her Viola.

It was a Friday so we all went to the pub. No one was talking about what happened but I caught first and second years stealing glances at me, the word having quickly filtered out. It felt like people from my year arranged themselves as far away as they could, like I was infectious. Aside from an amused arched eyebrow from Vanessa across the room, none of my year made eye contact. After an hour or so, when I'd been drinking too quickly, something I always did when unsure of myself, I noticed none of faculty were there. All the teachers except Jonathan would normally join for the end-of-week pub session. I decided their absence must have been down to what I'd done during my speech. I barged through a crowd out the door, went round the corner onto the square and saw lights shining through the windows of The Church. The teachers were inside. I imagined them in an emergency meeting in the moon-lit staffroom, deciding what to do with me. Nina arrived behind, snaked her hand into my pocket for my cigarettes and sparked one.

'Are they going to throw me out, Nee?'

'I don't know, mate.'

'But, you think they could?'

'You're missing the biggest problem.'

I turned to her, couldn't believe the situation could be any worse.

'Without his razor blade, what's my dad going to use to chop up all his drugs?' I smiled wide, not quite ready to laugh. 'Let's go home,' she said, linking her arm through mine. We got cans from the offy for the train back and had stepped over the threshold of tipsy by the time we were home.

We brushed our teeth together, I followed her into her room and we collapsed on the bed.

'You ever thought about it though?' she said after a few minutes staring at the ceiling, a silver lining of toothpaste around her lips.

'Thought about what?'

'Leaving. What it'd be like, to not be there,' she whispered as if they were listening.

'What, like, choose to leave? No, never.'

'You remember getting the offer letter?' she said. 'I literally ran around the house, three or four laps. It was the most exciting thing that had ever happened.'

'I felt like Charlie Bucket,' I said. The idea of drama school, an acting career, felt so distant when I left school. Even when my drama teacher Mrs Goody came to my house to ask me to do a play she was directing in Leeds, trying to convince my dad I had 'real talent'; after Vic Mantell, the former Ampleforth teacher who ran a movie club in Kippax, steered me towards The Conservatoire, the chances of me getting in always felt millions to one. They were.

'Mum and Dad's jaws dropped when I told them which actors had been there.' She turned away, breath caught, trying to stop herself crying. 'Now you're cutting yourself, actual self-harm, just to get the teachers to notice you. What the fuck!' I took her hand, put my other arm under her neck and pulled her into me. 'Sorry,' she said.

I squeezed her shoulders, her body was so warm next to mine, the edges of her so soft against my skin. 'Maybe we just don't have it,' I said.

The idea we simply weren't good enough at acting, almost unconscionable, hung in the air as we stared at the shadows on her ceiling. I thought about what being thrown out would actually mean. The Conservatoire was a fairy-tale forest, spooky trees, the threat of a wolf within but, although I tried, I found I couldn't envision a new path through the fog. But with my arms around Nina, smelling the orange of her shampoo, I remember a tremendous feeling of lightness when I thought about a future away from The Church, away from Jonathan.

I took Nina's chin in my hand and turned her face to mine. I looked into her eyes, we took a breath together and then I kissed her. Her lips on mine felt like a sort of truth I'd always been searching for. When we parted, she buried her face in my shoulder and made a noise between a sigh and a laugh.

'Wasn't sure that would ever happen,' she said, I think

hoping it would be too muffled by my jumper for me to hear.

'You glad it has?'

She turned her head up to mine, face dropping into an earnest frown.

'Shut up.' She kissed me. We fell asleep holding each other. I woke and she was still there in the morning. I watched her sleeping for, it could have been ten minutes, longer. I was grinning like a maniac. If she'd woken she'd have probably been terrified. I was teen-movie happy; it was ridiculous. It wasn't just that we'd kissed, something I think I'd been pretending I didn't want to do from the first time we met, but how it didn't feel weird, how it felt right.

We walked to the park the next morning. Nina went to the supermarket with Liv, I helped Tommy in the garden. We helped each other learn lines, snuck wine up to the attic and watched *Silence of the Lambs*. We did what we would have done in any ordinary weekend during term-time but every moment felt like it had shimmering silver dusted on it from above because we were together. And, of course, we kissed. A lot. And it sounds like something from some repressed Victorian novel but that's all we did then. Our hands explored each other's backs, our stomachs, hands, arms, necks, ankles even, but I didn't want to go any further, to sully the simple beauty of that weekend with sex. We'd crossed the threshold of our friendship and I could see now it wouldn't have happened without Jonathan. If he hadn't come into the studio that evening when I was rehearsing Giovanni and lit a fire under me, I never would have found the courage to make the move. They were the two most perfect days I'd ever had.

Nina and I walked from the tube that Monday morning holding hands. We kicked through mulched leaves, the late autumn light filtered through trees. I felt at peace, almost wanted Jonathan and Aggie to throw me out. It would be more merciful to kill my dream abruptly than let it wither in an industry wilderness for the next decade and none of that mattered anyway because I had Nina, she had me. A career, a future, a job, in that moment, none of that mattered. She pulled me back at the end of the road that led onto the square.

'I don't want that place' – she flicked an arm towards The Conservatoire – 'to have anything to do with this, you and me, whatever this is.' She laughed, pulled herself into me.

'I'm with you,' I said. It felt almost impossible, but we let go of each other's hands, stepped apart and walked into the square, up the steps of The Church.

But as soon as we walked through the huge entrance, we could both sense something was very wrong. Amongst the normal bustle of first and second years, Group 28 were hunkered around the corridor in conspiratorial bunches on sofas, by lockers, in the entrance to the showers. Vanessa gave me an ironic eyebrow. I was certain I had been chucked out and they'd told my classmates first. I walked into the hall, stomach like a bag of trapped animals, unable to compute why James was smiling at me.

Nina grabbed my wrist and dragged me back to the

noticeboard by the front entrance and pointed at a piece of paper scrawled in Aggie's handwriting in the 'Group 28' section. A cast list. The cast list.

It didn't make sense. I blinked as I read, ran my finger down the notice, trying to understand what I was seeing.

'*The Tragedy of Hamlet, Prince of Denmark*, directed by Jonathan Dors,' was written at the top and, as I scanned the names, next to the word Hamlet: Adam Sealey. It was me. I was Hamlet. I sprang away from the board like I'd seen the ghost.

I looked at the mass of bodies in the corridor and rising above them, torso swelling through his vest, Patrick stood staring at me. He'd been cast as Laertes, Vanessa was Gertrude, Nina a gender-switched Guildenstern. But could any of it be real? I glanced at the staffroom, expecting to see Jonathan's narrow eyes watching through the porthole window, but no one was there.

'You're Hamlet,' Nina said, arms half-spread, unsure whether we could hug with the school watching. Her words made so little sense to me, it was like they had been carried in on the wind, whispers from some other realm. Her eyes were huge, joy concealing a thread of fear like I'd just been called up to a far-away war. I didn't know what to say to her, what else could I say?

'I'm Hamlet.'

Act 2

II.i

We left for Heathrow the morning after measuredbella's post. Despite having the luxury of travelling like a toddler, not having to reckon with any of the logistics and having someone on hand to check if I needed a snack, I found traversing LAX an ordeal. I was accustomed to being stared at in public places but after the comment, every passing look seemed a threat, every nudge from one stranger to the other suggested the whole world knew about the disappearance of this student.

I was more insulated in the first-class cabin but I still couldn't sleep. Amber woke up mid-flight and came and sat with me.

'Want to watch something?' she said. I nodded and we went through the catalogue together on the screen in front of our seat. We stopped at *On the Waterfront* and she confessed that, to her shame, she'd never seen it all the way through, so we synced our screens and put it on. I spent most of the time watching Amber connecting to Brando's performance with a depth people rarely find in real life.

She held my eye for a moment during the speech I'd done for Jonathan in my first year, before turning back to the screen.

'He got the Oscar for it,' she said as the closing credits rolled, dabbing under her eyes with a tiny paper napkin.

'He did.'

'He's your hero?'

I nodded.

'Is that why you want to win one so much?'

'No.'

'Why then, the recognition?'

'People talk about there being nothing worse than being invisible but there is. Maybe if I finally won—'

'You'd exist.'

'It's stupid.'

Amber said nothing for a moment.

'He turned down the second one they gave him, for *The Godfather*,' I said.

'For the native Americans, I know, the way Hollywood depicted them.'

'Kind of amazing.'

'Maybe it was easy for him. Perhaps the first one didn't give him what he was looking for.'

I looked at her, raised an eyebrow, trying to figure out this young woman who sounded a million years wiser than I was. 'Are you sure you want to be an agent?'

'Wanted to work in radio as a kid but, travelling first class, going to the Oscars. It's not bad. And how else would I get Michael B. Jordan to fall in love with me?'

'Makes sense.'

'Try to sleep, Adam,' she said, putting in her headphones and returning to her seat. I spent the rest of the flight drinking Diet Cokes and mainlining accounts of Russian spies for my next project, *Night-train to Rostov*, knowing if I closed my eyes, I might end up back in Room 1.

I felt jagged by the time we arrived at our Covent Garden hotel and as I looked out the ceiling-to-floor window of my suite at the dome of St Paul's, the carpet beneath felt like it was spinning. Since Van moved us out to the States six years before, I'd not been in London more than a day or two, where I'd be sequestered in a hotel room doing press. Even before, I was only ever jetting back from location somewhere to work with Jonathan on whichever role I was in. So, with my formative years there at The Conservatoire, the city was tethered with him in my head.

I tried to focus on the lights of London twinkling off miles of gleaming glass, but felt a tremor in my chest at the thought of seeing him the next day for the photoshoot. I'd have to ask him about this girl, I'd have to, and then the following day, I was going back to The Church.

I messaged Van to come up and, in a few minutes, she was marching through the door of my suite clutching an enormous burger in dripping greaseproof paper.

'You rang?' she said.

'Was wondering what you were up to?' I said.

She crinkled her face, like I'd told her I'd joined the Nazi party. 'You look . . . peaky.'

'What do you mean?'

'You look like shit, that clearer for you?' She split the burger in half and left me a portion she knew I wouldn't eat on the walnut table.

'This workshop with the students,' I said.

'Which was your idea, yes?'

'Do we have to do it at The Conservatoire?'

'Where else would we do it?'

'BAFTA?'

'You want to do a workshop at BAFTA the day of the actual BAFTA awards? No, of course that can't happen. You don't want to go to The Church?'

'Do you?'

'I'd prefer Bora Bora but it might be a bit incongruous. I wasn't keen on the PTSD nostalgia tour, if you remember, but there has been a press release. It'll be on all their TikToks. Delilah's probably built them a *Woodsman* lumberjack emoji.'

I returned to the window, got lost again in the blinking cranes.

Van crossed over and lowered the blind. 'We'll be in and out of the place in an hour,' she said. 'I'll get Amber to brief you on how to talk to young people. Photoshoot tomorrow. Get some beauty sleep.' She moved towards the door to go.

'Stay tonight,' I said.

She stopped, stood up straighter.

'We can watch a quiz show.'

'A quiz show?'

'Isn't that what people watch? You can get a martini. Sit

on the bed. Try and get the answers. You don't even have to talk to me.'

She grabbed a bottle of sparkling water from the dresser, strangled it open and drank, the glass clicking against her teeth. I'd never asked her to do this before. It was always when I found myself alone in hotel rooms I imagined how my life would have been with Nina. If she'd been with me on the planes, the cars, the beautiful locations, the trailers, which, however luxurious, were still always caravans. Chomping through complimentary fruit baskets on turned-down beds night after night, ambling conversations that solved nothing but meant everything. The smell of oranges on the pillow-case each morning. Showing me a better way to be.

'I think we need to sleep,' Van said.

I leant forward, put my hand out to her. She looked at it like it was a landmine.

'I won't sleep,' I said. She pushed the air out of her nose, chewed the side of her lip. There had been a moment, before what happened at the end of our last year at The Conservatoire, where there could have been potential for something between Van and me, intimacy perhaps, at least comfort, but never a glint afterwards.

'I can't, Adam.'

'Why not?'

'Good night.' She plonked the empty bottle of water on the dresser and left me in my suite, alone.

There was a black van waiting out front the next morning. I was dressed for the photoshoot. Tan boots, dark jeans, check over-shirt and a fur-trim sherpa jacket – understated Americana was the stylist's brief for the campaign. When I first questioned Van about it, she said it was all the rage.

'Timberlake, Gaga, Tay Tay. Back to nature, frontiersman vibes,' she said. 'It's probably an alt-right thing, but it sells.'

I grazed on a few fingers of mango in my suite before meeting her in the lobby. She was barely off her phone in the car, my request the night before not mentioned. I looked out the window as we headed north, feeling nothing for the greyscale grandeur of the centre of town. It was only when we left Euston and headed into Somers Town, the shock of the open space above the train-track arteries running into the city, that the memories of heading in and out of town on the 168 bus returned. I opened my window and breathed in the tarry tang of the streets. Everything was different, the dodgy boozers had become an anthracite gastropub, the babs-café had evolved into a chain sandwich shop. The people seemed unfathomably young, eyes fixed on phones or looking up at the city perplexed, but still the feeling of hope I had when I first moved down returned to me like a mudslide. I was like Dick Whittington, my provincial world exploded into an overwhelming new galaxy, streets paved with glistering possibilities.

We emerged into Mornington Crescent and the copper-domed Camden Palace reminded me of Moondance nights in second year, stood under the strobe-light Nina and I called Terry, the memory coming to me so vividly I asked the driver to stop so I could get cigarettes. Vanessa told him to ignore me without looking up. I'd not smoked for ten years.

Amber, cocooned in a furry parka, met us at the entrance to Hampstead Heath with a golf umbrella and escorted me to the location for the shoot as Vanessa strode ahead to ensure all was ready for my arrival.

'I've prepped the make-up lady to get the trowel for the bags under your eyes,' Amber said, as we walked past a team of ducks sheltering from the weather.

'Does it look that bad?'

'Like you've just had a newborn,' she said.

'Now there's a terrible idea.'

She squawked out a laugh. In the distance I saw lights through a thicket, assistants tying trees back to create what I'd been told would be a 'pastoral Shakespearean mise-en-scène'. I guessed Jonathan was Lear, my co-star Emmy would be Rosalind, which left me as who? Hamlet never did nature.

'It's *Measure for Measure*, isn't it?' Amber said just before we got to the clearing.

'What is?'

'Measuredbella. Isn't it a reference to Isabella in *Measure for Measure*?'

'Remind me.'

'Angelo tries to blackmail Isabella into sleeping with him. She threatens to expose him, even though he's this powerful guy in the Duchy.'

'What's a Duchy?'

'There's a duke; it's not important.'

79

'Oh right, the Duke. It's that one. She does expose him, doesn't she?'

'Eventually.'

'So what are you saying? That this person is trying to expose us?' I asked.

'I don't know, expose what?' she said, rocking her shoulder into mine. 'Don't worry, Adam, it's the internet.'

We arrived at the edge of the glen and there he was, Jonathan, on a camping chair under a sycamore, Styrofoam cup in one hand, cigarette in the other. Although we'd emailed to discuss working on the Cold War film, this was the first time I'd seen him since the Wasatch Mountains. He wore a trench coat, woolly hat and had a blanket over his legs. He looked like an old man and for the first time the thought struck me that he would die.

'Talent's on set,' Van declared, making me cringe, assistants fluster over plastic sheets and the tiny, hirsute photographer look at his watch like our arrival had initiated a doomsday device. Jonathan lifted his head. I smiled and raised a flat hand in greeting. He blinked, conveying he was neither pleased nor unhappy to see me. Deflated, I looked around the crowd for Emmy, hoping she could be relied on for a warmer greeting.

'Emmy's on her way,' Amber reassured me. I looked for her agent Benny for confirmation, a lanky young man with a pencil moustache who everyone in the industry adored, but none of her people were there. Amber indicated a chair being put out for me next to Jonathan. After another glance around the trees, I went and sat down. He and I

80

didn't speak for a moment. I'd never managed to overcome the straitjacket formality his having been my teacher had instilled in me and it seemed the closer we were, the tighter the buckles were pulled.

The photographer waved a light-meter about, ranting in German to himself. Van was getting rained on beyond the clearing, frowning at her phone.

'How's it going, Jonathan?' I said.

'Damp.' He got out another cigarette. 'Not smoking still?'

'Heard it's bad for you.' Jonathan's mouth drooped, making me regret my joke. He'd never been vain, but I could see now his coat was new, an expensive old English brand, and he wore a silver watch he hadn't had before. He'd spent years turning down directing jobs and private work as an acting coach due to his commitment to The Conservatoire, but after word spread of his work on *Woodsman*, the floodgates opened. Several older actors doing villains in prestige TV and a few young starlets with enterprising management had gone to him and word had it the results had been transformative. On top of this, the director Danny Barrett-Hughes had done the impossible and convinced Jonathan to act, playing the leader of a crime cartel running operations from prison in a Netflix show. It was a surprising coup that got both Jonathan and the project a lot of press.

'You're off to sprinkle your stardust on The Conservatoire?'

I was surprised to hear him colour the name of the school like a disgraced relative. 'Tomorrow.'

Jonathan said nothing. The photographer barked and his assistants rushed to put coloured gels on a standing light.

'It was my PR's idea,' I felt I had to say.

He closed his eyes and tilted his head forward as if someone had switched him off. I fiddled with the net cup-holder in my chair. This missing girl seemed an elephant sat between him and me, but I didn't know how to ask. Twenty, thirty people shuffled through the wet leaves, moving equipment to keep warm while the two of us sat cocooned in strained stillness.

Until I heard Van say, 'Fuck sake!' under her breath. She darted over and tried to get me away from Jonathan using silent, emphatic gesticulations.

'Emmy's not coming,' Jonathan said without opening his eyes. She looked at him, then back at me.

'No,' she said.

'Shall we get on then?' Jonathan said, getting up and walking with the force of a much younger man into a cloud of mist someone had just pumped out of the hazer.

'What the fuck?' I said.

'Benny said she's got another engagement.'

'It's the *Times*. She needs this much more than us.' Emmy had been nominated as Best Supporting at the BAFTAs, the Globes, the SAGs and others, but hadn't received anything from the Academy.

'In some ways she does, but—'

'We insisted she be here. You said the BAFTAs was about . . . what did you call it?'

'A groundswell.'

The movie had done well at festivals. It first played to standing ovations at Berlin, which, although I always say I don't do it for the applause, was a rush. I won Best Actor at Cannes but then what was looking like an awards juggernaut started to meander in the press's opinion. We got one or two gongs at some of the other awards ceremonies, my win at the Globes helped pick up momentum, but we hadn't managed to establish ourselves as cast-iron favourites in any of the categories.

'And she's—Not a friend but we got on. All the press stuff so far, it's been great. Why would she pull out like this?'

'It's a busy time, Adam.'

'It's this girl, isn't it?' I said. 'When did Emmy finish at The Church? Two years ago?'

'Three.'

'She could know the missing girl.'

Van took one of her breaths, pushing the exhalation down into the floor. 'As far as we know, there is no missing girl. Emmy Reed is nuclear-meltdown hot in the industry, Adam. She probably does have another engagement.'

'I have an hour,' Jonathan bellowed through the artificial fog. Van pointed towards the set. I made my way over, leaning down so the make-up lady could powder as I went.

The shoot was painful. The concept required all three of us, three generations of British method acting, a lineage reaching into the past. As we stood waiting for the photographer to finish a lengthy phone call with the editor who'd set it up, I felt people behind us in the trees, dog-walkers peering under the canopy before being shooed away by assistants. At one point there was a scuffle in the bushes as production runners chased off a middle-aged woman with a huge camera around her neck. This wasn't unusual shooting somewhere public but, with Emmy's failure to show up, I couldn't help thinking these people had all read the comment, wondering why I was palling up with Jonathan. Or even that this person, measuredbella, might be hiding in the undergrowth, adding pictorial evidence to her case against us.

The photographer started shooting but didn't know how to arrange us. Jonathan was put several feet behind me because of his height, but with his refusal to wear make-up, Van told me he looked like Nosferatu. With each niggle and adjustment, although his face didn't betray it, I could see him getting more and more irritated, taking frequent breaks to smoke, which brought out a rattling cough he hadn't had the year before.

I found myself with him during one of these breaks. He clicked his lighter for one of his foot-long cigarettes and it failed to spark, making him throw it to the floor. It was disquieting to see him so petulant, so mortal. Amber, trying not to be noticed, picked up the lighter and put it in her pocket.

'Can't you find me a device that functions?' Jonathan snarled at her.

'I think it's got wet,' she said.

'Did I ask for your thesis?'

Amber looked at me to defend her, but I couldn't. I held my hand out for the lighter, which she gave me before scurrying off, rocked by his venom. I dried the lighter on my jeans and leant over to light his cigarette. His casual cruelty sat like a ball of static between us as he smoked in silence.

84

A rally of wind brushed through the trees above. I looked up and saw a strand of black rope, drifting on a bough high above. I saw the body, closed my eyes but still the image remained. A branch creaked somewhere.

'You saw this story?' I said, eyes springing open. 'A student who disappeared?'

Jonathan sucked his cigarette until the cherry glowed white at its tip.

'I didn't know you retired in the middle of the year.'

'Why would you?'

'Was it to do with this girl?'

He took a breath before swivelling round to me. Maxi, the photographer, called from under a waterproof cover and an assistant came to bring me and Jonathan to set. They positioned him behind me, had me stand in profile. When Maxi was back at his tripod, I felt Jonathan leaning towards me.

'It was, Adam.'

'What was?'

'The reason I left. It was related to the girl.'

I turned round to him.

'Can we stay like this, Adam, two moments.' The camera rattled and I waited for a break, desperate to know what he meant. Maxi paused and I snapped back to Jonathan.

'Her name was Raya Bilson,' he said.

'What happened to her?' I leant in, Van glaring at us from behind the lights.

'She left the school.'

'Why?'

'They asked her to.'

'Who?'

'The powers that be.'

I could feel the breath growing higher in my chest as I thought what he could mean.

'There was an altercation.'

'A fight.'

'Between two of the students. Raya was thought to be the aggressor so they threw her out. My appeals on her behalf fell on deaf ears so I left, to make a stand. The girl was working on a character and got carried away, lost her temper. They chose to make an example of her, which was a shame. She was talented.'

'Were you—' I said in a whisper, 'directing the girls?'

'They were second years. Barely knew them.'

'You left because of it, and you didn't even know them?'

Jonathan glared at me, eyes narrowing. I noticed Amber by a stack of sandbags, picking at her fingernails, seeming to question her existence after her brush with Jonathan.

'The bean counters at the University had been threatening a code of ethics ever since they swallowed us,' he said. 'The kind of oversight that would render Ingram's methodology completely untenable. I hoped my advocacy might change their minds about Raya but in truth, the incident confirmed to me that we had tipped fully into a puritanical inquisition. Even if I'd managed to save Raya' – he flicked sleepy eyes up at me – 'I felt I had no choice. I could have kicked up a stink but for the sake of the students there, and the many who had gone before, I withdrew from the faculty without even a whimper.' His fingers were tensed into claws, eyes glassy. It sounded like grief.

An assistant came and offered us coffee. 'They're just waiting for a cloud to move,' she told us in near-perfect English before sensing the thickness in the air between us and leaving.

'Did Raya know you'd been trying to keep her at the school?'

Jonathan weighed my question in the foliage above him. 'We kept conversations within the staff.'

'Could it be her, then?' I said. 'The comment, measuredbella. You were the figurehead of the school. Is it possible she's trying to get back at you?'

He hummed as if I'd reminded him of a joke. 'She was mercurial as a student. It's possible but—' He stepped back, appraising me like chattel. 'Your Rs have been hard since we've been talking,' he said. 'Russian. You've been getting into the mindset of a KGB interrogator working with the CIA. And this' – his long fingers traced the air in front of me – 'this thing on the internet. You seem to have taken it very much to heart. Is it possible your preparation for the character might be bleeding into your thoughts?'

I shook my head, trying to scrub away his nonchalance. 'Measuredbella, though, it's *Measure for Measure*.'

'I picked up the reference.'

'What if there's more? What if she's planning to expose—'

'What, Adam?' His tone gripped like a vice, urging me not to go further. Jonathan glanced at the crew pretending not to watch us and brandished an unlit cigarette. I got the lighter out of my pocket, sparked it and he leant in. 'Only you and I know what happened,' he said, face inches from mine.

'How about . . .?' I said, eyeing Vanessa.

'That's right, your manager,' he said, standing up. Van was in her usual pose, eyes on her phone, amused and pissed off at the same time. She'd spent her life building my career, I was her biggest client, our fortunes were intertwined. She was there that night, but it didn't make sense she'd endanger that.

'Your performance in *Woodsman*,' Jonathan said and, despite everything, I felt myself perk up for his feedback. 'It was wonderful.'

I had the sensation of dropping down a rollercoaster. He'd not said a thing about my work since leaving The Conservatoire. I made peace with it; after movies were finished what use would his analysis be when the performance couldn't be changed, but here it was.

'It could be a legacy for you, perhaps for our work. You once told me you sought immortality. In a few weeks' time you could claim it. You know my ambivalence to gongs and garlands, for most I'd discourage their pursuit, but I know you don't want it to show your greatness to other people, you need it to prove it for yourself. I want to support that.' Maxi arrived and fiddled with the lapel of Jonathan's purple suit. 'You think I'd put myself through this pantomime,' he said, eyeballing the photographer, 'if I didn't think it was essential?' Jonathan brushed Maxi away and headed to his mark, smoke billowing over his shoulders. I looked at the black rope above me, closed my eyes, saw nothing but trees when I looked again. Only the three of us knew, and there's no way Van or Jonathan would have told a soul.

How could you?

There had been no phone call that night in the cabin, the comment had to be a coincidence. Jonathan was right, the paranoia I'd been working on for Yevgeny was leaking into how I was seeing everything. It was in my head. 'Keep it sane,' Van always said, 'keep it sane.'

In the car on the way back to the hotel, I told Vanessa what Jonathan said about Raya. She seemed unruffled, so by the time I made it back to my suite I felt confident any concerns about blogposts and missing students would soon be resolved. The girl was thrown out after some minor incident at the school, no one had disappeared. I collapsed onto my bed and finally slept.

But Amber was in my room within the hour, rushing me to the hotel entrance where a car was waiting to take us to Van's office.

'She's found the girl?' I asked, euphoric Van had already put everything to bed.

'She doesn't tell me anything,' Amber said with a shrug. Twenty-five minutes later, I was in the lift at her building in the heart of Piccadilly.

There was a wave of excitement amongst the troop of young assistants who'd never met me as Amber took me through Van's open-plan London office. I glanced at piles of contracts, bound scripts, proof copies of new books sent for her clients to read. Part of me wanted to stop and talk to her employees, but knowing they spent their days booking flights for me, telling venues what I'd want for lunch, making sure there wouldn't be wine on the table, made me so embarrassed I couldn't. Being treated like a child sultan is easier if you don't have to look into the eyes of your subjects.

Van beckoned me in through the glass wall of her back office when she saw us. Amber opened the door and I was surprised to see a striking young black girl sitting across the desk from Vanessa. She wore a teal scarf and stood as she saw me, bunching her hands together when she noticed they were shaking. I looked at Van, so pleased she'd found Raya that I wanted to give them both a hug.

'Is this—'

'This is Lyndsey,' Van said, cutting me off. I held her look for a moment before turning to the girl.

'Oh my God,' the girl said in a cut-glass accent, breaking into a huge smile. 'I've seen everything you've ever been in. I'm, like, a colossal fan.'

'That's so nice of you,' I said, 'especially if you've seen absolutely everything.' She laughed too much at my self-deprecation. Vanessa nodded for me to sit.

'Lyndsey's in her final year at The Conservatoire, doing Nina in their production of *The Seagull*,' Van said. 'I've heard great things, so wanted to meet in case we didn't have time before we have to get back to LA.'

I smiled at the girl, whose eyes were eager and terrified

like prey. I remembered it, interest from an agent was like a visit from an angel. An acting career felt so distant when we were training that the promise of a champion, a partnership, seemed an ungraspable treasure. Although I still had no idea what I was doing in the room with them.

'You must be stacked with all the awards stuff,' Lyndsey said, turning to me. 'So honoured you could make time for me.' I noticed a patch of perforated skin on the lower part of one side of her face. The mark continued onto her neck, visible either side of the scarf and down to her right shoulder. The skin was darker, pearlescent. A burn.

'We were chatting about The Conservatoire?' Vanessa said.

'God, I knew nothing when I arrived,' Lyndsey said. 'I thought I did, but it's like they've taken that apart, everything I was doing before and remade it into something deeper, more powerful.'

'We'd heard the training had become a little watered down?' Van said.

'I hate to think what it was like before then.' Lyndsey raised her eyebrows. 'But that's what you need, isn't it? I mean, Adam, you've nearly *died* for roles.'

'Not quite.'

'It's the best job in the world, so it has to be hard, it has to be harder than anything you've ever even thought of because, otherwise, the audience will know, it won't be truthful and you'll be cheating them.'

'You sound like Adam!' Van said, noticing me staring at the girl's burn still. 'Did something happen though, last year? You had a coming together with another student?'

Van sounded casual but there was a tautness in her voice and I realised why she'd called me in. Lyndsey wasn't a prospective client. She was the girl who had the fight with Raya. I noticed a picture on top of a pile of actor's head-shots on Van's desk. A skinny girl with haunted hazel eyes and light brown hair in bunches. I glanced at Lyndsey's burn. 'If you don't want to talk about it—'

'It's fine.' She balled her hands, darted a glance at me, eyes wary.

'What happened?' I asked.

'A girl in my year, Raya. She' – Lyndsey blinked. I could see her remembering, trying not to remember – 'threw boiling water at me.'

'Fucking hell!' I said. Van darted me a warning look.

'I don't think she meant to. She struggled in first year and they gave her a bigger role in our second year showing. She put all this insane pressure on herself and . . . went a bit . . . funny? Stopped talking to everyone, stayed in character the whole time' – Van glanced at me – 'she snapped. I was in the wrong place at the wrong time.'

'I'm so sorry that happened to you,' I said.

'But it's like the training,' Lyndsey spoke as if she hadn't heard me, touching the top of her burn. 'It hurt, course it did, but it's healed now and I'm stronger. I can use the experience. And you know, I've got the lead in the final show, I'm meeting you. This might sound weird, but I'm grateful for what happened.'

'That's a wonderful way of looking at it,' Van said, the tone of someone wrapping things up.

'Is Raya still at The Church?'

'She was asked to leave, but we – my year – we didn't want that at all. Raya felt terrible about it and—' She picked at her thumbnail, eyes on the floor.

'We'd like to know, Lyndsey.'

'After how she'd been before, we were worried what she might do to herself, if they threw her out.'

I closed my eyes and saw the rope. I stood up and crossed to the back of the room, pretended to straighten a Korean poster of one of my films, *Lightwell Grange*. I felt sick. I knew the ardour The Conservatoire bred in its students, I'd felt it in my marrow, still did. I'd been ignored for the first two years as well. If I'd been thrown out of the school just at the point I'd won the teachers' favour, I couldn't imagine what it might have made me do.

'Is anyone in touch with her?' Van said, the breeze through the window tickling the hanging plants behind her.

'This last year has been so intense, no one's really talked about Raya. That's terrible, isn't it? I'm sure someone's spoken to her. I can ask?'

'That's sweet,' Van said, 'but we're just being nosy. Ignore us. Now, it might be a push coming over for your show, but you've got a great look and I can just feel you'd have a wonderful screen presence.' Van's compliments blew away the clouds and Lyndsey brightened like someone had turned up a dimmer-switch. 'My assistant will send some scenes over and you can put yourself on tape?'

'Oh my God, I'd love to,' she said.

'Great,' Vanessa stood. 'We have to run but, such a pleasure.' She extended her hand for Lyndsey to shake.

'Yeh, totally, thank you,' Lyndsey said, pumping Van's hand before turning to me. 'Can't wait for the workshop tomorrow!' I shook her hand and plastered on a smile at the idea of going back to The Church. Amber opened the door for Lyndsey. She stared at me for a moment longer, seeming like she didn't want to leave, before turning to go.

'What part was she playing?' I asked Lyndsey, stopping her in the entrance.

'Sorry?'

'You said Raya had been given a bigger role.'

'We were doing the Greeks,' she said, drifting back into the room.

I nodded – we always did the Greeks in second year.

'Medea,' she said.

'Great to meet you, Lyndsey,' Van said, giving me a basilisk-glare. 'But we do have—'

Lyndsey clasped her hands together, nodded to Van and left.

Van came and stood next to me and we watched Lyndsey passing through the office and out the doors. Once she'd disappeared, Van swished her coat off the back of the door and brushed past me, ushering me to follow her.

'Well,' Van said, motor boating a breath through her lips as she headed towards the lift. 'That seems conclusive.'

'What?'

'It's studio bullshit. Carl Dillane's people probably.' She backed into the lift. I followed her in.

'She didn't know where Raya is?'

'Adam, they're acting students, they live for the drama. If one of them had disappeared in mysterious circumstances, they'd know about it. This Raya's ashamed, has fallen off the radar. Happened to that guy Teddy who got asked to leave at the end of our first year.'

'Who?'

'Exactly, we didn't give him a second thought, it didn't mean something happened to him. He'll be an accountant now, sex tourist, blissfully content.'

'It sounded like Raya was unhinged.'

'Lots of people think you're unhinged.'

'I didn't scald anyone.'

Van stopped and gave me a look that chilled before the lift opened and she led us through the lobby to the street, where she walked into the bus lane to force an oncoming cab to stop for us.

'She was doing Medea,' I said when we were a few streets from her office.

'I heard.'

'She's playing the woman who kills her own children, murders her rival, the archetype of female rage and she does something like this to her classmate?'

'I said I know, Adam.'

'You think Jonathan had something to do with it?'

She shrugged.

'He said he didn't know Raya. He wouldn't lie to me.'

95

'He said it was an altercation, Adam. When I realised he'd underplayed it, it seemed prudent, if it were to emerge Jonathan did have some part in it, to get the student involved on our team.'

'That's why you got Lyndsey in?'

Van shrugged.

'You were never going to sign her?'

'I wasn't before, no, but casting directors would shit bricks for that bone structure. It's not like you're making me enough.' She smirked at her joke, but as cyclists buzzed past the window, one of whom nearly fell off taking a picture of me, all I could think about was the girl with the eyes, Raya, from the photo on Van's desk, sat in a room at The Conservatoire, working herself into such a rage she picked up a pan of boiling water and threw it at her friend.

II.ii

On the first day of rehearsals for *Hamlet*, I walked into
Room 1 after lunch to find Patrick leading the rest of the
company in a warm-up. It was a week after my casting had
been announced. A week where the initial honour I felt on
being chosen to play the role had dissolved into almost im-
mediate paranoia. It seemed like every conversation around
the school was about me, how I wasn't up to the part, that
it had to be Jonathan testing Patrick. I checked the noticeboard several times a day expecting to see a revised cast list,
almost hoping for it, to let me off the hook. *Hamlet* is the
ultimate challenge for the actor. There had been nothing
from my time at The Conservatoire, no stand-out second-
year performance or highly praised exercise, that made me
think I was up to it.

Things between Nina and I felt different too. Where
just a few hours before it felt like we were floating along a
rainbow road of endless possibilities, after we'd seen the
cast list, a heaviness hung between us. Our secret conversations, the little world of our own we were beginning to

imagine, became overwhelmed by *Hamlet*. Nina could talk of nothing else.

'Was it the *'Tis Pity* speech, do you think?' she asked as we walked from the train to her house, hands that were desperate to enfold each other before now held in uneasy peace. 'You never showed it to me, it must have been incredible.'

'I'm not sure.'

'Because, the razor-blade thing . . . Doesn't send a great message if they're rewarding you for that.'

I shrugged.

'I mean, sorry,' she said. 'It is so amazing.' For the first few days, she'd qualify everything she said like this. Both of us were baffled as to how I'd been cast, but even though she knew it wasn't particularly supportive, Nina couldn't help trying to make sense of it. Those sorts of conversations, trying to understand why certain people had been given roles ahead of us, were a huge part of our friendship. Except now I was the chosen one, so felt desperate to talk about anything else. I would put on music, stupid films, pull her face to mine and kiss her, hold her head into my neck so she couldn't tell me again how great it was, how proud she was of me. I wanted things to return to how they had been before because I felt like I had been pulled out of a quagmire at random, and with the small part she'd been given, had left Nina behind to rot.

Patrick made a point of speaking to me the day after the cast list was posted. I'd been trying to avoid him, but he saw me heading to the bus-stop from the Three Corners, where he was outside having a pint with a smart-suited older man.

'I'm made up for you, man, seriously,' he said, leaning against the pub window. 'Such a demanding role. Would terrify me, but we're all right behind you. I should get back but, this weekend, buy you a pint?' On the bus into town, I felt relieved Patrick didn't see me as I saw myself, a usurper to the anointed king. If I'd known the man he was with was Vanessa's agent father Alasdair, I would have seen our exchange as the reassertion of status it was, and his forgetting to mention he'd organised a warm-up on the first day of rehearsals would have been less of a surprise.

I didn't want to seem precious, so I ditched my bag and jumped into the set of burpees they were doing, but almost immediately Patrick jumped up and went into a long tongue-twister everyone joined in with. I watched the robotic speed of his lips and tongue, trying to keep up. He started another before I'd finished the first, waving his arms to egg us on to match his tempo. As I looked around the circle at the grins and steaming bodies of my classmates, my terror about the role started to melt away and for the first time I felt excited about the play.

Patrick broke us out a minute before nine and we clumped together, staring at the door, braced for Jonathan's arrival. We'd never been directed by him, but judging by his classes, it wasn't going to be a fairground ride. Bang on time he swung through, crocodile-embossed notebook against his chest, and the most astonishing thing happened. He opened his arms and smiled.

'This,' he began as the doors closed behind him, 'is a "big fuck-off" play.' I heard a few sucked breaths at his swearing for the first time in front of us. 'The sort of grown-up, sophisticated material Ingram's methodology is designed to help us tame. You must give all of yourself to the play or risk failing it, which, I'm sure you would agree, would be a mortal sin. Let us read.' He swept his arms towards the table and the group around me dispersed. Jonathan beckoned me to him.

'How are you, Hamlet?' he asked.

'Good,' I said, trying to stifle the thrill of him christening me with the hallowed name.

'This is a process. A long one. You won't get fourteen weeks in the real world. Nothing's expected of you straight away. I will help you get where you need to be, but I cannot do that unless you are willing to go there. Are you prepared to do that?'

'Definitely.'

He blinked and waved me towards the table to join the others to begin our first read-through of the play.

Once sat, Jonathan told us it was a 'reading not a performance' and we began. Although I had an insect-buzz of anxiety when I spoke my first words, things felt OK. I was tripping on the odd syllable, but my performance felt light, in control. When I got to the 'too, too solid' speech, assuming it was my Shakespeare showing that won me the role, I imagined the blood dripping down my arm as I spoke. I caught Nina giving me a secret smile and had the sense that I still had her and that with support, I might actually be able to do Hamlet.

Jonathan was stone-still as we read, face pointed to the roof, the model-box of the production's design on the desk in front of him, peopled by tiny tin figures. We got to the players' scene and James and I had fun with it, throwing lines to each other like we were fencing. I noticed Jonathan's shut eye flinching. I hoped he was hearing it like I was, enjoying it even. I began my soliloquy at the end of the scene. Jonathan began tapping the blunt end of his fountain pen on the pages of his notebook.

Halfway through the speech, the pen stopped.

'Back to the top,' Jonathan said. The room clenched.

'Sorry?' I said.

'Go back. Top of the speech.' He opened his eyes, forehead bunching into four thick folds. I cleared my throat.

'O, what a rogue and peasant slave am I! Is it not monstrous that this player here but in a fiction—'

'No.' Jonathan rubbed his temples. He tapped five heartbeats on his notebook. Silence spread like an oil spill. I was blushing, chest held, waiting for him to speak. 'Have another go,' he said.

I looked to Nina for help, knowing I was doing something wrong. Vanessa looked out the window, sucking on a pencil. Patrick stretched his hands above his head, muscles balling in his arms.

I started the speech and Jonathan stopped me again, five or six lines in.

'Stand?'

'Sorry?'

'Perhaps you want to stand.'

I stood. The room felt a thousand degrees. Nina's hands were on the desk, ready to jump as if she were watching a blind man wandering along the top of a cliff.

'Take your time,' Jonathan said. I took the speech slower, a pause at each punctuation point, giving each word a different intonation, trying to get it right.

Jonathan laughed. It stopped me dead.

'The metre, Hamlet?'

'Sorry?'

'The rhythm.' He spat the words, smile frosting his face still.

'Shall I go from the top?'

'Please.'

I stared at the page, began speaking.

After two lines, he stopped me. 'Clap it.'

'What?'

'Iambic pentameter,' he said, a friendliness that from him was terrifying. 'Five feet. Short stress, long stress.' His tone put a dunce's cap on me. 'Clap it.' My breath caught. I swallowed and started again, clapping the rhythm as I went.

'No words. Just clap.'

The room felt thick, insulated with my humiliation. As I clapped the heartbeat stresses, Jonathan rose from his desk. I lost the ability to count in clusters of five, the rhythm went awry, lost it entirely. Nina was tapping her hand on the desk, nodding encouragement. Vanessa looked up at me through anxious eyebrows.

Jonathan flipped the model-box on its head, sending it crashing back to the desk, metal figures spilling over the horseshoe of tables.

'Keep going,' he said. He started slamming the rhythm on the desk with his palm, goading everyone to do the same. He looked at me floundering, hyperventilating almost, unable to keep to his beat.

Something pinged into my chest. He was throwing the tiny figurines at me. He threw one on each stress, another and another. Everyone else stopped clapping, pinned to their seats. Jonathan circled, pinging the figures into me as I tried to count, one hit me in the neck, one on the side of the face.

'Dee dum, dee dum, dee dum, dee dum, dee dum,' he shouted, right behind me. He must have run out of little men because they stopped thudding into me, but I kept clapping like a possessed toy monkey.

'Speak the speech,' he said, separating the words like he was ordering an assassination.

'Oh, what a rogue and peasant slave am I,' I said, struggling to keep it together.

Three lines later, Jonathan started speaking over me, face inches from mine. 'Eee by gum. Down t'mine. Margaret, where's me gravy. Blah blah blah blah blah blah blah.'

I stopped. As did he, his childish mockery of my accent ringing around the nave. The room panted with adrenalin, though no one moved. Although I did everything I could to try and smother it, I burst into tears.

'The waterworks,' Jonathan said, sonorous tone returning. 'Hamlet isn't waterworks. Hamlet isn't slicing-yourself shock tactics. We don't want cheap pyrotechnics from Hamlet. We love him for his brain. His brain. You can't even understand the words he's saying. I'm talking to you.'

'I do, I understand it,' I said, his breath on the top of my head.

'Are you telling me I'm wrong?'

'No.'

'You are the Shakespearean scholar?'

'No.'

He stepped away from me. My body jerked, desperate to leave the hall.

'You want to leave?'

'No.'

'You can. Please do. Fuck off.' Every sinew was desperate to escape but I didn't move. Nina stared with wide, scared eyes, willing me to sit, so I sat. 'Let's get to the end,' Jonathan said. The heel of his shoe clacked against the stone floor as he went to sit on the stage where the altar used to be. He listened to the rest of the read-through lying back with his arm over his face.

As soon as Jonathan left, Patrick said the word 'Pub?' and the chairs couldn't be scraped back quick enough. As everyone left, I bent down to pick up the model pieces and started placing them back inside their cardboard stage one by one. Nina arrived beside me.

'I'm OK,' I said. She knelt down, scraped the remaining figures into her hand and shoved them into the model-box.

'There. Now come to the pub.'

'I'm just going to—'

'What? Wait for him to come back and throw something else at you?'

I shook my head, though of course that was why I was staying.

'I feel like, don't you think we should tell someone? Aggie or—'

'No,' I said, tone harsher than I'd intended. 'It was me.' I took her wrist in my hand. 'The rhythm, I wasn't doing it right.'

She looked away, put her hand over mine. The dying sunlight from the stained glass window painted a rainbow around her. Jonathan was right and Nina knew it.

'You go to the pub,' I said. 'I'm not going to be much fun.'

She kissed my neck, nodded, pulled away. It was the most loving she had been since we'd read the noticeboard. She couldn't help feeling jealous of my elevation to Hamlet, everyone was, but that afternoon we'd all seen what being Jonathan's leading man really meant.

I stacked the tables and chairs on the back wall after she left, reset the model-box on the front of the stage and waited for Jonathan to come back and retrieve it. I was staring up at Jesus on the window above the stage, bearing his cross through the streets, when the door opened. I swung round, expecting to see Jonathan, but it was Vanessa. She considered leaving, then sauntered in.

'Know the last time The Conservatoire did a production of *Hamlet*, Adam?'

'When?'

'Never. They've never done *Hamlet*.'

'Is that meant to make me feel better?' She wandered towards me, her posture so upright she always seemed feet taller than me though we were around the same height. She caught her hair in a clump and tied it up, exposing her long neck and collarbones that punched through her skin. Her beauty was so wrapped up in how intimidating she was, it was easy to forget it was there at all.

'None of us know why – honestly, everyone's scratching their heads – but you are Jonathan's Hamlet. Don't know if that makes you feel better or worse.' She walked over to the desk, closed my rehearsal text and took it up. 'I heard him say to you before we started, it's a process. Today was only day one.' Van handed me my script, flicked one of her eyebrows, turned and left me for the car waiting for her out front. As I watched her disappear through the huge double doors, I wondered why it was she'd come back into Room 1. She'd never taken time to talk to me like that before, so I thought she must have forgotten something, but as I scanned the room for a coat, a bag she might have missed, it became clear she came in just for me.

A sunbeam caught me in the corner of my eye. I looked up at Jesus on the window, head turned to Room 1, blood and sweat dripping onto his forehead, and I suddenly understood what Van had meant. Jonathan hadn't lost his temper. It was a call to arms.

I clutched my play-text to my chest, left through the emergency exit to avoid the rest of my year and walked to Camden Town Library, where I asked for a dictionary. The librarian handed me three volumes and pointed me to a desk in the reading room amongst older gentlemen with their heads in newspapers and students gazing into space. I proceeded to look up every word from Hamlet and started to write out the whole play, not just my lines, in language that made sense to me. It was slow going because my hand was still sore from where I cut myself and Jonathan had been right, I didn't understand the vast majority of the play.

When the library was about to close, knowing I wouldn't be able to take the dictionaries home, I shoved them through the small window in the ground-floor toilet and had to run round to collect them. By the time I got there a homeless man had purloined J to R and I had to give him a pound to get it back.

When I got home, Nina still at the pub, I swerved Liv's dinner to finish working through the play. I was onto the last act, head feeling like Angel Delight when, about midnight, Nina stumbled in and threw her arms around my neck. She noticed the books and stacks of scrawled paper on the floor around my desk and started laughing.

'Mate, I love you, you're so literal,' she said, trying to prop herself up. I wasn't sure she'd known what she said, but the three words made something fizz in my stomach. She stepped back, reached a hand for me, tried to make her drunk eyes look sultry. I stood up and kissed her. She tasted of fun, cigarettes and red wine. We shuffled across the room and she fell back onto the bed, arranged herself under the covers, made a space for me.

'I'm not quite finished,' I said, stood above her.

Nina raised an incredulous eyebrow.

'I'm on act five.' I flicked on the HiFi, brought over the glass of water on my desk and kissed her again – tried to kiss like I meant it, though my head was still in Elsinore. 'Half an hour.' She rolled her eyes and snuggled into the bed. I went back to my work, and ten minutes later she had passed out. I turned off the light, got out a pen-torch and scratched away with my biro, listening to Nina sleeping until I finished at about two. She was sprawled over my single bed so, not wanting to wake her, I lay on the floor beside her, fingers beating heartbeats onto the nearby chair-leg, as they had since I left The Church.

For the next few days, I continued my assault on the text, Nina taking it upon herself to be my coach. She recorded my lines on her dad's dictaphone, stressing the rhythm, which I listened to on my commute, while working at the Italian restaurant where I washed pots, even as I slept. She'd come on runs with me in the park, as I tried to build my fitness up for the part. But I started going out by myself later at night, wanting to run faster, further than she could manage. Liv lent me her rape alarm because Bexleyheath was rougher back then. When I ran through kids smoking weed, older folks spilling from the pub, veins angry with booze, it spurred me to run farther from the sanctity of the Dumas' two-up-two-down, deep into the halogen fury of the streets.

I engaged our speech teacher Lizya Abelard, who gave me a forty-five minute, once-a-day diction work-out, which I did four times a day. My lips ached constantly, and the root of my tongue was so sore I thought the whole thing might detach, but I soon felt the exercises working. My speech became sharper, more precise, tongue tapping around my mouth like a stenographer.

This was around the time Nina was due to go up in front of Jonathan to redo her emotional memory exercise. I was in the kitchen at their house and heard her berating her mum about it, something I'd never witnessed before.

'Everyone else has been through something,' Nina said. 'Adam's got his mum, James is gay, Anna was sexually assaulted at the cinema. Even Vanessa, most perfect girl in our year, her dad's had tonnes of affairs.'

'I don't quite know what you're saying,' Liv said.

'You and Dad wrapped me up in cotton wool.'

'We've just tried to look after you.'

'I had to hold your hand crossing the road until I was twelve!'

'Was I meant to push you into traffic?'

'I'm playing Guildenstern, Mum. Not even Rosencrantz.'

'Is that bad?'

'The teachers are always asking me to dig deeper. I'm digging down and there's nothing there.'

Shocked at hearing Nina, normally so positive, voice her frustration, I tried to help her find a way through in her room later that night.

'I work harder than anyone else in our year', she said. 'We did fifteen different plays in second year and I knew all my lines on day one. I've nailed every accent, read every book on the list, I cut my hair off to do *Marat/Sade*, spent a whole weekend doing laundry with a bar of soap and a bloody washboard for *Uncle Vanya*.'

'I've still got the holes in my t-shirt.'

'They talk about breaking us down so they can build us back up. I feel like they've cracked me open and found nothing inside but candy floss. A childish fucking fantasy.' Where before I could offer empathy, I now had this demanding role, this huge purpose, we were no longer in the same boat.

'People get noticed in smaller roles.' Everything I said felt patronising. 'Kimi Allendale was playing chorus in *Antigone* and got signed by IJM.'

'Kimi Allendale has absolutely gigantic tits.'

'Forget the industry then. If you give Jonathan the thing you're most scared of, show him the real you, it's going to make you a better actor.'

A week later, with only minutes before the class Nina was due to go up in, no one had seen her. At dinner the night before, she'd not been herself and when I'd gone to get her to leave for school, she'd already left. I started to think she'd run away from home, gone rogue just to miss her turn to face Jonathan, but just as the clock turned to the hour, she swept in wearing her dad's dressing gown.

'Nee, what the fuck?' I said as she sat in front of me on the right of Jonathan's desk. At The Conservatoire, wearing a robe meant one thing – she was going to get naked. 'You don't have to—'

'I think, maybe I do,' she said. She looked scared, pupils huge. She squeezed my hand, gave a weak smile and turned back to face the front. Jonathan walked in on the stroke of nine, sat down and gestured to the empty space.

My stomach clenched as she got up and walked to the end of the room. Nina didn't even wear revealing clothes in the summer. I could feel the room jostling for a better view. Patrick whispered 'chill out' to Victor and Ben. I'd felt jealous when she kissed Oban in their scene study the year before, but we were together and I hadn't even seen her naked. I wanted to crack the fire alarm, blindfold everyone, stop it somehow.

Nina, back to us, shed the robe. Although the room was warm, a shiver waved across the top of her shoulders. The room held their breath, but she didn't turn for some moments. She looked slim, body toned and firm. Nina had been bigger than some of the other girls when we'd started, school-girl chubbiness Varda's classes saw to. Jonathan looked up, the sign for the exercise to begin, unmoved by the naked young girl in front of him.

Nina turned around and began miming showering. I'd only once seen her in her bra and pants before, when she was brushing her teeth and hadn't locked the bathroom door, but there she was, naked in front of us, rubbing her breasts, her stomach, as if lathering in the imagined water raining down. There was a tension in Nina's wrists, a flicker in the eyelids that made me want to jump up and shield her, as if the watching eyes were a barrage of stones. Nina played out the scene, in which a boy she'd spurned had stolen her towel and clothes in the school showers. She kept stopping her arms coming up to cover her body, even though that's what she would have done in the reality of the scene. She was showing Jonathan her commitment, her courage, exposing all of herself, stripping away the 'polish' she was always accused of. It was so uncomfortable to watch, it hurt.

At the end she retrieved the robe and put it on facing the back wall. I realised I'd been holding my breath throughout almost the whole thing, not taking in for a moment whether the exercise had gone well or badly. Someone put a chair out and she sat to face Jonathan. He took a deep breath. I had the impression he was going to go for her again for choosing another childish subject, but he gave a satisfied sigh, a surprised twinkle in his eye.

'What were you working for, Nina?' he asked.

'Shame,' she said, confused, as if she had expected to be ripped to shreds and somehow it was worse that she hadn't.

'Mm,' he said, writing in his notebook. 'There are no memories more powerful than those embossed in the mind by shame. How do you feel?'

'Awful,' she said.

Jonathan cocked his head, said nothing.

'I mean doing that, it was exposing. I hated it. But I suppose I know what it feels like now.'

He bowed his head in a slow nod. Wind rattled the lattice windowpanes. 'To destroy the artifice of the self and be reborn,' he said. 'This is the job of the actor.' Jonathan pursed his lips and sat. Nina returned to her seat. I was buzzing for her. A response from Jonathan like that was so rare, it must have felt like being touched by God.

'Fucking flawless, Nina,' Patrick whispered to her, planting a hand on her shoulder.

'The casting in our production,' Jonathan intoned above the murmurs of the class, face in his hand. 'Nothing is set. The pieces can be moved around the board.' He turned, glanced at Nina. 'Who's next? Oh, Anna K.' He sounded bored saying Anna's name. It wasn't accidental. Anna was playing Ophelia. He'd given Nina a sliver of light. I squeezed Nina's elbow. She turned to me and gave me a little shrug, eyes hollow.

'How are we going to make it happen?' I said, after classes were finished and I'd got Nina on her own for a cigarette, hidden behind the pillars at the front of the building.

'What do you mean?'

'Maybe we could think of a duologue for Aggie, something like the Hamlet–Ophelia scenes, get Jonathan to come see it.'

'Oh right.' Since she'd been up in class she'd barely said a word, had a look in her eyes like she'd been in a car accident.

'Jonathan loved it. He said about casting, straight after you sat down. Ophelia could be so great for you and, you know, me, playing against each other. The real dynamic. I mean, you'd wipe the floor with me. So how do we make it happen?' She bit the side of her lip. I tried to take her fingers but she swerved me.

'Why though?'

'What?'

'Why did he like it?'

'It was so committed.'

'To what, taking off my clothes? What's that got to do with acting?'

'It tells Jonathan you're able to go however far the character needs to go.'

Nina looked past me at the trees on the square quarrelling in the wind. 'You're proud of me,' she said, an epiphany not a question.

I smiled, shrugged. I suppose I was.

'Your girlfriend, or whatever I am, gets naked in front of all your mates and you're proud?'

'I just—You went there, you know? Obviously I didn't like it, it was horrible to watch.'

'Charming.'

'I don't—You looked so beautiful, Nee, fragile.' She turned to me, hurt.

'I don't want to be fragile.'

'Ophelia's fragile.'

She stubbed her cigarette out on the pillar, ruffled her curls into a mess covering her eyes.

'Let's go back in,' she said, leaving me outside, alone.

That was early December and with a few weeks until the Christmas break, our classes began to give way to more *Hamlet* rehearsals. I knew my lines and Jonathan must have been satisfied with the technical work I'd done because he didn't mention my diction again, but his attitude was still that of a father tending to his least favourite child. Every time he stopped us in rehearsals it was always for me, addressing a lack of thought, questioning what intention underlaid my words. There were moments I hovered above myself and it was like watching a frog being dissected. It was brutal, but I was Hamlet, 'big-lead' The Boys had started to call me, it needed to be.

I became addicted to the feeling. I'd keep Nina up at night running scenes with me. When we started, these had the thrill of that first summer together when she was getting me up to speed, but as the weeks passed, things became strained.

'It's good,' Nina said one night, when I got to the end of my speech in the first ghost scene.

'"Good"? What can I do with "good"?' I snapped. It was about eleven and she'd been yawning theatrically for almost an hour.

Nina looked down at her script, sighed.

'Does it need to build more?' I asked.

'I don't think so, you're finding it.'

'If I'm only finding it, I must be doing something wrong.'

'I just mean, it's there, it's clear, the more we work on it—'

'I've just found out my uncle murdered my dad and I've got no rage, nothing boiling inside.'

'You're processing. I like the choice.'

'I can feel it's wrong though, safe. I'm mewling, almost,' I said, teeth grinding against each other, pulling at the flesh of my stomach. I stood, wanting to toss her chair onto its side in frustration. 'You don't have to sugar coat it. If it's shit, I need you to be honest.'

'I don't want to do this with you anymore.'

'You said you'd help me.'

'I'm trying.'

'By lying to me?'

'I'm not lying.' She came to me, put her hands on my shoulders. I felt the breath settle in my chest. 'I'm your biggest fan. I can't be a bitch to you for no reason, even if you think it's what you need. We said we'd keep The Church separate from us.'

I put my arms around her, she was right.

'Mark me!' she said, doing her spooky ghost voice that had had us pissing ourselves laughing weeks before. She put her duvet over her face to complete the effect. 'Mark me!' She stood on the bottom of it, tripped. I caught her and then we really laughed.

A few days later, Van came into one of the teaching rooms where I was working on the speeches, wearing a leotard that could have come from a Milan catwalk.

'Nina spoke to me,' she said. 'You want someone to run your scenes with?'

'Um, I did, yeh.'

Vanessa's nostrils were flared, eyes amused. 'Trouble in paradise?'

I blushed, said nothing. If she hadn't known Nina and I were together, she would have from my reaction.

Van smiled, brushed some dust from the door she was leaning on off her shoulder. 'I can get a room booked, for whenever we're not in rehearsals.'

'Do you have time, to help me?'

'I'm in the play too, it helps us both.'

So, whenever we found ourselves free from rehearsals, we worked on the play together. At first the heated

Gertrude and Hamlet scenes, our mother–son relationship, but then she worked with me on the rest of the show. She had an imperious knowledge of the play and what my performance might need and, even back then, I never had to ask Van to go harder with her feedback.

But even with her help, I was grasping at the essence of the crisis Hamlet was going through, lurching between numbness and overacting in an effort to get the tiniest hint Jonathan was pleased with where I was going. One afternoon, after the rest of the cast had left Room 1, I asked him whether Hamlet was mad.

'His whole being is addled by grief,' Jonathan told me. That night I opened my bedroom window as wide as it would go, kept the heater off and slept without a blanket. I woke stiff, mind numb to anything but the cold. I didn't eat, pretending to myself I'd forgotten. Nina brought sandwiches I'd have to find ways to dispose of without her knowing. After nearly a week of days and nights like that, addled was exactly how I felt. I was working on the speeches with Jonathan in Room 1 and couldn't warm up, bones feeling like iron rods. I struggled to move across the stage, get my lines out through chattering teeth. But when the words came, when I said I had of late lost all my mirth, despair swirled up from me into the vaulted ceiling and I saw a flicker of gold in Jonathan's eyes.

He called me to sit with him when I came to the end.

'You're working from the outside in,' he said. 'It produces an effect which is not unwatchable, but Hamlet must come from within as well. Every cell in his body has been altered by his father's death. Every glimmer of hope, any light, any joy becomes an affront. A trifling distraction to pass the minutes, only enjoyable to those who've never known your pain.' He wandered to the model-box, played his fingers over some of the figurines. Earlier that day, Nina and I had been on one of the sofas laughing, having a thumb-war if I remember, and saw Jonathan by the entrance observing us, greatcoat hanging off his thin frame. She and I flushed red, separated, like teenagers caught in the act by a strict parent.

'You may want happiness,' he said, eddies of dust swirling around him in the coloured light from the stained glass. 'But Hamlet cannot have any.'

Term finished two days later, and our class went to a Christmas fair in Regent's Park. Vanessa raided the costume store for bustles and ruffs and James did our make-up so as we wandered around the clanking Ferris-wheel we must have looked like Jacobean ghosts escaped from the crypt of St Mark's Church. Well-to-do forty-somethings and families with young children looked at us like predatory lepers, which only encouraged us to be more over-the-top as we danced ironically to the Spice Girls, East 17 and the rest of the Christmas pop playlist. When Patrick and The Boys turned up, the drinking became a championship event. Cans of Diamond White shot-gunned at speed, spumes of foam spilt on hand-stitched jerkins, chants and games only private schooling seemed to teach. Nina got into it, so I did too. Her mischievous side came out, stealing James' hat and throwing it on the hoopla, sneaking up the side of the helter-skelter, stealing hundreds of cocktail umbrellas and filling her and my hair with them. We didn't kiss or canoodle, but looking back, if anyone had been paying attention to Nina and I that night, they would have been in no doubt we were together.

The smell of bonfires swirling around us, the multicoloured lights shining in sloppy-drunk eyes, I felt the tension from rehearsals, the exhaustion of constantly trying to satisfy Jonathan, drift away into the cold night air. In the spring term, classes would stop and we'd go into rehearsals full-time. For our whole group, it felt like the last night of our childhood. Victor sparked up a joint, 'Uzbek shit,' he said.

'You don't smoke, Adam,' Vanessa said when someone passed it to me. 'You shouldn't. Jonathan says it kills the actor's intention.'

I smiled, passed it over to Nina, who was drunker than most of us, head leant to one side. She made a face at Vanessa, turned the joint around, put it in her mouth and leant over to me, blowing the smoke out the other end. I'd seen it done before, a blowback, but felt torn as to whether I should try. I glanced at Van before turning and tunnelling the smoke into my hands, face close to Nina as I inhaled. Nina took the joint out of her mouth, took a long hit, and passed it on, giving Vanessa a sarcastic smile.

'Fucking child,' Van said, standing up and moving to one of the other groups. Later in the night, she found me on my own.

'I think I've worked out what Jonathan sees in you,' Van said.

'Oh yeh,' I said, laughing, fumbling with a rollie I'd been trying to make for a few minutes.

'It must be your lack of complacency.'

'What does that mean?'

'He can see you don't think you deserve it, at all. Means you won't rest on your laurels. He can keep pushing you.'

'Er, thanks. I think.'

'Just don't, you know, smoking, boozing because the others are doing it. Make sure you don't fucking lose it.' She left, to an industry party. Later, sapped by another of Victor's joints, we all lay on the cold ground staring up at the flashbulb lights pulsing to 'I Saw Mommy Kissing Santa Claus'. Nina took my hand in hers, tickled my palm. Jonathan's words, Vanessa's warning, flittered into my head. It was a night of wonderful debauchery with the girl I adored. It was a distraction.

The thought passed. Nina and I were hammered by the time we were in the taxi home. We only had half the fare, so we had the driver stop a little away from her house and, after we'd shoved the rest of our money through the slot, Nina grabbed my hand and we ran home, giggled all the way up the stairs, trying not to wake Liv and Tommy, and bundled into Nina's room.

We closed the door and looked at each other, smiles faded. The fact we hadn't had sex yet seemed to charge the whole room with static. I lifted her onto me, her legs wrapped around me and we kissed, moving as we did over to the bed. We lay back, kisses growing more passionate. I pulled at myriad strings on Nina's bodice, her hands roaming under my ruffled shirt, bodies pressing together, becoming one. Nina pulled her face away from mine for a moment.

'I love you,' she said.

The words pinned something in my chest, seemed to open up a space inside me and, for a moment, I couldn't breathe. I hadn't thought about love, hadn't let myself. Ever since we met I had wanted to be with her. The moment we first kissed I realised it, but love, Nina's love felt like the completion of something, the end. And I found myself hearing Jonathan sirening in my head. Any hope, any joy, any light is an affront. Nina's eyes scoured mine for the response she wanted, expected, for anything now she'd stepped off the edge of the cliff. But my tongue was stuck to the back of my throat. Love. I wasn't allowed it. Hamlet, Adam. I couldn't be loved. So I said nothing, watched the fear in Nina's eyes melt into loss. She pushed herself from me, turned to face the other way, held her frog-pillow into herself.

'Nina—'

'Just go.'

By ten the next day, I was at Euston station waiting for a train up to Leeds. I'd left Nina's room and gone to my own up the stairs but couldn't sleep. I had to leave. I couldn't face Nina after how I'd let her down, nor imagine cracking out the mince pies and advocaats with her happy family over Christmas. I lit on Jonathan's words about my childhood grief and decided to go back to my family home and spend it with my dad, who I'd barely spoken to in months. I left a note in my room. It said sorry. It said I had to go home. I took a half-bottle of schnapps from Tommy's drinks cabinet and walked into town. It was a long walk.

But by the time I'd topped up with three pints at a tiny station pub and missed three trains up, it became clear I wasn't going back to Leeds. I bought spiced rum at an off-licence and went for a walk to the river. When I got to Waterloo Bridge, I found a payphone and called my dad.

'You're shitfaced,' he said with his smoker's growl after I'd sung 'We Wish You a Merry Christmas' at him when he answered. 'Are you alright?' I imagined him holding a chisel. Dad made cricket bats for a hobby, at least I assumed he still did. He'd come up to London once since I'd moved down, before Christmas of my first year, and we'd only spoken a handful of times since. He always asked the same two questions: 'Are you alright?' and 'Are you OK for money?' To both of which he expected me to answer, 'Yes.'

I can't imagine what he'd have done if I ever told him about what we got up to at The Conservatoire. He'd spent his life on building sites and had his own small company by then. He would have been disgusted by us giving every ounce of ourselves – graft, bodies and souls – to what he thought of as 'playing make-believe'. He had asked about my job at the restaurant once or twice, so perhaps he told himself, and probably anyone that asked, that I'd gone to the bright lights of London to pursue a career in hospitality.

'Finally doing the bathroom,' he said when I hadn't said anything for a while. Mum loved the bath. I couldn't go in that room after she died. Dad tried to force me to wash in there after he moved in to look after me, but despite him shouting at me, calling me a little shit, I wouldn't go in. After a while he gave up and let me use a flannel in the downstairs sink. It didn't take him long to give up trying to parent me.

I was eight when she died. I can't remember who I was before but when she went, she took the feeling out of the house. Life was quieter with Dad, near silent, but it thrummed with the hurricane-loud absence of her. I came to see my mother as this angel, red hair glowing like the electric fire in the TV room, dopey eyes, always in a thick fleece dressing gown.

I'd tell Jonathan grief was a fear of the bath. The thought made me giggle. Dad blew out a sigh. I could hear him deciding whether he could hang up. The streets buzzed past me, the sun having gone down at some point, head-lights blurring. The buttons of the payphone started to vibrate as I looked at them. I didn't feel well. I wanted my dad to be there, to throw his arms around me. I wanted to go back to Nina's, throw myself at her feet. But I was Hamlet.

'Don't need anything, no?' he said.

'Why did you never tell me anything about Mum?'

'I didn't know your mum.'

'Knew her well enough to get her up the duff and then piss off.'

'Is this that school? Dredging up all this crap.'

'I'm playing Hamlet, Dad.'

123

'Am I meant to be impressed?'

'We never talked about her, never.'

He heaved out a heavy sigh, sucked at his teeth.

'She was my mum.'

'You wanna know about that woman, Adam? Look in the mirror, you pisshead.' He hung up.

I looked at the receiver in my trembling hand for a moment before smashing it into its cradle again and again until it cracked into shards. I stood, catching my breath, staring at the knot of wires and diodes in my hand, wishing Jonathan had been with me to watch the moment of transcendent violence.

The rest of the night comes back to me as clipped rushes from the footage of a dream. Giving my coat to a homeless man. Walking down to the mud of the Thames in the sleet. Getting punched by a wide-set bloke in a suit for resting my elbow on his girlfriend's head at a riverside pub. Crawling onto the top of a barge moored by Tower Bridge before being chased off by a dog. Making the comedy and tragedy masks with my face in the scratched plastic window of a night-bus, hair in dirty blond wedges, dregs of make-up, bright red gums, grey teeth. The last thing I remember was being in a black cab, shivering uncontrollably, lights strobing when I closed my eyes, head leant on the shoulder of Jonathan Dors.

II.iii

The voice from the cabin had taunted me as I slept in my hotel suite the night after the photoshoot – *How could you?* I dreamt of sawing at a rope for what felt like an eternity but no matter how many strands frayed, I never managed to sever it. The body I saw was covered in burns this time. I was woken by the sound of wood cracking sharply. I must have screamed out.

'You're OK, Adam!' Amber was at the foot of the bed, clutching a stack of tuxedos for the BAFTAs. Van had sent her up to help with the workshop but, after I'd changed and joined her and the inevitable fruit plate, she admitted she had no idea what she could tell me about talking to drama school students.

'I keep thinking about that girl's scars,' she said, as if she'd been watching my dream. 'Trying to understand how this Raya could do something like that.'

'Do you think she's OK, Raya?' I said, eating a melon chunk that tasted like a mothball.

Amber glanced round the room as if it were filled with

listening devices before coming to sit close to me. 'The school gave me her address,' she said. 'It's her uncle's house.'

'Where is it?'

'South London.'

'We should go,' I said, hugging myself.

Amber looked scandalised but after a minute or two discussing why we absolutely shouldn't, the two of us were making our way to the lobby, looking round corners for Van, before escaping into an Uber.

'Were you having a nightmare this morning?' she said, as the car moved out of central London into streets lined with builders' hoardings, overlooked by a battalion of cranes.

'I can't remember.'

'I heard you,' she said. 'After *Woodsman*, padding around your room all night. You used to say her name.'

'Whose?' I said, chest fluttering with panic at the thought of what I might have revealed.

'Louanne. Does it feel real when you're in character? Do you forget who you are?'

'I suppose that's what I aim for.'

'Where does it leave you?'

'What do you mean?'

'When the film's finished. I played it down how you were to Van because I know you didn't want to go back to Ganymede, but you didn't speak, barely left your room.'

'We hung out,' I laughed. 'Watched movies. I made dinner. I'm no Jamie Oliver but—'

'That was one night, Adam. We watched the Brando *Julius Caesar* and you made carbonara.'

I blinked at the overcast sky. One night can't have been right, but as I tried to think what else we'd watched, the other dishes I was sure I'd cooked, what we talked about, my mind was blank.

'Then you were straight into press mode, the campaign,' she said, 'constantly having to talk about being Harrison. I felt so bad I hadn't told anyone how I'd found you in the bath—'

'You did the right thing,' I said, cutting her off.

'Every journalist, every panel, all anyone asked about was the scene at the end,' she said. 'It felt like they were trolling me because, for me, that bit was like watching a snuff movie. That's rude, I'm sorry, but, having seen you afterwards.'

I had to look away for fear of bursting into tears. I couldn't remember anyone showing concern for me like that, for Adam the human being, not the actor. Not since Nina.

The taxi turned off the road from Camberwell and stopped at a terrace of new-builds. We got to the house and stepped through a front garden where every shrub had been cut down to the stump. I paused at the door, brand-new and still in its cellophane wrapping, no idea what I was going to say to this girl's uncle, but I was due at The Church in an hour's time, so I knocked.

The man who answered wore a snug gilet and a short-back-and-sides too severe for someone in his fifties. He took in the beanie hat low on my head and, for a second, I think he thought I was there to rob him.

'Excuse the intrusion,' Amber said, 'we're looking for Raya Bilson?' The man's face fell.

'This isn't a great time,' he said, looking back into the house.

'Is she here?' I said, trying to see past him.

'Do I know you?' he said, blocking my view. There were murmurs in the background, rat-a-tat gunfire coming from a television. The man scrutinised me and a whisper of recognition came into his eyes. 'Is it you?'

'Adam Sealey,' I said. I took my hat off and extended my hand to shake, hoping it would disarm him. He put the door on the latch, came outside and shut the door.

'Raya always said you might—She didn't say you'd come here! Bloody hell.'

I glanced at Amber, hoping what he had said made sense to her, but she looked as blank as me. 'Is Raya not here?' I asked.

'Let me try her—' He got his phone out and called. 'Answerphone,' he tutted, thought about leaving a message then hung up.

'Could we come in?' Amber said.

'Raya was obsessed with you,' he said.

'Is that right?'

'Talked about you all the time. Thought she'd meet you after the . . . the thing. I told her you didn't even live in England but she was convinced. And now you're here and—' He shook his head, genuinely upset for Raya.

'Do you know where she is?' I said.

'She moved out when she went to drama college.'

'That was three years ago? You haven't seen her since then?'

'I'm Barry by the way,' he said, finally deciding to shake my hand. Barry looked like a man who always feared the worst. Amber glanced at the street behind us, uncomfortable, and I realised she was worried about us being spotted, photographed lurking around South East London. 'Every cunt with a smartphone's a paparazzo these days,' was one of Van's mantras.

'Can we come in?' I said. Barry looked at his pathway for the answer before nodding. He led us through a spotless hallway to a living room where some sci-fi shoot-out was playing on TV and invited us to sit on brand-new sofas that, like the door, were still in their packing covers. There was a hairdryer going upstairs, presumably whoever it was he'd been hiding us from on the doorstep.

'Did you know Raya had left The Conservatoire?' I asked once we'd sat.

He nodded. 'Wasn't surprised. Always was a loose cannon,' he said. 'Her mum ran off when she was eleven and my brother Al, her dad, passed five years ago.'

'She lived here with you?' Amber asked.

'We were in a flat in Streatham. When she moved out, Andrea and me finally got a house. With stairs.'

'We heard Raya might have disappeared,' I said. Amber gave me a look she'd learnt from Vanessa. I was being too brusque, too blunt, but I wasn't going to dance around, however skittish Barry seemed.

'Disappeared? Not that I know of.'

'Then you've seen her?' I asked.

He scratched his face with his shoulder.

'When was the last time?'

Barry glanced at Amber. 'It was before Christmas.'

'December?'

'More like summer last year, July maybe.'

'You've not seen her since July?' It was February.

'She's texted, not for a month or two but, that's Raya. When she lived with me, she was hardly ever in once she got to fifteen.'

I bit the side of my index finger. Barry was doing nothing to reassure me his niece was safe, but there was something else. Something he'd said outside was rankling me, but I couldn't place it. I went to the mantlepiece to look at a studio-shot photo of Barry clutching a severe-looking woman like a limpet. The woman, Andrea he'd said, was lit so harshly it was difficult to make out her features.

'Did she tell you why she'd left The Conservatoire?' Amber asked.

'Didn't rate the place, she said, but I thought there might have been more to it.'

'Why?'

'She was off on one when she was here. Upset the missus,' he said, indicating upstairs. 'Manic, like someone was coming for her. She said she wasn't, but I think she must have been off her meds.'

'She was on medication?'

'What did she take?' Amber said.

'Hello.' Andrea stood in the doorway, Farrah Fawcett

hair, grinning but furious. Barry jumped from his seat and crossed to her. Amber and I stood with him.

'They're here about Raya, my love.'

'She doesn't live here,' Andrea said, voice like vinegar.

'Someone told us she was missing,' I said, ruffling my hair as I stood, hoping she'd recognise me.

'It's that actor,' Barry murmured, 'you know, the one,' he said, raising his eyebrows. I was about to go and shake Andrea's hand, but I wasn't sure she was a fan, of mine, of movies, possibly of anything.

'What are you doing turning up at our house?'

'I'm Amber,' Amber blew one of her wisps out of her eye. 'I work for GNM talent agency. We have an interest in Raya but no one knows where she is.'

Barry looked over to Andrea, a glint of being impressed she squashed with a glare. I guessed she wanted Raya's acting career to founder.

'Who said she was "missing"? Was it online?' she said. She spotted a concerned look passing between Amber and me. 'Someone on social media saying she's disappeared?' Andrea made a face – well? To some people she'd be attractive. I could see how Barry might think he'd won the lottery snagging her, but there was nothing under the surface. Her eyes flicked around like a lizard's. I found myself going out of focus as I looked at her. I'd played a serial killer called Paul Dettins eight years before. Whenever he felt like a woman was lording it over him, they started to become a blur of his abusive grandmother and great aunt, all the other women he'd ever hated. He'd climb into their bedrooms many months later, drug them and cut them into pieces.

'It was a comment online actually,' Amber said, because I wasn't saying anything. 'About Adam.'

'Not disappeared then if she's leaving comments online.' The woman crossed her arms like she had Miss Marpled the case.

'Are you saying you think Raya wrote the comment about her disappearing herself?' Amber said.

'The girl is a *rampant* attention-seeker. She's done it before; they nearly chucked her out of school for it. She set up an Instagram and catfished a perfectly nice girl because she got the part in the school play Raya wanted. You two probably think doing something like that over a play is fine, but the girl is, quite frankly, toxic.'

'Could you—' Amber went to her bag and rifled for the papers with the comment from measuredbella and took them to Barry's girlfriend. 'You think Raya did this?' The woman took the page with an elaborate huff and squinted to read.

'That's your niece,' she said, handing the pages over to Barry, making it clear it was his fault there were strangers in her living room asking questions. 'Tell me it isn't?'

Barry read and nodded his agreement. He hadn't looked at us since Andrea had come in. I started to imagine what it must have been like for Raya losing her uncle, her only family, to a woman like this, what it might have done to her. I held my eyes closed, beginning to feel what Paul Dettins called his 'fog' descending.

'Do you have any idea why Raya would choose to involve Adam?' Andrea looked at Barry, expecting him to answer, but he wasn't quick enough.

'That girl doesn't care who she damages with her little fantasies, but I imagine it's because of the grant.'

'What grant is that?' Amber asked.

Andrea looked from me to Amber, eyes widening with pleasure.

'Oh my God, I wish she was here to see this!' She burst into laughter.

'You gave her money,' Barry said. 'A bursary for the drama school.' He darted a glance between Andrea and me, desperate for her to stop laughing.

'The grant was in your name!' Andrea couldn't control herself. 'She thought you were going to be her mentor, boasted about it like you were her husband, not just given her a few hundred quid. And you don't even know who she is!' The woman pointed at me, laughing still. I found myself bolting across the room towards her. Barry was stuck to the spot as I got up in her face, feeling the hours cutting up sides of beef to understand Paul's sadism twinging in my tendons.

'You're being very rude,' I said in Paul's reedy Florida twang, raising my fist slowly. Andrea stopped laughing, lips trembling as she tried to take in my complete change of persona. The room was paralysed for a moment but before Barry or Andrea had time to react, Amber had grabbed my wrist, pulling me away.

'Sorry to intrude,' Amber said, rushing me into the hall.

I looked behind to see Andrea trying to work out what had happened, lighting on Barry, who would bear the brunt of her indignation. As Amber bustled me towards the front door, I felt horrible for putting her in that position, for Barry, Andrea even, scaring her like that.

What I was most ashamed about though, was that the woman was right. When we set up the bursary years before, a thousand pounds to a working-class Conservatoire student every year, there had been an idea I'd have some involvement with the students. But I'd been so consumed with my own career, I didn't even know who Van awarded it to. Raya thought she'd won a mentor and all she'd got was a cheque. Obsessed with me, Barry had said.

Out on the street, Amber glared at her phone, willing our car to arrive as a group of lads holding a football approached on the opposite side. I pulled my hat on, but it was too late, one of them had seen me. Phones came out ready to capture us, so Amber hurried me towards the main road where she hailed a cab.

'What was that, Adam?' she asked as we drove back into town. 'I thought you were going to hit her. And the accent?'

I said nothing, stared at a lurid line of chicken shops as the car took us north.

'How could you not know you gave the girl money?'

'Vanessa handles money. If anyone should have known, it's you.' Amber bit the side of her lip and looked away.

'I'm sorry, Adam,' she said, blushing, tone becoming painfully formal. 'I should have known.' She buried her head in her phone, the sense of connection we'd had since coming to London seeming to petrify in the back of the cab as she googled Raya, trying to find out what else she should already have known.

I leant into the side of the cab and pretended to sleep, wondering how I didn't know about the bursary, how Vanessa didn't. Or if she did, why she hadn't told me.

She was waiting for us in a lime-green coat as we turned off Kentish Town Road onto the square of Georgian houses The Church stood at the heart of. I took a sharp breath as I took in the building. I tried to see Nina waiting with me on the steps as I smoked, in the houndstooth blazer she wore over her movement gear, hair in a hundred different directions. She and I had been the unlovable ones, the chaff, and now I was back like the messiah.

'Give me the look if you want to leave,' Vanessa said, straightening my jacket. The news about the bursary sat on my tongue like an ulcer, but it could wait. I needed Van with me if I had to go back to Room 1. 'And agree to nothing. You're their golden goose and they'll be desperate for you to lay a big fuck-off egg. Keep it contained, have them show you a scene, give a few pointers. I'll be there with a cattle-prod if things get spicy.'

Across the square, I noticed a man in leathers, cameras hanging from him like shrunken heads, pointing his lens at us.

'Van—'

'Smile,' she said, walking up the stairs, opening The Church doors and wandering in. I followed but stopped at the entrance, paralysed at the thought of crossing the

135

threshold. My breath grew shallow, the adrenalin from my run-in with Barry's girlfriend still not dispersed, and heard the paparazzo snapping as I put my hand to the singeing pain in my ribcage. Amber took me by the elbow and led me in.

I was hit by the familiar stench of sweat, made sickly with a chemical suggestion of strawberries. The walls had been repainted, but the lockers remained, so rusted it looked intentional, and although the sofas in the corridor were new, the layout was identical. Drumming flooded from one studio, piano sonatas from the other. It could have been the week before *Hamlet*. The double doors to Room 1 were shut.

Van was calling whoever it is she'd arranged to meet us, when a slight man burst into the hall.

'Adam!' he said, clasping his hands. Manicured beard, a straight back, he reminded me of a waiter. 'Adam Sealey, wow, just wow.' He shook my hand with both of his for some time, nodding in awe.

'George Pivac, Head of Acting,' the man said. 'Group 28. Legendary. Group 39,' he said, pointing to himself. Of course he'd been at The Conservatoire.

'Shall we get started?' Van said, arranging her hair onto her shoulder.

'I thought Room 1's the most photogenic,' he said, leading the way. Vanessa flashed me a look and followed.

As soon as I walked into the old performance space, my eyes went to the balcony above the stage. I expected to see the black curtain tied onto one of the balustrades, the body swinging from it below. I stared at it for some time, almost willing myself to see it, but there was nothing there.

'Adam?' Vanessa indicated the rest of the nave and far more people than I'd expected. A camera crew. A huddle of teachers to one side, Aggie, Varda, I wasn't surprised to see still there, but Max Webern was too, along with seven or eight others I'd never met. Without Jonathan, they seemed like bleached coral.

'Feels like fucking Children in Need,' Van said under her breath, nodding to the students over by the stage. They stared at me, nudges to ribs, claps on shoulders, the same easy physicality we had in Group 28, that we took for granted because we didn't know it would go away. Lyndsey was amongst them. She eyed us, hoping others wouldn't clock we'd met, wanting to keep our meeting to herself.

Aggie shambled over, sphere-shape having thinned out, and gave me a theatrical double kiss. Varda sprang forwards next, white hair the only clue to the passing of years. Max told me he always showed his students the train scene from *Coward*. In the scene, Charles Coward meets a teenage girl he had a hand in saving from Auschwitz – it's near the end of the film. The girl asks Coward why he exaggerated the number of people he'd saved from the death camp, making the world think him a fraud instead of a hero.

'It wasn't enough to be ordinary,' I said as Charles, then made a sound between anguish and revelation, eyes rolling back as I realised how much I'd failed my own legacy. One critic said it revealed the soul of character and actor, meshed in perfect symbiosis. I thought it was hammy, a lot of 'acting'. Acclaim is powerful; it rewrites the narrative indelibly.

The Head of Acting dragged me down to the students, whose eyes drilled into me, sending paranoia wriggling up my spine. Their fascination felt more loaded than their being run-of-the-mill star-struck, it felt like it had something to do with Raya.

'Hi everyone,' I said, Leeds accent swelling to how it was when I first arrived at The Church, causing a thrilled ripple of surprise. 'Thanks for having me.'

'Adam wants to do some scene work with you, lucky things, but sure he'd love to answer a couple of Qs first?'

I felt exposed in Room 1, the balcony above humming like a fridge.

'Who'd like to kick us off?'

'Arthur Forbes-Masson,' said a tall boy with dark blond curtains. 'In *Coward*, I thought the weight you lost gave you this hunger in your eyes, even later, like it never left him.'

'Thanks,' I said.

'How much weight did you lose exactly? I read it was four stone.'

'We had a couple of weeks before the prisoner-of-war scenes, I shed as much as I could.'

'You wanted to lose more, didn't you, but the studio stepped in?'

I swallowed, glanced at Van. This wasn't common knowledge, very few people knew the execs had sat Van down and got her to promise to make me eat. The class leant forward for an answer.

138

'I wanted the audience to see what Charles had put himself through. Once I saw how I could change my body, it never seemed enough.' I caught one girl, pale skin stretched tight over fine cheekbones, nodding. 'That's why it's so important to have good people around to help you keep perspective.'

'But ultimately, you, the actor,' a girl joined in, so posh she hardly moved her lips. 'You're the person who knows what you need to prepare. That's why it was so inspiring what you did on *The Bends.*'

'What was inspiring?'

'We discussed it, didn't we, Malia,' George said to the girl.

'The stuntman's not the guy ripping his heart out,' Malia said. 'You were doing what you needed for your character' – my smile started cracking at the edges – 'it shouldn't have been you, the artist, vilified for it.'

The group murmured their agreement. A photographer snapped photos of me while another took the reverse of the students.

'I picked a fight with someone. My behaviour was completely unacceptable,' I said. 'I want to make that really clear.'

'We thought it was understandable,' Malia said. 'We made placards, did you see?'

'Placards?'

'"Free Adam Sealey". About that rehab place they sent you to.'

'I wasn't in prison.' I tried laughing it off, glanced at Van again. What had these kids been told?

'But a doctor did send you there?' Arthur said.

139

Van moved to George. I saw a psychiatrist after *The Bends*, and we agreed I should go to Ganymede, to stop the divemaster suing. These kids were making it sound like I'd been sectioned. Lyndsey seemed to sense my rising panic.

'I wish you'd finished the movie,' she said. 'They should have rolled straight after they got you out. Imagine what that would have brought to the scene!'

'It's like the *Hamlet* you did here,' Arthur said. A cold hand gripped my throat. 'After your classmate died. The teachers told us you fed the emotion directly into your performance and it was unbelievable.' The class grinned like child cannibals, blood dripping from pin-teeth.

'Listen, the teachers should not have said that,' I said. The students beamed like I was joking.

'Shall we go for this scene?' Van said, fixing me with a look. George clapped and the students jumped on stage. The photographers circled, snapping, flashes I could normally ignore felt like being blasted with pellets.

Van came over as I leant on the stage, running my fingers over the masking-tape map marking out the set of their show.

'How do they know about *Hamlet*?' I said under my breath.

'It's not a secret.'

'Who told them? Jonathan can't have—'

'It's a war story, the best one, this place lives for that shit.'

'Using what happened as a motivational tool?'

'Let's remember why we're here, yes?' Van said, eyeing the photographers.

I walked to the middle of the aisle, purple and green from the window pouring onto my face. The photographers liked that, me looking up at Jesus carrying his cross, pretending I wasn't aware of the metaphor.

The students started the last act of *The Seagull* but I barely took it in, too shaken by how much they seemed to know about me. They thought I'd been put away in an institution, but worse, someone, Jonathan maybe, talked to them about *Hamlet*, telling them I'd used what happened to galvanise my performance.

Most of the characters went off, leaving the tall boy Arthur up there alone. There was a gush of water off stage and Lyndsey entered soaking wet, teeth chattering with cold. Through her sodden dress, I could see the burn went about halfway down her back. I looked at the thin white scar on my wrist from where I'd cut myself for the Shakespeare showing. Before *Medea*, Raya had been out of favour with the teachers. Was her attack on her classmate an attempt to prove she was up to it?

Lyndsey was wonderful. The cold gave her a bird-like frailty, which made you care for her instantly. She touched her burn when she talked about the hardship she'd suffered in Moscow, and I found myself drifting closer to the stage.

'I know that in our work,' Lyndsey said. 'It doesn't matter if it's my acting or your writing, what's important isn't fame, isn't glamour, the life I dreamt of, it's about the ability to endure.'

I felt a lump in my throat and couldn't help feeling such love for the school. Jonathan emboldened us, pushed us to become intrepid explorers of the human condition. I caught Vanessa's eye; she could feel it too.

'I think about my vocation,' Lyndsey said, 'and I'm not afraid of life.'

She spoke with such penetrating truth, it felt like magic.

'You've found your way,' Arthur said, breaking the spell. He was diluted cordial next to Lyndsey. 'I'm wandering around a maze of dreams and symbols, with no idea what use they are. I have no faith.'

'I don't believe you,' I called out. Arthur stopped, gave me a shit-eating grin. I took off my jacket, rolled up the sleeves of my shirt and walked to the stage.

'What happens next, Konstantin? When she leaves.'

'I go outside and shoot myself.'

'Why do you go and shoot yourself?'

'Because I love Nina and she leaves.'

I paused, swallowed a lump hearing this boy say the name. I cleared my throat, recovered myself. 'Would your lover leaving be enough for you, Arthur? To kill yourself?'

'Is it because she's in love with someone else?' Arthur said.

'Who is Nina in love with?' I said, slamming my hand on the edge of the stage, making the room flinch. 'A writer. Everything Konstantin wants to be. But worse, a popular writer, a hack who's bored of it but who both Konstantin's mother and the love of his life find themselves obsessed with. He could go and shoot his rival, but instead he kills himself. Why? Because his being spurned for this specific writer, tells him the world does not want him. It doesn't want his idealism or originality, it wants mediocrity.' The students were in thrall to every word and it was a quiet kind of euphoria. I sat on the stage facing them.

'Arthur's the favourite in your year?' I asked them.

'We don't really—' George said, standing from his seat.

'Yeh, big time,' Malia said. I pushed myself up and joined Arthur stage-left.

'Got an agent?' I asked.

'Lot of interest.'

'Lyndsey had a meeting with my agent yesterday.' Room 1 shifted. Lyndsey's face crinkled into an apologetic half-smile. 'Why would she pick Lyndsey over you?'

'We probably should break,' George said.

'Why do you think, Arthur?'

'I don't know.'

'You do.'

'Because she's a girl.'

'Come on, we're not judging.'

Arthur said nothing, his eyes looking around the room. 'I—I don't know.'

'Because of her ethnicity, perhaps?' The room took a collective breath, Van glared at me.

'Er, no,' Arthur said. George cleared his throat, knotting his hands in front of him, not liking where I was going but unsure how to stop it.

'Konstantin thinks Nina loves Trigorin solely because he's famous,' I continued. 'Just as you think things will be easier for Lyndsey because the industry wants people of colour and is no longer as keen on posh white guys.' Arthur caught Malia's eye in the crowd, prevaricated with

143

a docile smile. 'But that would just be the story you tell yourself, Arthur, because you know' – I walked to the front of the stage and looked up at him, lowering my voice to a murmur – 'deep down, that Lyndsey is, quite simply, a better actor than you. That she has a talent you'll never have. Why does Konstantin kill himself? Because he knows Trigorin is brilliant and he's just so-so. You and Konstantin feel the same. So let's have the scene.' I stepped off the stage. Arthur looked like I'd just wrenched his spinal cord out.

They did the scene again. He was better, brought an authentic self-hatred. The moments after Lyndsey left the stage, the moment before he'd go off to shoot himself, were quite affecting. He was too broken perhaps, the cracks in his psyche so overt it was, at times, unpleasant to watch. But he was better.

After they finished, I clapped like a seal and told them they'd done a fantastic job. The colour came back into Arthur's cheeks. Van dismissed the photographers and Amber brought me a cup of tea.

'What did Jonathan say, that night in the cabin?' she said.

'What?'

'What you did to that boy. It was just like the last night on *Woodsman* when Jonathan chucked us all out.' She looked at me with a directness I'd not seen. 'Did he tell you you were mediocre too?'

'That boy gave a much better performance,' I said.

Amber was about to speak but clicked her mouth shut, smiled and went to check on the photographers.

I looked at the scar on my hand. Amber had held a

mirror up to what I'd done to the boy, and I felt something in my veins like corruption. I started to think about what the next few hours would hold for him, the next few days, months. He seemed the sort of person who'd be able to brush most things off, but what about when he was alone, facing himself as he lay his head on the pillow at night? In the guise of showing him what he had in common with the character, I, an Oscar-nominated actor, told him he'd only ever be ordinary. I did it as easily as giving someone directions to the tube.

The speakers on the pillars seemed to fuzz and I heard the distant sound of a choir, the Requiem. I had to be imagining it. The candles lining the wall weren't lit, but the wax seemed to drip. I backed down the aisle, needing to get out. I looked up and there it was again, the body swinging beneath the balcony.

'How could you?'

I swung around. The words had come from behind me. Not the voice. It couldn't be, not there. But from where? The students were looking at me still. Had it been one of them, defending their classmate after my evisceration? Van, George, the photographers even, were all staring as I gawped at the balcony. All of them, in that moment, knew exactly what I'd done.

I bolted, Amber reaching for me as I escaped into the corridor and out into the daylight. From the top of the steps, I saw ghosts everywhere. Patrick and Victor wrestling on the grass. Nina whiteying from one of Anna's spliffs behind one of the plinths. Van stepping out of a chauffeured town-car just in time for class. I ran fingers over my fore-head, trying to massage calmness into my brain.

I spotted Arthur behind a pillar, watching me as he rolled a cigarette, and composed myself as if someone had called cut on a scene.

'Can you do me one?' I asked. He handed me his rollie and lighter and began rolling another. I smoked and it tasted like doing something wrong, which, having been a good boy for Vanessa the last six months, was delicious.

'You were much better the second time,' I said as Arthur lit his cigarette. I imagined myself apologising to him, but we continued to smoke in silence.

'Do you think your agent will sign Lyndz? She should.' He didn't mean it. He would do well; he had the chutzpah you needed if you weren't much of an actor.

'Was Raya good?' I asked.

He leant into the wall, making himself smaller. 'Why do you want to know about Raya?'

'We heard what happened, between her and Lyndsey. Have you seen her since she left?'

Arthur looked at me like I was a baited trap. 'Did Lynd-sey say something about me?'

'What would she say?'

'Me and Raya had an on–off thing all through first year. I had to end it.'

'Why?'

'She was wild, great fun with it, got on with everyone even if she wasn't tight with any of us. But in second year, it was like she was a different person.'

'Because she was playing Medea?'

Arthur raised his eyebrows, surprised I knew as much as I did. 'She'd done small parts, maids, servants' – the school always cast anyone with a regional accent as the help – 'then she's cast as the mum who eats her kids and threw herself into it. Stopped talking to me, to any of us, was in rehearsal rooms doing exercises on her own for hours. She did one where she ate a whole calf's liver in front of us, imagining it was her children. She'd been vegan for years and was retching as she shoved it in her mouth. It was horrible.'

I pictured shimmering flesh torn by incisors; had to stop a smile at the girl's ingenuity. 'Who directed Medea?' I asked.

'George.'

'Did he push her to do all that?'

'Tried to steer her away from it. She whipped herself in an exercise.'

'What?'

'With a belt. Getting into her guilt or something. George told her to stop.'

I remember the razor blade searing into the flesh of my palm, how much hurting myself in front of everyone gave me in that moment. The hardest exercises I did at The Conservatoire and beyond, the ones that brought the greatest insight, although I thought they were my idea, I realised later Jonathan had led me there. But Jonathan said he didn't know Raya.

'Has anyone seen her since she left?'

Arthur grappled his head with his hand, whether genuinely tortured or a performance it wasn't clear.

'After what happened with Lyndsey, we all met with the teachers and people from the University, without Raya obviously. They were considering throwing her out and wanted to hear what we thought.'

'What did you think?'

'We said go for it.'

'Lyndsey said you stuck up for Raya, that you were all worried what she'd do to herself.'

Arthur raised an eyebrow. 'The only thing Lyndsey was worried about was what part she'd get, same as the rest of us. You know. Raya was one less person to think about.'

'But you told her you'd all backed her to stay?'

'Yeh, but she knew, she would have done the same.'

I clenched my fists. Despite the dressing down I'd given him, Arthur still wore his arrogance like burnished armour.

'And Jonathan, did he say anything at the meeting?'

Arthur cocked his head, something in his eyes I didn't like. 'He wasn't there.' He went into his pouch of tobacco and began rolling again. I needed to find out what he knew about *Hamlet*, what they all knew. If Raya was disturbed, writing comments about me and Jonathan with a sizeable axe to grind, if she'd somehow found out what we did that night before *Hamlet* and had plans to expose me, the Oscar was gone, my career over. I needed to know, but this boy was cleverer than he seemed and preternaturally ruthless. I couldn't just ask.

'Do you think Raya's OK?'

Arthur's eyes widened, as if he'd never considered she might not be. 'Did you not meet her?' he said.

'What?'

'She said she met you. After a Q&A at the Film Festival. We thought she was bullshitting but was there some—' He waggled his finger at me suggestively. 'Is that why you're interested?'

'I've never met her,' I said, regretting how strident I sounded. 'When was this?'

'Our first year, so, two years ago. *American Wrath*, I think you were doing?'

I had been at the London Film Festival and it was *American Wrath*, a thinky film. We'd hoped it was going to be my Atticus Finch, but the public found it too worthy. I'd always tried to put the audience first, but I'd begun to hate the way their tastes were taking cinema and, at the time, was very down on cinemagoers. I would have escaped the BFI and dashed back to my hotel as soon as my talk was done. If I had been collared by a fan, I wouldn't have been very gracious.

'What did she say,' I asked, 'about meeting me?'

Arthur began to smirk, turned his head to the side.

'There you are!' Van arrived over my shoulder, Amber pulling a carry-on case behind her. 'Thought you'd re-enrolled.' She looked between me and Arthur and sniffed like someone from a Roald Dahl book. 'The British Academy awaits.'

II.iv

I was befuddled when I woke under an oriental blanket in the small orangery at the end of what I realised was Jonathan Dors' kitchen. I was caked in sweat, so my first thought was to detach every part of my body from whatever I was sitting on, so as not to soil his furniture. But getting up wasn't as easy as I thought. Sitting, blanket pulled up around me, was the best I could do, and it was in this state he found me.

'I'm making dinner,' he said, his voice making me feel I was being tended to by a huge-winged crane. I had imagined him in a large house with grey walls, minimal furniture, a lawn outside of Chekhovian aristocracy drinking tea from a samovar and postulating on the futility of their existence. I'd discover he lived in a one-bedroom garden flat. The kitchen teemed with thick-bottomed pans hung from the ceiling, utensils poking between them like bunches of bananas. There was an upright piano in the living room, a television surrounded by towers of videos. Bookshelves lined most of the downstairs, but the books were disordered, random piles stacked at strange angles. The front window had columns of them up to about half-way, blocking light into the room.

After a hot bath, I felt less shaky. I looked in the mirror and even though the person staring back was grey, skin candle wax, I couldn't stop smiling. Jonathan had found me wrecked like Hamlet and brought me home, to his inner sanctum, to nurse me to health. It was fate, as if the de-votion he inspired at my first audition was a prophecy of salvation and this its fulfilment.

We ate together, a curried vegetable pie he'd made, as he told me he had found me passed out in the graveyard behind The Church the previous day and that he would have taken me to hospital had it not been Christmas Eve. It still took him making a quip about Tiny Tim for me to realise the two of us were there sharing Christmas dinner. He drank brandy from a decanter, didn't offer me any.

'How do you feel?' he asked after we finished. I held his gaze for a moment before laughing. Jonathan smiled and I almost thought he'd join in. I don't know if it was his concern that set me off, or him using the exact same tone he did in his classes after an exercise. I started to become hysterical and had to grip my knee hard to stop myself laughing, apologising when I got myself under control.

'You live with Nina?'

I nodded, imagining he was about to telephone her par-ents to come and get me.

'But you don't want to go back.' He leant forward to snuff out the candles in the middle of the table. 'I'm going to bed,' he said, gesturing to the sofa I'd woken on. He'd made it up like a bed, sheets, a new duvet. And that's how I came to stay with Jonathan for the week between Christmas and New Year.

For the first two days, doing anything more than lying down caused a coughing fit and, although Jonathan left me a curated selection of videos, if I tried focusing on anything, my brain felt like fruit reducing in a saucepan. And then, on the third day, we began working on the play. At first, we read, Jonathan playing the various other parts. His acting was extraordinarily precise. He spoke huge chunks of text without taking a breath and his voice, normally so removed, was vital, punctuated by infinitesimal bursts of emotion, just rare enough to be thrilling every time.

We stopped to discuss where Hamlet was in his emotional journey. The conversations were open, considered, Jonathan leapt up to his shelves to bring me down essays, told me stories of past productions, the travails of some of the greats playing the part: Gielgud, Richard Burton, Mark Rylance. He retired to his room that night after a dinner of fish stew, but I couldn't sleep. I'd never felt such rapport with an adult before. He treated me like an equal, a partner even. It was like being resuscitated.

The next day we took a walk on the Heath. We stopped at an empty playground. He told me to go on the swings on my own for ten minutes to see how it felt. After a few minutes, I started thinking back to evening walks with Nina in Bexleyheath, jumping the fence to the play area, her showing me how to get the swing so high it felt like I'd fall to the ground.

To my childhood, crashing off the top of a slide in floods of tears, wrist in agony, desperately looking for my mum but unable to find her. As I swung alone, I began to sink into a deep pit of loneliness and felt a relish for it Jonathan had prodded me towards but until then I'd found elusive.

'Unhappy people are born to be so,' he'd said to me in a rehearsal at The Church. 'It's how they relate to the world, where they draw their energy from. Embracing that darkness is the only freedom they'll ever find.'

We climbed up Parliament Hill and gazed at the skyline, a blanket of cloud above the BT Tower, St Paul's, the brand-new Canary Wharf, the lone skyscraper in a city still resisting them.

'Why did you never act?' I asked. 'You're brilliant.'

'When I was at The Church,' he said, leant on the stone plinth at the summit. 'San and Ingram controlled everything, none of the committee nonsense we're forced to go through now. San liked me from the start. He was an old queen and had his . . . favourites.' He flicked his eyebrows laconically. 'Ingram was less convinced. "All arms," he used to say.' Jonathan waved his pipe-cleaner arms around then stopped so quickly I wasn't sure if I'd imagined it. 'I was desperate for him to like me. I worked on his method over everything else, got barracked by the voice department, skipped singing, didn't turn up for half a term of ballet.'

'Really?'

'Spent every minute I had on exercises for him. I didn't know if it made them any better, he never let on he was pleased. Then we worked together in the final year. San

must have let Ingram do horrible things to him in the bedroom because I got cast as Cassius in Ingram's *Julius Caesar*.
That rehearsal process was the most fascinating time of my
life. Not just for my craft, but in the way he worked with
other actors. He had cast a council-estate fellow, Omar, as
Mark Antony and—'

'Omar Fox-Daniels? He was in your year?'

'Group 9. Omar could never keep still on stage. Frantic.
Ingram could've done all sorts of things to stop it, strapped
his hands, interrupting every time he moved, but instead,
knowing Omar was desperately poor – the state paid our
fees then so many more of us were – Ingram started bringing in gourmet sandwiches. Roast pork, salmon and capers,
chicken escalope. If Omar moved superfluously on stage,
he would give these sandwiches to other members of the
cast and have them eat them in front of him. In time, Omar
stopped moving.'

'And he is, on screen, Omar Fox-Daniels is always
motionless,' I said. A border collie ran up and danced a
figure-of-eight around Jonathan's legs. He raised an eyebrow at me before leaning down to ruffle the dog's head
before it scampered away.

'Seeing him changing students like that, inspired you to
teach?'

Jonathan inhaled deeply on his cigarette before huffing
out a dragon's breath of smoke.

'Nine months after I graduated, San told me Ingram
wanted to see me. I'd done a fetid season in Colchester, so
I hoped he was getting me in to meet one of his contacts,

but he told me he was dying. Throat cancer. Smoked like a munitions factory.' He flicked his cigarette to the floor and ground it with his foot until the leaves formed a paste. 'They asked me to study under him with a view to my taking on his mantle. They'd seen a faith in their methodology, which gave them hope I could become its custodian.'

'You said you would, even though you still wanted to be an actor?'

He fixed me with those languorous eyes. 'They chose me. It was an honour. I didn't hesitate for a second and haven't spent any longer regretting it.' Damp air had soaked through the sweater Jonathan had lent me and I started to cough. He clapped me on the back with surprising force and wrapped his scarf tight around my neck. 'Let's get you back,' he said, leading back down the hill.

'Nietzsche said we killed God,' he said as we walked towards Kenwood House. '"Is not the greatness of this deed too great for us? Must we ourselves not become gods to appear worthy of it?"' His long stride stretched beetle-shadows behind us. 'I think he meant who are we, as a species, without God? What is it we can do with our capacity for thought, our faith, our boundless love without him? The world has diminished by God's demise, no doubt about it in my mind. But, if there is something into which we can pour the entirety of our belief, our love, a purpose which we can dedicate ourselves to, we can live for something greater than our own selfish desires and that, in my view, is the last remaining path to heaven.'

*

The following day Jonathan took me to buy my Christmas present. He rapped on the shutters of a shop on Essex Road and a Turkish man emerged, who he introduced as Menem, and ushered us inside. It was like being brought onto the set of a horror film. The walls were overwhelmed with stuffed animals, talons, teeth, gills even, pointed threateningly towards us.

'We're here to find Yorick,' he told Menem, who looked at me with a new sense of wonder. He pulled a cord, lighting up a back room filled with hundreds of animal skeletons, the colour of sandstone. Jonathan urged me forward, to my left birds, to the right woodland creatures and the skulls of larger animals, cows perhaps, at the bottom something even larger, an elk or moose. On the far wall at the back of the room were six or seven rows of human skulls.

I went and studied them one by one, Jonathan shifting in the light behind me.

'What am I looking for?' I asked, trying to picture skin wrinkled on foreheads, eye-sockets filled, cartilage noses hanging like prosthetics.

'The text.'

'Alas, poor Yorick! I knew him, Horatio, a fellow of infinite jest, of most excellent fancy.' I saw him amongst the small mammals. Dustin. A mutt Jack Russell mix who belonged to an old lady called Rachel on our terrace in Kippax. She'd give me KitKats if I walked him. I'd take Dustin out for hours, along the Aire down to Allerton. When Mum was ill, he'd cuddle in the folds of her scratty dressing gown and as she got worse, he used to turn up unannounced, sat outside the back door, desperate to be with her. After she died, he'd sniff around the sofa for hours, trying to find her. Dad went round and told Rachel to keep Dustin locked in. He died a couple of years after.

I took up the skull, looked in its eye-sockets. I was on the recreation ground near our house in Kippax, throwing the ball for Dustin. I heard Mum singing. Low with a crackle of fuzz, a song-bird vibrato at the top end. She sang before I was born. Choirs, pubs, a wedding band. She met my dad doing a wedding; he was an usher at a church hall affair. Lust at first sight she told me. She got headhunted by a proper band too, one that was going on a tour. But then she fell pregnant, so the band had to find someone else and a couple of months after I was born, my dad did the same.

People at the Old Tree would sometimes cajole my mum up to the piano to sing something and only then, the world would see her grace. It was natural talent. She didn't nurture it, never worked on it. At best, she was a distant memory of a few dozen nobodies in a village no one's heard of. Extraordinary but pointless. I felt her hand in mine, her hair against my cheek like a nest of caramel.

Jonathan was watching me, the bare lightbulb catching an intensity in his eyes that might have been pride. He went to Menem and bought me the skull.

The following day, the phlegm had lifted. Jonathan let me smoke again as we worked on the closet scene together. He read Hamlet's mother Gertrude with a sensuality I was amazed he could inhabit, internal conflict squeezing through every word. He wasn't happy with me though.

'How did your mother die?' he said, stopping me in the middle of the line where I tell Gertrude she's sleeping in the rank sweat of an enseamed bed with my uncle. The morning was so dark it could have been the night, a lamp with a marbled shade casting a ring of gold onto Jonathan's shoulder.

'She had cancer.'

'That's not true.' His soothing tone had returned, always on the edge of a sigh. My mouth filled with spit.

'She—Organ failure.'

'How old?'

'Thirty-one.'

'Organ failure at thirty-one?' I knew he knew, but he needed me to say it.

'She drank,' I said. A grandfather clock struck eleven. We waited in silence until it had finished. It was the first time I'd told anyone who had anything to do with The Conservatoire the truth.

'You lie about it why?' Jonathan said. I plugged my fingers into the holes of his Chesterfield sofa.

'I suppose it's easier.'

'People drink, Adam. The world is littered with alcoholics. What is it about your mother's drinking that makes you hide it?'

'Just less questions.'

'The audience only have questions. They come to the actor for answers.' I fumbled for the packet of cigarettes.

'Look at Yorick.' Jonathan nodded at the skull on the coffee table between us. I took it up and stared into the cavernous eyes. 'Tell me what you remember of your mother?'

'I—I don't know.'

'Tell me about her eyes.'

I cleared my throat. 'They were yellow at the end. The whites went yellow. She limped. Hips had crumbled, the bones in them.'

'What else?'

'There were times she held me and I felt tethered to something, but mostly it was like her soul had left her body. She'd try to focus, really try, like seeing me was the most important thing in the world, but the lines of me were never clear enough. I thought I must be translucent, like a cartoon ghost. She tried so hard.' I wanted to show him tears, but nothing came, my voice a detached monotone.

'Why did she drink?'

'I don't know.'

'Why did she drink?'

My mouth was dry, I couldn't say it.

'The speech,' Jonathan whispered, closing his eyes.

'Alas, poor Yorick—'

'To be or not to be.'

I gave the famous speech. The first part to Dustin, the rest to Jonathan. I was messy on the text, but I felt a depth of despair so terrifying, I felt desperate, truly desperate for the sweet release of death.

'That,' Jonathan said when I finished, circling a finger

in the air, every word a separate sentence. 'That. Is. The. Method.'

Although almost entirely recovered from my illness, I was shaking as I walked up the path of Nina's house on the afternoon of New Year's Eve. We didn't have mobile phones then, weren't constantly texting and checking in with each other. We were more comfortable not being in touch, but aside from my note, the only contact I'd had with Nina was an answerphone message on Boxing Day wishing them all a Merry Christmas, explaining I hadn't called because I had come down with flu. She would have been so hurt by what happened, so confused at how I could have left. My absence would have tarnished the whole family's Christmas, sucked the cinnamon air out of their festivities. I found myself upset, clammy hand slipping off the key as I put it in the door, a deep dread at facing Nina. But she wasn't at home.

Liv wrapped me in a hug, told me I looked peaky and made me tea.

'We've missed you,' she said, voice dripping with concern. 'All of us. An awful lot.' She was telling me without telling me that if they hadn't known about Nina and me before, how she was in my absence had revealed it to them. Nina was at a New Year's Eve Party at The Boys' flat in Highgate. Liv told me I should go, surprise Nina, said it was my last year, I should be amongst my friends. I wanted to turn back out the door immediately, desperate to see her. At night, when Jonathan had left me to my sofa, I'd thought of going back to Nina, taking her in my arms and telling her I loved her too. The thought of her at the party, face splashed with glitter, swigging from a bottle of Lambrusco, demanding The Boys put on her Destiny's Child CD, filled me with the most luminous warmth. I could have told her at midnight, she would have forgiven my hesitation before Christmas because Nina was built to forgive.

But I knew that I couldn't. In the middle of the play Hamlet is sent to England. His uncle sends a letter with his two friends which says that on his arrival, Hamlet is to be put to death. Hamlet finds the letter, instead murders his two friends and returns to Denmark stripped of his philosophy, his self-reflection, concerns for family and friends, driven only by his vengeful purpose, an entirely different person. In the same way, the week with Jonathan was like special forces training, a re-education camp, I felt transformed. However much I wanted to see her, to make things right between us, diving back into wonderful debauchery with Nina and my classmates risked undoing all the work Jonathan and I had done in one halcyon night. I pled illness to Liv, went to my garret, unplugged the heater and slept.

I woke at four and waited in my room working on the text until ten, when I took Nina a cup of tea that felt like a peace offering. I stood outside her door for some time, then turned on my heel, not ready, but the floorboard squeaked beneath me.

'Ad?'

I cleared my throat and went in. 'Hi.'

'Hello stranger.' She shifted herself up in the bed, hair so dishevelled it was like it grew from three or four different places. She reached for the tea like it was water in a desert, gave me a sleepy smile of thanks, in pieces from the night before but putting on a brave face. She shifted up, making space for me on the bed. I sat, couldn't face her yet.

'So, that was dramatic,' she said.

'Yeh.'

'Did you miss me?'

'Course.'

'Barely noticed you were gone.' She pulled me round to her, grinning. I couldn't help smiling back, so pleased to see her. I put my hand on her cheek and she nuzzled in, closed her eyes, before a wave of nausea sent her back into her pillows. 'I was fuming when I found you'd left. I mean, it's great you went to see your dad,' she said. I blinked hard, wondering if there was any world where I could tell her the truth about where I'd been the previous week, deciding in an instant there wasn't. 'Just, after what you said, well, didn't say.'

'I know,' I said, shifting myself towards her on the bed. I still couldn't say it. I wasn't sure why. I loved her, I knew I did. I felt even then that I probably always would. But it's like the words were trapped at the bottom of a well. Nina sat up, squared herself to me.

'Listen,' she said, swallowing some horrible taste in her mouth. 'God, I'm hung-over. Anyway—'

'It's alright, Nee,' I said, taking her wrist in my hand.

'No, I need to say, I get it. We're friends, we were friends, it makes it all way more complicated. And then—' She bunched a bit of duvet up, pulled it up into a cone. 'There's

162

the play. It's a challenge, bit of a headfuck and you have a lot going on trying to do it justice. Exactly as you should be.'

I clenched my jaw, finding it excruciating her being so reasonable. I wanted recriminations, resentment, not un-conditional understanding.

'But please,' she took my hand in both of hers. 'Please don't lose sight of who you are, Adam. Because I'm your biggest fan and I'm going to say it when we're not shit-faced, I do love you.' She searched my eyes, giving me a moment to say the 'I love you too' she wanted. It would have been so easy, but Jonathan was there in my head talk-ing of God's death, putting my purpose over the selfish desire I had to be happy with the woman I loved. So I leant forward and kissed her for a long time.

We parted, settled back on her bed and, although she relaxed into the nook of my shoulder, our bodies felt sep-arate, a gap between us, guardedness clouding around. My eyes dotted her salmon-pink walls, the lightbulb mirror make-up desk, the framed posters of Broadway musicals, postcard-pictures of Judi Dench, Maggie Smith on stage. It was the bedroom of a fangirl. How many times had she told me she was my biggest fan, how great my work was, how I should back myself more. 'Your friends are your enemies, and your enemies are your friends,' Jonathan had told me that day under the rhododendron. Nina started explaining with relish how messy the New Year's party had got. I felt a tremor of irritation, then instant guilt to be thinking of Nina as vapid. I was unmoored by this new ambivalence but tried to bank how it felt. It would be perfect for my scenes with Ophelia.

Term started two days later. When I walked into The Church everything seemed too bright, colours an assault, like the saturation had been blasted up in post-production. The rest of Group 28 seemed to pinball around the halls, more vibrant, louder, overjoyed to be together again. It felt like they had spent the whole holidays in each others' pockets because the cast-iron edges of cliques and alliances seemed to have melted away, leaving only them and me. I observed Anna K, James, Ben half-dressed around the entrance to the changing room, The Boys yanking people's boxers down, pinging the girls' bras as if they were kids at camp. I found it appalling, looked around for Nina to agree with me, before hearing her screaming laugh inside the changing room as Patrick ran out carrying Victor through the halls by his jockstrap. I swerved to avoid them, the whole building bellowing with laughter at the melee. I looked at Nina, head thrown back in joy at the sort of public-school horseplay we used to bitch about on the train home. I went to my locker at the far end of the hall, desperate to separate myself from the festival atmosphere, climbing inside almost to get changed. When I re-emerged, Vanessa was there.

'My father asked about you,' she said, pretending she didn't enjoy being the herald of the kingmaker before indicating to walk with her to ballet class.

'Hasn't he already met with Patrick?' I said, catching up.

Her father rarely took on new graduates; his taking two in a year was unheard of. She pushed open the door to Studio 2, where our ballet teacher Bempe was at the mirror doing his port de bras, many of the class already at the barre stretching.

'*Hamlet*'s the one play people in the industry know. Patrick's a honeypot, but, whatever else is wrong with my dad, and the list is ever-growing, he only ever wants the best actor.'

'Aren't we all so lucky to have arms?' Bempe said, turning to the class, his childlike voice always surprising from his body carved from marble. Bempe was a beacon of light at The Church, obsessed with the human form, the shapes of nature, he spent his weekends in Epping Forest dancing with the trees. 'Pas de deux today,' he said, gliding over to the cassette player. 'Find a partner.'

Vanessa raised an eyebrow, extended her hand to me. I glanced at Nina stood at the front of the barre, laughing with Anna T. She clocked me stood with Vanessa, gave me a confused half-smile. I took Van's hand. I couldn't remember us ever being paired together and as I led her into the middle of the room, the unctuousness of her expensive perfume in my nostrils, I felt a quiet sense of power over the rest of the room. I tried not to look at Nina.

'So, what did you say?' I said a few minutes after Van and I started working through the routine, supporting her as she stepped towards me en-pointe. She jumped down in a pas de chat.

'I said you could be good. He wants to meet you.'

The thought of meeting Alasdair Nixon ran through my ribcage like a surge of heat. He represented movie stars, theatre sirs and dames. His clients weren't jobbing actors, they did epoch-defining plays, seminal movies. With first Jonathan and then Alasdair in my corner, I'd have opportunities to do the sort of important work Ingram set up The Conservatoire for. I'd be able to become someone.

One of our moves was a high lift that went into a dip, the music unbearably slow. I lifted Vanessa, limber as a reed, as far as I could before bringing her down to the floor. As we held our bodies horizontally, her eyes looking into mine, I felt a heat from her belying her exterior coolness. My arms strained to hold her, so she rose up early to save my blushes. I watched James and Nina as they messed around doing a mock *Dirty Dancing* lift, pissing themselves laughing as they crumpled onto the floor. Van looked at her, a tired sigh. She put her hand on my shoulder as we waited for the music to end, gave it a squeeze when it did.

With the carrot of a meeting with Alasdair dangling, I threw myself into rehearsals where, in the first few weeks, we were working on exercises exploring our characters in private moments. Patrick hit a punchbag until he was sick finding Laertes' anger; James applied elaborate make-up to explore his Player King's gender; Nina, perhaps subconsciously nodding to how we still hadn't had sex, bound her breasts to explore her version of Guildenstern suppressing her femininity to please the men of the court. People were going for it; Jonathan seemed impressed.

166

I felt imperious as I strode up onto the stage for my exercise. The rest of the cast sat semicircled behind Jonathan, anticipation collecting like smoke in the vaulted ceiling. I sat on the stage-bed for some time and did nothing, allowing them to take me in, to be held in my spell.

Then I took my shirt off, went to look in the mirror, traced my cheekbones, pulled apart my lips until the flesh turned white, scratched at oily skin. I looked for the boy I was, the lonely child, the chaff, hated myself for my callowness, my naivete. I let the hatred build then produced electric clippers from my back pocket and began to shave my head. I could feel the room breathe as one. My eyes widened, pupils huge as I stripped my hair back to the skull. Though not as shocking as the razor blade, this felt more powerful, a physical rejection of everything Hamlet was, the death of his father moving him from child to man, killing my very self. I looked down at the hair piled on the stage below, about two-thirds across my head.

'What kind of infant-school literality is this meant to be?' Jonathan stood over his desk like a dictator mapping a conquest. 'How, Group 28, how is it that all of you have succeeded in mining your intrinsic pain to bring out the characters' psychology through action, and this boy,' he hammered the word like it was a broken bell, 'hands us pantomime cliché? Tell me. Guildenstern, tell me.' He wheeled himself round to Nina, making her scrabble to sit up. 'What was Hamlet, your friend, working for?' She looked at me, lost, desperate to help.

'Um, I don't know. Anger maybe?'

'Anger! The go-to emotion for children, soap operas and the ill-educated. I'm sure that's exactly what it was meant to be.'

I cleared my throat, came down-stage. 'I was working for grief.'

'Grief?! You watched your mother drink herself to death' – my chest caught as I felt the room making sense of what he had said – 'and the best you can give us is a haircut.'

I stared at him, aghast he could air my most guarded secret, but he was unmoved, nothing on his face but a crease of disdain. Nina's eyes burned into me, foundering that I could have lied to her about such a fundamental pillar of myself.

'Break,' Jonathan said. He flipped his notebook closed and walked out the double doors. The blazer on the back of his chair wafted in his draught before settling to stillness.

It was after Jonathan revealed how my mother died that the edges of me began fracturing. Nina found me in the graveyard at the back of The Church afterwards and the cruelty I had felt bubbling in a secret pit in my stomach burst out.

'I would never have judged you,' she said, taking her hand off a gravestone she'd leant on. 'You didn't have to make something up. You never have to lie to me.' She reached her hand to mine, I shrugged it away.

'Sounds like something from a TV programme.'

'I'm just saying, it's a big thing, I could have helped you.'

'How? With all the life lessons you read in *Just Seventeen* magazine?'

She sucked a breath in like she'd seen a dead body. 'It's not my fault he didn't like your exercise,' Nina said, threads fraying in her voice. She opened her mouth to say something else, then turned, shaking her head, and left me to the mildewed graves.

The following day, I felt the collected curiosity of the whole Conservatoire pressing in on me like I'd swum into deep, deep water. Jonathan dismissed me from rehearsals until lunch to work with James and the other players on the play-within-a-play. His coldness, compared to how he'd been with me over Christmas, felt almost physical. Van perched next to me on the sofa I'd succumbed to.

'How did he know about your mother?' she asked, so directly I found myself telling her. About how he'd found me passed out and on the way to pneumonia behind The Church, how he'd taken me in, gave me the most rousing, most enlightening week of my life.

'I couldn't tell Nina,' I said as I came to the end.

'She's not your keeper.' She angled away from me, scratched the back of her head. 'My father's known Jonathan twenty-five years,' she said, changing the subject as if she'd found the thought hidden amongst the cobwebs on the ceiling. 'He's never been to his house, never met someone who has. Yet, he let you in.'

'Only to rip me to shreds? Tell my closest friends my mother was a drunk.'

'This is what you wanted, Adam. I used to watch you in his classes as he tore Patrick new orifices, found fifteen different ways to call me an ice-cold bitch. You sat watching like a Victorian orphan looking through a toy-shop window. Now you've got Jonathan's attention, his full, both barrels and several RPGs attention, and you want to disappear into the furniture. Fucking do something about it.'

I looked at her, felt a caffeine-spark thrill across my skin and had an idea.

'Fetch me a paper and pen, mother,' I asked.

Van raised a trademark eyebrow but got up and went to her locker to bring back expensive writing paper and a fountain pen. Nina came out of one of the teaching rooms and saw Van and I together. The two of us had hardly seen each other since my outburst in the graveyard. Van smiled wide at her, kissed me on the top of my head and left me on the sofa.

I spent the next three hours writing sections of script for the players to perform my own version of the play-within-a-play. I worked on the dialogue, revision after revision, writing out the individual parts as Shakespeare would have done. The first years came out of a class and watched, which made me write more furiously. I was Hamlet; jealousy, exhibitionism, rage, grief, swirling like sands in a vacuum. This felt right, losing myself to Hamlet was what Jonathan wanted from me. He didn't want to be my friend, my confidante, he didn't want to see Adam anymore. He was sick of Adam. Everyone always had been.

I finished ten minutes before I was due back in rehearsals but felt sure Jonathan would want to see what I'd done. When I opened the doors of Room 1, I was confused to hear Patrick's mellifluous baritone. Laertes wasn't in the players scene. I drew the curtains and saw him on stage, alone, James and the rest sat behind Jonathan, who stood in front of the stage.

'What's Hecuba to him, or he to Hecuba, that he should weep for her?' Patrick was speaking my lines. The 'rogue and peasant slave' speech, without a script. I twisted the reams of paper I'd spent hours writing until they were a pulpy mess in my hands as Patrick did my speech. It was nothing like my performance. He drove through the rhythm like he was pulling up a tree, dynamic and, although superficial, compelling. He looked like a God.

'The play's the thing,' he said, knelt at the front of the stage, the idea catching him like a sharp wind, 'wherein I'll catch the conscience of the King.' Patrick finished and spotted me, sadness in his eyes.

Jonathan turned, not surprised I was there. 'Adam,' he said, using my name for the first time in months. 'I've had thoughts about the production.'

Act 3

III.i

Under a monsoon of lights, the red carpet at the foot of the Albert Hall steps glowed nineteen-fifties technicolour.

After The Church, I was taken to the hotel to be tailored into my suit, but spent the afternoon wanting to find Amber so we could piece together whether it was possible I had met Raya. Her uncle said she was obsessed with me, that she thought I would be her mentor. She'd tried to meet me; said she had met me and I couldn't even remember it. This wasn't about Jonathan anymore. A student had been hurt, maimed almost, and the girl who did it was off her medication, had gone missing and someone, perhaps even Raya herself, was trying to implicate me and my mentor in the disappearance. But worse, her year knew about *Hamlet*. Even if they didn't know what really happened, if Lyndsey's scalding were to get out, would it be too much of a stretch for someone to dig a little deeper into what happened that night? No Oscar, no career, no walking about a free person, that's what Van had said. I had to find Raya. I needed to find her safe. But Amber had looked everywhere – the missing persons database, the police, various hospitals – Raya couldn't be found.

Van barged into my suite an hour before we were due to leave. She'd dashed from The Church in a different car and, perhaps it was just because she'd kept the scholarship from me, I couldn't help the feeling she couldn't meet my eye.

'What?' she mouthed when she caught me glaring as she sat on a call to Delilah. The photos from the workshop had gone on social media and had gone down very well. In one, I was with Lyndsey, conjuring something in the air. Another showed the whole class listening to me like I was Jesus; there was a video of me talking about playing things for truth. The buzz was how wonderful it was that I had chosen to give something back, rather than spending the day of the ceremony under seaweed facials. Although Delilah reminded us Carl Dillane was still Carl Dillane, so we'd have to assume I was in second place for the BAFTA that night, after the call Van floated around the suite, distributing bowls of macadamia nuts with an air of triumph. It seemed like being back at The Church, in Room 1, hadn't affected her at all. Compartmentalising was key to her success and however much I wanted to talk to her about what it had felt like being there, I couldn't unlock the box where she'd buried what she saw.

She stood behind me on the red carpet, wearing an understated dress by an Iranian designer she liked. I wore a regulation black tuxedo. Not making a statement was the statement, I'd been told by the gentleman from Tom Ford.

We were held in a queue by a fierce-looking woman with

pulled-back red hair, who flashed honeydew eyes at all of us 'stars' while looking at her underlings like they were in a competition to undermine her entire existence. As I neared the gauntlet to face the photographers, I saw Emmy, my *Woodsman* co-star, bursting in front of the lights from no-where. Even with a pixie cut and a sheer golden dress, she was still my Louanne, the woman who brought me back to life and destroyed me all at once. Seeing her so resplendent with the press, made it seem even more unlikely she swerved our huge *Times* profile on Hampstead Heath for a 'schedule clash'.

The red-haired woman tried to beckon me to join Emmy but, head full of Raya, I waved her off, not wanting my proximity to a beautiful, much younger woman to be misinterpreted by the cameras. But Van was pushing my elbow, admonishing me forward. I stumbled as I got past the queue, felt the swarm of camera clicks as I moved to embrace my former co-star. I was used to her throwing her yoga-toned arms around me like a loving child greeting their father back from a work trip, but instead I got a polite hand on a shoulder before she turned back to the on-slaught. I put on a half-smile, realising my suspicions that she swerved the profile because of measuredbella's blog post had to be true.

Emmy moved down to the interviews; an assistant arrived taking me to join her. As flashes flashed, I scanned the faces in the crowd for my image of Raya, light-brown bunches, haunted eyes. I got down to Emmy and heard the tail-end of one of her answers.

'It's actually how it subverts the traditional narrative I was drawn to,' she said. 'Because, despite her tragic fate, it's Louanne who saves Harrison, not the other way round.' She gave me a hooded side-eye as the journalist spotted me.

'The man of the moment,' the young reporter said, idiotically considering Emmy, the film and Bryce the director were also nominated. I had become synonymous with the film in the public's mind, my Cannes win and the comeback narrative becoming the fulcrum of the marketing effort that elevated *Woodsman* from an old-fashioned indie in a handful of arthouse cinemas into a worldwide critical darling. Of course, it still made about two per cent of a *Spider-man*. I looked down the line of journalists thrusting the back ends of smartphones at whichever star's attention they could grab and felt absolute certainty that every question would be about Jonathan, about Raya, it had to be. Perhaps one of them had found her, perhaps the girl with those haunted eyes would be stood with one of them, ready to expose me to the world's press. But, 'It looks like you've had a shower for tonight!' was all the idiot said. The press loved I hadn't washed my clothes throughout the shoot for *Woodsman*.

'Had two, not one for half-measures,' I said, the contempt I had for these things returning like a reassuring blanket. I'm sure the journalists at awards ceremonies don't want to be raging sycophants, but at some point their gushing praise and our earnest enthusiasm became the contract. The red-headed lady moved Emmy and me on to the next one, then the next one. None of them asked anything more

178

pressing than what it was like being back in London, what project I was doing next, whether I'd be going Method for my Soviet flick, which gave me a chance to make the joke Delilah's scriptwriter had suggested about only eating Borscht for a year. We got to the end of the queue, and just as the red-headed woman was about to whisk us away, Amy Dawson, the journalist from the *Times* who'd done the interview accompanying the photoshoot, appeared at the front of the hoardings.

'Adam, Emmy,' she called out. I could see Emmy considering whether to leave, but she composed herself and came back down to Amy.

'Magical night,' Amy said. 'Emmy, you and Adam went to the same drama school' – my throat tightened; I searched the crowd for Van – 'did you look up to Adam when you were training?'

'We talked about Adam a lot,' Emmy said, treating the journalist like the most important person in the world. 'The teachers held him up as the pinnacle of what we should be aiming for in our work, that absolute single-mindedness.' Emmy glanced at me, a sliver of something I couldn't place. 'But I've learnt so much since then, from every project, about what I need to give the best performance.'

'I learnt a lot working with Emmy,' I said, uncertain as to where Emmy was heading. If Lyndsey and Arthur's group knew about *Hamlet*, of course Emmy would too. She'd known about the hanging, about the echoes it would have with our movie, but never mentioned it. 'She has incredible instincts, far better than mine were at her age.' I knew

179

instantly how patronising I'd been. Emmy's face didn't move. I needed to get away from the cameras. I started to go but Amy stopped me again.

'If either of you win tonight, the world's your oyster. Quick-fire, if you could choose any role, real or imagined, who would it be, Adam?'

'Let's go with that,' I said, trying to escape. 'The first man, Adam. That would be a challenge.'

'Emmy, would you be Adam's Eve?'

'Speak to my agent about that.'

This drew a huge laugh from Amy. 'Emmy, same question?' Amy asked as she was just starting to move off.

'I'd love to do some Shakespeare,' Emmy said. 'You've put me on the spot but—A play that has a lot of resonance today, maybe *Measure for Measure*?' She turned, pierced me with a look and walked up the stairs.

I found myself reaching out, wanting to grab her before the volley of flashes reminded me where I was. I joined the queue eight or ten behind Emmy, expecting her to turn round and wink, as if the whole thing were a big joke.

We were ushered into the hall, which was as quiet and stilted as these things always are. No one knows where they're meant to be until they're told, so we stood around in purgatory, the neuroses of nominees pretending they're not desperate to win sitting around our ankles in thick clouds.

Someone led me to my table where the director and producers greeted me like a lost son. All the seats were filled but Emmy wasn't there. Across the room, I could see her air-kissing the cast of the other movie she was in that year, taking a place at their table. It was a campus movie in which she was part of an ensemble cast, whereas she was nominated for *Woodsman*, the next biggest character after mine. I couldn't understand why she was shunning me. Working together had been the best thing about the shoot. Then afterwards doing press, in every Green Room, every city, we'd find that old-friend wavelength. But that night, she seemed disgusted by my very presence.

I looked for Van amongst the tables at the back, needing to tell her what Emmy had said, but before I could find her, the lights dimmed and I was being urged into my seat, ready for the ceremony to begin.

After the first few awards, I managed to relax, convincing myself whatever I was imagining with Emmy was just the pressure of the occasion. Her table was filled with gleaming youth and mine with crusty, older white men. If I was her, I would have sat over there too.

The ceremony washed over me and two hours in, without the booze the other guests used to alleviate their boredom, I had to do everything I could to stop yawning. Then Cate Blanchett came on to present the Leading Actor award. I felt the cameras locking me in their crosshairs. As she read out the nominations, roughly the same list I'd heard seven or eight times at these ceremonies now, I closed my eyes. Her presidential voice muffled and flattened out until all I could hear was my own breathing. The air in the room seemed to empty, all was still.

I heard the thunk of a rope slamming down taut and the cavernous hall seemed to erupt with applause. Someone manhandled me onto my feet, and I found myself looking around the Albert Hall as my rival Carl Dillane led the room in a standing ovation. I had won. I manoeuvred towards the stage and saw Emmy on her feet with the rest of her table clapping, her body turned away from me. As I made my way up, glistening eyes, applauding as if I were their child getting married, I saw Van stood at a table near the back with some of the financiers. Two seats to her left, the only person in the room sitting, was Jonathan Dors, chin balanced on pointed index fingers, not clapping, nor smiling, the same as at the end of every student show. As I climbed the steps, my lip shivered with joy. We'd invited him to everything, but he never came. But there he was, there for me.

I paused at the top of the steps. Cate stepped towards me, hair slicked back with some wet-look product, which reminded me of the soaking Lyndsey that afternoon in The Church. I strode across and she handed me the trophy. As she leant forward to kiss my cheek, I looked down at her shoulder and saw Lyndsey's burn, writhing in whorls. When I blinked it was gone.

I got to the lectern and paused, bubbles of awe in my throat.

'I feel sick,' I said. Vanessa perked up. This wasn't the beginning of the speech we'd discussed. Hundreds of faces staring at me, expecting the world, and I could have thrown up over my statuette.

'I'm so grateful. So grateful. I know you will have all spent the last few months sat in gold chairs clapping for a

182

few hours a day to get in character for tonight.' The audience pealed into laughter. 'I've been in this tuxedo for three weeks. The socks for longer. Don't let me get too relaxed at the after-party.' I looked at Emmy, beaming but not happy, in the sea of glistening faces.

'But, seriously,' I said, dialling up my Northern vowels. 'There are times in my career I have been a massive pain in the arse. But more than that, I crossed a line with a fellow professional on the movie I was making before this one, and I'm sorry. Truly sorry about that. But the thing that makes us human, I hope, is the capacity to forgive, something we have the potential to do because' – I stared down the barrel of the camera lens – 'every single one of us is broken.' The room was silent with the sense I could say anything. 'It's the one thing we all have in common. And I believe that's the actor's job, to go down to the depths and come out the other side, to remind the audience that whatever we might have been through, whatever we've witnessed' – I looked at Jonathan – 'though we may not heal, we can grow to love the damaged parts of ourselves, which, more than anything else, define who we are.' Eyes were moist in the front row. Keanu nodded a few back. Jess Chastain kissed her husband's fingers. 'I was drawn to act because I was searching for redemption. Tonight, you've shown me it's possible and, for that, I thank you all from the bottom of my ridiculous heart.'

I went on to thank yous. The film's producers, Bryce, Emmy. I thanked Vanessa. I was running out of time. A man with a shaved head at the side of the stage gave me a smile telling me to finish. I looked at Jonathan, arms by his side, sleepy, almost bored. He wasn't smiling. I gripped the base of my award and felt an intense burst of indignant rage. He could have been a great actor, a director or writer, he had the intellect and discipline to make vast sums of money in business or the law, live in mansions, have fast cars, a loving partner, children even, all the things the world aspires to have to live a happy life. He had given that all up to help people like me aim for greatness, to create performances that transcend the everyday and live in the memory. But the University drummed him out of the institution he'd dedicated his life to, away from the students who were the closest thing he had to family. Now some anonymous coward was trying to make it seem like he was responsible for doing something to a girl he was trying to protect. And we – me and Van – despite everything he'd done for us, hadn't done a thing to defend him.

'Being here tonight,' I found myself saying, 'amongst my betters, reminds me we're part of a lineage, standing on the shoulders of those that have gone before, the sacrifices they made. It was my teacher Jonathan Dors who taught me that. And it was working with him again on this film that pushed me to a performance I hope might inspire another generation. Jonathan.' I shook the award in his direction. He looked to his right, took a deep breath in, then out again. I prayed he was pleased.

Although I'd alluded to my team in other speeches, I hadn't namechecked Jonathan in any of my speeches before. I was guided to the post-award interviews and photoshoot backstage, leaving thunderous applause behind me, and as I stepped through, shaking hands and hoisting up my gong, all I was thinking was that he had to be pleased.

I thought Van would be furious in the Green Room afterwards, but she was over the moon. I'd made the speech she'd written seem off-the-cuff, and she thought adding Jonathan gave a noble humility and, combined with the workshop at The Church, felt like a PR masterstroke. The narratives of the movie and our campaign had aligned at just the right time. Delilah had messaged to say there was now no doubt I'd become the Oscar frontrunner.

'Did he leave?' I asked when Van had finished gushing.

'After your speech.'

'Did he say anything?'

'He's proud of you, Adam. We all are.'

Emmy wasn't at The Grosvenor for the dinner, but with everyone desperate for face-time, I didn't have much space to worry about it. I mentioned to Van what she'd said about *Measure for Measure*, but she dismissed it.

'It's a coincidence,' she said. 'Her trying to sound intellectual.' She said she'd reach out to Benny to find out if there was anything we had put out that upset Emmy. 'Rice-paper-thin-skinned the kids coming through now,' she told me, but Van hadn't seen the way Emmy looked at me as she walked up the stairs.

After the starters, we went to the Chiltern Firehouse for the after-party. Everyone told me how wonderful I was, how inspiring they found my speech. A couple of people enquired whether I thought Jonathan would work with them on their next project. I found myself prevaricating, protective, like Jonathan was my secret ingredient. At around one, I was so exhausted I felt as if I'd surfaced from a natural disaster and Van escaped us to the hotel.

The car took us around the back where Van escorted me through the kitchen up to my suite. We faced each other at the door. She straightened the jacket hanging over my shoulders.

'Well done, darling,' she said. 'You exceeded my expectations.' She'd drunk a little and had a soft-focus glow. Her arm brushed mine as she reached past me to open my room. We held each other's gaze a little longer than normal.

'Do you ever imagine it?' I said. 'If we'd just gone home together that night. What life would be like?'

She went back, I could see it in her eyes, just for a moment. She touched my cheek, took the weight of my head in her cupped hand. 'You and me?' she said. 'Would not have lasted twenty years' – I laughed, nodded – 'We wouldn't be here. And—' She nodded to the BAFTA I had cradled by my hip. 'You wouldn't have that.'

I shifted away from her hand, stepped back, stomach feeling empty.

'It's a good night, Adam, enjoy the good nights.' She turned and glided down the corridor out of sight.

In my sleep, I heard the voice again. The words *How could you?* again and again like a glitching record. After about three hours, the voice was replaced by an insect buzzing, which woke me. I looked at my phone, the phone I'd had in the cabin, expecting to see it vibrating on the bedside table but it lay black and dormant. I sat up. The air in my suite felt disturbed. Light washed under the door from the corridor. I jumped up and opened it but there was no one there, just the empty procession of mystery doors. I went back in and flicked on the light. When I walked over, I noticed an indent in the pristine coverlet on the empty side of the bed, as if a dog or cat had been curled up for the night.

I went to check the bathroom, the cupboards, set about taking pictures off the wall looking for, I don't know what, before I stopped and slumped into an occasional chair. I needed to get away from hotel rooms, voices, The Church. I was due to meet Jonathan before we left to discuss how we'd work on *Night-train to Rostov*, but it felt like I was already far deeper in the weeds of paranoia than the role would require.

After an hour and a half, I went to our booth at the back of the restaurant for coffee, fruit plate, etcetera. I knew Van would be tapping on my door as soon as she was up to get me on the phone to the *Today* programme, or whoever else had space to squeeze me in, so I could tell them how grateful I was. Which isn't to say I wasn't. Being recognised in Britain, having exiled myself from the country of my birth, really did mean the world to me.

I saw Amber before she saw me, skittering around the lobby looking for something. I called over and could tell I was who she'd been trying to find.

'Van needs to see you,' she said, as she got to the table

a little out of breath, clutching an iPad like she was trying to suppress a grenade.

'What's going on?'

'I think we need to wait for Vanessa?'

I indicated to sit. She fiddled with the headphones hung around her neck like a choker, glanced over her shoulder, before sliding into the booth opposite. She gave me a plastic smile. Something had gone to shit. I proffered my hand for the iPad. She tapped an empty coffee cup, imploring Vanessa to arrive, before reluctantly handing it over.

A headline:

BAFTA-WINNER SEALEY CHANGED MOVIE TO GO FULL METHOD

Hours after Adam Sealey picked up his first BAFTA, an online commenter made an extraordinary accusation against the Leeds-born actor. @measuredbella claims the thespian changed the script of his movie Woodsman, winner of three awards on the night, to make it resonate with a real-life tragedy from his time at drama school.

@measuredbella writes:

'In an earlier draft of Woodsman there's no hanging. A student in Adam Sealey's year from The Conservatoire hung themselves and they changed the ending, exploiting someone's tragic death, just to help his performance. How could you, Adam?'

My heart thudded into my stomach.

'Where was this? Where was it posted?'

'Van's just coming.'

'Amber, please.'

She bit her lip, pity in her eyes. 'A comment on the BAFTA website, the video of your speech.'

'I didn't see another script.' I shoved away from the table, cutlery clashing to the floor, causing waiters to pop up like meerkats.

Vanessa arrived at the entrance, implored heaven at the sight of me and marched to our table, asking Amber to leave us. Once she'd gone, Van sat and poured herself coffee. She arched her fingers on the table and took an enormous breath in. The story wasn't tabloid bullshit.

'Why didn't you tell me?' I said.

'You think you see the first draft? That I involve you in every wrangle about how the screenplay works? By the time you're reading anything it is the final, the best version I've run through an excruciating mill to get to you.'

'You changed the ending?'

'I made suggestions.'

'When?'

'What?'

'When did you change the ending? You brought the script to me, what, four, five months after *The Bends*, so when did you change it?'

'Why does that matter?'

'I was not well, Vanessa,' I whispered, leaning across the table. 'And you brought me a script in which I had to cut down and hold the dead body of someone who had hung themselves.' She placed her cup back on its saucer.

'I talked to your nurses at Ganymede every day, Adam. They told me you sat like a zombie in group therapy, refused every medication, every private session I was paying for, that the only thing you'd said when they managed to get you to talk, was that you were never going to act again.'

'You were there that night, you saw, you—'

'I couldn't let you become a ghost,' she said. She wiped her lips with a napkin. 'We weren't sure the script would be enough to shake you out of your . . . your funk. Giving you a chance to use what happened felt like something you wouldn't want to refuse.'

I caught my face in my hands and started laughing. Hotel guests began filtering in, ordering omelettes, eating the only grapefruit they'd have that year.

'We've released a statement saying your team was involved in the development of the script with the execs, the distributor, but that you had no knowledge of any other versions of it. Delilah's swerving requests for interviews this morning while we see how this escalates.'

I looked at her and thought about the voice in the Wasatch Mountains. It couldn't be a coincidence anymore, I wasn't sure how, but I heard those words that night, then again and again in my dreams, and now through measured-bella. I should have told Van after the cabin, but the way she'd looked at me since *The Bends*, how she'd booked me a no-pressure-to-attend appointment every month with Dr Shandell, the psychiatrist I saw before Ganymede, confessing I'd had a phone call from beyond the grave would have convinced her I'd tipped over the edge.

'Will I have to talk about it?' I asked her.

'We play a straight bat. We've never spoken about what happened in our last year out of respect for the family, which is true, and maybe we say it was what you were alluding to in your speech. "Sacrifice of others" etcetera.'

'What? No!'

'Delilah has the prestige media in her pocket, which is the only thing the fossils at the Academy pay attention to so, Oscars-wise, we're OK.'

'What about the other one?'

'Other one?'

'The comment about Raya. Won't they connect the two?'

'The *Hollywood Reporter* isn't exactly the *Guardian* when it comes to journalistic integrity. We had it taken down.'

'Who's doing this? Who is measuredbella?'

'She doesn't exist. Granular massively overpaid for distribution of Carl Dillane's Armenian genocide yawn-fest, so they'll have got an intern to toss a few buckets o' bullshit around the routers, hoping something lands.'

'This story is true, Van, you did change the script, which, fucking hell—' I paused, attempts at cogent thoughts like a headrush. I bit down on a chunk of blood orange. 'Even if it is Dillane's people, someone is telling them this stuff, about Raya, about *Hamlet*. Maybe they already know what happened and they're just waiting.'

'Delilah has assured me no one ever remembers the smears around the Oscars if you win. So, we keep sane, keep quiet, we don't engage with it.'

'It has to be someone close to the school?' – Van sighed – 'But then how could they find out about the script? I was in the film and I didn't know.'

'Adam, just—' She made a calming gesture, nodded at waiters bussing trays around busy tables.

'You said we,' I said.

'What?'

'When you were talking about changing the screenplay, you said we.' I leant forward, clattering fork against plate. 'Who's we, Vanessa?'

'Adam Sealey,' she talked through clenched teeth as if I were a toddler who'd broken their great-aunt's ornament. 'Two million people watched you on television last night. We are in a public place. You will behave yourself or risk shitting in the punchbowl.'

I could feel someone at the far end of the restaurant standing to take a photo of us.

I stared at Vanessa, picked up my knife and began to poke it into the side of a glass of beetroot juice, making it tip. I kept pushing, Van's face telling me how close I was to knocking the contents over her. She grabbed the glass and put it on the other side of the table.

'Jonathan,' she said. 'We met for coffee a month or so after *The Bends* debacle.'

'The two of you met up?'

'He reached out, was concerned, said you spoke the night after the fight with the divemaster.' I stood up, looked around the room and a waiter scurried up. Vanessa ordered more coffee. I sat down again.

'You moved us across the Atlantic to get away from Jonathan.'

'He was convinced you just needed the right project. I shared some scripts with him, sought his counsel, which wasn't easy for me, as you can imagine, but I didn't know what else to do. I never dreamt you'd ask to actually work with him again.'

I thought back to phoning him in the middle of the night, the day Paulo had dragged me out of the tank. We'd not spoken for a few years, but Jonathan listened to me in silence as I told him it'd been the thought of him seeing me on the diving film that drove me to do it. I told Jonathan my dad had died, that he was the closest thing I ever had to a father and without him in the preceding few years, I'd lost the sense of who I was, why I'd done any of the things I did. I admitted that whatever I'd told Van, told myself, about detaching myself from the safety harness for my performance, I realised I really had been trying to drown myself. I told Jonathan I didn't think I could go on, that I needed help. He said nothing for a long time then he spoke.

'You don't need help, Adam. You have a purpose,' he said. 'Do you know how few people reach the end of their life having found theirs?' He ended the call and, although he'd sounded irritated having to field my neurosis, he'd lifted me more than any friend or therapist could. I was lucky, I had a purpose. But for him to reach out to Van, who I knew he blamed for taking me away to the States, it seemed he'd been more touched by my confession than he'd let on.

'Did he suggest the change?' Vanessa bit her top lip, shook her head.

'He and I discussed it, Louanne poisoned herself, Juliet-style, in the other draft, but no. Hanging was my idea.'

'Why didn't you tell me?'

'I don't know, Adam – you, Jonathan, big vat of Freudian gumbo . . . Managing you, particularly then, it felt like walking a tightrope across a tank of bipolar sharks.'

'What does that mean?'

'It means I never have a clue as to how you'll react because I have no idea who I'm getting – you, whichever character you're playing, some terrifying melange of the two, three, however many are swimming around in there. I keep you in the dark because it's easier. Fucking shoot me. This is . . . not a non-story, to be frank, but until we give it oxygen, it won't be an albatross. Hope is it makes it across the pond now and is gone by the time we're back tomorrow night. Today we lay low. You hang in your suite. I send a masseuse up. Maybe a Pilates guy. Could even see if they'll send up someone with a cooking trolley to make you a crêpe suzette like it's nineteen eighty-seven but, headline, stay in your room, please.'

In my suite, all I thought about was the ghost. In *Hamlet*, the ghost was all the academics and theatrical historians in Nina's books ever wrote about. With the modern ambivalence to God and the afterlife, it's the element of the play that offers directors the greatest potential for re-interpretation. The ghost has been played straight, as a corporeal spirit of Hamlet's father visiting his son and demanding he avenge his murder. But he's also been played as a figment of Hamlet's imagination, borne of his grief and overwhelming melancholy. The lines have been spoken by Hamlet himself, as if he's in denial about the crime he knows his uncle and mother have committed and his subconscious is rebuking him for standing by and doing nothing. And it's been played as a delusion, a psychotic episode manifested from Hamlet's having gone completely and utterly insane.

But the words I heard that night in the cabin, the voice of the dead, *How could you?*, had been written online too. More than once, erasing all hope it could be coincidence. Van, Amber, everyone could see them. Unless my subconscious was creating the whole thing, unless it was me making comments on my own videos, it couldn't be a ghost. It had to, somehow, be real.

An hour and a half later, Amber and I were in a car out to Portobello Road. Whoever was doing this knew The Conservatoire, knew about what happened in the final weeks of *Hamlet*, they knew more about the script of *Woodsman* than I did. And, as I discovered looking back through Conservatoire newsletters that sat neglected in an ancient email account, Emmy was cast as Isabella in *Measure for Measure* in her final show at The Conservatoire but, for some undisclosed reason, never got to perform the role. I needed to speak to my co-star.

III.ii

I was back rehearsing as Hamlet the afternoon I discovered Patrick had been working on the role with Jonathan. I hadn't been replaced but Jonathan wanted to 'keep casting fluid, for the sake of the production'. He had told us the chess-pieces could move but none of us had imagined he could mean the character who has nearly half the lines of the entire three-and-a-half-hour play.

As we ran the scene where Hamlet watches the play-within-a-play, my former insecurities scratched at me like I was cassette-tape, glitching the words as I spoke. I wanted Jonathan to attack me for these mistakes, but he spent most of the time with his head in the script, muttering with Rakka the stage manager about designs. I may as well have been reading pages from the phonebook.

'Learn Laertes, Adam, obviously,' was all he said to me as he swooped out at the end of the day.

That night our year were going out to Marathon, the kebab-shop-cum-nightclub opposite The Roundhouse, but I lingered by my locker waiting for them to leave, intending to work the speeches alone in Room 1 while I still had a shred of Hamlet to hang on to. Nina came in from outside for me, stinking of cigarettes.

'About yesterday,' she said, leaning against a locker three or four away from mine.

'What?'

'In the graveyard?'

'Oh yeh, don't worry.'

'Don't worry? You were fucking rude to me.'

'I mean sorry. I was in shock.' I was looking past her, brow furrowed, cogs were clicking around, wondering how it was I'd ended up in direct competition with an actor I could never beat.

'You should come to the party,' Nina said. She moved her head down, trying to get my full attention.

'I can't,' I said. 'Got to—' I waved my scuffed copy of *Hamlet* at her.

'I can't imagine how disappointing it must seem, but maybe it could be good for you.'

'What?'

'Not doing Hamlet,' she said. I looked at her, incredulous. 'I think you'd be amazing, of course. I'm your biggest fan, always will be, but, with your mum . . .' Her cheeks were flushed from the cold, curls falling over her face. 'If it's something you couldn't even talk to me about, dragging it all up for a part in a play?'

'Hamlet.'

'You already seem different.'

'Different?'

197

'I don't know, heavier, weighed down with it. I worry if you go too far into it, losing your mum when you were so little, her drinking?'

'Can we not, now—'

'This is what I mean. You've become this amazing person, despite how things were when you were a kid. Maybe that's because of what you've overcome, maybe it's why I love being with you. But digging back into all that shit, you have no idea how painful it will be. It can fuck people up, change them, permanently. I don't want that; I don't get why you would. So, long-term, not doing it, maybe would be for the best.'

'That why you didn't want Ophelia?'

'What?'

'Too scared to go down into the dark places?'

'I haven't got any dark places.'

'Jonathan opened the door for you, the first time in two and a half years, and you did nothing, like you didn't even want it.'

'Maybe I don't. I get naked then what else do I have to do? Start sleeping in Greenwich Park, picking flowers singing "Hey Nonny Nonny" until I lose my mind? Jonathan liking my exercise should have felt great, but all I could think was where does it all end?' She put her face in her hand. 'I don't want to argue with you. This sniping at each other, it's not you, it's not us. It's this fucking place.' She reached her hand out for me. 'Let's get out of here.' I looked at it, stomach clenched. Perhaps she was right, maybe Hamlet wasn't worth it, maybe I'd been saved from going into a cave within myself from which I might not return. I took her hand, squeezed it. She looked up at me, gave a satisfied sigh like she'd passed an impossible test. Behind her the front door bashed against the stone wall as it opened.

'Let's get polluted,' Patrick bellowed at the head of a bunch of our classmates. 'Big-lead!' he called through the corridor. 'You're coming, that's final.' Then he was there, splitting me from Nina, arm around my waist, almost lifting me into the January air and the rabble of classmates, adrenalised by the promise of three-paper spliffs and corner-shop vodka. I looked back, Nina was laughing at me in the middle of the exuberant roughhousing she suddenly found so funny and I had a wringing sense I had thrown in the towel, acquiesced, that she had won.

'Will you have a bump?' Patrick thrust a key loaded with white powder at my face as he sat down next to me on the sofa. I'd spent most of the hour or two since we'd arrived at the flat sucking down beers, wondering when they'd open the crisps. 'Come on, you big ride.' Someone had given me coke once back home and I didn't much like it. But Patrick was Patrick and I thought I'd lost Hamlet, so I leant forward and snorted, nostrils burning so hard I checked my nose wasn't bleeding.

'Jesus, what is that?'

'Ketamine.'

'Right, cheers.'

Patrick gave me a cocked-head smile, a hint of cruelty.

I'd never had ketamine before. Vanessa would have disapproved, but she wasn't there and maybe I was just Laertes, so fuck it. Patrick dug his key in and snorted, far less than what he'd given me. I closed an eye as the chemical sent waves of wonkiness around my skull.

'It's hard, isn't it?' Patrick said.

'What?'

'Hamlet, speaking the words, weight of history. You want to throw them away but also make every one count. You know what I mean?' Patrick shrugged, like we were playing the part in separate productions rather than rivals for it. 'All those words as well, fuck! I've been up 'til two every night getting them in.'

'When did Jonathan ask you to learn it?'

'Mentioned it, like, beginning of term.' Patrick drank down the rest of his pint of gin and tonic. I couldn't make sense of it. I'd left Jonathan's house feeling so understood by him, Hamlet finally starting to click. But he came away from that week thinking he'd need to prepare my replacement. 'I was loving Laertes,' Patrick continued. 'Good casting for me, what agents have said but—Whatever happens, I'm psyched about the production. Doing a show with you bunch of eejits after the last couple of years. Feel like it's going to be so fucking—' His jaw clenched, eyes bulging. I wanted more of what was in his bag. 'You know what I mean?' he said, 'Just like, fucking rawrr.' He roared like a tiger. 'It'll be an amazing showcase for the both of us.' He threw an arm around me. I took the bag from him, wishing I could be as magnanimous. The sofa began rocking like I was on a boat. Anna K bounded over and sat between us.

'What we doing?' she said. 'Knife fight before the dress rehearsal, last man standing gets to do the Dane.' She laughed too much at her joke. 'Jonathan would cream himself.' She leant into Patrick, laughing. I thought they'd slept together in first year, but I could never keep up.

'He's fucking with us,' Patrick said. 'Dorsy would never have wasted eight weeks rehearsing with someone who wasn't going to be big-lead.' He slapped me hard on the knee.

'Do you really think so?' I said. I turned the baggie in my fingers, feeling great, so good in fact I shovelled more on a fingernail and sniffed it up.

'Sure, I'm just his meat puppet.'

'But you still learnt the whole thing?' Anna said, grabbing a purple scarf off the back of the sofa and wrapping it around my neck. I looked around for Nina, saw her chugging cans of K cider with The Boys in the far end of the kitchen, proud of her for a moment.

'Good for auditions.' Patrick levered himself up from the sofa and headed towards the kitchen. Anna found a fur hat on a side table and plonked it on my head. I was being sucked deeper and deeper into the sofa and was sure that, as she continued to dress me up, I wouldn't be able to stand. Anna found a camera and took a picture of me, laughing her head off.

'Do you think he's right?' I asked, through at least three scarves. 'That it'll be me?' She couldn't hear. I think my mouth was closed. Perhaps my eyes as well. But I felt good. It was all going to be good.

The next day, I stewed in a bucket of ketamine and lager-induced guilt. Hamlet hadn't been taken away from me yet, but Jonathan wanted me to earn it. But when I tried to work on the script, the words moved like grass-cutter ants were carrying them around the page. Perhaps it made Nina happy I'd gone to the party, it had felt good to submerge myself again in the warmth of Group 28's camaraderie, but the only thing I had over Patrick was my dedication, my lack of complacency as Van had put it, and I'd managed to incapacitate myself. I refused Nina's offer to take me for a hangover fry-up, instead threw open my attic window and smoked cigarette after cigarette, hoping the January air would shock me out of my come-down, but it only worsened the hacking cough, which had lingered since Christmas. I slept that night under the window without a blanket. I don't think I was trying to get sick but at the same time, whether it was Hamlet or Adam then, I felt I deserved to be punished.

'Let us give Patrick the conch today,' Jonathan said on the Monday morning. 'Act five scene two.' The only scene shared by Hamlet and Laertes.

Patrick did the first part with Oban and was very fluent, very fast, grounding himself to the stage like he was tree-rooted, with a solemnity he'd never shown before. But as the scene went on, he couldn't help doing his charming fall-in-love-with-me Patrick thing. Head still throbbing from the weekend, I had one eye on Jonathan as Patrick became further enamoured with his own performance, expecting to see boredom, disappointment, perhaps anger in our teacher's eyes, but he revealed nothing. I turned to the back of Room 1, found Nina and made a face at Patrick's antics, expecting her to mouth 'I know', but she couldn't keep her eyes off the stage.

Jonathan got up just before my entrance, face fixed like a tribal mask. I bounced to the front of my chair, grinning with the anticipation of Patrick being torn apart because there wasn't an ounce of truth in anything he'd done. But Jonathan's eyebrows rose to the top of his pate, owl-like surprise, worse, the glazed eyes of inspiration you see on the faces of religious paintings.

'Hamlet the King,' he said, using the name he'd given me. 'I've never seen it. The prince would have become the King.'

'Are you kidding?' I said. The whole room turned. 'It's the same tricksy bullshit he always does.'

Jonathan swept his hands over his head, eyes burning.

'No, but—He thrusts his groin out and he's suddenly Mr Regal?'

'Thus spake the oracle.'

'The ending's his ballpark anyway. Let's see him do the early bits when Hamlet's head's fucked.'

'I think we almost certainly shall, Adam.'

'It's a fucking piss-take.'

Jonathan looked at the ground and swallowed a smile. 'Do you know the lines here, Laertes?' he said. I nodded. 'Shall we continue?'

My hissy-fit fed Patrick in our dialogue. If it had been a boxing match, he would have delivered several knockout blows before the actual fight scene had even begun. He'd worked on Hamlet's side of the fight choreography already and I hadn't, so we had to skip it for safety reasons. Patrick made excuses for me, reminded everyone I hadn't had as much time to prepare, which made it more embarrassing.

For most of that week, I was sent to work on my own on Laertes' scenes. I vacillated between indignant rage and the callow resignation I'd had when I thought of myself as 'the chaff'. Back then, at least I'd had Nina to lean on, but things felt stilted between the two of us. At home, we'd still watch films together on her bed, still listen to whatever she'd bought from Our Price that weekend, but as it got later each night, the spectre of our sexlessness would loom over us. I'd feign a moment of inspiration, hearing something in the music or something similar, and use it as an excuse to escape upstairs to work on my script or smoke out the window.

At The Church, on the few occasions I wasn't squirrelled away on my own or with Van in a teaching room, we play-acted our friendship, but whether we were talking about *Hamlet*, what we were getting for lunch, even the normally safe ground of bemoaning the laddy guitar-bullshit The Boys blasted in the changing room, every interaction felt loaded with what we weren't saying. Nina seemed to spend more and more time out drinking with the others in our year who didn't have a lot to do in the play. They'd start at the Three Corners at two, three o'clock and still be there when I'd come out at nine. When Nina was drunk, her guardedness melted but, although there were moments she'd link her arm through mine and we'd walk from the station in contented silence, more often than not, it would open the dam that held back her jealousies and resentment. Vanessa and I had continued our work together and I'd sometimes find Nina, having snuck back from the pub late-afternoon, glaring at the studio door as we emerged from one of our sessions.

'I'm just saying she's ignored you for two years,' Nina said after I picked her up from the pub one evening. Van and I had spent the afternoon reliving an imagined time from childhood when Hamlet had caught Gertrude and Old Hamlet having sex. 'And what, now you're besties?'

'She's helping.'

'Van's a proper Mother Teresa.' She was leant against the window, opposite me on the train.

'You asked her. You didn't want to do it anymore,' I said, clearing my throat.

'She called you a worm the other day, I heard her. Are you, like, into it?'

'Into it?'

'Like an S and M thing?'

I sighed, turning away to look out the window. Drunk, jealous, listening in at studio doors, trying to provoke me — it wasn't Nina. And I knew it was my capriciousness, my aloofness, which had created this cynical version of her. The more she reached for me, the further it pushed us apart.

'Most of her scenes are with Hamlet. Van's doing it for her own performance,' I said.

'Except you might not be Hamlet,' she said. I shut my eyes tight. 'Yet, she's spending way more time with you than before.' This was true, but I'd put it down to my having more time out of rehearsal. I exhaled, let the air sag out of me. I had been so delighted to have Van's forensic brain, her total disregard for my feelings as we worked on the play, I'd never thought to ask why. I didn't care. 'Do you think she's hot?' Nina asked, slurring a little. I locked eyes with her, found myself not wanting to soothe the insecurity steaming off her. 'You do, don't you?'

'I don't want to do this,' I said, burying my head in the open script on my lap. Van was beautiful. Tall, perfect skin, hair, contained entitlement, which made it seem as if gravity attached her more firmly to the ground than the rest of us. I'd always been attracted to her but it was in the way a teenager might be with a pin-up on their bedroom wall, a thrilling idea but out of reach. But by that point in our last year, the reason I found myself drawn to her, why I sought her out in the halls of The Church as I had with Nina before, was that she seemed to believe I was a good actor. At the time, I couldn't be sure anyone else did.

Which is why I shouldn't have accosted Van in The Rose Garden the next week about her father. In a professional preparation class we'd had at the end of second year, we were told not to talk to each other about interest we'd had from the industry, but it didn't stop us lingering at the wire pigeon-holes in the corridor hoping there'd be a letter from an agent for us. Patrick had already had some letters based on his headshot, Vanessa likewise, although not from anyone exciting. Before the *Hamlet* cast list went up, Nina checked as soon as we got to school each day, but afterwards I noticed her changing her route around The Church to avoid it. I hadn't paid it much attention but after Vanessa said her father wanted to meet, every time I saw a letter from across the corridor, my stomach fizzed at the thought it could be for me. It was always for someone else.

On one occasion, after being let down by another envelope for Patrick, I went out to smoke what could have been my hundredth roll-up of the day and heard Vanessa around the corner, talking on the phone. Van was the only one who had a mobile phone, which were the domain of yuppies and the military in nineteen ninety-seven, and the technology felt magical. Her tone was serious so I came out of the shadows, assuming it was her dad, and waved to get her attention.

'That your dad?' I mouthed. She covered the receiver.

'I'm on the phone,' she said.

'Is it Alasdair? I can meet whenever's good for him.'

'What?'

'You said he wants to meet me.' I spoke louder, hoping he'd hear. 'I'm such a fan of the work he does with new actors.'

'He wants to meet Hamlet,' she said, nostrils flared. 'Now can you fuck off?'

*

The following week I had to redo my character exercise for Jonathan. He'd quipped I could do Laertes if I didn't have anything. The truth was he was right, hours before I was due to go, chest rattling, having barely slept the night before, I still had no idea what I was going to do. I kept going back to what he'd said to me on the first day of rehearsals about how he could get me where I needed to be, but only if I could 'go there'. But where? Where was it I needed to go?

He had called a full company rehearsal with Varda that morning to work on the Ghost, who was being played by several different actors in neutral masks like a Greek chorus. As Hamlet, I'd got to miss these sessions, but now I was part of the wider company, I needed to know Patrick's parts. Group 28 buzzed into Studio 1 discussing the weekend's partying. Anna was ribbed by Victor for sleeping with someone, because it wasn't him; James bragged about the dive bar he wished everyone had come to; Ben called Nina an 'absolute animal' as if it were a compliment. They threw their heads back laughing, wide grins, limbs slopping, imprecise. I found myself shaking my head, mumbling to myself in cold fury as I glared at the relish, their self-satisfaction. Nina glanced at me, skittish with hangover anxiety, looked away and seemed to swallow back her spit. When she was out, Nina was one of the lads, smiling along with The Boys in their self-satisfaction, but in the mornings, she always seemed hollowed out by her excesses. Just weeks ago, I would have bought her Lucozade, checked why she was getting quite so hammered all the time or, more probably, been at the parties with her so she wouldn't have got so drunk in the first place. But I was trying to make something of our last year while she seemed content to fritter it all away.

'Claim your personas,' Varda said, wearing a playsuit that would have fitted a child, carrying her box of dark-wood half-masks. Everyone took theirs and got in formation to do the warm-up. I grabbed the last one and looked at it for a moment, as we had to do. There was no expression on the faces but as I stared, I saw eyebrows pinch together, nostrils flare in fury, the lines on the forehead tensing. I slid the mask on and took a space next to Anna T. I looked at them all in their masks in the mirror, a dozen blank expressions taking on characters of their own, the backs of bodies I knew, after two and a half years together, better than my own. Victor's gym-built neck, Vanessa's muscles casting shadows down her back, Nina's arms, once softer but now sinewy and strong. But Patrick, the frame that dominated every room since our first day, wasn't there.

We followed Varda as she pivoted her hips to the Underworld track on the sound system. She dropped to her hands and feet and stretched her limbs like a cat. We copied, torsos juddering with strain as we looped our legs under our body. I couldn't focus, checking to make sure I hadn't somehow missed Patrick. But he wasn't rehearsing with us, the company, the cogs who would whirr behind him, sacrifice ourselves on the altar of his brilliance, because Patrick and Jonathan were together, working on my speeches.

After ten minutes sweating under our masks, bodies hot

and alive, Varda broke us into two to work on the movements, our group going into the corner to wait our turn. Nina
came over to where I was by the back wall, leant into me.

'Was Patrick out with you all at the weekend?' I said.

She looked at the floor, wrapped herself up in her arms.
'Everyone was. Wish you'd come, really missed you.'

I couldn't take my eyes off the door of the studio, willing Patrick to come in, rejoin the ensemble. I was now the
ensemble.

'Patrick has . . . everything. And now he's Hamlet,' I said.
'Landed in his lap, like it was always going to. Probably
doesn't even want it that much. It's a game to someone like
him, play-acting to get laid.'

'On Saturday night, he and I, we talked about it. Proper
deep and meaningful.' She laughed off the phrase. I was still
looking at the door. 'He is, honestly, really serious about it.'

'A three-day bender couple of weeks before the show?
Must be.'

'His dad basically thinks he's gay because he wants to be
an actor, at best has him down as a dosser. His brothers
are insanely successful. Apart from with his little sister, he's
the family joke.'

'Are you seriously sticking up for him?'

'I'm just saying it would have been easier for him to do
literally anything else. And when he was a kid—He has
been through some stuff.'

'It's too dangerous for me to go into my childhood,
but it's fine for him, with all the terrible "stuff" he's
been through?'

'I didn't say that.'

'You want him to be Hamlet, don't you?'

She looked at me like I was a child who wouldn't share their toys.

'You want it to be him?'

'I honestly don't—'

'If you're not on my side, Nina, then what's the point of you?'

Her face seemed to hollow out in shock. She looked around me, desperate to find an answer to the starkest of questions she'd never thought to ask herself. It was a question I'd been asked when I was a child and, in that moment, I knew exactly the scene I had to give Jonathan.

I abandoned Nina, burst through the rest of our group in the middle of their movements, out the double doors of the studio, and marched through the empty corridor towards Room 1. At the entrance I stopped, closed my eyes and sent a memory wringing down my throat, my breastbone, until it settled in my guts – the bathroom at home in Kippax. I threw open the doors, tore through the curtains.

'Mumma?' I said. Patrick and Jonathan swung around to look at me, but I didn't see them as I made my way down the aisle and bounded up onto the stage. 'Mumma? Are you asleep?' I felt the lightness of a child in my feet as I hopped over to a block of staging, seeing it as the bath my mother was lying in.

I lifted a sodden lock of her hair off her forehead. Her skin was cold. Panic skittered my skin. I was seven. A primal fear gripped me. She was dead. I was certain. 'Mum?' I took her shoulders. 'Mumma! Mumma!' I shook her with all my childish strength. 'Please! Wake up, Mumma!' I leant into her, desperate to hear breath. She was dead. My eyes rolled back in my head. I'd found my mother dead in the bath.

'What?' The word croaked out of Mum's mouth. I sat back, breath stuttering in relief, clothes soaking though there was no water. Mum coughed a bitter laugh, making me flinch. In a different world, the real world, I felt Patrick make some movement, Jonathan stilling him.

'You've hurt your head?' I said. She touched a cut on her forehead that had started to crust over, a ruby of wet blood at its heart.

'Threw meself downstairs, didn't I?'

'Why?'

'Why do you think!' she barked. I stumbled up to standing, terrified. There wasn't a sound in Room 1, my audience couldn't hear her, couldn't see how she looked at me, but it was real for me. She looked like a waxwork, body slack in the long-cold water. This was four, five months before she died in the hospital. I didn't understand any of it. She started coughing, the sound of thousands of cigarettes, and wrenched herself away from the tub. I reached forward to give her a hug, but she pushed my arms away. 'Why have you got soup in your hair, Mummy? It smells.' Her head turned, snail slow. She opened her eyes and gave me a salamander stare.

'New recipe,' she said, lip twisting as she shook her fetid hair. 'Got it off *Floyd on Food*.' She laughed too much before closing her eyes and lying back, exhausted by the effort. I picked up the first thing I found on the stage, Patrick's jumper, and began to clean the vomit out of her hair, just as I did thirteen years before. I became aware of more people coming through the doors of Room 1.

'I used to be beautiful,' Mum said in a mumble. I leant my head closer, muscle memory from this scene I'd lived so many times, controlling each movement.

'You are beautiful.' I picked chunks of vomit out with my fingertips.

'Look,' she said, grabbing the tyres of flesh around her middle, the flaps of her breasts. I wiped my elbow across my eyes, tried to stop the tears coming. 'You think your dad wanted to stay around for this?'

'Mumma?'

'Or the screaming, screaming, screaming from the moment you climbed out of me.' She raised herself out of the bath. 'Puke everywhere, everything you ever ate sicked up on me, so I'm wearing rotten milk like eau de toilet. He couldn't even look at me. Barely lasted a month before he's off with anyone else who'd looked at him.'

'Sorry. Sorry, Mumma.'

'Bunch of dogs, all of them. But who can blame him! Compared to this! You sucked it all out of me.'

'Don't like it when you shout at me.'

'You never stopped shouting at me.' She was half out the bath. Tears streamed down my face as I held the jumper in front of me like a shield.

'It's not on purpose,' I said, 'I didn't do it on purpose.'

'You ruined my body. Ruined my head and for what?' She burst into a fit of coughing. I wanted to go to her but I was so frightened. 'What's the point of you, eh? You're nothing. Just like your old mum now, you're nothing.' I was almost keening, body doubled over, tears dripping out over the mask I hadn't realised I still had on.

'You need to stop him.'

I heard Nina's voice and part of me was back in the room. There was a commotion, Vanessa said something, but I didn't want to be back in Room 1. I wanted to stay with Mum in the little bathroom with its dolphin tiles. Her breathing slowed and she looked at me, shoulders hunched, body like a rack. I put my arms out, desperate for her to hold me, take my head in the crook of her neck and kiss me. I blinked, trying to find a way to make her better.

'You don't understand, I could have had class,' I said, squinting, in my cod-American Brando accent. A glimmer of light came into her eyes for a moment, our quiet time together in front of movies swimming in her memory. 'I could have been a contender.' I leant on it too much, too much acting, made it a caricature.

'Get out!' she screamed, leaping out of the bath. 'Get out, get out, get the fuck out!' I slipped on the imagined bathmat and scrambled out of the room. I lay like that, face covered in snot, mask on the top of my head, one arm over the edge of the stage for some time. When I looked up, I saw the whole of Group 28, Jonathan, Patrick, watching in abject silence. Vanessa stood a little in front of every-one, a smile teasing onto the side of her face. Behind her

Nina was turned away from the stage, leaning on a chair. She glanced at me, tears streaming down her face, shook her head and stormed out.

Jonathan was devoid of expression. He glanced at Patrick who looked lost, possibly for the first time in his life, before coming back to stare at me. It was almost imperceptible, but as the double doors swished shut again after Nina's exit, he gave the tiniest raise of his eyebrows.

Act 4

IV.i

I'd been prodding the intercom for a minute when Emmy pulled me into the entry hall of her Portobello flat.

'You can't be here,' she said, hair up, nostrils flared. In gingham pyjamas without a scrap of make-up, it was shocking to see the genetic miracle that was her face. She went to a narrow window and saw two men with telephoto lenses approaching.

'Is it you?' I said.

'Is what me?'

'You were cast as Isabella in your final show and last night you treated me like I was covered in radioactive dog-shit, so is it you, measuredbella, trying to make it look like I've done something terrible?'

'Haven't you?' she asked.

The room went dark as bodies blocked the window.

'Emmy! Emmy!' The paparazzo banged at the door.

'Adam Sealey in there, Emmy?'

'Getting back into Emmy's character, Adam?'

'Daddy issues, Emmy?'

She shrank like a wounded cat, blue eyes ashen. 'Fuck sake,' she said, marching upstairs. The locusts continued heckling and although I wasn't invited, I followed up. I walked through into her small flat, Moroccan blue with an overwhelming array of houseplants, the scent of expensive candles.

Emmy was in the kitchen cutting up what sounded like fruit. There was a stack of screenplays on a side table. I thought about the script of *Woodsman*. Did Emmy know Jonathan had been the one who'd got it to me? She re-emerged, having changed out of her pyjamas into athleisure, and placed a chopping board of mango chunks on the coffee table. She saw me eyeing the scripts, picked up the pile and began tossing them onto the sofa one-by-one.

'Dystopian thing for Apple, indie shooting in Bulgaria, another in Northern Ireland early next year, this one, I've got to learn how to be a freestyle skier, me, the girl who hid in the toilets during every school gym class. You honestly think I have time to be slagging you off on the internet?'

'Yet you know what I'm talking about?'

'I've spent the last six months plastering on a grateful expression, giving you adoring glances every ten seconds, trying to help journalists understand how you gave such an incredible performance. So, if all of that – and honestly that was the hardest acting – was going to be shat up the wall because you've tied your horse to the wrong post, I was going to make absolutely certain I still came out smelling of roses.'

'That's a lot of metaphors,' I said.

She looked at me, steel-firm for a moment, before curling herself on the sofa like a circus tiger at the end of a show.

'I saw the story about the girl who'd disappeared. You know what happened? Why they chucked her out?'

I nodded.

'I left just before their year started, but I had a mentee, Alice, a couple of years below who I asked about it. She told me the school had cut this Raya loose, even though she clearly had issues, and brushed the whole incident under the carpet. And then you and your team, when you find out about it, did the same. When I heard you'd gone back to The Church, the day of the BAFTAs, it just felt like the most cynical PR bullshit.'

'It was,' I said.

'That's why I skipped the photoshoot, how I was with you last night. I couldn't continue the charade of you being my hero any longer.'

'All of it was a charade?'

She took a deep breath, pulled off a dead leaf from a spider-plant.

'You were always nice to me and rehearsals were cool. Staying in character the whole time with you felt like being at The Church. And maybe it helped. But honestly, if the script hadn't lined up so well with how we wanted the next few years to go, there's no way I would've done a film with you.'

'You said I was the reason you did it.'

'I know what men your age like to hear.'

I held my hands in a tight ball.

'I think you're a brilliant actor. Course I do. I get why people were fascinated when you came on the scene; people used to love the tortured male genius shit. But I was taught by Jonathan too and it was obvious you'd drunk his Kool-Aid, had maybe irreversible portions of it. I wasn't desperate to involve myself with all that again.'

'What, you don't believe in what we were taught at The Church? You've done pretty well out it.'

'The place gave me a good grounding, but all the method stuff, it's not for the audience, it's not for "the work", it's an excuse for having a public wank. If there's one thing we've learnt in the last few years, it's that some men are unusually into that sort of thing.'

I turned away, feeling like a little boy who had wet himself.

'You must have noticed on set, I didn't speak to Jonathan once, not a single conversation. He knows exactly what I think of him.'

'I didn't change the script.'

'You took the part though. You still used your friend dying, didn't you? I remember Jonathan telling us how he'd never seen such authentic despair as your Hamlet, how it was basically a religious experience for those who saw it, and thinking to myself, "Christ, how could he do that, a few weeks afterwards." '

'They put it back, it was a month.'

Emmy scoffed, looked at the floor.

'Look, you might win an Oscar, good for you, but I'm

not going to keep smiling along as you hold up that bully as some great genius.'

I felt a hot fury in my stomach at what she was saying, wanted to throw her not winning the BAFTA in her face, break a window. I settled for going over and opening one on the far side of the room and watched pigeons trying to haul each other off a ledge by the neck.

'Was it Jonathan who took the part away from you in *Measure for Measure*?' I said.

Emmy blinked slowly, telling me he had.

'You can tell yourself whatever you like about him, but you probably just weren't doing it very well.'

'He took the part away from me because I refused to give up my therapist,' she said, losing her composure.

'You were seeing a therapist, while you were at The Church?'

'It should have been included in the fees, but Jonathan said it would ruin me, told me I had to keep the contradictions, the fractured psyche, so I could "imbue" them into the character.' She clutched her throat, a blush coming into her cheeks. I thought of what he'd said to me about seeking help on the phone after the incident in the diving tank, of Raya's uncle telling me she'd gone off her medication. 'The guy's a sociopath. Even the way he did it, letting me rehearse the role for weeks then acting like the therapy was a big betrayal so he could get me in his teaching room on my own and make me an ultimatum. Exactly like the play, the scene Isabella has with Angelo forcing her to make the impossible choice. He did the whole thing as some big

223

character moment.' Emmy stopped, hostility draining into the carpet. 'You're working with him,' she said, 'on the next film?'

'Meant to be.'

'What's the film, what happens?'

'It's a spy-thriller.'

'But what happens in it?'

'My guy defects and works with the CIA. Starts to think they're in cahoots with his Russian handlers and he's a patsy, sort of being sacrificed.'

'Let me guess,' she said. 'He doesn't know if any of its real and starts to lose his mind?'

I crossed my arms, put my tongue to the roof of my mouth, of course she was right. 'What are you trying to say?'

'Jonathan doesn't see students as people, Adam. How could he have treated us like he did otherwise? He's evil fucking Geppetto, but you're so desperate for him to see you as a real boy, you can't see he's still holding your strings.'

I looked above me, unable to speak as I took in what she was suggesting – that it was him. That measuredbella was Jonathan.

He had all the facts. It could have been. Emmy didn't even know he'd seen the original script before me, perhaps been involved in changing the ending.

'No,' I said, not knowing what else I could say. 'Sorry, no.'

'This is getting toxic, Adam.' She crossed the room and opened the door for me to leave.

'*Woodsman* would be a footnote without what Jonathan did with me, you know that, don't you?'

'Maybe. Or maybe you would have given a brilliant performance because you're really fucking talented. Or maybe it would have been even better if someone else was in it. Who knows? There's a fire escape at the end of the hall outside.'

'Louanne, don't—'

'That's not my name, Adam. It's never been my name. Now, please.'

For three months it was the only name I called her. I blinked, cocked my head, the answer to the mystery of Raya hitting me like a poison dart.

'Adam?' Emmy said.

I shook myself back into the room, went to the door and stopped in front of her. I needed to get out to Amber, but it was clear this would be the end for us.

'I'm sorry I brought Jonathan to set,' I said, my voice sounding oddly formal. 'I didn't realise how much you hated him.'

'I don't hate him, Adam. I don't hate either of you. I don't think about you at all.'

'That's good,' I said, meaning it, before nodding an awkward goodbye and rushing past her into the dark corridor. I shoved open the fire escape and saw Amber looking vexed at the bottom of the staircase as a furious driver got into his car and slammed the door.

'Van got the driver's number,' Amber said. 'She's apoplectic—'

'Medea,' I said as I got down to the street.

'What?'

'That's how we'll find Raya. Wherever she is, she might think she's Medea.'

The cab driver drove away when we said we weren't going to the hotel. Struggling to look through databases on her phone, Amber suggested we walk the backstreets to the Notting Hill Library. I didn't want her to be fired, so told her to go back and tell Van she'd tried to stop me going AWOL, but she said Van was in meetings all day and she wanted to come even if it cost her job. I got the sense finding Raya had started to mean almost as much to Amber as it did to me. Emmy's suggestion that Jonathan could be behind the comments made some sense, I knew better than anyone the lengths he'd go to improve his actors' performances, but Emmy didn't know what had happened that night at The Church. She didn't know Jonathan had almost as much to fear from being exposed as I did.

We got to the library and climbed the magnolia steps to the second floor with its bank of computers.

'Oh my God, that smell!' she said, sitting at one of the machines. 'I spent my whole childhood in places like this.' She pulled a chair out for me, a fizz of excitement in her eyes that we might be about to find Raya. I couldn't believe I hadn't thought of it before. If she was off her medication, if she'd lost touch with reality enough to attack her classmate, it was possible she still thought she was in character: Medea, the archangel of self-destructive vengeance. First Amber went into the missing persons database, putting the name Medea in and searched.

'This is mostly remains of bodies,' she said. 'Some of them have names but are unclaimed.'

My stomach hollowed out at the thought Raya could come up dead, but thankfully the page came up with no results. Amber went to a missing persons charity next, put Medea in, but again nothing. She leant back to think, before typing 'Medea, missing' into the search engine. Thousands of pages came up, but they were all academic papers relating to the Euripides play. She tried to narrow it down, adding UK, England, London, and then Raya's name, but still, nothing came up. Amber looked over, dejected. I thought back to *Hamlet*, back to the work I'd done to prepare for the role. One of the first things we did was write a biography, to fill out the character's life from birth to the point they're in the play.

'Surname,' I said. 'Try a surname.'

'What's Medea's surname?' Amber asked.

'I don't know, she's just Medea. Like Madonna or Prince.'

Amber raised an eyebrow before turning back to the computer. She searched Medea and found she was the daughter of the King of Colchis. She searched Medea Colchis, it was still all articles about the play, about Jason and the Argonauts.

'Missing Medea of Colchis,' I said.

Amber typed it in and still nothing, but then she added 'female twenties'. And there it was. A link for Essex Police. Amber looked to me, scared. I closed my eyes, nodded, and she clicked on it. The page loaded and there she was, the girl from the photo. She wore a grey sweatshirt, hair hanging lank, enormous dark circles under eyes that had lost the spark that had made them so striking.

'Is she alive?' I asked Amber, unable to make sense of what I was looking at.

'It's a request for information on a female in her early twenties calling herself Medea of Colchis.' Amber scanned the page for other details. 'Any information please call Essex Police Missing Persons department or the Essex Mental Health Crisis team.' She stood up and walked to the far end of the room, hand to her forehead.

'This is good,' I said, following. 'It means she's OK.'

'Mental Health Crisis?'

'She's alive.'

'That's a pretty low bar,' she said, looking out the slit of window. I put a hand on her shoulder and turned her towards me as a decrepit photocopier chuntered behind us.

'Let's go and find her,' I said.

'You think she's measuredbella?'

'One way to find out.'

'Then what? If she is, if she isn't. She's—' She looked down, overcome for a moment, the green light of the copier painting her forehead. 'She's under the care of the mental health service, she thinks she's Medea.'

'Maybe we can help her.'

'How?'

'I can do her a bit of *Macbeth*.'

Amber laughed despite herself. Five minutes later, we were back outside, waiting for a car to take us out to Essex.

*

As we travelled east, we called the Essex Mental Health service team and although they thanked us for providing the name of the girl claiming to be Medea of Colchis, without being family members, they couldn't share any more details. We rang the police, two local councils and a few Essex mental health numbers we found, but no one could give us any information. Amber came off yet another phone call, and I could tell she was trying to find a way to say it was time to give up, but I had one last idea.

'How many psychiatric units are there in Essex?' I said.

Amber sighed a laugh, hoping I was joking, before shaking her head and going back to her phone to find out.

We drove to a converted old house in Billericay with no inpatients, on to a hospital in Wickford where an officious older woman told us she couldn't share personal details of patients with us before asking me to record a video for her niece. Looking at the map, I became convinced someone who thought they were Medea of Colchis would have gone to Colchester, but it was in the less aptly named Basildon we got the breakthrough.

We trailed through the identical corridors of the small hospital until we found the psychiatric ward at the far end of one of the wings. There were cameras above the entrance, the glass in the door reinforced with metal wires. After we buzzed an intercom, the nurse who emerged on the other side of the door saw my rollneck jumper and sunglasses and peered behind us to make sure we weren't part of a documentary crew. But when we mentioned Medea of Colchis, he opened the doors and told us to wait on a line of plastic chairs while he went to get someone. Within minutes, a doctor in her early fifties arrived.

'Good lord, it's you,' she said when I'd taken off my sunglasses.

'Adam Sealey,' I said, getting up to shake her hand.

'I used you in a conference speech once.'

'Did you? What was it about?' I asked.

She gave a sheepish smile. 'Dissociative identity disorder and the potential for intentionality in the narratives the brain creates in patients.'

'Right,' I said, going full Northern to excuse my ignorance.

'I was positing actors often intentionally dissociate and was discussing what the long-term psychiatric effects could be.'

I felt Amber looking at me, knowing she was thinking about those weeks after I wrapped on *Woodsman*.

'What did you discover?'

'It's an area that needs more research.' She angled her head, scrutinised me like a steer at auction, before shaking away the thought. 'We had a message from the mental health service an hour ago giving us Medea's real name.'

'That was us,' Amber said.

'The police hadn't come up with anything, which, for the number of days she's been with us, is unusual.'

If she'd been with them for some time, I thought, even just a week or so, she couldn't be measuredbella.

'Would it be OK to see her?' I asked.

The doctor looked over her shoulder. 'We should have family permission.'

'She doesn't have any family,' I said.

'There's an uncle registered.'

'He hasn't seen Raya for nearly a year.'

'What are you to her, Mr Sealey?' She arched an eyebrow, implying I might be some predatory older man.

'Raya was one of Adam's scholars,' Amber said, handing her phone to the doctor. I saw a page open from a website with a headline talking about the Adam Sealey Bursary. 'We were very concerned when no one knew where she was.'

'We want to check she's OK,' I added.

'Raya's not OK.' The doctor stared at the floor for a moment before looking up at me. I saw her memory of me forty-feet high on a cinema screen, a little spark of wonder. 'Give me a moment.' She disappeared through opaque doors, which sounded a howling alarm when they opened.

Amber and I waited in silence before the doors screamed again and the nurse who'd met us in reception ushered us through. We walked down what could have been a hallway in any other under-funded hospital, a world away from the leafy environs of Ganymede with its patchouli spirit burners and overwatered grass. I must have been expecting a *One Flew Over the Cuckoo's Nest* situation, full of raving inmates, because I was shocked at how quiet it was. Through windows in the rooms, I saw patients lying on beds reading, playing video games. It could have been a university hall of residence.

I noticed a patient doing something on a communal computer in the corridor, quashing my theory Raya couldn't be my internet tormentor. We got to an open area where several patients sat staring, ignoring daytime TV on the screen above them. They had the slackened mouths and sunken eyes of the heavily medicated, and I understood why the place seemed so subdued. I had to stop myself going to sit down and study them, get myself into their heads, to try and see how they saw the world. But the nurse ahead had stopped in front of a door further down the corridor.

As I walked down, the realisation we'd found her, that we were going to meet Raya, measuredbella perhaps, made me want to sprint back along the hall and out of the hospital. I'd become so wrapped up in the search, I hadn't thought about what we might find. I closed my eyes and tried to put myself in the headspace of Kai Brandt, the opioid-addicted young detective I played just after I did *Coward*. I felt my jaw tensing with the muscle memory, the itching under my skin. I'd gone to a beekeeper and had some of his hive sting me for prep as I'd read an addict's need for heroin felt like insect stings. I hoped if I found Kai's conviction, his desperation for the truth, I might be able to silence the voices asking me why I was in a psychiatric ward about to disturb an ill young woman I'd never met.

The nurse opened the door and ushered us into a private lounge and there, stood in front of an ugly chair, was Raya, chewing on her thumb. She was shocking to look at, so much thinner than the picture we'd seen. The loose sweatshirt and joggers made her look like she was wrapped in a duvet. Her hair was braided on top of her head, cheekbones so wide and prominent it felt like the other parts of her face had been erased, hazel eyes saucer-wide. On seeing me, her shoulders shook and she began to cry, sitting back down, hiding her face in her huge jumper.

'I'll be outside,' the nurse said, unaffected by the weeping girl as he closed the door. Amber and I sat opposite her.

'Raya, isn't it?' I said.

The girl took a deep breath and looked at me like I was a messenger from the gods. 'I waited for you,' she said, rippling her shoulders into the chair, composing herself.

'What do you mean, Raya?' Amber said.

'Who's she?' Raya said, a savage edge in her voice reminding us this was the same girl who had thrown scalding water at her classmate. She looked at me as if to say, who's the civilian?

'Maybe wait outside,' I said to Amber.

She stood, grinding teeth behind pursed lips, and left.

Once she'd gone, Raya stared at me, neither of us knowing what to say. 'Do you want me to do a handstand?' she said.

'That's OK,' I said, trying not to let on how confused I was by the suggestion.

'Listen to this then,' she said. 'What a to-do to die today at a minute or two to two she said at a minute or two to two.' She finished the tongue-twister, trying to gauge how impressed I was.

'That's amazing.'

'I've had a lot of time to work on my technique since I left.' She pulled up the sleeves of her sweatshirt to reveal sinewy forearms. 'Got a truckload of auditions to prepare for.'

It took a few moments to realise she was serious. I had planned to throw measuredbella into the room as soon as I could, but it seemed implausible such cogent messages could have come from this girl.

'We were at The Church,' I said. 'We met Lyndsey.'

Raya turned her body and stared at the wall. Light reflected off a coffee-table book of wildlife photography onto her face, making her look like a Renaissance maiden.

'I saw the scars. What happened?'

'She stole my husband,' Raya growled, voice an octave lower. She smiled, shook her head with the vigour of a wet dog before composing herself. 'I was Medea,' she said, voice gentler. 'I'd been a scullery maid for the whole time I'd been at The Church. Medea was what I was there to do. But I couldn't get it right.'

'What couldn't you get right?'

'The anger wasn't real.'

'In what way?'

'What Jason and Glauce did. Abandoning me.' She chewed her lip as she talked about Medea's husband Jason and the woman he left her for, the abandonment that leads her to stab and kill her own children, as if they were real people. 'It was because they weren't real for me.'

'You hadn't personalised them.'

'I'd tried my uncle and his girlfriend—'

I was about to tell her we'd met them but didn't want to throw her off.

'I spent hours reliving some of the stuff Andrea said to me, how she'd pushed me out of my house, trying to transfer that onto Lyndsey. But it wasn't right at all. Barry, my uncle, I didn't care enough about him to really—' She hit herself hard in the stomach. The violence was shocking, but I knew what she meant. She swivelled in her chair and stared at me. 'I realised I had to use you.'

'What?'

'*Casagemas*,' she said, turning back to her spot on the far wall. 'The way you moved in that film, the looseness in your muscles, like booze had saturated your ligaments. That was when I knew we were the same. My mother drank. I know yours did too.'

I swallowed. How did she know about my mum? I'd never talked about her in interviews, no one had written anything about my family life, we'd been careful about it.

'You were the reason I wanted to be an actor, why I went to The Conservatoire. You'd been my whole purpose for so many years. You were the only one who could be my Jason. But however hard I tried, I couldn't get it to connect. Someone told me you would be at the festival and said I should try and see you.'

'Did we meet?'

She raised an eyebrow as if she was keeping a secret.

'At the talk before the film, your co-star was this flighty thing, Abi something, a lightweight, she wasn't going to work as the woman you'd jilted me for. But then I saw your manager Vanessa in the front row. You kept looking at her, checking, scared almost. She was perfect. As the talk finished, I tried to get through the crowd to you, but they stopped me, so when the lights went down I slipped out and headed to the stage door. I waited in the cold for nearly an hour, but I knew if I could get you to look at me, if I could touch you, I'd have the connection I needed. Eventually the door opened, and she came out, your manager. "I'm a student at The Conservatoire," I said to her. She snickered at me before turning back into the building, where I could see you waiting through the half-closed door. The next thing I knew she was blocking my way as you dashed out, then she took you by the arm and jogged you towards a car. Running for your life to get away from me. I was distraught.' She looked around, seemed like she wanted to get up but couldn't see where to go.

'I'm sorry I didn't stop,' I said. 'I wasn't in a good place, but it was still very rude.'

'It was perfect.'

'Perfect?'

'I was so hurt, it stung, so physical. Exactly what I'd been missing. The next day we did a run of the play and I still felt so worthless. I got into The Church early, locked myself in a teaching room and went over the moment again and again. I'd got pictures of the two of you from a magazine. I stared at Vanessa posing at some awards thing and imagined her laughing at me again and again and again.' Raya tried to swallow, her mouth suddenly dry. 'That was when I saw Lyndsey walking past with the guy who was playing Jason, Arthur.'

I nodded.

'Did you meet him?'

'Mm-hm.'

'Lyndsey was smiling, gazing adoringly at something he'd said. And, I can't explain it, it was you. He was you. And Lyndsey was your manager.' I could see it in her face. A year later, the memory of the poisonous jealousy was still there, disturbingly vivid.

'What happened then?'

'It was too much, the rage. I knew I'd be out of control for the run of the play, so I went to make a cup of tea, to calm down. As I stood in the kitchen, I saw scrawls of graffiti on the inside cupboards, all the furious, fucked-up students before me, scratching some sense of themselves into the building. I remembered the story I'd heard about you, from your last year at the school.'

My breath stuttered. I felt sure she knew, I wasn't sure how, but it seemed so obvious she knew what I'd done.

'That you'd had a girlfriend in your class you'd discarded to be with that horrible woman who'd laughed at me. And I was that girl, I didn't know her name, but I was her and, I can't tell you, but I felt like I was channelling another person entirely.'

That wasn't how it was, I wanted to tell her. Her name was Nina and that wasn't how it was.

'Then I heard her laughing,' she said. 'Lyndsey was laughing at something down the corridor but to me it was Vanessa, and I was your girlfriend. Then I heard the kettle click. I carried it down the corridor and into the showers where Lyndsey was, she wasn't even with Arthur by then,

237

but I didn't notice. I took the top off the kettle and threw it at her.'

'I bet it felt amazing,' I said.

Raya looked at me, breathing fast out of her nose. She edged forward on her chair and leant into me. 'It really did,' she said. 'Going there, really going there. So savage. If it'd been a knife, I would have stabbed her.'

I closed my eyes, bile at the back of my throat. I knew exactly how she had felt. 'Was Jonathan proud of you?' I asked.

Raya narrowed her eyes. Since I'd heard what she'd done, I kept telling myself he wouldn't lie about something like this, but hearing her talk through the process, the desperation to go so much further, she had to have been driven there by him.

'You were working with him?'

'It was the best few months of my life,' she said, so relieved it seemed like she'd been keeping the secret for decades. 'Jonathan changed everything I'd ever thought about acting, about myself.'

'Months?'

'We had to keep it a secret, the University didn't let him work one-on-one with students anymore. He was always pining for the good old days.'

'It was Jonathan who told you about my mother, the girlfriend?'

Raya nodded, knelt a few feet away from me and leant forward as if the room was listening. 'I reminded him of you, he said, if I could really go there I would have a career like you. The way he talked about you, Adam! His voice changed. It was like—' She broke off, considering how to phrase what was coming next. A few weeks ago, hearing Jonathan went gooey when he talked about our work would have felt wonderful, but this time I was scared to hear what she had to say. 'It was like you were the shining example that proved his whole methodology. Do you know what I mean?'

'I think I do,' I said, wishing I didn't.

The doctor let herself in. Raya stood and returned to her chair.

'Raya, we should get you back to your room,' she said. I looked at the girl, expecting a kickback of fiery temper, hoping to see it, but she nodded and moved towards the door. She stopped in front of me and reached open palms out as if for me to handcuff her. I looked at the doctor who nodded her permission, and I took Raya's two hands in mine. I could feel every bone, so delicate I wanted to crush them. Her lip quivered, eyes growing dewy.

'Will you speak to them,' she whispered, 'about the auditions?'

I nodded, wanted to tell her we'd get her out, but she let go of my hand and left. The nurse handed her a small cup of pills and lead her down the corridor.

'What are the pills?' I asked.

'Lithium and antipsychotics.'

'What's wrong with her?'

'We treated her as schizophrenic and having seen her records now, she was diagnosed as such as a teenager and,

239

possibly down to the instability of her upbringing, it seems there was suspected borderline personality disorder.'

I put my hand on the chair in front of me. Raya had been diagnosed with a mental disorder, she was medicated from a young age, and it was impossible not to see the echoes between her childhood and my own. I'd always thought the fragile, unhinged roles they'd thrust me into were down to my youth, my sunken eyes that made me look on the brink of fight or flight, but perhaps it'd been there from the start, perhaps that's why I got into the school in the first place because, like Raya, I was unstable. But the industry, and Jonathan, knew they could sell it.

'What happens if someone like her stops taking their pills?'

'There's no single prognosis for how symptoms could manifest. She'd been off her meds for some time before we found her but to reach that state, we'd expect a certain amount of mental stress and environmental factors.'

Environmental factors, I thought, like being thrown out of drama school. But Raya left The Conservatoire almost a year ago.

'Can I ask,' the doctor said, 'are you here for a part?'

'What?'

'Are you studying Raya for a role?'

'No.'

'I don't judge, it's fascinating.'

'I'm not, no.'

'I hope you don't mind my asking, but have you ever been diagnosed with anything?'

I thought back to before Ganymede, sat in front of the psychiatrist like a Kafka protagonist, a white room and a barrage of questions for which I only had wrong answers. His prescription was to rest in a nice facility in the hills. If I had been diagnosed, no one ever took the time to tell me what was wrong with me.

'I've not been, no,' I said, not wanting to go into it. I glanced at Amber, who was leant against the corridor wall, eyes closed. 'What state was Raya found in?'

'I thought you knew.'

I shook my head.

'She was in Southend, by the seafront, waving a kitchen knife in the air, howling for her children. When the police got to her, they'd just had to stop her walking into the sea.'

IV.ii

Jonathan didn't say anything to me after the exercise with my mother, but the next day I was Hamlet while Patrick was consigned to go and work on his own. I was in flow as we worked on the scene where Hamlet rejects Ophelia, receiving Jonathan's notes in focused silence, an athlete listening to their coach with aloof detachment. I would have thought the lack of deference would infuriate Jonathan, but he seemed younger, more vital, enjoying being more mentor than tormentor. The rest of the cast gazed in envy at the two of us in hushed congress, looking at me like I was someone new, a super-soldier drafted in from an elite programme they'd never heard of.

Van found me at lunch, sat in a sunbeam on a bench in the graveyard. She thrust a tray of what I'd come to know was sushi in front of me. I picked off the fish, ate the sweetened rice. In so many more ways than I knew, I was a child then.

'Yesterday I saw something I'd never seen before on a stage,' she said, pulling her skirt down as she sat beside me, staring at the headstones. 'Patrick, he acts for love, wants everyone watching to fall in love with him. Nina wants the feeling of getting it right, top marks in the test, a pat on the head from the teacher. For me? I don't know, a sense of power perhaps, having a roomful of people all forced to listen to me, psychoanalyse that. But you, it honestly seems like survival, like your very existence depends on it.' She seemed to take me in almost for the first time, grabbed a handful of edamame pods from my tray, squeezed one into her mouth.

'Nina was very upset afterwards,' Van said, flicking salt off the ends of her fingers. 'She tried to get on stage and stop you. I managed to head her off, but she ripped into me in the corridor afterwards.'

'What did she say?'

'She thinks I'm egging you on, that Jonathan and I may push you into hurting yourself in some way.'

'What do you think?'

'I think you've just arrived. How Jonathan was with you just now, fucking hell. He said it was a process, Hamlet, and it seems like you're getting where he wants you to be. But perhaps your whole time at the school has been a process.'

'What do you mean?'

'Nothing is accidental. Maybe he gave you smaller roles in the first couple of years to make you question yourself, your desire, so he could build you up to this. I hadn't spotted it before, but he's never been so engaged with a student, even from stories Dad's told me from over the years.' She massaged the ends of her hair. 'My concern, Adam, moving forward, is that you've always been a life-raft for Nina. She clung on to you because if the two of you weren't alone in the doldrums, you each still had hope. But now you've risen above the surface, she may become desperate and try to drag you back down with her.'

'Nina would never sabotage me.'

'Not intentionally, it'll be dressed up in care, concern for you, love even.' Her eyes darted to mine for a moment before looking away. 'You're just so close to the summit. I don't know if you can carry the extra weight.'

When the afternoon rehearsals had finished, I lingered in Jonathan's teaching room, listening to K-CI & JoJo on Nina's Discman, trying to stem tears at what I knew I had to do until the night porter threw me out. I thought about not going home, finding a hostel or turning up at Vanessa's door, the dread at facing Nina almost insurmountable. By the time I got back to Tommy and Liv's, I had almost convinced myself it was funny how I'd been treating her, like I'd reveal the distance I'd intentionally put between us since Christmas had been an elaborate practical joke. When I got in, I tried to sneak past the living room, where Nina was mainlining a bottle of red she was sharing with her mum, but she must have heard because she stopped me as I was halfway up the stairs.

'You're back?' she said and straight away she saw in my eyes what was going to happen. I thought she'd cry but she just looked to the side for a long moment before turning back, eyes feral, and nodding me up towards her room. I waited outside for her as she came up the stairs, let her walk in front of me and inside, where she sat on the end of her bed. I edged in, closed the door and leant against her dressing gown hanging from it.

'Nee,' I said, swallowing, barely able to get words out. 'We need to—'

'Yeh, I get it,' she said, picking at her thumbnail. 'Actually, actually I really fucking don't.' She looked up at me. I could see her cuticle was bleeding. I half-turned into the door, wishing her dressing gown and towel were a portal to a different place.

'I guess, the play is at a stage—'

'Oh, fuck off!' She shook her head, annoyed at herself for getting angry and reached behind her for a cushion of hers that had a teddy-bear face on it. She held it to her chest. 'I had a friend at school, Lilly,' she said. 'We were in the choir together. She used to change the words in the hymns, like, not objectively that funny, but good when we were kids. Kevin for Heaven, whisper "Edmonds" after the Noel in "First Noel". Stupid. She went to a Christian camp thing in the summer, must have been about fifteen, and when she came back it was like she was a different person. She wouldn't laugh at anything, told me off if I slagged one of our classmates off, constantly wanted me to think about how I was choosing to live. She prayed for me once, which really pissed me off. Like how you were before the mask class yesterday. Never thought *you'd* be judgemental like that. I was so angry about Lilly, not with her though, with Jesus. Used to lie awake at night fuming with actual Jesus for taking my best friend from me. Really hurt me.'

She looked at me, a look that cut into my sternum, pulled the flesh down to my guts. 'But this is so much worse. I can't compete with God, but I'm losing you to Jonathan.'

'This isn't about Jonathan.'

'He probably put you up to it! Said you can't possibly play Hamlet with a girlfriend. It's insane.'

I was about to speak, stopped, looked at my shoes.

'After the exercise where I got naked, it was like the blinkers fell away. All his bullshit. Someone does a good bit of work, say "well done", lift them up, make them feel like they could do a show in front of two thousand people.'

I put my tongue behind my teeth, trying not to ask whether she learnt her directing style from her years of Musical Theatre. She saw the impulse.

'No? Am I wrong? You honestly think it's better to slate people until they're shambling around the stage, shell-shocked, like they're about to face a firing squad?'

'Nee, I'm sorry but the work I'm doing—'

'The "work" you're doing is because you're a brilliant actor. He's finally let you feel like you belong, like you're an actor, so we're seeing it. Even that wasn't enough, no, you had to rip open your heart for him.'

'I needed to go there.'

'Fuck sake, I love you! I'd love you if you were the shittest actor in the world. If you swallowed your words, tripped over your feet, made funny faces to sell a joke like a twat. You're kind, before he got to you anyway – sweet, funny – well, occasionally funny . . . All of that despite what your mum was like to you, despite being ignored by your dad. And we were happy. Weren't we?'

'Yeh, yes.'

'Even before we got together, since the day we met. However hard it was at The Church, I always had you. We always had each other.'

'This is it,' I said, mouth dry. 'You're . . . we've been like a life-raft for each other and—'

'This isn't you! It's a fucking play. You don't need to do this; we don't need to end things.' She looked up at me, wanting to stand, wanting me to come to her, but neither of us moving. Tears began to well under her eyes, reddened with emotion. 'He's a sadist. How can you not see?'

I took a stuttering breath in, needing to say something but no idea what it should be. She was wrong about Jonathan, upset, desperate. He was tough, incredibly tough, we all knew that. But what I felt on that stage, reliving the scene with my mother, I could feel myself crossing into a deeper part of myself, a sort of transcendence. When I'd rehearsed the play after it, my words didn't feel like something that had been written four hundred years before, they felt like my own.

When I said nothing, Nina's head collapsed into her hands and she began to cry. I wanted to go to her, had to clench my hands behind my back to stop myself reaching out to her. Instead, I knelt from where I was at the door and took in the image of her, limbs tangled over each other, fingers twisting her curls in wringing despair. After some moments watching her, so grounded, raw, I began to feel myself as an observer, an audience watching a masterful performance. I had to look away to stop it.

'You're not going to say anything?' She looked up at me, brown eyes hot with venom. 'Thought Hamlet couldn't stop talking?' Her voice was lower, the cynicism of someone twenty years old, teeth red with wine. 'Well, you can get yourself to a fucking nunnery.' She stood up, marched into her ensuite bathroom and slammed the door. She turned on both taps, maybe even the shower, but it didn't drown out the sound of her crying. I listened for a moment, took in the sound of what I'd done to someone I loved. It felt strained, painful, like trying to pull in my final few breaths.

I moved back into the squat in Limehouse after rehearsals the next day. After the ceiling collapse, my old stablemates had converted the disused warehouse and for twenty-eight quid a week contribution to bills and food, I got a room of sorts with plasterboard walls, rather than sharing the main living space as I had previously. There were eight or nine who were still there from before, led by a drug-addled performance artist called Rudy, who didn't like me because his on–off girlfriend Loz wanted to sleep with me. On top of that, there were anywhere between ten and forty others who'd come in and out, some treating the place like a rave, some as a doss house. I didn't like any of them but nor did I hate them. No one cared what I did or who I was. I was another body. One of the revolving door of characters, some colourful but most bland, which was how I wanted them to think of me. The walls dripped in their self-loathing, and I drank it up like it was good for me. The kitchen in the squat was the epicentre of the partying, so I didn't eat much, no real food – sweets, crisps, a pasty. There were always mountains of cigarettes and tobacco knocking around, so whenever I felt hungry, I smoked.

It was in the squat that I started talking to Dustin. The real Dustin had been a good listener; Mum used to look into his eyes and he didn't look away, unusual for a dog. The skull slept next to me on the pile of clothes I used as a pillow. I'd talk to it, imagine a past where Yorick and I would roam the wilds around Elsinore, pulling him from a sucking bog, he alerting me to some ambushers on the treacherous road back from Copenhagen. I stared into his eyeholes and could see the glassiness of Mum's eyes near the end reflected back, and sometimes I'd hear her voice. In better moments, I'd look into the empty space and try to imbue it with the star-like capacity to love Nina had given me, that I'd tossed on the bonfire. All of it couldn't have been more perfect for the last stages of the play.

After a couple of weeks there, I started to get sick again. I began walking the halls of The Church talking to Dustin's skull. My body was weak from my cigarette diet and the lack of sleep, so at times I stumbled, struggling to put one foot in front of the other. I looked like shit, skin sallow, always wearing the same threadbare black coat I'd found in the wardrobe in the cellar of The Church, and my perambulations whenever I was out of rehearsals became a cause of twitching concern for the staff and the rest of the student body.

It felt magnificent. People who cut themselves become addicted to it, those who go in for tattoos the same. There are endorphins that come from the pain but it's more than that, there's an extraordinary rush in wilful self-destruction. Destroying the sacred self seemed to me the ultimate form of empowerment. The weakness, the exhaustion, hunger, choosing to alienate myself from Nina, happiness, everyone else, it felt revolutionary. I started to think of myself like a religious martyr, tried to tap into their fervour. The idea of being Adam again when the play finished, re-entering a world of compromise and quotidian suffering, felt like something I would never be able to do.

Three weeks before the production, I was shocked to catch a glimpse of the back of Patrick's head through the slit of glass in Aggie's office. Putting the tremors of paranoia I felt down to my immersion in *Hamlet*, I tried telling myself I'd observed an innocent catch-up between teacher and final-year student. But the next morning, Jonathan wasn't there at nine o'clock. In our whole time at the school, he'd never been late. We broke out of our warm-up and formed a massage chain to distract from the spreading unease. Anna T mumbled about him dying in his sleep, that was how unexpected Jonathan not being there was.

He marched in twenty minutes later like it was nothing, accompanied by Aggie. I went to him, but Jonathan didn't acknowledge me as the two of them sat behind his desk. I followed Aggie's glance to Patrick who was sat, headphones in, eyes closed, and had the sensation of losing my balance.

'Jonathan?' I said.

'One more exercise,' he called out, opening his notebook to a blank page. Patrick clenched every muscle in his face before opening his eyes and looking to the teachers, who nodded at him to begin.

He got up on stage, affecting a younger, more callow physicality. I glanced at Aggie and Jonathan. Jonathan was still, but she was jiggling in her seat, so excited her wet-dream favourite was being given another bite of the cherry. I caught everyone in our year stealing glances at me as Patrick pulled on furniture to set up his space. They were happy to see me squirm; hubris, they were thinking, delusions of grandeur to think someone like me could ever be big-lead.

Patrick sat on the far chair of three plastic seats lined up in a row, the theatre shorthand for a sofa. He opened his eyes and shifted to his left, in the scene. He looked down at his leg, shocked.

'Linda, what you up to?' Patrick said, sounding surprised. He reacted to whatever Linda replied with a swallowed breath.

'That's my—' He laughed, a strained smile. 'I do like you. But, this is my dad's office.' Patrick crossed the stage and pretended to look out a window. He turned and acted Linda approaching, his body shimmered and you could see her arms wrapping around him, a sucking in of his navel as she grabbed at his crotch again. He swung round and we could feel him pushing Linda away, moving past her back to the sofa.

'I'm still in school like,' he said. That was the moment he lost it. Although Jonathan's face remained unchanged, I could read him by then. Patrick had deviated from the truth of the moment for the sake of spelling out the story for us. I wish I could say that, as I watched him revealing his father's assistant starting a relationship with him when he was fourteen, I felt sorry for the boy Patrick being sexualised too soon, or the adult Patrick trying too hard to win back the role he thought he deserved, but I didn't. I wanted this moment of defeat to be a bigger trauma for him than the one he was using in the exercise to try and top mine.

Jonathan didn't stop him, letting Patrick limp on to a conclusion.

'Stay there, Patrick,' Jonathan said, taking off his jacket and swinging it onto the back of his chair. I saw a flicker of excitement on Patrick's face, ready for Jonathan's praise, his adulation, his confirmation that he'd been wrong, and that Hamlet was once again his. 'Act one, scene three, Polonius' advice to you, Laertes.'

Patrick's face dropped as Ben stood up to join his friend rehearsing a scene that didn't feature Hamlet. Jonathan strode in front of the rest of us and looked up towards the pipes of the organ on the far side of the nave.

'This above all else,' he said. 'To thine own self be true. And it must follow as the night the day, thou canst not then be false to any man.' His eyes lit on Aggie. 'Agatha, if you please.'

The principal wrapped her shawl around her and left

without saying a word. I had the uneasy sense that whatever private power struggles had led to Patrick's exercise,
although vanquished for now, might not yet be finished.

This was borne out a few days later. Vanessa found me
smoking behind the greasy spoon on the main road, sleeve
to her nose to block out the smell of reused oil.

'They have concerns about your health,' she said.

'Who?'

'The school. Aggie said students had mentioned it to her.'

'She spoke to you?'

She nodded.

'What did you say?'

'I said you got food poisoning from a dodgy Chinese
behind Waterloo station. Let's go in, I'll buy you some
chips.'

Inside she ordered me a huge breakfast and I felt com-
forted as she watched me eat.

'Patrick was in Aggie's office, the day before that fiasco
with his dad's secretary. He's trying to steal it from me.' I
crossed my knife and fork over my plate. Vanessa glared at
the breakfast I'd barely touched as I slid it across the table.

'So, don't let him. I want your performance to be real
for you, but Dad's always said people can only tolerate so
much ugliness. And if given the choice between truth and
beauty, the masses would probably choose the latter.'

'Hamlet's dad has died. He's grieving.'

'I'm just saying wear a jumper and eat a couple of
burgers.'

'There's a conspiracy building.'

'There always will be, so play the game a little. Agents don't want to have blood coughed up on them, however "in it" you may be. I meant to say, I'm sorry I told you to fuck off the other day.'

'I was being a dick.'

'It was my mum. She'd just found out about another twenty-four-year-old my father was running around with.'

'Shit, sorry.'

'Oh, don't be,' she said, as dismissive as if I'd forgotten to return her Tupperware.

'Don't you mind, the affairs?'

'Not really.' She looked to the side before leaning over the table a little towards me. 'Sort of fascinates me. I meet them sometimes.'

'The girls?'

'At openings, parties. I can always tell. I chat to them, sometimes the whole night.'

'I can't believe you talk to them?'

'Dad's never been that affectionate to me. The odd impromptu squeeze around the waist on a holiday balcony but not much more, enough for me to crave it. The agency's his life. He makes no secret of it. Perhaps I talk to the women he does lavish attention on, often only four, five years older than me, because I think they'll have the key to unlocking his love, I don't know. They're all fantastically beautiful, self-possessed. I find myself feeling almost proud of him.'

'For cheating?'

'Not the infidelity per se, but my mother is limited, no ambition, not enough for him, so he takes what he wants. He never lies to the girls, never promises to make them stars.'

'Clients?'

'Sometimes. They don't sack him after the relationship breaks down.'

'Isn't that because he has a lot of sway?'

'He gets them the work they want. They wouldn't get it anywhere else.'

'So, you're saying it wasn't a great time to compliment your dad about his work with young clients in front of his cuckolded wife?' I said.

Van laughed. 'Not perfect, no.' She held my gaze for a moment, took a deep breath and looked away.

'Has your dad met Patrick?'

'He hasn't, no, but he's sent his headshot out, here and in the US.'

'And me?'

'Your photos are terrible, and he'd get you on stage anyway. Patrick's a movie star, you're an actor.'

The Conservatoire wasn't interested in movie stars. A-listers, blockbusters, commercial success were like junk food to us, so it was wonderful Van and her father made the distinction. Although Patrick was the one Alasdair was touting to the industry and not me.

'Why are you so nice to me?' I asked.

'I'm not. What do you mean?' she said too fast, the suggestion of a blush.

'We're not friends though.'

'No, right.' She glanced out the window, frowned. It struck me for the first time that the fact that no one in Group 28 would count Van as a friend might not be something she would actually want. She glanced at my hand splayed on the table and, for a moment, I thought she was going to touch it. 'I've never wanted for anything Adam. I click my fingers and am brought whatever I want, live wherever I want. My dad could help me be an actor, a singer, film director, run his company, job in publishing, production, whatever I chose to do, within reason, I could do. Where you're the total opposite. My whole life has taught me I'm worth so much more than you, and you've grown up thinking that that's basically true.'

I smiled at how right she was. 'Yet here we are, at the same school, you're blossoming and I remain consistent. Perhaps I hope a bit of it will rub off on me.'

I was grateful to have Vanessa because by the following week it felt like everyone was against us. There was a massive night out on the Saturday that everyone in our year was oddly quiet about when they came in the following week. Conversations would halt when I came into earshot. I caught Patrick giving me furtive looks, Nina going to even greater pains to avoid eye contact with me. It was like there had been some meeting between them all, some secret agreement to oust me. Aggie and Jonathan passed in the corridors with barely a look between them. Every time I witnessed her talking with someone from the faculty – Max, Daniel – it felt like she was rallying the troops. I'd watch her classes through the window convinced she was telling second years how ill I looked, encouraging them to back her intervention. She was the principal. At the time, she was negotiating with the University absorbing the school to secure government funding. She had the power to overrule Jonathan.

One afternoon I saw Patrick working on the swordfight with Ricky, our fight teacher, who invited me in when he caught me loitering outside.

'We're fixing it so Laertes wins. Know it's not in the script,' Patrick said, laughing at his own joke.

'Let's run through it, men,' Ricky said, throwing a foil at me. The two of us crossed swords. I looked at Patrick and saw the man I'd respected, who I'd wanted so much to like me, take me under his wing like a treasured little sibling even and felt a deep sadness to have lost him. But then we fought. Patrick was fast, striking hard, precise, but I matched him.

Ricky retreated to his drum and as we were going through the choreography, the tension fell away and we were having fun, like it was before I got the role, the joy of performing with someone came flooding back. Patrick threw an arm around my neck, brought me into him, and as we looked at each other we smiled. I wished we could do the show as brothers-in-arms because I loved him and he me. I loved them all.

He shoved me off, catching me under the chin with the hilt of his sword, perhaps on purpose, perhaps not. It hurt but I didn't care.

'Do that in the show,' I said. 'Hurt me. Don't tell me when. Sucker-punch, cheap shot, whatever.'

Patrick nodded. 'Whatever you say, big-lead,' he said, mocking, some secret knowledge in his eyes.

I turned away, feeling feral, certain he had some ace up his sleeve he couldn't wait to play.

So, it was after that I started following him around The Church. I'd heard he'd been calling Alasdair's office to arrange a meeting and became convinced he was winning the cold war to steal the role back from me. But Jonathan and I spent much of that last week hunkered down on the speeches and thus, if there was any plot afoot, I wouldn't have seen it anyway.

Until I did, just over a week before the show was due to go up. Stood in the shadowy end of the corridor by a piano, I observed Patrick finding a note in his locker. He looked around to make sure no one was watching before putting on his coat and leaving The Church. I followed, reeling through the options of where he could be going to try and undermine my career. Vanessa had told me that he'd spent his time out of rehearsals going to the Groucho and the Garrick clubs to schmooze industry people ahead of the show; perhaps I'd find him getting a cab to Soho.

I got out just in time to see him disappearing down the steps, heading towards Kentish Town. I hid myself around a corner house as he stopped on the junction with the High Street. He looked back towards me, waiting for something. Over my shoulder, I caught a flash of pink and ducked into the basement steps of a Georgian house. It was Nina coming from the other side of the square. I hid in my spot next to a wheelie bin until she passed, then edged up and watched as Patrick spread his arms to greet her.

I still didn't realise. I still thought she was on her way to the station to go home and he was being his magnanimous, flirtatious self. But then she stepped towards him, tentative. My fingers gripped at a loose brick. Patrick threw his arms around her, pulled her into him and kissed her. I leapt over the low wall, brick in hand. I was going to bound over and batter him off as if he was forcing himself on her, but then Nina snaked her hand around his waist, kissed him back. I stopped, disembowelled. Nina broke from Patrick, smiled nervously and glanced around her. Patrick put his arm around her waist and almost carried her away from me. I rushed towards them, certain he must be coercing her, taking her against her will. But she started laughing at something he'd said. As the two of them, Patrick and Nina, my Nina, disappeared around the corner towards the tube station arm in arm, she was laughing. I gripped the brick tighter. Dust crumbled off the corners, reddening the pavement below.

IV.iii

On the journey back from seeing Raya, I had Amber call Jonathan but he didn't answer. I needed him to know the girl he'd pushed to scalding her classmate had been found walking into the sea, to ask him how he could have lied about it and to ask, outright, if he was the person doing this to me. If he'd sent an unstable Raya to see me at the film festival when I was avoiding fans like the diseased, knowing how crushing that would be for her, was it so inconceivable he was the anonymous phantom haunting me online? Driving me into a paranoid mess, making me doubt myself, doubt everything for the sake of my next film. Could he even have been the voice calling me after we wrapped *Woodsman*? I'd seen when I stayed with him he was an uncannily good mimic. I couldn't make sense of it. I didn't think he'd know what film I would do next but, if he and Van had met about one project without my knowing, who's to say he hadn't dictated my next one as well.

When we got back to the hotel, I steeled myself for telling Van what we'd discovered from Raya but as I pushed into the revolving door she was there, Van, going out the other way. She looked so angry when she saw me, I wondered whether I could stay in the door indefinitely. She emerged onto the street and waited until I came out.

'Are you actually trying to put me in a fucking ashram?' She thrust a phone into my hand, turned and walked down towards the street. On the phone's screen was the *Daily Mail* website. Images of Amber and I, sunglasses, hats, leaving the hospital in Basildon. A dizzying number of pictures showing us talking, agitated, shell-shocked. We looked like criminals deciding where to hide a body. There was a close-up of the sign for the psychiatric ward. Raya's name; a picture of her in a school play accompanied by the phrase 'raving mad on Southend beach'; an image of The Church; a screenshot of the webpage saying she'd been awarded a thousand-pound bursary by me. A still of me giving my BAFTAs speech; a decades-old picture of an unsmiling Jonathan. Then the image that shocked me the most. A screenshot of the initial comment from measured-bella about the missing girl – the one Vanessa had told me had been deleted. I blinked, the overcast day seeming too bright, before casting around the street for Vanessa. A black cab purred ahead; door swung open for me.

I slid in next to her, she was on the speakerphone to Delilah, the taxi drove off. Delilah used the same kinds of phrases as before, things being 'all the fun of the fair', but she was clearly terrified I was going to ruin her unblemished Oscars record. She told us it made sense for Carl Dillane's studio to ramp up their campaign against us, but

261

I didn't have to make it quite so easy for them. The car stopped on Dean Street in the heart of Soho. Van ended the call, reached past me to open the door and walked into a restaurant. We hadn't talked and I had the sensation of having not been in the car with her at all.

The driver squinted at me through his rear-view mirror, so I got out and went through the building Van had disappeared into. A curtain was drawn for me by a model-beautiful woman who ushered me through to a dining room. I was shocked to see Arthur, the cocky student from The Church, sitting in a booth, snapping a grissini like he owned the restaurant and possibly several others.

'Arthur's come to talk to us,' Van said, in a rusted-metal voice. The boy stood and shook my hand like I was an old school chum. I sat and Van poured us all sparkling water. 'Journalists have reached out to the students,' she continued by way of explanation.

'No one's said anything,' Arthur said. 'But' – Van darted her eyes to me, near apoplectic beneath her mill-pond expression – 'I thought you should know, and I'm pretty certain, Raya was working with Jonathan. I didn't want to say when you came. Felt disloyal.'

Van and I didn't tell him we already knew.

'Disloyal to whom?' I asked, finding myself in the accent of the prosecutor I'd played in *American Wrath*. Arthur gave me a wry smile that said 'Who do you think?' before looking at the table, play-acting he was going to find the next part difficult.

'He was still working with her though, a long time after she left. That's what I thought you should know.'

'What do you mean? Working with her how?' I said.

'He was helping her, coaching her for auditions.'

'What auditions?' Van said.

'I went to see her a month or so after she left. Booty call, mea culpa.' He held his hands up like a footballer trying to avoid a yellow card, a smirk to me as if I'd understand. 'She told me she'd gone to his place, working through different characters. He was going to get her auditions, prepare her for them. I thought it was fucked up, but it was like what she did to Lyndsey proved to Jonathan that she had what it takes.'

Nothing showed on Van's face, but I could tell by how she pushed her water glass across the tablecloth how catastrophic this could be for us. Jonathan had chosen to mentor and teach, pro bono we had to assume, a girl who'd displayed violent mental instability. He'd kept her in a state of obsessive readiness for auditions, which may or may not have materialised, potentially kept her off her medication in the months leading up to her losing her mind and handing out posies to strangers on the seafront.

Arthur fiddled with the silver knife in front of him.

'If this were to get out,' he said, 'after what you said at the BAFTAs, it could be problematic. Potensh.' He measured his words but the way he looked at Van and I was so brazen, there was no doubt what he was insinuating.

'Great to know,' Van said. 'Forewarned is forearmed, although, as Adam will tell you, I've got one of those big underground vaults of weaponry, like Arnie had in the

263

nineties, but mine's full of favours, threats and all sorts of other big fuck-off grenade launchers I can turn to when I feel my clients are being threatened.'

Arthur pouted his lips a little and gave a sharp sniff, seeming unmoved by Van's response.

'There's also the student who killed themselves when you were both at The Church. If Raya's lost it like this after working with him, isn't it possible that Jonathan pushed things too far back then too?' The boy scratched at the tablecloth with the serrated part of the knife. I wanted to snatch it off him. 'But, my year, we don't want to have to get involved. We want to do our show, graduate, get an amazing agent' – he raised an eyebrow at Vanessa – 'go into the industry and do the work we've trained for.'

Vanessa stifled a laugh and put her hand on mine. 'We have to go,' she said. 'Thank you for coming to see us.'

Arthur looked baffled as Van stood, nodded at me to do the same. Arthur got up, cleared his throat, thinking he'd been too subtle in his attempt at blackmail. Van placed her hands on his shoulders, put him back into his seat and knelt to his eye level.

'The main thing I look for in a client, more than talent, looks, more important than the ability to put in the graft even, the main thing I'm looking for is someone I can trust. And I get it,' she said, 'if your conscience demands you speak about Jonathan, I would never stand in your way. But the industry is very, very small and it has a long memory. And for actors' – she pressed her index finger into her thumb and held them up to Arthur's face – 'the line between success and oblivion

264

is so thin you can barely even see it.' She stood, an arm on my back to usher me out of the restaurant. 'If you're that hungry, Arthur, have another breadstick.'

Although we had left Arthur floored for a second time, I could tell as we got in the cab to our hotel his news had rattled her, and we spent the ride in silence save for the sound of Van tapping on her phone like she was trying to dig to the earth's core with her thumbs. She didn't speak to me until the lift we got opened onto the floor of my suite.

'I'm not going to tell you what a fucking idiot you are for going to see the girl. You're aware of my feelings on that in general.' She flicked her eyes at me, a sliver of a smile. Despite what she said, firefighting was her favourite part of the job. Whether it was a natural predilection, or borne of having to deal with me, neither of us had ever been certain. 'The Oscars is in a fortnight,' she said, walking out into the corridor. 'We cannot ignore this story, so please, if you don't want my frontal lobe to pop like a car going over a fucking Capri-Sun, stay in your room, get some sleep, essentially do nothing.'

She marched down the hall to her suite and I did what I was told, went to my room, laid on the bed to try to sleep. But the tumbling thoughts were far too loud and after a few hours, I found myself sitting on the floor, facing the open mini-bar. I stared at the tiny bottles for some time. From my earliest memories, alcohol had been forbidden fruit to me. I knew how it had corroded my mother from a sparkling young woman into a rusted shell, but still felt myself drawn to it. She drank vodka mainly. Clear bottles with shiny red writing. I drank some once thinking it was water when I was seven or so; it burned my throat. I didn't hate it. Even after she died, I would steal sips of my dad's beer then, when I was twelve, thirteen, cans of it, sneaking down at night and making myself sick drinking whisky. My teenage years I dived in, getting drunk with friends because that was all anyone did, but never enjoying it, always knowing its promise of fun times, worldliness and escapism were nothing more than a chimera. At The Conservatoire it became a necessary evil, social glue, anaesthetic for the neuroses, saturating our rivalries for a few hours. But after what happened near the end of *Hamlet* – I was a little drunk that night, perhaps it made a difference – in twenty years since, I hadn't touched a drop.

But still I reached into the little fridge, took out four vodka miniatures and placed them on the desk above in a row. I snapped open the lid of one and sniffed it, got notes of paint-thinner and nostalgia for the front room of our little terrace in Kippax. I placed my tongue over the top of the bottle, upturned it and held it there for some time, the chemical tang more scent than taste. All I had to do was take my tongue away and I could swallow the whole thing in one. Oblivion felt almost overwhelmingly appealing, having not drunk for so long it would take no time to get there. I could make it all go away. In the mirror I saw my BAFTA glinting on the mantelpiece behind me. I put the miniature down. We were so close.

I lay back on the bed. I remembered Amber had sent me recordings of some guided meditations after the flight over. I went onto my phone, clicked one and held it to my ear. There was a gong, tinkling bells, a man telling me to breathe. I closed my eyes, tried to give myself to it. My mind kept drifting to Raya's frightened eyes, imagining her in Jonathan's living room, working on Shakespeare, feeling like she'd been anointed by God. I closed my eyes, tuned into the static, the hiss around the man's words, a glitch on the recording. I fell asleep.

I woke up early the next morning to banging on the door, but the first thing that struck me was that there had been no dreams, no voice asking me how I could have done what I'd done. The door knocking still, I reached for my phone and scrolled through the call history. The ghost had only spoken after I'd been with Jonathan, after I'd praised him, defended him, measuredbella's attacks the same.

I went back to the night we wrapped on *Woodsman*. There were no calls, I knew there were no calls, I'd checked. I scanned back and saw there hadn't been any calls for three weeks before. I tried to square it. Van had been on set for the last week, there would be no reason for her to call, but was it possible she wouldn't have tried to contact me at all for the two weeks before that? I could only remember that time as Harrison, sat with Louanne by the fire we'd made, axing wood on freezing mornings, prizing rabbit-fur out of traps with my knife. I have no memory of my phone ringing, but did that mean it hadn't? I tried to hear the voice as it'd come to me in my dreams. Just like the meditation, there was a glitch, a click on the line. Always a click before the words. How could it be that I would imagine, dream about, a click? It had been the same in the cabin.

'Adam,' Amber said through the door. Her voice brought me back to myself and I stumbled out of bed to let her in.

'Can calls be deleted?' I said, holding the phone out.

'What?' she said, pushing a rail with several outfits past me into the room.

'Can you tell, is there any way to tell if calls I've had have been deleted?'

'I don't know, that thing's ancient but—' She spotted the miniatures on the desk and looked at me, concerned.

'I didn't drink them.'

She scanned me for the truth, before going to sweep them into the wastepaper bin.

'Have a shower and get dressed,' she said. 'We're going to the BBC.'

Van was waiting in the car as I got in wearing my high-fashion-meets-Country outfit. She explained Raya's uncle Barry had been in touch and it had given her an epiphany as to how we were going to deal with the fallout of my psychiatric ward visit. I thought she'd be anxious, angry, fingers tapping her nerves out on the screen of her phone, but she spent the whole journey staring out the window at the sunny morning.

They put us in a Green Room where pastries grew stale on a composite table, presented cups of machine-coffee and told us it'd just be a few minutes. I was there to do an interview with Jed Francis and Ally Carver on the 5 Live film show. I'd done a segment for them about *Woodsman* remotely a month or so before. It had been made clear I wasn't there to discuss the film.

An assistant walked us into the studio. Jed and Ally were finishing off a review of an animation they'd found tedious, making gestures when they saw me, he a thumbs up, her a chef's kiss. Highbrow left-leaning journalists have always loved me. I represent purity to them, a throwback to when film was a serious art form for serious people and for people, read pompous men.

'Now, we have a wonderful surprise,' Jed said, flipping cartoonish eyebrows. 'Freshly minted BAFTA-winning screen legend, Adam Sealey. Are you OK being called a legend?'

'Not really,' I said, laughing into the character of the self-effacing guest.

'Adam's come to see us before heading to the States for the Academy Awards, but as an extra-special treat, we're joined by Adam's long-time manager Vanessa Sanjeev-Nixon, to get a little behind-the-scenes intel. Thanks for joining us, Vanessa.'

'They normally keep us bloodsuckers nailed in our coffins. I'm happy they've let me out for this.' She looked at me, eyes bulging. I was glad she was nervous.

'Adam, first thing,' Ally chipped in. 'Who's designing your ball-gown?'

I smiled, pretending I didn't know Van would've taken them aside beforehand and told them to 'keep it light' with the handshake of a CIA-enhanced interrogator.

We talked around the BAFTAs for a few minutes, letting Jed make mediocre jokes about Dames, Vanessa joining in to make another self-deprecating comment about how the agents spent the night going into the actors' goody bags to steal their iPads. Then they asked me about *Night-train to Rostov* and I, as I was told to, spoke about how great the script was.

'Are you happy to talk about the script for *Woodsman?*' Ally said, modulating her tone from frothy to robust.

'Sure,' I said.

'The movie only came out over here a few weeks ago, so it's hard to discuss without spoilers, but it was reported you had the script changed to make it similar to something which happened when you were at university?'

'Drama school,' Van interjected. 'They'd kill you for calling it a university, but yes, there had been an earlier draft of the script that had a different ending. Now, without delving too much into the dull nitty-gritty of how a movie comes to be made, scripts are changed throughout their development all the time. But it's true that *Woodsman's* ending was altered at a late stage and that the change came from our side. What's important to make clear though, is that Adam never saw an earlier version. He read the final script of the movie that audiences have taken to their hearts. I was the one who suggested we echo—God, it is hard to talk about without spoilers, um, but it was me who thought it might be powerful for Adam's performance to echo a difficult time for him.'

'At The Conservatoire of the Dramatic Arts.'

'That's right,' I said.

Ally looked at Jed. Jed looked at Vanessa, who gave the tiniest nod.

'Now, you went back the day of the BAFTAs to do some work with the students there?' Ally said.

'It was great to go back,' I said.

'But there have been a few tails wagging after you went to see a former student?'

'We were made aware a girl I'd donated financial aid to had had to leave the school due to struggles with her mental health.' I could feel Vanessa's eyes boring into me. 'When I heard about her from her peers, what her upbringing had been like, she reminded me of myself. And, maybe it's just because I'll forever have Harrison in my DNA after *Woodsman*, but I felt like I had to help her. And um, sorry—' I stopped, cleared my throat for a moment, injecting the ambiguity of some kind of emotion. 'Often in life we hesitate to do the right thing, we miss our chance to act, perhaps worrying whether it's appropriate. I probably shouldn't have gone to the hospital where she's a patient, but I wanted to reach out, ask if I could help. I knew once I got back to LA, I would've got swept up in the Oscars and Raya would have been forgotten.'

'You even went to see her uncle!' Jed said, laughing like a nineties radio DJ.

'Having given her a bursary to attend the school,' I said, chuckling along, 'I felt responsible things hadn't worked out for her.'

Vanessa looked so pleased with me, I thought she'd pat my hand. Uncle Barry had called Van to say they were going to sell their side of things to the papers. But when Van laid out our version, that I'd given his niece money to help with her studies and, on hearing what she'd been through, had made more effort to help her than her own family, it silenced Uncle Barry and Van realised how well what I'd done aligned with the campaign 'narrative' they had crafted – the man who can't help but be the hero.

Van made a face at the producer; they knew we were getting a flight that night. Jed started to guffaw about some other film they'd reviewed, asking if the ultimate method-acting challenge would be to play an anthropomorphised animal, when I noticed a shadow come over Ally's face. She glanced at her monitor for a few moments and then to her producer.

'Adam, can I ask,' she said. 'Is there anything off-limits, in terms of what you'd use for a role?' Ally Carver had started out interviewing politicians before moving into culture and, although she was as genial as ever, I heard a gladiatorial relish in her voice.

'Before I begin a new project, I've no idea how I'll find a way into the character, but I'm not quite sure what you mean?'

'An email's just come in from a . . . Bella?'

Van and I stared at the two presenters, poker-faced. The air in the studio felt like an electrical storm.

'She wanted us to ask you if you thought about the close friends and family of your classmate who—'

'Spoilers,' Jed said.

'Who passed away.'

'As I was saying' – Van came in fast – 'Adam didn't read any other version of the script so—'

'But he chose to do the film. What our listener I think is asking is, when you use something like this, are you conscious it was a real tragedy, that there were people left behind, grieving, in pain? Pain you pick at as and when you need to use it.'

I blinked, felt static building behind my eyes. I wanted to tell her it was my grief too, my pain. I wanted to tell her every time a chair scraped the floor, I thought of it, how I still couldn't see a balustrade on a staircase without needing to sit down in the brace position. But I couldn't say that.

'Losing a friend at that age . . . is very affecting.'

'But the—The email's from a Bella, she says she was very close to your classmate who died.'

Vanessa stole a glance at me. It felt like we'd been lured into a clearing and were now surrounded on all sides by pointed spears.

'She says the family and friends were torn apart, driven into depression, lives ravaged by alcoholism.'

Vanessa clenched her jaw. Ally adjusted her headphones and gave an expectant shrug.

'Throughout their lives people go through unimaginable pain,' I said, eyes closed still, head bowed. 'They have to deal with tragedies that come from nowhere, sometimes with no warning and, most damaging of all, no explanation.' I looked up at Ally. 'I think one of the functions of stories, films, TV shows – one of the reasons we watch them – is to try and understand the random brutality to life and that, maybe seeing an actor going through something like that, even if it doesn't prepare you, it can cleanse you of the fear, just for a little while. And if that's what I'm here to do, to go to that impossible place so you don't have to, I have to give it everything I have, everything I've been through. And perhaps it makes that pain, the trauma when it does happen, a little bit easier to cope with. I don't know. Probably the most pretentious thing you've ever heard, but I guess, maybe that's why I do it.' Jonathan could have written it for me, so ingrained in his ideals was everything I had said. I didn't know if it had answered the question, wasn't sure I believed any of it anymore, but Ally leant back on her chair and the producer made a thumbs-up sign to move on.

Bella had been in touch while we were on air. We hadn't been billed as guests on the show, so she must have been listening. Van and I didn't speak as a researcher led us through the airless corridors and out into the square where the air was limp with the hangover of rain.

'I feel like I've been molested,' Van said. 'You did good.' She darted her hand out at the nearest cab, but it slid past, the wake of a puddle crashing onto the curb, making us jump back.

'This isn't Carl Dillane's management,' I said. 'It's not a studio. They wouldn't do this weird shit.'

Van stared at the traffic meandering in front of us, her silence telling me that however much she didn't want me to be, I was right.

'Family and friends,' I said. 'Alcoholism.'

'Yes,' she said, looking ahead with a faraway fear.

Jonathan, Van, they had too much to lose exposing me. Raya was unwell, institutionalised and barely knew me, what would she gain from bringing me down?

'It has to be,' I said. 'Doesn't it?'

Vanessa did one of her yogic breaths before she said, in a voice like rolled steel. 'Don't even think about it.'

IV.iv

'Adam?' Nina said as she saw me sat with Liv, Tommy and several finished cans of lager in her living room a few hours after she'd walked off into the sunset with Patrick. I'd gone back to The Church after seeing them together, back into rehearsing the scene where Hamlet considers killing his uncle as he prays for forgiveness. When I finished, mind on fire with the depth of her betrayal, I went straight down to Bexleyheath to drop in on her parents. Feeling her discomfort at my being there, Liv and Tommy left for the kitchen.

'Been at the pub?' I asked, though she didn't appear drunk as she sat in the armchair opposite. She seemed distracted, upset, perhaps by my being there, perhaps something else.

'Cinema.' She moved over to the fireplace and flicked off the electric heater. She was too hot, couldn't look at me. 'I wanted to say—'

'What did you want to say?'

'About your mum.' She moved to a different chair, leant towards me. I picked up the citrus from her hair, but there was something else, some other smell that had to be him.

I pictured her curled in his arms, eating popcorn from his lap and everything tensed. 'After the other night—' Her breath stuttered as she thought of how things had ended between us. 'Even so, as your friend, seeing that exercise—' She couldn't help colouring the word with disdain. 'I'm sorry you had to go through that, with your mum.'

I shrugged, broke into a smile. 'Don't be. I'm lucky,' I said. 'I can use it.'

Nina sat back, frowned, confused. 'No one should have to hear that when they're a kid, don't make out it's fine.'

'I am fine. Look at Patrick.' I couldn't look at her. If I did, I'd confront her about him, which would have been no use to me because I wanted it. The jealousy, the bitterness, my peasant's rage. I wanted all of it to marinate inside until the show. 'The best he had was some schoolboy smut.'

She looked at me with calculating eyes, didn't react, leap to his defence. I had realised it must have been the party I'd missed on Saturday when they got together, why everyone in Group 28 suddenly couldn't look me in the eyes. They all knew. But it was worse than I thought. That afternoon she'd been to the cinema with him. Not just the drunken fumble I'd hoped, Patrick taking advantage after one too many Strongbows. An actual date.

'It's not your fault, Adam, your mum, what she said to you. You know that, don't you?'

'Not really.'

'Well, it's not.' She began a shadow-move of taking my hand before resting both of hers on her knee. 'Did she even have cancer?'

'Fatty liver disease. I always thought my dad had dumbed it down for me, but that's what it's called. Turned into cirrhosis. She died.'

'You sound so cold.'

'Not a very warm topic of conversation.'

'I understand why you didn't tell me the truth.'

'Dinner's on the table in T-minus one minute,' Liv called from the kitchen.

'Beer or wine?' said Tommy.

'Wine,' Nina shouted. 'A man-size dinner portion for Adam. Says he's famished.' She gave me a half-smile. Vanessa was right about Nina. She had seduced me into staying with her in the depths of mediocrity. She allowed me to believe it was us and only us so she could keep me as her life-raft. And even after she'd found someone better, a real man, she couldn't help trying to control me, feeding me up like the children in a fairy story to water down my preparation for *Hamlet*.

'I've been working out,' I said, eyes sparkling. 'Do I look bigger?'

'You look skeletal.'

'You must be worried.'

'You look unwell, all of us are worried.'

'Worried enough to speak to the teachers?' I held her eye, she didn't flinch.

'Pretty worried.'

It *was* her that spoke to Aggie. She was on their side.

'Chicken Kievs,' Liv said, arriving in the doorframe. 'Always got them in the freezer. You've got to really, haven't you?'

I slipped on the attic steps much later that night as I climbed down. I thought about leaving before dinner but couldn't do it to Nina's parents and their infectious chirpiness soon turned the meal into a facsimile of the good times we had before. But their hospitality, their joy, watching Nina play the entertainer like she hadn't taken up with the man who'd become my nemesis, felt to me like thrusting a freezing limb into warm water. I drank too much wine and by the time I got up from the table, Liv had gone to bed and Tommy was making eyes at Nina to take me upstairs.

She took me up to my old room, laid a towel on the end of the bed. I took her hand as she was about to leave me, a test, or perhaps I just wanted to.

'Adam, don't,' she said.

'Why not?' I slurred accusingly, gearing up for a confession.

'Because you broke my heart,' she said, looking me in the eyes. It felt like being stabbed in the guts with a shard of glass. Nina put a hand to her neck, pulling the flesh at the back of her head, breath short, trying not to cry. Her head began shaking, wanting me to do something but not wanting me to be there, seeing her broken like that.

'I love you, Nina. I know you're with Patrick, but I've always been in love with you.' That's what I should have said. In the film version, the sight of Nina, hurt, desperate for me to fight for her, would have thawed the ice in my veins. Everything would have ended differently. But as she turned to leave, I said nothing, made an indecipherable noise, let her walk away.

I passed out soon after I lay down but woke in the middle of the night, throat arid, sinuses feeling like they were blocked with garlic powder. I'd dreamt of Patrick fucking Nina and scrabbled around for one of my old notebooks and a pencil to write it down. His body cut like an oil-rig, her hands gripping his muscular back, eyes closed, face tensed with what, pain? Ecstasy? All of it was wonderful for *Hamlet* but writing the words made me want to slam my head onto the pencil. I went and held my face over the sink and spat several times, expecting to be sick. I'm not sure who I hated more, him, her, myself, but I found myself walking down the stairs to her room.

I stopped outside the door, stepped over the squeaky floorboard and went in to see her sleeping, arms wrapped around a pillow.

I went to her make-up table and looked at the photos and cards stuck into the lightbulb-mirror. There were pictures of the two of us. Others of Group 28 together. Some from Youth Theatre groups. There were new things as well. An index card with a line from *The Seagull* written in Nina's neat block capitals, 'There's no worse feeling than knowing how badly you're acting.' I looked at her, cherubic in her sleep, a space next to her. I could have curled my body around hers as I used to. The quote was how she felt, she was the chaff still, but now alone. At the start of The Conservatoire, she'd been everyone's favourite spark of life, committed, passionate, joyful. Within weeks of being there, she started to believe it wasn't enough, she wasn't enough.

I tiptoed over to the bed, watched Nina's eyelids flickering in her sleep. She was dreaming of him, gripping the pillow, imagining it was him making love to her, not me lying on the bed next to her, clothes on, touching her fingers like a fucking eunuch.

I knelt, so close I could feel her breath on my face. Wine and oranges. I slipped the pillow out of her hands, stood and wound the ends of it in my two bunched hands, pulling it taut. I stared at the strand of hair she disturbed every time she exhaled. I dropped the pillow on the floor, walked down the stairs and out the front door into the night.

On the last Friday before we went into performance week, it was tradition to do a final exercise as a whole company. It usually took the form of a party or celebration to allow for all the characters to logically be there. The Church was kept open and in past years it had become an all-night affair, drinking always, but also rumours of drugs and almost certainly sex. We stayed in our characters all night and had objectives Jonathan gave us to stop it becoming too much of a free-for-all. Previous years had gone outside, but, after a group of girls were thrown out of Regent's Park for dancing naked around a fire for a production of *The Crucible*, the teachers decided to keep it in the lawless international waters of The Conservatoire. Guided by Vanessa, we had decided to have a party to celebrate my uncle Claudius' coronation a month after the death of Hamlet's father.

We'd been running the play again and again that week but on the Friday morning, Jonathan surprised us by having Patrick and I swap roles for the penultimate run-through.

Aggie was there with three other grown-ups, one suited and official-looking, the others more crumpled, industry folk. A week before, this would have caused me a seismic wobble, but the needless cruelty of Nina and Patrick having got together extinguished any lingering light I felt for the world, stripping away my neuroses and replacing them with a granite core. I would shine brighter in Laertes' scenes than Patrick could in the whole play as the Prince. Although he seemed to have prior knowledge of the change, Patrick gave a rushed performance and fell back on his locker-room nudge-nudge schtick, always both in front of the play and trying to catch up. It was glorious.

In the afternoon run-through, I was reinstated. The bigwigs who'd been there in the morning were gone but Aggie remained to watch. I gave my speeches straight to her, sat on the stage and eyeballed her as I said 'Man delights not me. No, nor woman neither.' I caught Jonathan grinning. The rest of our year sat out in the auditorium watching, Patrick up front, perhaps trying to put me off, or understand how it was he, despite everything he'd done, was no longer 'big-lead'. Nina was in the back corner, headphones in, eyes mostly closed. After we finished the run-through, Jonathan gave us a speech before we left to prepare for the party.

'Although the rehearsal process is over,' he said, massaging the underside of his chin with the steepled tips of his fingers, 'the sandpit remains open. The play has seeped into your marrow, it lives in your subconscious, and you are free to play with it, to surprise yourself, to surprise us.

We have three or four more runs next week and I want you all to know' – he looked at me, then Patrick – 'the door is not and will not close. Even when the performances have begun, my mind is open regarding casting. We are building a piece of art that must function in and of itself but also change our audience. It will change all of you. The exercise tonight is a last opportunity to explore, to push yourselves beyond your limits, to show me who you really are.' He twisted his prayer hands, so they clutched in a ball, and looked at each and every one of us, not stopping longer at me or Patrick. Then he rested his gaze on the stained-glass window behind us, light beaming through the balcony onto the stage.

'And indeed, there will be time to wonder, "Do I dare?" and, "Do I dare?" Time to turn back and descend the stair, with a bald spot in the middle of my hair.' He waved a hand at our stage manager Rakka, continuing to stare at the sun as she told us to be back at nine.

Patrick, Nina and most of the others went to the pub. Vanessa went home. I stayed in Room 1 and worked on the script. It seemed from what Jonathan said that Aggie was lobbying hard for Hamlet to be, at least, shared between Patrick and me but I couldn't let that happen. I wanted Alasdair to be my agent but, more than that, I wanted to be The Conservatoire's first Hamlet. I took Jonathan's little bit of poetry, T. S. Eliot though I didn't know that then, as a reminder to me that, where I had a whole career in front of me, his thoughts were turning towards legacy. I could be Jonathan's Hamlet. He had chosen me, perhaps, if Van was right, had me earmarked from the moment he walked into my audition. I had to transcend, to be extraordinary. So, while the rest of Group 28 drank, I worked.

They were well-oiled when they returned, clanging their lockers as they changed for the party. Jonathan came back wearing what looked like his old movement gear, loose-fitting, black. He sat at the back of the stage with his notebook like the resident theatre ghost. Patrick and The Boys bundled in first. He gave me a wink as he came in and looked messy-drunk, something we didn't often see. Oban as Horatio came over to me with drinks to ask how it was with me. His objective was clearly to look after me at the coronation and I appreciated it like the love of a sibling.

Nina arrived with Anna T, and I was shocked to see that in the break, rather than being at the pub, they'd gone off to get matching haircuts, short bobs. Nina's wild, Anna's dead straight.

I bowled over to them and embraced Anna like a long-lost friend.

'Rosencrantz, Guildenstern. How was the journey from Wittenberg?'

'Very good, my Lord,' Anna said.

'The sight of you is salve to my fractured heart.' I gripped Nina's shoulders, pulled her into me, but her body felt limp in my arms, eyes blank when I pulled away from her. I glanced at Patrick, wondering if he'd done something, said something to upset her, but he was occupied with The Boys, pouring shots of gin into their mouths.

The exercise began properly when Vanessa and Greg, a

lovely actor who was playing Claudius, walked in accompanied by a fanfare. Van wore a couture party dress, which I found out later she'd stolen from her father's office, one of the many freebies sent to his clients. It was coral pink, halfway between a meringue dress and something out of the Sex Pistols. Perhaps it was that she looked dressed for a wedding, but I found myself dumbstruck by the sight of her and, for the first time, thought about what it would be like to take it off.

'Hamlet,' she said, throwing Greg's arm off. I strode through the crowd, kissed Vanessa's hand and put my arm around her waist, claiming her. My objective was to break up my mother and uncle and, taking Jonathan's words to heart, fired by a last-days-of-Rome lust for Vanessa I'd never acknowledged before, had no qualms about going far beyond what was appropriate.

Sat on a chaise-longue together, my hands in hers, Van and I watched the rest of the room go about their actions and manipulations. Nina stayed with Anna T and James, drinking too much, avoiding The Boys. She'd glance over from time to time, pretend she wasn't looking. As the evening wore on, I spent time with Anna K, Oban, James too, but avoided Patrick and he me. I got caught in a corner for about twenty minutes with Ali, the guy playing Osric, I think trying to seduce me. When I managed to escape, I noticed Van and Patrick were gone.

I went into the hall, the cold light of normality allowing me to breathe outside the pressure cooker we'd created in Room 1. I'd drunk more than I should have and was feeling spacey. I darted through the corridor, gripped by the fear Patrick and Vanessa had left together, finally deciding to realise the power-couple that had always seemed on the cards. I felt possessive of her, jealous, looking through the windows of teaching rooms, expecting to see them tangled together, fucking. He'd always wanted to and she knew it.

'Hamlet,' a voice trying to call me back into Room 1, so I went outside to smoke.

'You said he'd be there this morning.'

I heard an angry voice as I approached the main entrance. From just inside, I saw it was Patrick.

'He said he might,' Vanessa said.

'He wined and dined me for fuck's sake. I turned down ITM, Green and Wells, Alan Winter, all for your father. And what, he's binned me off now? For no reason.'

I edged out and saw Patrick, hoary with drunken anger. Van had her arms crossed, smoking from a cigarette holder.

'I'm just his daughter.'

'And I'm gonna be a fucking movie star.'

'You're drunk.'

'It's been you and me here, from the start. Every play, every scene they've given us. I thought you'd have my back.'

'I don't owe you anything, Patrick.'

He grabbed her wrist, pulled her to him.

'Mother?' I said, leaping forward from where I'd hidden myself. Patrick let go of Vanessa, and I got between them, my body close to Patrick's. He loomed down on me, a glint of something in him that wanted to hit me. I gave him the widest lunatic grin I could.

'Calling her mother? You ever listen to yourself?'

'Good Laertes, your temper is too hot,' Vanessa said, adopting Gertrude's low voice. 'Think upon what it is can be done, not what has been.'

I turned back to Van, took the cigarette holder out of her mouth and puffed on it, staring at Patrick, throwing my arm around her shoulder. Patrick swept past us.

'Fucking nutcase,' he mumbled as he burst back into The Church.

A few hours later everyone was hammered. The Boys had coke and people snuck off to the showers to do it. Jonathan disappeared from his spot from time to time but even as the night became looser, we were always aware he was somewhere in the building, watching. We started to lose our characters and people coupled up, either for some fumbling or deep and meaningful chats. Although it was meant to be an exercise, there was a sense it was our last night together. Once presented to the world not as students but as actors, our collective would no longer be our own. We knew it wouldn't take long for us to be torn asunder.

I grew too tired, drunk, bored of attempting to be clever, so I found a sofa and lay my head in Vanessa's lap, perhaps to sleep. We said nothing as she stroked my stubble-hair. It was painfully intimate, more so knowing the room was watching. Patrick glared from the knot of drunken men he'd formed at the far side of the room at Van and I, at Nina too who looked desperate to be anywhere else.

I caught her eye at one point, she looked ten years older,

lost. A memory in me wanted to get up from Van, wrap Nina in my arms and carry her away from The Church. We could go back in time, to the moment we were outside before we saw the cast list, go back to her house, pack our bags and go, somewhere warm where people didn't care who you are, what you'd achieved, where no one cared about Stanislavski, weighed you up against *Taxi Driver*, Olivier's *Henry V.* Up on the stage Jonathan loomed down at me, disapproving, like he could read my wavering thoughts. So, I lifted myself up to sitting, turned Vanessa's face to mine and, with Nina watching, kissed her. Van kissed back then jerked away, shocked more by her reaction than my kissing her. She put my head back in her lap. We'd talked at length about the Freudian element of Gertrude and Hamlet's relationship, done exercises where I'd straddled her on the bed, where we'd imagined her bathing me as a child, but her kissing me hadn't felt in character. Perhaps none of us knew what was real by then. Nina stared at the floor, then walked calmly out. She'd wanted to go anyway, I told myself. Not long after, Patrick followed.

Sometime later, there was a huge crash from outside in the hallway. By the time we got out to see, Vincent and Ben were on each side of Patrick, dragging him out the front doors to take him home. He was shouting at them to take their hands off him, angry but limp, raging through tears. In the changing room, a metal bin had been thrown against something, a huge dent in its side. Laertes, I thought, the anti-Hamlet man of action. Jonathan would be impressed.

We all looked around for our teacher, expecting him to

287

want to check in on the night's most exuberant transgression but he was nowhere to be seen. If he'd gone home, it was odd he wouldn't let us know, but we were used to his idiosyncrasies by then. People broke away from giggling about the bin attack to get changed. The night was over.

My head felt heavy, as if my impending hangover had got an earlier train, so I ventured into the darkened corridors off the main thoroughfare, looking for quiet. Nina found me. She had been crying.

'Guildenstern—' I said.

'Don't.' I swallowed, no idea what to say. 'Are you two, together? Is that why—'

'It's an exercise, we were in character.'

'It doesn't matter,' she said, wrapping her arms around herself, voice like candle-smoke. 'I have this feeling. Like I don't want to be anymore.'

I blinked, taking in what she was saying. I wasn't angry about Patrick anymore. I knew I'd driven her into his arms, I knew I had turned the most joyful presence in my life into a dizzying mess of pain. She looked up, moved towards me, held her arms open.

'Can you just . . . give me a hug?'

I stayed where I was, arms squeezed behind me against the corridor wall.

'Please, just for a moment. I don't know what I'll do.'

I looked into her eyes, despair opening up a portal to her soul. I found myself unable to go to her, couldn't make it better.

Behind us in the main corridor, Vanessa burst out of Room 1, billowing cigar smoke. Nina looked around to see who I was looking at before turning back to me, a light of an epiphany in her eyes.

'It's hopeless,' she said. She smiled at me. A horrible smile, eyes lost in unfathomable bewilderment, before turning and barrelling back into the main thoroughfare.

I walked to the end of the corridor but by the time I got there, Nina was gone. Van sauntered over to me, magnum of champagne in her hand, back to her imperious best after the contretemps with Patrick. I glanced over to see the staff-room had a light on, but whether it'd been left on or Jonathan was still inside, I didn't feel brave enough to find out.

'Stay with me here tonight,' I said when Van got to me.

'Why?' she said, leant against the doorframe, blowing a smoke ring into the air.

'I can't go home.'

'I'm not going to sleep with you.'

'Don't you want to?'

'It's not a good idea.'

I took the bottle out of her hand and twined my fingers with hers. She looked at the rest of our year leaving and gave a small nod.

'Not in there,' she said, meaning Room 1. 'All the Jesus shit will give me nightmares.'

'For in that sleep of death what dreams may come,' I said.

'Definitely not sleeping with you now,' she said, rolling her eyes at me as she bowled past.

In Jonathan's teaching room we found two sofas I pushed together as Vanessa unhooked the dress and found a mannequin on which to hang it. She was wearing a leotard underneath, completely unselfconscious of her near nakedness in front of me. I remained fully clothed.

She found a blanket hung over a stack of chairs, lay down, finishing her cigarette, and submerged herself in it on the bed we'd made. I laid down next to her.

She took my head in her hand and kissed me, our bodies squeezing into each other, before she pulled away.

'Good night,' she said, an alluring half-smile promising more, but not then.

'Night.' I went to take her hand, but she turned over and faced the other way. I took Dustin's skull out of my coat and stared at him until I drifted into sleep.

'Hamlet.'

A voice threaded through my dreams. A dark figure stood in the doorway of the teaching room but when I blinked my eyes open, it was gone. I sat up. Vanessa had wrapped herself around a sofa pillow. Steps echoed far away on flagstones. I lay back, shoulders slumped as I gave in again to sleep.

'Mark me.'

I swung round to the voice, but it was just the wind on the windows. The rhododendron flowers pulsating in the darkness outside like sea anemones. I glanced at Vanessa again, a patch of spit against her pillow making her just imperfect enough to seem perfect. I stood up, walked to the door and followed a faint light into the main corridor. The lockers stood in the darkness like monoliths, the bolt of the main entrance rattling. The light came from the gap under the doors of Room 1. I went over, put my hands on the ridges of the door and pushed it open.

Choral music carried to me, Fauré, from the *Requiem*. The house lights were off but the candles lining the walls were all lit. A black figure stood in the centre aisle looking up at the stage, posture so upright it had to be Jonathan.

On the stage someone I couldn't make out was sat hunched over a table, writing. As I got closer, I saw it was Patrick, wearing the doublet he wore when he was playing Hamlet. He was sweating, hair askew, but so acutely focused on what he was doing he didn't seem at all drunk. I realised it was a character exercise. He was doing one more exercise to convince Jonathan the role should be his. I should have been angry, but he was so captivating that our former rivalry seemed to drift away into the candle-smoke. A spell surrounded him, freezing the moment in time, making it impossible to look away.

Jonathan took a deep breath as he felt me coming forward, he too unable to take his eyes off the stage. Patrick stood, legs pushing back the chair. He folded what he'd written, put it in an envelope and looked at it on the table with such intensity it felt like anything could happen. He could rip it apart, grab it and stuff it into his pocket, set it alight, but after a long moment, he took a few steps back from the desk, almost frightened of the letter.

I stopped in line with Jonathan, separated by a bank of

pews, and spotted black material spilling out through the balustrades of the balcony above the stage. Patrick took the top of his chair in both hands and didn't move for some time. When he did, it wasn't a cheap plastic school chair anymore, his physicality made it solid oak as he dragged it across the stage. Even when he placed the chair under the material, I couldn't see where the exercise was heading. But when he stood up on it, threw his arm through what became clear were not discarded theatre blacks but something he'd tied there, it became plain. Something caught in my throat, I glanced over to Jonathan. He was transfixed.

Patrick checked the noose once, twice. He mumbled a prayer we couldn't hear and turned to face us with a look of resolve barely masking the most radiant vulnerability. All of his bravura, the confidence, his charisma had gone, to such an extent I could hardly recognise him as the Patrick I'd known.

He put his head through the noose and looked down at the floor. I took a deep breath, certain it was about to be over, that he'd break character back into Patrick, take his head out and step down, ready for Jonathan's feedback. But his face remained down and his arms went above him to tighten the knot round his neck, eyes blazing wide. I didn't look at Jonathan but could feel he was enthralled. True transformation, this was the work, what he'd been wanting from all of us, perhaps from every student who had been to the school.

Patrick stood with the noose around his neck for what felt like hours, sweat dripping down his forehead, closing his eyes then opening them, a wild desperation. Then he looked at Jonathan, expectant, in character but I could see a sliver of Patrick emerge too, pleading. I glared at Jonathan, willing him to say something, to stop it, knowing he just had to say 'OK', 'Right', any syllable of anything.

Patrick swayed forward, the chair teetering onto two legs. My stomach flipped like I'd fallen from a great height. Patrick looked to me for help. I'm not sure if he even knew it was me in the darkness, but I did nothing. I couldn't. It was Patrick's exercise, Jonathan was the teacher. He was going to stop it. Patrick was going to take the noose off and step down onto the stage, perhaps be crowned Hamlet then and there. But Jonathan's face remained the same blank canvas we'd spent three years painting with our insufficiencies, what we hoped, what we feared. Patrick went back to Jonathan, whose eyebrows arched slightly as he gave one of his slow, purposeful blinks. Patrick looked up, beyond us both, eyes rolling in their sockets. He stepped off the chair. His body dropped. The swift snap of a butcher's knife cleaving through bone.

I watched. Jonathan and I watched. Something slapped me back into the room. My legs didn't move with my mind, so I stumbled as I bolted forward. I fell, struggled to get up, feet slipping as I ran towards the stage. I bounded up the steps in one and ran towards Patrick, reached my arms forward ready to do, I'm not sure what.

'It's too late,' Jonathan said, long and resonant. And it was. His neck had snapped. A hangman's fracture I would later discover they called it. Instant death. 'Don't touch him.'

I put my hands in my pocket. Machines whirred behind Jonathan's eyes. I waved my arms at him, tried to speak.

'He's gone, Adam. If you touch him, it remoulds the rest of your life.'

Patrick's eyes were open, swollen, but no life in them. Nothing.

'We have to get him down,' I said but didn't move. I looked at the door, desperate for someone to arrive, the police, Aggie, any other human being but Jonathan. 'Don't we. We have to get him down?'

'I'm going to the staffroom,' Jonathan said. He walked up the aisle and pushed open the door. In the dim light of the hall, I saw a sleepy Vanessa, a velvet robe over her leotard, emerging from the corridor where we'd been. She smiled when she saw me. One of the candles blew out as Jonathan closed the door behind him.

Act 5

V.i

She was crouched in a hedgehog-tight ball in the 'six' of a hopscotch court when I arrived at the gates of the school. I watched her body unfolding, arms extending, chin rooted to her chest until she straightened herself out with the wringing effort of a ballerina's port de bras to become the perfect embodiment of an oak tree. She opened her eyes and watched her little disciples, around seven I thought, several stages in the growth cycle behind her, reaching their arms out with imprecise gusto. There was a skinny girl with Dutch braids whose movements were more refined than the others, eyes steely as she unfurled one knuckle at a time. Nina spotted her too and went over.

'Cells split at the end of the twigs, Abigail,' Nina said, 'growing up to the heavens over many, many years.'

Abigail moved her torso up so slowly her body shuddered with the strain. 'Hold it,' Nina told her. 'Don't break it.'

'It hurts,' a voice from deep in the girl's throat.

'The tree is destroying itself and regrowing, that's its journey.' Nina put a hand on her pupil's hip to steady her.

'I can't,' Abigail said, pleading. The rest of the class had come out of their trees and stood mesmerised by the rawness of the moment.

'Up, keep in it, up,' Nina said, creating a bubble for the two of them. Abigail's neck wound up, braids becoming knotty scars, finger-leaves infused with a gentle breeze. 'Stretch above the canopy,' Nina said. 'You need the sun. This is life or death, survival, your entire purpose.'

The girl bit her bottom lip as she strained onto her tip-toes. She was magnificent.

'OK, beautiful,' Nina said. The spell was broken. Abigail returned to the ground, looking at Nina like she was a witch. 'Did you feel it?' Nina knelt in front of her. 'How what you were doing affected everyone?'

Abigail nodded, eyes roaming at the realisation she could shape-shift.

'Miss,' a boy said, noticing me in the shade of a horse chestnut outside the school fence. Nina followed the boy's gaze and our eyes met. She didn't seem surprised. 'Shall I get Mr Walker?'

'That's OK, Ronit.'

I felt a pang like hunger as she walked over to the fence. Her hair was shorter, the curls on top of her head accentuating her heart-shaped face. A thousand images of our years together flashed through my mind.

'Hi Adam,' she said, voice lower than I remembered, a huskiness to it, gravel in syrup.

'I liked your tree,' I said. I expected her to look angry, wary, something.

'I've got another class after this,' she said. 'There are three shelters on the seafront. Down that road and turn right. I'll come down when I'm done.'

I bought an ice-cream at the front. The man in the kiosk recognised me from *Coward*. He said he liked the bits in Auschwitz but wasn't convinced about the rest. I told him lots of people felt the same, didn't like it when the archetypal hero began to unravel. I strolled on the pebble beach of Hythe, a little town west of Folkestone. The wind felt like insect stings so once I'd finished the 99, I settled into the nearest of the three shelters, stomach fluttering.

I told Van I was going. I didn't have the energy to lie. She tried to make me see that, if Nina was measuredbella, it was good. She didn't know we'd been at The Church that night, so there was nothing to be gained from going to see her. But I always thought, somehow, Nina had known I'd been there when Patrick died, that I'd watched him do it and done nothing.

Van came into Room 1 straight after Jonathan left and saw me standing next to Patrick's body. She almost vaulted onto the stage but, as Jonathan had to me, I told her not to touch his body.

'I don't know,' I said to her when she asked me what happened.

'You found him like this.' I nodded, unable to make the sounds to lie but knowing there's no way I could explain the truth. She stood staring at Patrick's body, but I couldn't look at him. I thought he'd speak, ask me why I hadn't

299

stopped it, because we both knew with Jonathan watching an exercise, always wanting us to go further, there's no way he could have stopped himself. Van started crying, tears raking eyeliner down her face. After a few moments she caught me watching, brushed the tears away, wiped the smudges with a tissue and composed herself. It was as if, in that moment, she'd decided emotion wasn't going to be of much use in her life going forward.

'We should take him down?' I asked her.

Vanessa weighed her head in the air, considering. 'Let's—' She escorted me down the stairs, along the aisles, candles dripping wax into molehills on the flagstones, out the door to the staffroom where we found Jonathan at the window, staring into the pitch-black Rose Garden.

She led me to a battered sofa; I sank deep into its cushions. Van paced, eyes darting around as if the answers were hidden in cubbyholes on the walls. It was that night, I think, I became a spectator in everything but my work.

Van wanted to go to the police, call the ambulance, do right by Patrick's family. Jonathan must have known it was a performance because he said nothing, allowed her avowals of the righteous courses of action we should take to dissipate.

'Sit with Adam, please,' he said in a lull. She seemed relieved to be told what to do and sat, allowing her arm to rest against mine. 'None of us expected this,' Jonathan said. He went over to the kitchenette and poured milk into two mugs, put them in the microwave and, thirty seconds later, served them to us. 'Let us consider,' he said, before going out into the corridor, leaving Van and I alone.

'We need to get him down from there,' I said, not moving.

Vanessa reached forward and drank her mug of warm milk.

A couple of minutes later, Jonathan returned.

'The letter Patrick wrote was addressed to "mother",' he said, taking off a pair of leather gloves. In the letter, Patrick had written he couldn't find a reason to be in the world anymore. The sense he'd failed his father had become so overwhelming he couldn't bear it. He told mother not to mourn him but to take heart he was no longer in pain. Jonathan glanced at me after retelling what he'd read. He and I knew it was Hamlet writing, we had watched him, his body, his gait, his whole physicality was nothing like Patrick. He was in character. But with what Nina had told me about his real parents, the letter got the two of us off the hook. Seeing us with the body, Van could have asked more questions. When we'd found him, how long since it had happened? She could have asked about the music, the candles, why the stage looked set up for an exercise, rather than a random collection of leftover furniture. But she didn't.

The most shameful thing was, as I sat muffled by heavy cushions, all I wanted to do was talk about how brilliant Patrick had been in his character exercise moments before, how much I wanted to see that man play Hamlet, how, if I were ever to get the chance to do the role, I had to work far harder, go much further.

Jonathan sat opposite, steepled fingertips rubbing his eyes.

301

'We have an opportunity to choose whether or not we play a part in this,' he said. 'Of course, I worry for the school's integrity, but we shouldn't allow that to be our concern. Your futures, however, are yours to forge, and that should not be taken away from you.' The music in Room 1 stopped, casting the building into silence. But I could hear a creaking sound. Wood against wood. Balustrade against socket. I looked at Jonathan, Vanessa, neither of them seemed to hear it.

Van stared up at a line of black-and-white photos beside the door. Alumnae. Legends. Far younger than we knew them as, but with a steeliness you rarely saw in an actor's headshot. She glanced at me, seemed to look into my soul, before standing up.

'I'm going to go home,' she said.

Jonathan closed his eyes, bowed his head towards the floor. That was how the pact was sealed. I didn't even have to make a decision.

Jonathan went to the hatstand and took his hat, coat, a bag. He put his palms together and pointed them towards us, once, twice. Van pushed open the staffroom door, I stood with her, and the two of us walked out into the hallway. I found myself drawn towards the flickering candlelight under the entrance to Room 1, but Vanessa walked towards the main doors, cleared her throat for me to follow her. We left The Church together and walked to the main road. She gave me a twenty-pound note and hailed a cab. I watched her drive off then walked south for a while, until a taxi stopped next to me and I felt I had no choice but to climb in. I lay on the mattress in my cubicle of the warehouse and heard the creaking of the wood all night, insistent as a ticking clock.

Vanessa had me meet her on the Southbank for a roast on the Sunday. Everyone in Group 28 knew Patrick had died by then and there'd been tentative attempts to get together for a vigil that evening, which Van stifled on the grounds it would be better to find out details first, for fear of offending the family. Any question of our burgeoning intimacy was pulverised by what happened to Patrick, but that aside she seemed unmoved. I was a wreck.

'You look like a wreck,' she told me when I sat down. But that was fine, she said. She suggested, if anyone asked me how I was feeling, that it might be prudent to focus on whether or not the play would go ahead.

'What kind of arsehole would ask about the play?' I said.

'You need to remain consistent with how you've been the last few months, stay in character essentially,' she said, placing her knife and fork together.

The next day the police came to The Church and, as Vanessa had hoped, didn't talk to us individually. They'd spoken to the staff and Jonathan had told them he'd been the last to leave, which was true, and had no idea Patrick was still in the building. He said he felt responsible because Patrick had expected to play the lead in the play, and he didn't cast him.

A policewoman came and talked to us. She was in uniform, a civilian liaison called Claudie. She told us how sorry she was, that it was a horrible thing to happen to a group of young people. She mentioned support services, asked Aggie whether The Conservatoire had any counselling facility – it didn't – and she said she'd make sure we had an NHS contact. It was only as she was wrapping up, she started to ask questions.

'Did any of you suspect Patrick might harm himself in some way?'

'He'd not been himself for a few months,' Ben said.

'Lost his confidence,' Oban added.

'There may have been some stuff with his family,' Vanessa said.

I couldn't believe how easy it seemed to be for her.

'Did he have a girlfriend?'

'Nothing serious,' Victor said.

I couldn't help glancing at Nina. It was only the second day she'd been back. She'd tried to speak to me before Bempe gave us a healing three-hour ballet class the day before. She asked how I was with eyes that knew nothing would ever be the same again. I felt if I spoke to her, I might not be able to stop myself telling her everything. So, I shrugged, said nothing. She walked away, shaking her head.

'He'd had a lot of agents interested,' Anna K said. 'But none of them had taken him on.'

'Your teacher said Patrick didn't get the part he wanted in the play?' Claudie the policewoman said.

'He thought he was going to be Hamlet,' Van confirmed.

'So young, all of you,' Claudie said, casting her eye over us before fixing on Aggie. 'Everything seems so important.'

Seven of us went to Ireland for the funeral at the end of the week after he died. Ben, Victor, Anna K, Oban, James, Vanessa and I. Aggie made the trip too, albeit separate to us. Jonathan did not. The family put us up in an outbuilding on their estate. The father didn't want us there but Patrick's older brother Cillian, the rugby player, had insisted. He came down to see us the night before with a crate of beer, already hammered, and continued drinking at a pace that would have floored any of the rest of us in an hour. I wasn't drinking. I couldn't. Cillian was shorter than Patrick but bigger, the kind of neck only rugby players have. His hair was lighter, but that and a few crunches to the nose aside, the two of them could have been twins. Everyone else crowded round him with condolences but I had to get away. He found me outside smoking half an hour or so later.

'You're Hamlet,' he said when I told him my name. 'Pat mentioned you.' He looked into my eyes, granite jaw tensed. For a moment I was sure he knew what happened. 'He thought you were brilliant,' he said. 'I'm sorry this happened, for you.' He threw a hand on my shoulder, the same beefy machismo as Patrick that always made me feel so special. It was torture. 'I had to get away from that old prick,' Cillian continued, sloshing his whisky bottle at the main house, referring to his dad. 'He was saying you'd have to be mentally deficient to want to prance around on stage. Said it was inevitable.'

I wanted to scream it wasn't, Patrick didn't mean to do it, that it could have been stopped. I could have stopped it.

'What happened to him at that place?'

'What do you mean?'

'Pat loved himself. More than anyone I'd ever met. How does he do something like this? Something must have gone on?'

'Acting gets full on. It's just you up there, the feedback, criticism, it can feel personal.'

He glared at me, one eye closing with the booze. 'Pat said the principal promised him the lead role, did you know that?'

'I didn't,' I said. It didn't surprise me.

'Little brother acted like he had a hide thick as concrete but, under it all—Something, someone, got to him.' He looked out into a row of trees jostling in the wind. Cillian upturned the bottle into his mouth for too long, reddened eyes locked on mine.

'Will you do a bit?' was what he said. 'Of your play. At the funeral.'

'Won't your dad—'

'They need to see what Patrick wanted to do with his life, what it meant. Bit of fucking grace.' I nodded yes, animal scrapes of anxiety in my stomach.

The next day I had the shakes, whether from the countless cigarettes I'd chain-smoked or the circumstances, I couldn't be sure. Vanessa held my hand throughout the taxi ride to the ceremony. The church was small, reeked of incense, the ceremony endless, and mostly in Latin. After an hour and a half, the priest invited me up to speak. I walked up the aisle, didn't introduce myself, nor tell the family how sorry for their loss I was. I just spoke, 'To be or not to be'. It wasn't good. I realised as I spoke, his fractured family glowering up at me, that the stories I'd told myself, about Patrick dying doing what he loved, the transcendence of his transformation in the exercise, it being a form of martyrdom even, were just vain attempts to blind myself to the waste of it and how straightforward it would have been for me to have stopped him.

The wind howled around the shelter, and I thought every figure I saw in the distance was Nina. We did *Hamlet* a month after Patrick's death. I got the lead in a new play, *Eye of a Needle*, at the Royal Court a few weeks after, so I left The Conservatoire before Group 28 graduated. Nina and I weren't in contact at all after that. Alasdair and, within a year, Vanessa, had me auditioning non-stop and I had my first film lined up, a supporting lead in a period thing, as soon as I finished at the Court. Then *Casagemas* happened and everything exploded. I knew the onus was on me to fix things between Nina and me, I'd destroyed it and was the busy one with the world at my feet, but I couldn't. I was too ashamed. But I thought about her constantly, wished she was with me every step of those first few years when everything was new and extraordinary. I wanted to share all of it with her. Perhaps it would have killed her watching me soar as she struggled and, from what I heard from Van, she really did struggle.

Her drinking from that final year crept into something all-consuming after we left. Binge drinking was all the rage at the beginning of the millennium, and there are not many who can binge like a group of out-of-work actors, so I imagine her addiction flew under the radar of whoever it was she was with. She finished at The Church without an agent, so she didn't work. Vanessa tried to help at one point, got her a meeting with the people who cast the soaps at ITV, but she turned up looking like she'd been out all night. I imagine she did it on purpose, a fuck you to Vanessa, to me. Or she really did have no control at that point. The last I heard was that she'd moved to the seaside and was working at a school. I didn't know if she was married, had kids, none of it. I'd stopped asking Vanessa and had lost touch with everyone else from those days, mostly on purpose.

Then Nina was there, wrapped in a huge puffy coat, looking totally different and barely changed at once. I motioned my arms for a kind of hug, but she moved past me onto the bench. I sat and the two of us stared at the seagulls flapping with everything they could just to stay where they were against the wind.

'Glad you've washed,' she said.

'Sorry?'

'My housemate sent me an interview which spent the whole time talking about how you didn't have a bath for two months on your last film, so, just saying, I'm glad you washed before coming to see me.'

'Not washing and losing four stone. People think that's all it is.'

'Such a hard life you have, Adam,' she said with a grain

of bitterness. The space grew between us. A paper wrapper got trapped on the inside wall in front of me.

'In fairness to the person interviewing, I probably was quite pungent at the time.'

Nina gave me a sniff.

'Lynx Africa still?'

I looked at her, wanted to laugh but it didn't seem appropriate. 'Do you like teaching?'

'I'm only a TA.'

'You'd be a great teacher.'

'No, it suits me. Don't need much to live down here. It gives me time to do other things.'

'Like what?'

'Just what I need,' she said. 'To keep my head straight.'

'Sounds nice.'

'Got to "do the work", haven't you?' She looked at me and, although her face was the same as I remembered, I saw the years of drinking in her eyes. The blackouts, the waking up in strangers' beds, the vomit, the euphoria, the self-loathing.

'You look really well. I heard you had a time of it.'

She leant forward, sighed. 'No one wanted me. After what happened with us, then Patrick.' She took a deep breath in through her nose, steadying herself at the mention of his name. 'I needed to work. It was my dream, what I'd trained for, so I tried. Worked my arse off to get myself auditions, all sorts of shit. But when I was in the room, people directing me, after what happened to all of us in that last year, it all seemed rotten. But I tried still, and

309

no one wanted me.' She turned to me with a grim smile. 'I fucking hated you.'

'Did you?' My chest caught at her bitterness. When I saw her in the playground, I felt ridiculous coming down on the train to accuse my Nina of slandering me online, but I could see she was nothing like the girl I'd known.

'Anyone who asked me about you, in the pub and whatever, I told them you were a fraud. All your method stuff, just a load of wank. When we were together—' She stopped herself, shook her head, looked at the floor. 'If nothing else, I was your best friend and you tortured me for it, started treating me like fucking Guildenstern, not worth the shit on your shoe—'

'It wasn't—'

'We were in love, weren't we?'

I turned my head to her, no fear, no doubt in her eyes. She wanted to know the answer. 'Yes,' I said. 'I was in love with you. But Hamlet couldn't be in love.'

'No.'

'I had to cut you out, and it had to hurt. I felt like I had no choice.'

She nodded, a world-weary smile. 'You did. But then you're going to have an Oscar on your mantelpiece, and I've got a bunch of badly spelled Christmas cards, so maybe you made the right choice.'

The two of us said nothing, both took a deep breath, watched the waves colliding.

'I hadn't seen a single one of your films until about ten years ago,' she said.

'What changed?'

She shifted in her seat, got a phone out of her coat pocket, checked it. The sun had broken through a cloud, but Nina remained frosty. 'I wrote to you, second time you got nominated, to say congratulations. Couldn't help myself. I know you got the letter.'

I blew into my hands. They weren't cold but I didn't want her to see my face. I remembered getting the note. One of Van's assistants brought a pile of correspondence to the place I was staying the morning after the nominations were announced. I was loosely with a French musician called Olivia then and she was there as I read through the congratulations.

Nina had spent money on it, embossed card, silver trim. The message was lucid, beautifully phrased. It couldn't have been done when she was drunk. She said how proud of me she was, how much she missed having me in her life and ended saying if I won, even if I weren't to say his name, she hoped I could dedicate it to Patrick.

I was so surprised to see his name, so bewildered by how I should respond, Olivia making us smoothies at the breakfast bar, that I shoved Nina's card under a sofa cushion and left it there when I went off to shoot the next project, knowing I wouldn't return to that condo.

'No? Nothing?' Nina said. 'Again?'

'I don't know what to say.'

'Sorry?'

'I am sorry.'

'You not replying, not responding even, because it had

taken a lot for me to send that to you, it was a Road to Damascus moment. I realised you weren't the love of my life, nor someone who'd betrayed me, you weren't a God, not even my friend anymore, just some actor I'd once known. The bitterness left me and it was like I suddenly had space in my head for something better. I went to see *Coward* the next day. You were so brilliant it made me realise everything I'd told myself I wanted was just me trying to carry on being a kid. It was never the acting bit I loved, it was the people, pissing around, the fun. It was never meant to be work; it's meant to be play. So, I gave up, moved down here, an old schoolfriend Nats lived in Folkestone, and got a job.'

'You seem good at it.'

'I'm really good. I teach a drama club Saturdays and Sundays too. From four years old up to eighteen. It's not why I do it, but I've had a few go off to drama schools. One or two doing OK. One guy, Benoit, got into The Conservatoire.' She gave me a look, hooded eyes.

'Is he still there?'

'Left the year before last,' she said. He would have been a couple of years above Raya but there's no reason he couldn't have fed back to his audition coach what happened. I wrapped my hands around my waist and rocked forward. On the train I'd thought about why Nina would attack me online, attack Jonathan. An ignored telegram, resentment about an acting career unfulfilled, sadness about her new boyfriend's suicide, none of them seemed to be enough. But if she'd heard what happened to Lyndsey, if she'd had inside knowledge of Jonathan's part in pushing Raya to violence, watching me talk about how I owed the man everything, it made far more sense.

'How you were with that girl, Abigail, it was very Jonathan.'

Nina stared out at the sea. I'd expected her to react, to shout me down for comparing her to him. If she was angry enough to campaign against us online, would she be able to help herself?

'I suppose he's up here,' she said, massaging her temple. 'How could he not be? I use a lot of his principles but in the way someone who's a human being would.'

'You don't think he's human?' I asked.

'I don't know. Being that in love with an idea, putting it above everything even though it can never, ever love you back.' She checked her phone again before standing up to wave at a group of women emerging from cars parked on the promenade. She took off her coat to reveal a bathing-suit. 'Come on,' she said.

'What?'

'Not missed a day since I came down. Eight years. I wouldn't break that run if you had ten Oscars.'

'I'm OK.'

'I've told the girls you're coming in. Go in your pants, I've got a spare towel. Your jumper's probably unicorn cashmere, so you'll warm up quick.'

The 'girls' waved at me as they de-robed on the beach in front of us. Nina pulled off her trousers, deposited them in a bag and walked off to join them. I'd played to thousands in the West End, got naked and simulated sex in front of a crew of hundreds; undressing to boxer-shorts in a shelter on the South Kent coast shouldn't have felt as exposing as it did. Nina and her friends didn't wait, so I had an audience as I hopped over jagged pebbles before staggering towards the sea. I launched myself in and the cold punched all the breath out of me. I came up to the surface, skin shredded so my nerves sang from every pore and shouted, a primal scream. Nina burst into laughter and, for a moment, she looked like the girl I loved.

Afterwards I bought the Hythe mermaids – that's what their WhatsApp group was called – coffee and chips at a beachside café. I sat next to Nina, and we laughed at one of the women's stories about her having buried her husband's ukulele in their garden to stop him playing it. There were creases around Nina's eyes as she smiled that weren't there before, but we could have been back round the table with Liv and Tommy. It felt like I was being allowed to live a parallel life for an afternoon, fulfilling the fantasy I daydreamed in location trailers, first-class cabins and over-perfumed hotel suites, blissful and excruciating. The time crept on until I had to leave for the train that would take me back to London, then to LA and the glory of an Oscar-winning future I'd yearned for for twenty years. I didn't want to go. I wanted to stay with Nina. But she wasn't asking me to. I stood up, gave hugs, kisses on cold-blushed cheeks. I told Nina to stay but she insisted she take me back.

'Thanks for doing that,' she said as we walked side-by-side. 'Loved it.'

'Julie, the one who offered you her hat, she identifies as a cineaste, nearly wet herself when I told her we went to college together.' She paused, turned to me. 'I'm not angry with you anymore, Adam.'

'OK.'

'I'm flattered you thought it was me, though. Putting the stuff about you and Jonathan on the internet.'

'I didn't—'

'Why else would you have come to see me?'

I said nothing, we kept walking.

'Fifteen years or so ago, I could have, maybe. I was that hurt. But now I try not to think about that part of my life.'

'I thought, you might have seen *Woodsman*, the ending and—I always thought you blamed me for Patrick.'

Nina pulled her hat further down over her wet hair and hugged her arms around. The taxi rank where I was dropped off came into view, a people carrier bound for the train station there waiting for me.

'You fossilised in that final year. Every grain of humanity replaced with stony conviction. I didn't watch *Woodsman*, couldn't, but I know about the scene and honestly, it's terrible to say, but it didn't surprise me you used Patrick's death, that you changed the script even. The boy my parents took in, the boy I slept next to, kissed, who I wanted to lose my virginity to, would never have done it, but he died that year as well.'

We faced each other at the end of the promenade as seagulls fought over an ice-cream cone. Nina shook her head, chin quivering, the veneer of serenity shattering.

'But I never blamed you, Adam,' she said, 'because Patrick did it because of me.'

'What are you talking about?'

'I broke things off.'

'You weren't together, were you? I thought it was a drunken snog.'

'We went out, a fair few times. Patrick was sweet. I thought he'd be pushy, try to get me to sleep with him, but he was lovely.'

The taxi door slid open behind us. A man in a too-tight suit came round the car, flipped his eyebrows at me. Nina puffed out her lips to stop herself crying, shook her arms in front of her. I grabbed at one of her hands, took it in mine, the years disappeared between us.

'It honestly wasn't about you,' I said, feeling the truth of that night burning up the back of my throat, desperate to come out.

'Everyone was so indoctrinated they thought it was *Hamlet*. But he was into me, or maybe, with what was going on, he needed something to be going right and I just—' She slid her fingers between mine, gripping on to me. 'Then you and Vanessa, right in front of me. I felt so powerless by the end, fucked around for so long, that when Patrick asked why I hadn't come to the pub with him, wanting me to leave with him, talking about making things official, I snapped. I—I was so brutal. It was in the changing room, I've played it in my head so many times. All the anger with you, I drowned him with it. Called him a Ken doll, said he was only on the planet to look good in a vest.' She looked down, I thought for a moment she might be sick. 'I said life had been so easy for him, he'd never really become a real person. Wasn't even what I thought of him, I'd got it from you. But then he was dead.'

'Nee—' I squeezed her hands, wanted to scream it had nothing to do with her.

'That was why I couldn't go to the funeral. Having to look them all in the eye. It ravaged his family,' she said. 'Victor told me a few years after. Catholics and suicide, there was so much shame. His dad wouldn't let any of them talk about it. Made it like he never existed. The mum left with his sister; older brothers became estranged from them all.'

'I promise you, look at me, Nina, it wasn't your fault.'

She pulled away from me, threw a hand out telling me to go, telling me I'd come down to this safe, happy place and dragged her back to the thing she'd spent her whole adult life trying to heal from. She turned and walked away.

'Nina,' I said too quietly, knowing the truth could cauterise the wound I'd reopened. But she'd put her hood up and was disappearing towards the grey of an overcast sea.

V.ii

On the train back, I felt like I was below decks in a disaster movie, guilt flooding around me and, with no way out, all I wanted was to give myself to the rising water and find peace. The train stopped at a tiny rural station, and I found myself stepping out onto the platform. Nina blamed herself for Patrick. She'd dedicated her life, wasted it, trying to recover from what happened in that last year. Having her heart broken, but so much worse, believing herself responsible for the suicide of our talented, beautiful friend. If I had told them Patrick killed himself doing an acting exercise, Nina would have been spared decades of self-loathing, strangling her dreams, plunging into an addiction she'd had to realign her very being to fight. But I still hadn't told her. She'd held on to my hands like she was hanging over the white cliffs, tears in her eyes, and I still hadn't told her. I think it was that which sent me to the newsagent opposite the station, had me buy a bottle of vodka, sit on a kerb outside and, without pausing to consider whether I should, led me to drink most of it. Having not touched a drop for nearly twenty years, I was very quickly shitfaced, so the exact details of the following few hours come back to me somewhat fragmented, but much later, Amber appeared in front of me and bustled me into an enormous town-car. I couldn't understand how she'd found me, later worked out it must have been the GPS on my phone.

We drove for a while and ended up on a motorway, though I could barely focus on the cars flying past my window. At some point the driver pulled into a petrol station to fill up. Amber had headphones in, though I couldn't make out any music coming from the MiniDisc player nestled in her lap, just what sounded like an occasional high-pitched giggle. I stared at her, her wisps of hair straggling forward as they always did. She'd been so kind getting me in the car, so lacking in judgement, so unlike Van had ever been, as if I were a child battling a nasty illness rather than a drunk middle-aged man. Amber wasn't much older than we were at The Church, all potential, hope, a life she could forge stretched ahead of her, and she was choosing to spend it babysitting me. Patrick died, Nina's life was a living death, who knows what Van's could have been if she hadn't been chained to me by our secret, and me, Nina said I died that year too. Something about my not deserving the care of this bright young woman, or perhaps not wanting to be responsible for wasting yet another life made me blink myself to some lucidity and turn to her.

'Amber,' I said. She didn't hear. I touched her shoulder. She turned, smiled as she took her headphones down from her head.

'You OK, Adam?' she said. 'Do you need anything?'

'The boy who died when I was at The Conservatoire,' I said. Amber took a deep breath, leant back into the seat behind her and I told her everything. As the car jetted along the motorway towards London, I told her the story of our time at The Conservatoire, from my first audition for Jonathan to the moment I left The Church that night, leaving my friend's body hanging above the stage, to be discovered by a stranger. I told her how I lied, to protect myself, my career, knowing I could have saved his family, and Nina, so much pain.

When I came to the end Amber said nothing, stared forward at the driver's headrest. The silence became excruciating.

'I'm drunk,' I said, though talking about Patrick had gone a long way to sobering me up. 'Shouldn't have told you that. I can help you find a different job back in LA.'

'Why didn't you stop him, your friend?' she said, voice in the distance.

I didn't know. Having just confessed to standing by and letting a boy die, to lying about it, I couldn't admit it to Amber, but I still didn't know.

'If it had just been you there watching, without Jonathan,' she said, turning to me. 'You would have stopped him, wouldn't you?'

I pinched my eyes in my fingers, took a deep breath in. I should have been able to say yes, emphatically yes, of course I would have stopped him. But I couldn't. I had asked myself, not for years, but I had wondered many times whether I was waiting for Jonathan, but I could never be sure. Even if I had been, what kind of person would that make me? Worse almost, a cipher, a callow pedestrian. After I'd told her a tragic story peopled by characters she'd never heard of, it was the only question Amber wanted the answer to, and I didn't have it.

'Can I listen to something?' I said, a bubble of nausea coming up my throat. She frowned, shook her head a little. 'Music, anything. I just—Have you?'

Amber stopped the MiniDisc player blinking in her lap, took out a disc she stowed in a jacket pocket, and selected something from the front pocket of her bag. She handed me the headphones, barely looking at me, and it struck me I had told someone about what happened. Someone who had nothing to do with The Conservatoire, who didn't know anything about Group 28, knew what Jonathan and I did. As I told her, it felt like I was dragging a great weight off my shoulders but the reality of what I had confessed to filled my head like mustard gas.

Then Radiohead started playing. Fucking Radiohead. The cooler members of my year, Patrick, The Boys, went apeshit for Radiohead. I always used to think it was a pose. Misery by association, for people who'd never really known it. I closed my eyes, shutting out Amber's disquieting coldness and tried to lose myself in the music. But the recording was fuzzy, the static sound again, seeming to grow with the vibrations of the car window. The car clunked over a pot-hole; it became the sound of rope-curtain thudding against balustrade. The track ended, a click before the next one began.

I remembered the click I'd heard before the voice that

night in the cabin, the buzzy static on the line, the same click in my dreams. I blinked my eyes open, thoughts surfacing through drunkenness, as I realised the voice on the end of the phone that night wasn't a ghost. But it was Patrick.

I lurched forward in my seat, reached for the button for the screen to the driver and lowered it.

'We need to go to The City,' I said to him.

Amber glared at me, about to protest, tell me we had a flight, that Van would fire her. 'No more Nancy Drew shit,' she'd made us both promise, but then she blinked, sat back in her seat, teeth grinding as she stared at suburbia expanding out the window as the car took us up into the financial district.

'*The* Adam Sealey?' the receptionist said from behind her desk in the foyer of an office building decorated like the death star. 'What are you doing here?'

'Cillian Moran?' I said, blinking my eyes further open, feeling far sloppier from the vodka outside the relative safety of the back seat of our car.

'Shit. You just said. Lol!' She grabbed her phone, flustered. 'Buzzing up.'

While we were on the radio, measuredbella had talked about the friends and family. I'd bumped into Patrick's brother Cillian, the rugby player, twelve years or so ago in a restaurant in Smithfield. I hadn't seen him since the funeral but he seemed delighted by my success and apologised when he told me he worked in insurance. It was a punt he still worked at the same company, but it seemed he did.

'He's in a meeting,' the receptionist said. 'His assistant will let Mr Moran know when he's out.'

'I'm back to LA this evening,' I said, swallowing, before turning on a Hollywood smile for her. 'I bet you could get him down for me?'

'I'll try,' she said with a flirtatious smile, getting back on the phone. She pointed me towards a cluster of brightly coloured pouffes. I looked for Amber as I crossed the reception area before remembering she'd stayed with the car to make sure it didn't abandon us. I sank into the seating, massaged my temples to try and head off the headache I could feel rumbling towards me.

'Adam.' Cillian was stood there. I don't know if I'd nodded off for a moment, but no time seemed to have passed. Although the muscle had softened and his bulk now strained against an expensive suit, he still looked so much like Patrick I had to look away to gather my breath. I stood up, unsure whether to hug or shake hands, but Cillian's arms stayed by his side. He looked me up and down and I realised how dishevelled I must look and panicked for a minute that he might have been able to tell I'd been drinking. 'Do you need coffee?' he said, reading my mind as he sat opposite, too big for the pouffe he was on.

'Thanks.'

He signalled something to the receptionist and turned back to me with a short sigh. People are usually pleased to meet me, but Cillian seemed wary. He'd seen the stories online, perhaps seen *Woodsman*. What must it have been like to have watched a man who spoke at your hanged brother's

323

funeral in a scene with a different body, cutting it down, holding it as Cillian must have wished he could have done.

'They said you were in a rush?' He scratched at his stubble.

'Got a flight in a few hours.'

'What is this, Adam?'

'The story, the papers writing about what happened. I wanted to see how you and your family were?'

'Are you playing someone who's brother has topped himself? Want to get in my head, have a nice little toss around?' This man was nothing like the Cillian who'd cried on my shoulder at the wake telling me he'd spent every minute in the gym, on the training pitch, ignored his brother's calls, missed his brother's shows, so he could get to play for Ireland. And even though he had, that it now meant nothing. That his brother was gone and a handful of games for his country no one would remember was the price he'd paid for it. No, this man was angry, rage bulging with his flesh against the tailoring as he leant forward.

'I never meant to disrespect Patrick's memory,' I said. 'It wasn't me who changed the script of the film.'

'Then why are you here?'

I looked into his eyes, the same bottle green as his brother's, and I heard the thud of the theatre curtain slamming down against the balustrade. Over his shoulder, I saw Patrick's body swinging from one of the glass balconies. I closed my eyes tight, trying to blink away the image of the corpse.

'Um, sorry, sorry,' I said, slurring a little, opening one

eye to see the body had gone. 'Listen, um, Cillian. There's a good chance I'm going to win an Oscar,' I said, trying to make the sentence seem as normal as I could.

'Good for you.' He adjusted his cuffs as if preparing for a fight.

'I was wondering,' I said, clearing my throat, trying to focus on what I'd come here to do. 'If you would mind me mentioning Patrick. If I win.'

'In your speech?'

I nodded. The receptionist arrived with a tray of coffee. She poured us a cup each, pot shaking a little in her hand, left a milk jug on the Perspex table between us and gave me a shrug before going back to her desk.

'Twenty years,' Cillian said, gripping his face in his large hand. 'I've spent half my life, every single day, trying not to think about Patrick.'

'I've been reflecting, that if he hadn't done what he did—'

'Hung himself, Adam,' Cillian said in a clenched whisper. 'Let's not dice with euphemisms. He hung himself.'

I took up my cup, drank half down despite it being too hot.

'His death,' I said. 'Perhaps it drove me to work as hard as I have. I thought it might be time to remember him.'

'You're not listening, we don't want to remember him. We want to forget. But we can't. You've already got journalists calling us all up, asking us what happened, why he did it, what we thought of that school, if you two were friends or enemies or lovers, dredging through the mud like fucking gannets.'

'You did think though, didn't you, you blamed The Conservatoire?'

'I've blamed that school, my dad, Rory, myself. I've spent thousands on therapists. But no one made Pat do it. No one. It's on him. So, whatever this is—' He waved his hand towards me. 'Whatever reason you'd have for talking about Patrick, whatever PR shite you're going with. Just don't. If not for me, then for my mother, she—She couldn't take it.' He poured most of the milk jug into his coffee and took it up in his fist, looked to the exit, willing me to go.

'Is your mum OK?' I asked.

Cillian looked at the floor for a while, sighed then sat up, aware he had to continue to play the role his workplace expected of him.

'The old man died last year.'

'I'm sorry.'

'Liver was full of holes. Drink was always going to get him but, after Pat died, he grabbed the bull by the horns.'

'How's your mum, how's she managing?' I remembered Patrick's mum as kind, where he got the twinkling eyes from. She was slim, face drawn with wrinkles and had a nervous smile. His dad was a huge guy, the two of them a reverse Jack Sprat situation.

'They weren't together, split two, three years after Patrick but, father of her children. Not sure how well she's doing.'

'I didn't know they'd split up.'

'He didn't leave her much choice.'

It drove the father to drink, the mother to leave the

father, the brother to work in insurance. The ripples of what I did had turned into high-walled waves. I drank the rest of my coffee, wishing it was something stronger, head beginning to throb.

'Do you go back home at all, to see her?'

'Rory's the only one of us still in Ireland.'

The epiphany in the car, that one of his brothers might have been measuredbella, now felt like another sodden fancy, but, with Cillian shuffling his body up off the pouffe to leave me, I felt I had nothing to lose asking him.

'Did he ever record anything?' I said.

'What?'

'Did you guys and Patrick ever record anything? When you were kids.'

'Like films? Not sure we had a camcorder.'

'Voice recordings, maybe a dictaphone or something.'

Cillian frowned, took a deep breath, mind going somewhere else.

The voice from the cabin didn't sound like it was a real person speaking through the line. I'd spent countless days in studios over my career re-recording dialogue, ADR it's called, so I was attuned to listening to recordings, clean audio, messy phone lines. The call had too much static, but the voice was distorted too, detached. And there was the click, the click that came each time. It'd been in my dreams too, a click as if someone had pressed a button. Twenty years ago, we didn't have phones in our pockets that could take pictures, shoot movies, make voice notes. We had camcorders, tape recorders, dictaphones.

'You want to hear his voice again?' Cillian said. 'This is for a movie, isn't it?' He rattled down his coffee cup and stood, bashed his shin on the table.

'It's not—Honestly, I—I remember him saying something about playing around with a dictaphone as a kid. I used to do the same.' I was making it up as I went, sensing from his reaction there was something, because there had to be or I had stepped over the edge into complete insanity. 'And, yeah, I did want to hear his voice again. Being back here brought it all back and—' I flicked the nuclear button and made myself cry. I covered my head with my arm, felt Cillian panicking, putting an arm on me, half to comfort, half to cover me from embarrassing him at his office. 'I'm sorry,' I said, composing myself. He sat and a silence breathed between us.

'Aoife,' he said. 'Patrick and Aoife used to do radio shows. She was mad on them. Rory and I thought it was dead embarrassing.'

'Who's Aoife?'

'Our little sister.'

I looked at him, blinking for a moment. The sister, she was much younger, we never knew much about her. But Nina had mentioned it. Patrick's mother left Ireland with their sister.

'I didn't meet her,' I said. 'When we came over.'

'Father didn't let her go to the funeral. She was seven, begged him, but he said she was too young. He didn't let her say goodbye. I always thought it was what led to mum leaving. Old bastard wouldn't let any of us talk about Pat. Mum was used to doing what Father told her, but Aoife couldn't, and it was her that drove the two of them apart.'

'They were close? Aoife and Patrick.'

'Two youngest, she idolised him.' Something caught his attention, and he looked behind me. I turned and saw the receptionist holding a phone receiver, making eyes at him. Cillian brushed his trousers and stood.

'We all just want to be able to get through the day. All any of us want.' He extended his hand to shake but I wasn't paying attention. A sister who idolised him. The truth was dangling above me. I looked to the balcony behind Cillian, but Patrick wasn't there. I tried to picture a younger Patrick, a female version, in Room 1 with me, looking up at the empty space where her brother should have been. A life crushed by tragedy before it had even begun. I could almost see her.

Cillian seized my hand and squeezed it like he needed to end our encounter without bitterness. There was something forever jaded in his face, a dullness in the eyes, a downturn of the mouth I recognised. I had an arresting moment of déjà vu because I felt I'd seen it that day. Cillian put one of his bearish hands on my shoulder before moving swiftly back towards his office but my mind was racing towards the answer, sweeping away the swathes of drunken fog.

'The radio shows,' I said, stopping Cillian. 'What did Patrick and Aoife record them on, a dictaphone or—?'

His bludgeoned features pinched in confusion.

'We never had one, no. Pat had one of those, ah,' he said, struggling to remember. 'They don't have them anymore, like cassettes but—'

'MiniDiscs,' I said.

'That's the one.' He gave me a nod, turned and continued back into the office. I walked out the front entrance and looked at my town-car, hazard lights blinking on double-yellow lines, windows fully tinted.

MiniDiscs. Amber. I couldn't wrap my head around it. Could Amber be Aoife? Patrick's baby sister? Her eyes were green, but nothing like Patrick's sparkling gems, nor even Cillian's. The red in her hair, her colouring . . . Celtic for sure, but she was Scottish, I'd never heard anything in Amber's accent to make me doubt it. Where Patrick owned every room he walked into, Amber was so unassuming Van and I would often forget she was sat in a car with us. But the downturn in Cillian's lips from moments before, it was Amber I'd seen. She'd been oddly adamant about staying with the car rather than joining me in the office, saving time on our way to Heathrow. I hadn't even considered that if she was Cillian's sister, she couldn't come in with me. And Amber knew everything. She was on Van's agency system, she knew about working with Jonathan, the script, she had been with her every step of the way . . .

But did it fit? Could it make sense? Amber had been with us from well before the *Woodsman* shoot. Why play a recording of her brother down the phone to me the night I cut Louanne down? Could that have been what started it? She had been there, watched me cut down a hanging corpse, an image like her dead brother, again and again. Had the trauma of reliving it made her snap?

But after that, why nothing for nearly a year, and then the comments? If she wanted to hurt me, Jonathan, avenge her brother's suicide, why not share that story with the world straight away? Unless she didn't know it. I walked down the steps and crossed over to the car, paused with my hand on the door handle before opening the car door. Could it really be her? The young woman I'd sat with on the plane, in countless cars, who'd brought me water bottles, fruit salads I didn't know I wanted, the woman who'd held an umbrella over my head to keep my hair looking just-so. The person whose quiet, undemanding presence had been such a salve to me in the weeks coming out of *Woodsman*. Could all of that be a fiction?

I took a deep breath and opened the door, eyes closed, not wanting to see, but when I opened them, she wasn't there. A single MiniDisc rested on the seat where she'd been, I reached in and read the label: *Radiohead*, ancient biro on yellowed paper. The MiniDisc was Patrick's. Her brother's. Then it came back to me, the blinking light on the device in her lap as I told her what happened to him, and the other disc she'd placed with unusual care in the top pocket of her denim jacket. She knew what happened to her brother now. I'd told her in excruciating detail and she had it all on tape.

V.iii

I nearly missed my plane. Shock-addled from discovering who Amber really was, clearly still drunker than I thought, I spent half an hour searching for her around Cillian's office, thinking, praying, she might just be hiding from me. But she was gone. I spent the car journey trying to get onto news websites on my ancient phone, assuming Amber would have uploaded the recording to social media as soon as she left me, but, after they had hurried me through the airport onto the plane and into my palatial seat, even moments before take-off, it still hadn't happened. I waited for the seatbelt signs to darken, locusts in my stomach, feeling like I was sat outside the headmaster's office waiting to be expelled. I knew I had to tell Vanessa.

'Are you pissed?' she said, almost doing a double-take as I sat down in the empty seat next to her. She studied my face, saw something cataclysmic in my eyes, and her instant anger fell away. 'Oh fuck, what have you done?'

I told her.

'She had an Irish fucking passport,' she said afterwards,

index fingers tracing the sinus ley-lines on her forehead. 'I've got a copy of it on file with her contract. Collins! Her surname was fucking Collins. Michael Collins. That's Irish as fuck.'

'Her mother's, I guess.'

'But—How did I not see it?' She looked above her, staring for the answer in the air vents in the cabin roof before turning to me, shaking her head. 'I'm so sorry.'

'Why are you—'

'I employed her. Fucking welcomed her in.'

'Do you think,' I mumbled, 'do you think she was planning, all along, when she got the job?'

Van waved her hand at me, dismissing my question as irrelevant. She turned back to the cabin, seemed to be looking amongst the mostly empty other seats for a solution. She looked at her leg, pushing invisible shapes over it as if she were playing a game of chess.

'What's she going to do?' Van said. I was about to try to answer but she stood up, headed towards the deck where the air hostesses were. I watched her showing them her phone, asking to use theirs. When they said she couldn't, she pointed them towards me. One of them recognised me, turned to the other, her superior. Eventually, Van was admitted into their area, a curtain drawn over them all and I had the intrusive thought of Hamlet stabbing Polonius through a curtain.

I felt paralysed in my seat, helpless. Although I should have been grateful for Van jumping into action, trying to save me once again, I found myself conflicted as I imagined her speaking to Delilah, the two of them letting loose their flying monkeys on twenty-something Amber, Aoife. She lost her brother, her hero, to suicide when she was a child, watched it tear her family apart, mark her indelibly before she'd had a chance to form any kind of identity.

I tried to make sense of what Amber had done. She had Patrick speak to me on the last night of the *Woodsman* shoot, then found me in the bath, then nothing for nearly a year. Until after the roundtable, when measuredbella first spoke up, hinting at some impropriety involving Jonathan, who I'd just lauded to the world. Then again, after the BAFTAs, revealing we'd changed the script to make it more like her brother's death, again invoking his words, *How could you?*, which had played in my dreams. But had they? I remembered the indent on my hotel bed, the feeling someone had been in the room with me. Had she been playing his words to me in my sleep? But what was her endgame? She had it now, a confession. But what was she doing to do with it? What was she ever trying to achieve?

I watched an air hostess bring another passenger a whisky and thought about asking her to bring me seven or eight vodkas, which I could stow in my pocket, but managed to stop myself. Whatever was to happen on our arrival at LAX, presumably the end of my career, diving back into drunkenness was unlikely to help. I lit instead on the screen in front of me. Movies, sanctuary. I scanned the catalogue, went into the list of classics, and found him, Brando, *Mutiny on the Bounty*. When I'd seen it before it seemed enchanting that the bull-headed, angry young man of *Streetcar* could transform himself into a dandyish British naval officer, but as I watched this time, everything he did seemed mannered, ridiculous. I started to hate him for what he'd made me believe, the example he'd given me to follow. I was about to turn it off when one of the hostesses came over to me with two white pills in a silver dish. Van had migrated back to her seat, on her laptop, and turned to indicate the pills had come from her and to take them. I swallowed them dry and went to sleep, thinking of egoist men arguing in tricorn hats.

When we landed there was nothing, no news had broken, though the halls of the airport still felt to me like the main street in a Western, empty yet thrumming with threat. When we got in the car, Vanessa finally explained what she'd been doing on the plane.

 'I didn't want to say until we'd landed in case the shit had somehow made its own way into the wind tunnel, but when she joined the agency, Amber signed a cast-iron, balls-to-the-wall NDA, standard contract stuff. So, if she speaks to the press, writes anything online, posts anything that could be construed as confidential, like a recording of a client, while being under my employment, she's fucked. Financially, reputationally, any fucking way, essentially. Delilah's informed every editor on the East and West Coast about a disgruntled employee threatening us, mentioned the NDAs, litigation, etcetera. UK-wise, the team should be able to get an injunction if anyone contacts us to say they have the story. I have sent Amber, whatever she's called, a

335

brief and, in the main, polite email, which indicates all of this to her.' She took a deep breath in, sighed out, somehow looking pleased.

'She might not care,' I said.

'I'm not with you.'

'Her brother died. She holds me and Jonathan responsible. The Raya thing, Jonathan's involvement, only proves it to her.'

'All we did that night is walk away,' she said. 'If Amber decides to be a fucking moron, which it appears she certainly isn't, and chooses to spend the rest of her life in court by leaking the tape, we say you were barely twenty, a student hopped up on melodrama, Pro Plus and supermarket gin. We were scared, Jonathan even—well, perhaps not, but that's his lookout. It doesn't look great, true, but all we did was walk away.'

I took a breath in. She still didn't know the truth, the bare truth I'd confessed to Amber. But as our car thumped past palm trees, California sun fighting through the tinted glass, I couldn't find the words to tell her.

There were ten days until the Oscars and although in Van's mind the Amber issue was settled, I spent every minute waiting for the bomb to drop. I sleepwalked through a fog of jetlag, flashbulbs and people with microphones asking who I was going to be wearing. I smiled, shook hands, humbly received every awe-filled pronouncement about my talent, my craft, my mastery, as the reality of what Amber was going to reveal spun in my head like a rodent on a wheel. Everywhere I looked, every crowd, every screening audience, the rivulets of pedestrians passing the car, I saw Amber turning to stare at me. The slight downturn of the mouth I'd only noticed when I'd seen it on Cillian, the green eyes, though now they were Patrick's coruscating emeralds staring at me, dripping with malice. But she was never there. Van kept trying to contact her but received no response. She had disappeared. Amber, Aoife, measuredbella had become a ghost. I knew it wasn't over. Ghosts don't leave unfinished business.

But as the night approached, I got so immersed in the role of the grateful veteran, being bused from meet-and-greet to luncheon to screening, in a haze of proffered water, cut-fruit and terrarium-boxes of salad, I found myself forgetting the sword dangling over my head as my desire to win the Oscar flared back into the roaring bonfire it had been before. An Oscar. Mount Olympus, Valhalla, the indelible mark of greatness. I was the favourite. Everyone around the campaign was always so pleased with me. Vanessa kept touching my arm.

On the morning of the ceremony, our condo was awash with bodies. A woman wearing a clinical outfit stood bereft in the hall for about two hours, until I realised she was there in case I wanted a massage. I sent her home with a couple of fruit baskets. I tried to send the barber away too, but Van overruled me. He clipped my hair short, my burgeoning beard into clear lines. 'Grizzly bear with a heart of gold,' I heard Van briefing someone at one point. I tried to stay out of everyone's way, but they kept finding me to have something done to my nostrils, to try on watches,

suits, at one point a sash, which stank of cultural appro-
priation so was dismissed. I wanted to be anywhere but
around these people, who seemed so amped by the occasion. I was surprised I didn't find cases of energy drinks or
troughs of cocaine littering the kitchen island. I missed the
grounded presence of Amber, her old soul and throwback
style, personality frozen in the past by her brother's death.

About midway through the afternoon, I'd shifted to the
pool to avoid the opinions stinking out the condo and, as
a man was doing something to my feet, I spotted Van by
the back wall glaring at her phone, the nonchalant triumph
in her eyes replaced by something else. She disappeared
inside and for the rest of the time before our car was due
to arrive, I couldn't help feeling she was avoiding me. I
sat through good-luck video calls from my director Bryce
without her; with the whole production team of *Woodsman*;
an extensive call with Delilah in which she, very subtly,
managed to remind me of her so far unblemished record
at the Oscars. Emmy didn't call, she wasn't even attending.
Filming a disaster movie in Chile.

Van and I rode over to West Hollywood together. She
was using masking tape to remove dust from my velvet
jacket and I noticed her fingers were shaking.

'You OK?' I said.

She looked up, blinked a few too many times. 'You should
know, Delilah has arranged a few of her own people, security, to be there tonight.'

'What's happened?'

'Nothing. It's belt-and-braces. Amber could ... it's

possible if she were to want to make a statement . . . tonight would obviously be a very public place.'

'Why are you saying this now? You told me you'd got rid of her accreditation, spoken to people at the Academy. She can't waltz in.'

'Exactly. Exactly. Just, if you do see her, if anyone mentions they've seen her, tell me, straight away. I've got a big red Batphone to Lyndon, the head of security for the whole shebang. They can put her in the hold,' she said, not quite selling the joke. 'Anyway, sorry, just a lot at stake,' she said. 'But you need to be relaxed. Did you see the massage woman?'

'Sent her home.'

'Dickhead.'

'I'm fine,' I said.

She raised an eyebrow at me, sat back in her seat and went back to the refuge of her phone. She was right about what was at stake. As it became more likely we'd win, Van started to get scripts and messages from directors who'd never countenanced working with me before. Apple and Disney wanted me for their upcoming slate, Marvel wanted to talk to us about an art-house origin story of some super-villain, not work I necessarily wanted, but a level of interest I thought I would never have again. Nominations had never stopped the industry thinking me an oddball, but it seemed having my name read out as the winner might. I'd spent so many years seeing an Oscar as an endpoint, it felt thrilling to think it could be the beginning of something, the guarantee of an enduring career that a year before seemed to

339

be wrecked on the rocks of public opinion. But, if Amber's tape were to surface, it wouldn't be rocks I'd have to worry about, they'd be out for me with torches and pitchforks.

When our car pulled into the motorcade waiting to drop us off at the entrance of the Dolby Theatre, Van leant over, gave me an unexpected kiss on the cheek, and exited on the side opposite the hordes of press. She wasn't coming to the ceremony as my date. The team thought attending with my manager sent out the wrong message for how they wanted me to be seen by the industry moving forward. No longer the damaged boy with his handler or his teacher, I was a fully formed man. I had no wife, no girlfriend, no mother to go with. I would be winning my Oscar as I deserved to, alone.

My car came to a stop, someone opened my door and it was as if the thousand camera flashes screamed 'Action', because as soon as I'd swung my leg onto the road, any thoughts about Amber's tape were erased. I was back in the role of Oscar frontrunner, raised hands to the crowd, pumping my fist in triumph, prayer poses in humble thanks. I went further in the character that night, puffed myself up with an old Hollywood insouciance I'd never worn before in public. The crowd ate it up like greedy children. I prowled the red carpet triumphant, the once dissolute prince at his long-awaited coronation. I leant into the interviewers with genuine interest as they asked questions, which allowed me to trot out platitudes about magic, lineage, 'standing on the shoulders of giants', the annual deluge of hot air that keeps the Hollywood machine afloat. I made jokes. Good jokes. The female reporters cocked their heads at me with a novel interest, male ones strained to shake my hand, stars I knew, stars I didn't, patted my shoulders, took my elbows in their hands.

Carl Dillane hugged me just as he was leaving the main photocall area, which the cameras adored. We'd known each other for ten years, he was also a losing nominee the first time I was at the Oscars, but this was the first time I'd been treated to one of his world-famous Arkansas embraces. It felt like crossing the Rubicon, being grabbed in from the outside into the industry's inner circle. Acceptance. It was almost unnerving.

'Can I be honest, Adam?' he said as he put his arm around my lower back and walked with me through the entrance of the theatre. 'Always had doubts about the method. Felt like us actors made it all up to convince the world we weren't just playing dress-up and doing funny accents, that we were serious people. Maybe we were trying to convince ourselves.' He took his arm away to shake a hand that was thrust in front of him, before replacing it, patting my lower back like I was his son. 'Even the performances. *Raging Bull*, *My Left Foot*, the transformation is impressive, but losing the soul of the actor, becoming the character, I don't know, always had me feeling a little removed.' Faces on all levels glowed down on us. I noticed a young woman with auburn hair on a balcony above. For a moment thought it could be Amber, but her hair was cropped much shorter. 'I went back and watched your other movies, *Coward*, *Casagemas*. Very detailed performances but they never hit me here,' he pounded his chest with his free hand. 'But this picture? I felt like I saw you.'

'A lonely dude in the forest?'

'"Every single one of us is broken", you said it at the BAFTAs. We all learn to hide the darkness, but you found a way to share it with the world.' He stopped, stepped away. 'It moved me, really did, and what else are movies there to do?' He took my hands in both of his. I felt a wring-ing feeling in my stomach at the idea that it was only him seeing the glint of what I'd done to Patrick that had fi-nally touched him. He was still holding my hands, half a dozen bystanders capturing the God-touching-man Sistine Chapel moment on their devices, when my phone buzzed in the inside pocket of my tuxedo. Amber. It had to be Van telling me Amber was there. I thanked Carl for his kind words, called him a legend, before he got whisked away to-wards the auditorium.

I glanced around for Van, assuming she'd be flaring through the masses to get to me, but she was nowhere to be seen. I left the steady flow heading into the hall and se-cluded myself in a corner to check my phone.

It was an email forwarded to me by Van, from Lyndsey Okori. I read quickly, feeling eyes from the bustle trained on me, and felt the blood draining from my face.

Raya had tried to kill herself. She'd stockpiled pills and taken them all at once. Her nurses hadn't found her until the morning, by which time it was too late to pump her stomach. She was in a coma, stable, but in a coma. Lynd-sey had reached out to the ward, and they'd told her that the day before, Raya had begged the nurses to release her to audition for Ophelia in an Actors Church production of *Hamlet*. George Bryant ran the theatre and was an old friend of Jonathan's. Raya had had an audition, Jonathan might have even been in touch with her, gone to see her, encouraged her to make herself available. The details didn't matter. Raya had tried to kill herself.

I spotted Van hunkered with Delilah and some greying fossils from the Academy at the far end of the hall towards the entrance to the auditorium. I caught her eye, she raised her eyebrows, nodded – OK? I went back to look at the email. The original message from Lyndsey had been received at three, around the time I'd seen Van ashen on reading something on her phone. Van hadn't forwarded me the message, there's no way she would, just minutes before I was due to go in for the start of the ceremony. I looked up to the balcony where I'd thought for a moment I'd seen Amber, but now it was empty. She had all Van's passwords, access to the agency's client system. Vanessa wasn't techy, so even if she'd changed them after we found out who Amber really was, it's possible she would have been able to guess her way back in. It had to be her who had forwarded the email to me. But what did it mean? Was it meant to be a threat?

I beckoned Van over. She made her excuses and came over.

'We OK?' she asked, seeing the anger in my eyes. I handed her the phone. She scanned it, blinked before handing it back. She looked around, spotted a room covered by a red rope between two brass posts, pointed me towards it. She removed the barrier, opened the door and walked in, thumbs already busying on her phone.

'She's in my fucking emails,' she mumbled as I arrived at the entrance of what appeared to be some kind of maintenance room, a table, a couple of chairs, hundreds of pipes. 'How do you change the fucking—' She looked up, holding the phone out to me for help, perched awkwardly on the edge of the table, dress too tight to sit. 'Will you close the door.'

I slammed it shut, making the tassels of her toreador jacket flutter in the draft. 'You weren't going to tell me, were you?'

'Jesus Christ, we are so close, Adam,' she said, a growl in her voice. 'We weathered a plague of poison fucking frogs in London. So, let's just—' She mimed lifting a tempestuous pile of air up before pushing it back down with a yogic breath, before going back to her phone.

'She took an overdose!'

'And we can send her something in the morning.'

'Fuck!' I bellowed, face to the ceiling, a primal roar.

Van jumped down off the table, put her phone in her bag, crossed to me and put a hand on my wrist.

'We can do something for Raya. We should. A trust perhaps, get on board with a mental health campaign. I agree with you, it's totally fucked up. But let's—' She indicated the hallway outside, the voices dimming as the crowds went into the auditorium. 'We can do something impactful, but in a few days. I mean, she's not going anywhere,' she said

it with a laugh. She laughed. I put my hand over hers, holding it onto my wrist.

'I watched Patrick kill himself,' I said, looking into her
eyes, measuring each word as if for its funeral.

Van blinked or perhaps it was the strip lights flickering
like the candles in Room 1. The sound of the announcer in
the hallway outside began to be overlaid with the voices of
Fauré's *Requiem*. Van gave a rictus grin, trying to unhear what
I'd said, but I could see the memory playing like a reel of film.
Her in the corridor, looking through the open door of Room
1 to see me stood next to the hanging corpse of our friend.

'Jonathan and I, we watched him do it. He was doing an
exercise, Hamlet writing a suicide note to his mother and
hanging himself. And we watched him do it.'

Her face cycled through shock, disgust, before flatten-
ing into the reality of where we were, the practicalities of
why we were there, surrounded by the mechanics of the
most famous auditorium in the world.

'Why are you telling me this?' she said.

'It wasn't suicide, Van, Patrick didn't want to die. He
was doing an exercise to impress Jonathan and win back
Hamlet.'

'You didn't push him though, Adam, he . . . he did it. He
decided to do it.'

'When Jonathan was watching, we didn't decide anything. We didn't think, didn't have a will of our own. And
he didn't stop him, didn't end the exercise, demand he step
away and not jump off the chair with a curtain tied round
his neck.'

She looked down at her nails for a moment, painted brilliant orange. 'Be that as it may—'

'I stood next to him and watched.'

'You were in the wrong place at the wrong time.'

'Are you listening to yourself?' I growled, raking fingers down my face. I couldn't tell whether what I was doing to Van in that room was just another performance. She grabbed my hands and clutched them together.

'Get yourself to-fucking-gether, Adam,' she said in a tone so surgical I expected to see blood gushing from my wrists. 'You're about to win an Oscar. Everything we've ever wanted. I understand that may bring up all sorts of feelings—'

'I should have stopped him.'

I started to cry, she grabbed my cheek and brushed a tear away with her thumb. 'Twenty years later. Who does it help?'

I shook myself from her and crossed towards the door. The sound outside grew quieter as people took their seats.

'Raya, the girl has an illness, nothing like Patrick. This has nothing to do with you.'

I smiled at her, the incredible ability she had to elide Jonathan's involvement, our complicity, from what this girl had thought she had no choice but to do.

'When she's better, I'll speak to people, get her meetings maybe, get her back on her feet.'

I looked at the floor in front of me. 'I wanted you to know the truth,' I said.

'What you said to Amber, what she recorded you saying. Was that . . . the truth?'

I nodded.

'OK,' she said, almost swallowing her tongue. 'OK. I'm going to go and find Lyndon and, um—'

I noticed a bead of sweat on her top lip as she half-turned, forgetting for a moment how to get out of the room. I thought about telling her I might have seen Amber. The girl on the balcony was the right age, frame, she could have had a haircut. But then there was a knock on the door. Van and I turned back to one another, eyes locked. The door opened a slice, Delilah there, hair startled into an updo, face a little swollen from a last-minute cosmetic injection.

'There you two are!' she said, with false bonhomie. 'We've got to be in place for the start, then we can hide in cleaning closets as much as we need. Ready?'

Van and I pasted on smiles. She turned to me, flicked dust from my jacket that wasn't there and pointed me through the door.

'Just one little surprise,' Delilah said as we passed her.

Jonathan stood next to the entrance to the back room wearing a dinner suit, leaning on a cane. Van glanced at Delilah.

'It was touch and go,' Delilah said. 'I didn't want to tell you because we weren't sure you'd make it, were we, Jonathan?' She raised her voice a little at the end as if he was hard of hearing. 'But you just got in in time.'

I stared at him. He did look old, dark bags under his eyes, face cracked with wrinkles, a feature I hadn't seen on a single person all night. And he was fragile, leaning on the stick too much, skin dust-grey, as if the long-haul flight had sucked all the blood out of his body.

'Jonathan, hi, thanks for coming,' Van said, brusque. 'Sorry to rush but we must go in.'

'We got just one moment for the Mr Miyagi money-shot,' Delilah said, summoning a photographer she'd clearly kept hanging around. Jonathan raised an eyebrow at me, almost amused. I looked at Van, wanted to say no, that there was no way I was having my picture taken with him.

'Shall we do it later?' Van said.

'We got time,' Delilah said, with her legendary steel.

'I had no idea,' Van said under her breath, turning into me. 'But let's—'

I took a deep breath and walked towards Jonathan.

'Look at you,' he said as I got to him. 'All trussed up for market.'

I put my tongue on the roof of my mouth, trying not to rise to his disparagement. I positioned myself next to him, Delilah's fake teeth grinning as she got the photographer in place. Vanessa stood to the side, looking at the two of us like a grenade could go off any moment.

'Not going to put an arm around me?' he said. He would have clocked my coiled rage towards him but I couldn't tell whether he knew about Raya and was mocking me or was just amused by his journey through the Looking Glass to the glitz and glamour he'd spent his life disdaining. The photographer took his pictures. Delilah entreated me to smile. I smiled. The PA announced the doors were closing, Van grabbed me by the arm and whisked me away.

348

I looked back at Jonathan, Delilah propping up one elbow, making sure he didn't fall, hobbling after me towards the entrance to the ceremony, a twinkle in his eye. He nodded, smiled at something Delilah said to him. I'd barely seen it before. He was enjoying himself.

They had me three rows from the front. I had shaken all the hands, had my shoulder slapped, air-kissed Americans, cheek-kissed Europeans, embraced comedy types as I made my way towards the stage. Bryce, my director, vaulted over legs to hug me in the aisle, dragged me back to the production team who I high-fived one after the other. We wouldn't win best movie, original screenplay was a possibility, for costume design we had a decent chance. But I was the banker, the thing that would keep *Woodsman* in the cinema, give it a wider re-release across the US in the following few weeks. A greater audience, a chance for more eyes, more minds to see my performance, to see how I took my friend's death and exploited the tragedy of it without a thought for his family, his loved ones, his baby sister.

I sank into my seat, shook more hands, nodded at stars, smiled as I drank down their adulation though it tasted like bitter medicine. Then the lights dimmed, the praise abated, the ceremony began. During the opening number, I cast around for Jonathan, found him glassy-eyed four rows back from me. My eyes darted around for Amber, expecting to see Patrick's bottle-green eyes lancing me from some dark corner, ready to bring the firmament down on top of me. The host started his monologue, the lights swished over

349

my row, cameras turned on me. I had to find my insouciant smile at his joke about my post-*Woodsman* jockstrap being the source of the next pandemic.

But as soon as the awards began proper, I was out of my seat and straight to the bar in the lobby. I was certain I'd see Amber looking at me from a rail above, but she wasn't there. It occurred to me that forwarding me the email about Raya must have been her last act. She had seen Van and Delilah at close quarters, she knew how scary they could be when under threat so, of course, their threats of a life in court would have been enough to frighten her off from exposing me. Making sure I knew how culpable the man I'd supported was in Raya nearly losing her life, just as her brother had lost his, just at the moment I took the stage for the crowning moment of my career – that would have to be revenge enough for her. I was safe, but part of me wished I wasn't because every time I thought of Amber, her question to me in the back of that car, almost the last thing she'd said to me before she disappeared from my life, had haunted me almost as much as Patrick's recorded words. The same question he'd asked almost. 'Why didn't you stop him?' *How could you?*

From where I'd stationed myself, concealed at the far end of the bar away from the waves of guests escaping the tedium at each ad-break to get more champagne and artisan popcorn, I saw Jonathan emerge, brushing off one of Delilah's entourage. I watched him glancing over at the main men's toilet, brow knitting at the sight of a large group of young, muscular actors, the Marvel brigade, laughing too loudly at their own jokes by the entrance. He peered at a disabled toilet by the front but there was a crowd there too, managers holding it for their venerable clients. I put down the soda water I'd filled with crushed maraschinos and went to him.

'Come upstairs,' I said. 'No one uses the dressing rooms during the show.' He looked embarrassed, bodily functions were never something that had come up between us. He had one last look at the lobby but saw he had no choice but to accept my help.

'Thank you, Adam,' he said.

I walked away up the stairs, not slowing to accommodate his age and waited at the top for him, heard the slight pant in his throat as he got to me.

'This way,' I said, opening the door of a dressing room I remembered from the last time I was at the Oscars. 'At the back,' I said as he hobbled past me. Although the long room had been adorned with the signature red plush and gold-plated plastic of the Oscars, it was pleasingly utilitarian, a world away from the *Architectural Digest*-designed Green Room on the floor above. And it was empty. I looked at the monitor showing the ceremony, an hour or so still from Best Actor. I looked at my fingers on the door handle, gripping so hard they had turned white, veins popping like I'd never had a meal. I thought of Raya, skeletal in bed, fed by a tube; Nina throwing up bottles of red wine in pub toilets for years; Patrick's eyes protruding too far from their sockets from the pressure of the curtain on his neck. I locked the dressing-room door from the inside and sat down in the middle of the row of chairs facing their individual mirrors.

'I wanted to say thank you,' Jonathan said, emerging from behind the wall hiding the toilets and shower cubicles, wiping his hands on a black hand towel. He didn't seem at all surprised at my glaring at myself in the mirror in the empty room. 'For your kind words at the BAFTAs. For the actor, these gongs can be incredibly toxic. Not winning anything when you were younger was one of the more fortuitous parts of your development.'

I pulled a tissue out of a box in front of me, wiped sweat from my eyebrow, balled it up in my fist.

'But the recognition you gave me felt . . . rather wonderful.' He had a smile in his eyes so uncanny I had to look away. 'Like ice-cream, not good for you, but probably alright for children and the elderly.'

'The script,' I said. 'You suggested the change, didn't you?'

Jonathan's eyebrows rose to his head, he placed the towel on a nearby table and crossed to me, resting his weight on the chair next to mine. Van told me it was her but from what Emmy had said about her *Measure for Measure*, how Jonathan had clearly coached Raya until she was waving a knife at strangers in Southend, that even if Van made the final suggestion, it would have been him who led her to the idea.

'Did you know I'd ask for you to work with me on it? Is that why you did it? Feeling abandoned by The Conservatoire, you wanted to stir up what happened so I'd be forced to bring you out of purgatory?'

'Hmm,' he said, sitting down next to me, ironing out the folds in his forehead with his hand, not surprised I wanted to spend the evening in some kind of contretemps. 'Very few people in life are chess-players, working out several steps into the future in the hope things will play out as we wish. Although life is brutally random, people, most people, remain largely consistent. Their motivations are usually what they have always been.'

'What, so you did it for the work?'

'The film, yes, but to a greater extent your work, moving forward. You were in absentia, stuck in a funny farm, stagnating. The despair you felt on the diving film came from the sense your life up to that point, your method, your whole meaning, might have become redundant. I needed to show you, for the sake of your audience, that you were incorrect.'

'It's not my method,' I said.

'The method itself is irrelevant. It's a commitment, an understanding that we as individuals are less important than what we can give to others. The Greek actors weren't stars, their audiences didn't worry about their emotional wellbeing. They understood they were bringing catharsis to their fellow man and that there was no greater service. You always understood that, intrinsically. I couldn't let the world lose it.'

'We spoke, the day they dragged me out of the tank. And you still wanted me to go back to Patrick. It could have killed me.'

'Or given you the conditions to perform alchemy. Icarus, Adam. Immortality always trumps existence.'

353

I took a sharp breath, eyes wild as I stared at him in the mirror. How nonchalantly he talked about how little my life was worth. Or was it that I still agreed with him? I stood up, chair rattling as I did, making Jonathan flinch.

I leant on a table at the back of the room, which held four enormous bouquets of flowers. Someone had stowed a multipack of Advil behind one of the vases. I started laughing as I realised something.

'It was therapy,' I said. 'The thought of me going to therapy. That's what had you meeting Van, demanding the two of you do something to get me back to the coalface.'

Jonathan half-turned in his chair, scratched his cane on the floor.

'Emmy Reed had therapy and you ditched her.'

'Emmy Reed is not an artist because an artist knows they cannot heal, that they need their wounds to drive them. Talking, talking, talking, constantly being told one is good, that you are enough, when we all know, deep down, that it's a fallacy. You would have adored talking to a therapist, thrown yourself body and soul into curing yourself of the exact thing that makes you as extraordinary as you are.' Someone had left their Oscar security accreditation lanyard on the table. I glanced at the picture, a glamorous woman in her fifties I thought I recognised.

'Raya tried to kill herself,' I said.

I turned around, saw his head bowed, looking at the floor.

'Did you hear me? Raya, who you worked with, who you told to stop taking medication a doctor had prescribed, took a bunch of pills and tried to end her life. Jonathan!' My voice cracked, desperate for some response. I took up the lanyard from the table, pulled the branded Academy chord taut like a garotte. The TV screens around us erupted into applause at the end of someone's speech.

'I'm glad she wasn't successful,' he said, still not looking up. 'Raya's good, with what she's been through, she had the potential to be a unique talent. The hope is, she still can be.'

'She nearly died. Patrick did die, trying to convince you he was a "unique talent".' I dropped the lanyard on the table behind me.

'He could have been.'

'What?'

'A truly great actor. I never thought he had it, not really. But that night—He was magnificent.'

I looked at him in horror, appalled he could say it, appalled I understood what he meant. I'd clung on to the idea I was a good person, that I'd dedicated my life to my work to make up for what I did to Patrick, but it struck me that I was, in fact, the monster Jonathan always wanted me to be.

'You should have stopped it,' I said.

He turned around in his seat, took a long breath before darting his eyes directly into mine. 'So should you.'

'I was young.'

'Old enough.'

'You were the teacher.'

'You his friend.'

'Why didn't you stop him?'

I was in front of him now, crouched down at his level. Jonathan looked at a point past me on the ceiling as if he were on a higher plane.

'The same reason as you.' He flipped his eyes to mine, cocked his head at me. 'I wanted to see if he would.'

I took his words in, breath becoming heavy through my nose. My eyes roamed the space around him, unable to look at him as it sank in that he was right. Of course he was right. It wasn't about our rivalry, wasn't about Nina. I didn't intervene because I wanted to see someone pay the ultimate price for the work.

Jonathan heaved himself up from his chair, cane rattling against the chair-leg, muscles trembling with the effort.

'I would change nothing,' he said. 'For what you've become, for the millions of lives you've touched and will continue to touch.'

I thought of Patrick, his family. Of Nina having spent years blaming herself for his death. Of Raya, Lyndsey, Emmy, even that boy Arthur and the rest of their year. I thought of myself as a young boy on the sofa with my mum watching Marlon Brando and falling irrevocably in love with an idea, with a fantasy. Then of Nina as a girl, doing musical numbers in sports halls with Liv and Tommy watching enraptured, of the girl in the playground transforming into a tree in front of my eyes, discovering a force within her she'd never even imagined. Jonathan was right in as many ways as he was wrong.

He put his hand on my shoulder. I wasn't sure he'd ever

touched me before. It didn't feel unpleasant. Jonathan moved to the door, found it locked, unlocked it.

'Bertolt Brecht, for all his theorising about what theatre could mean, had a favourite phrase, very simple, against which he tested everything he did,' Jonathan said, pausing before he opened the door to leave. '"The proof of the pudding is in the eating."'

I looked up, expecting him to turn, wanting him to look at me, but he stayed fixed on the gowns hanging on a hook in front of him.

'The past is the past. Look at where you are.'

He opened the door and left.

I stood up, retired to where he'd been by the toilet stalls, doubled over almost at the thought I'd let a boy die to please some brainwashed curiosity. My eye was drawn to a clothes rail, mostly empty hangers, on the end of which were three thick leather belts. I took one of them off, pulled it taut, tested its strength. Opposite the toilet stalls there were two large shower cubicles, obscured by shower-curtains. I went over to look at how the shower rail was fitted on one of them, metal brackets screwed into white tiles, before yanking hard at it, seeing if it would come away in my hand. I threw the belt around my shoulders and pulled down on the rail with both hands, most of my weight. It bowed in the middle but supported me.

I looked at the ends of the belt lying over my lapels like I'd loosened my tie, trying to work it out. If a person wanted to, I'd read it was possible for them to hang themselves by attaching a rope to a door handle and leaning forward. I put the belt around my neck and tried to loop it around the rail. It seemed too short. I watched myself struggling to get the loose end through the buckle when I heard the dressing-room door slamming open.

I stepped out from behind the dividing wall back into the main room and Amber stood in front of me, hair cut short, wearing a cheap, strappy lilac dress. She looked at me, startled, before her eyes went to the security pass I'd been fiddling with standing on the table. I remembered I'd seen the woman pictured on it chatting with the girl who looked like Amber on the balcony when I'd been with Carl Dillane. Amber must have seen her without her pass and gone looking for it. I crossed swiftly and picked it up, twisting the chord around my wrist.

'Adam,' she said.

I shook my head, took my phone out, got Vanessa's number up, ready to get Lyndon and his attack-dogs to escort Amber out of the building.

'I only wanted to feel close to Pat. It wasn't some plan. When I went for the job, I just wanted to feel close to him.'

I paused with my thumb over the button. She blinked, closed the door behind her, moving forward. '"I know you all, and will awhile uphold the unyoked humour of your idleness. Yet herein will I imitate the sun—"' Patrick's audition speech, Prince Hal. I remember watching him do it in our first week at The Conservatoire, feeling sure I'd never have what it took if that was the standard expected of me.

'He did it for me hundreds of times before he got into that place, I was five years old but I can still remember it, us hid in the utility room so Dad didn't make any comments. He was the sun for me, Adam. When he died, everything felt dark, for so long.' I noticed strands of Irish woven into her Edinburgh burr. I couldn't believe I hadn't noticed it before. 'I didn't even find out how he died until I was sixteen. We'd moved to Scotland, but father still wouldn't let my mum tell me. Can you imagine?'

I couldn't.

'I went to Uni, tried to do plays, Pat had given me a love for it, even so young, but I wasn't any good. I had no idea what I wanted to do after Uni, so when I came out and saw a job for Van's agency and found out she represented you, it felt like a sign.'

'You knew I trained with him?'

'I saw *Coward* when I was a teenager. Playing this guy everyone thought was a hero who was so deeply flawed, so vulnerable, for me that was Patrick. Mum told me you'd been in Pat's class. I applied, as a punt, but got the job. When I found out Vanessa had been at The Church as well, I wanted to tell you, I did. I kept thinking there'd be some moment at Cannes, sipping champagne on the Croisette as the sun went down, where I'd be able to tell you both without it feeling like some stalker-y surprise.'

'Better than on Oscar night.'

'But also, I really liked the job, didn't want to risk losing it. When I saw how seriously you took your craft, how much you cared about the audience, I felt like Pat would have been the same. And Van was inspirational. She didn't take any shit, wasn't always easy to work for, but she was so dedicated to you. I felt like I'd finally landed in a good place.'

'What are you doing here?' I said, phone screen having gone black as she spoke. The awards on the screens around us tumbled onwards as we stood in uneasy conference. I would have to leave soon, I had to call Vanessa, but somehow, I didn't.

'I didn't think I'd need to be here. But you just kept defending him.'

'Jonathan.'

'I'd see you after rehearsals with him on *Woodsman*, like you'd come back from a massacre. I started to get a horrible feeling. Mum told me Cill always blamed The Conservatoire for what Pat did, and I knew Jonathan had been directing you both at the time. After that last take, I was sure. I didn't hear what he said to you, but your performance, watching it on the monitor, felt like being stabbed. That night, playing you his voice, it was too much. I read too many plays at Uni, managed to convince myself some Banquo's ghost, *Play's the Thing* crap would get you to face up to whatever it was you'd done to Pat. But finding you in the bath, nearly—' She looked at me, the memory of her rescuing me vivid in her eyes. 'I had no idea what happened with Patrick. I realised I had to just leave it, move on. But then months later you said you owed that man everything. And after that first post I was sure you'd stop. I didn't expect some big thing disowning Jonathan, but it would have been so easy to just step away from him. But you all, you closed ranks, went further, even after we knew what happened to Lyndsey, bigging him up at the BAFTAs like a God. I went into Van's emails, saw they'd changed the ending of the screen-play to make it more like Pat and—' She sighed, shook her head before fixing me with those eyes, Patrick's eyes. 'I was so sure, as we learnt more about what happened with Lyndsey and Raya, I was certain you'd come out and take a stand. But I realised I'd bought into the characters you'd played. Damaged but eventually heroic, that was your stock-in-trade. I kept expecting it to happen.'

'Why didn't you say something?' I said, phone still poised, twisting the security pass in my spare hand. 'If I'd known you were Patrick's sister . . . Why didn't you just tell me?'

'"Who will believe thee, Isabel?" That's what Angelo says in *Measure for Measure*. Who's going to believe a girl no one knows against a movie star, his untouchable teacher, the most intimidating talent manager in Hollywood with her NDAs, her army of lawyers.' As if Amber had sum-moned her, my phone started vibrating in my hand, Van's name on the screen. I'd been gone a long time. I glanced at one of the plasma screens as the camera swept over the audience, almost expecting Van to be stood in the aisle waving, telling me to pick up my fucking phone. I glanced at a mantelpiece behind me – miniature Oscar-shaped creams, shower gels, lotions, sitting in baskets – let the phone ring out.

361

Amber came closer, leaning on the table next to us. I almost thought she'd take the phone out of my hand.

'I do not forgive you, Adam,' she said. 'You should have stopped Pat.'

I felt my chin quivering, thinking about what Jonathan had said, that I'd wanted to see, see if he would do it, horrified anew at what I'd done.

'But you told me you wanted to confess, after seeing Nina, you needed to tell me.'

I thought of Nina, of the life we could have rebuilt if I hadn't left Patrick in The Church that night, how the light in her eyes from our swim together had been extinguished by the thought she'd been responsible for his death. I felt my grip on the lanyard loosening, the pass slipping towards the floor.

'Maybe you think your life, your career so far, has been to make up for what happened that night, but submerging yourself in characters, in imaginary worlds, it's not atonement. Lyndsey, Raya, Patrick. How many others?'

My phone buzzed again, Vanessa. I heard voices outside in the hallway.

There were only four or five awards before mine, a search party would have been sent out. Amber reached forward and took hold of the lanyard's chord. The woman whose it was, was one of the Academy directors. The pass would give Amber access to anywhere in the auditorium.

I answered the phone.

'I'm upstairs, first dressing room you get to,' I said, cutting off Van's machine-gun swearing about where I was.

362

Amber held her breath, eyes growing wide, grip tightening on the pass.

'On my way back down.' I let Amber take the lanyard from me, made my way out of the dressing room, taking the stairs two at a time and, on hearing the swelling applause of another award waning, jogged towards the doors to get in just before they closed.

I was hurried down the aisle by an assistant, like Amber had been to me just a few weeks before. Carl Dillane gave me a raised eyebrow at my extended absence. Van caught my eye and blew her fringe up theatrically in relief. I ambled towards my seat and glanced at Jonathan who was staring at me as I passed. He widened his eyes in expectation. I gave him nothing, face a blank page as his had been to me so many times before.

I took my seat and watched, unblinking though not taking in anything going on around me. When Brendan Fraser strolled onto the stage to present the award before mine, Best Actress, my veins started to itch like I was going cold turkey. I stared at where he'd walked on from, looking to see if Amber was lurking in the wings, no idea what was going to happen, what I wanted to happen. As the winner was announced and the old-stager Lydia Bray was helped up to receive her award, I felt the camera turn on me for my reaction, knowing I was next.

As they led Lydia off, I felt like I was on fire and had to grip the armrest to stop myself hyperventilating. My phone felt large in my pocket, still time for one last call to Vanessa, to her Batphone to security.

Last year's best actress Michelle Yeoh came onto the stage and gave her introduction before reading out the nominees. Just as she was about to get to my name, I saw a flash of shimmering purple behind a knot of black-clad technicians standing in the wings.

She got to the end of the list, the envelope in her hand seeming to glow to me as if radioactive. Clips of our performances played on the enormous screen above the stage and just as it got to mine, the moment I first see Louanne's body hanging, I turned round and looked at Jonathan. I tensed my jaw, face breaking into a sustained smile. My heartbeat seemed to grow to double, triple the size in my chest. Jonathan's brows knitted together, confused, for once unable to decipher what it was going on in my head. I turned back to the stage, closed my eyes.

'And the winner is,' Michelle said. I heard the envelope snap open like a knot slamming down on a wooden balustrade. She scrabbled with the paper for a moment, paused. 'Adam Sealey.' Shockwaves of whoops and applause spread out from where I was sitting. Hands were thrust out for me to shake, arms laced my shoulder, my head, but I kept my hands in my lap. I remained where I was. One or two bemused faces got in front of me, offered to help me stand up, as if I was paralysed by shock, but I didn't take their offers, stayed in my seat.

Amber emerged from the wings, holding something in her hand. People in black clothing tried to stop her, the presenter, bigwigs at the side looked to me. I stood up and the clenched room relaxed. But I didn't move from where

I sat, just made a gesture to the suited men on each side of Amber trying to remove her, telling them to stand down. I turned and saw Van, somewhere near the back looking at me, mouth pursed in cold, resigned fury.

Amber got to the lectern, a confused Michelle raised a whimsical smile at the audience, the cameras, shrugged and then proffered my Oscar to Amber, but she rejected it, refused to take it. She brought her hand up and I saw she was holding a little shiny red disc, my confession. The room was in a state of mild uproar so I swung around, put my finger to my lips, demanding silence. They obeyed.

'My brother Patrick Moran was at The Conservatoire of the Dramatic Arts with Adam Sealey. And he died there,' Amber began.

I turned and made the long walk towards the exit as Amber told the world as much as she could about what happened in the forty-five seconds before she was escorted off stage. I didn't look at Jonathan as I passed and, as I came out into the blistering light of the main lobby, I prayed Nina was sat watching in her little house by the sea.

V.iv

I expected Van to come home to our house; I'd got a car back as soon as I left. I wasn't sure what she'd do, barrack me, cry into my arms, stab me in the throat with an iPad stylus. But she didn't come, sent a message saying we'd talk in the morning.

Amber released the tape to a British paper. Because of how big the story had become, there was no question of getting an injunction, undoubtedly it was in the public interest. I wasn't sure about the NDAs but I couldn't see Van or Delilah would want to further besmirch their ravaged brands by going after Patrick's baby sister. My confession tape from the back of the car on the M20 went viral. I sounded much drunker than I thought I had been. The incident overshadowed the Oscars ceremony. I was barred from the Academy and all the discussions we'd been involved with for future projects were abruptly ended.

The following afternoon Van and I parted company.

I was swimming when she arrived, done about a hundred lengths, having no idea what else I was supposed to do with myself. She had brought me a vat of cut mango and smoothies we allowed to grow warm in the California heat.

'I have to try and save the agency,' she said, once I was wrapped in a towel and sat opposite her on our rattan sofa. This was inevitable, I had left her no choice, but the idea of being cut adrift was as hollowing as a bereavement.

'Can we hug?' I said after a few minutes where we didn't know what to say to each other.

'I'd like that,' she said with the only waver I'd heard in her voice since Patrick died. I came over to sit next to her and we held each other, listening to planes flying over us into LAX, before pulling apart and smiling at each other like old friends.

'You're a fucking nightmare,' she said.

'Your nightmare, least I was.'

'You'll always be my nightmare,' she said. Soon after, she left.

The furore led several ex-Conservatoire students to go public about their run-ins with Jonathan Dors. Some defended him, but most didn't. Although he didn't work there, the scandal gave the University the excuse they needed to upgrade their death-by-a-thousand-cuts policy to a more brutal beheading as they closed the school permanently.

There was a boy who'd left four years before who revealed he'd fallen into self-harm after working with Jonathan. His family, rich with the right lawyers, kicked up enough of a fuss to launch a criminal investigation into Jonathan and the school. Fourteen people came forward.

Neither Raya nor Lyndsey involved themselves, though ironically Arthur did. I'd seen him in a commercial where he popped his head out of a bath of coffee beans, so I'm not sure how much he added to the case.

The investigation would run out of steam after several years, but by that stage, Jonathan was unwell. The damage to his reputation, his work, everything he stood for had been terminal, which, as anyone who knew him would agree, was a far worse punishment than prison.

By that time, I'd moved down to the coast by Dungeness. I'd visited on a whim. The landscape reminded me of the moon or the Wild West, bereft like a vacant movie lot. I found a converted train carriage on the beach for sale and offered to buy it that day. Without a career I had nothing tying me to London, to LA, to anywhere anymore.

I didn't really visit on a whim. I'd started my trip driving down to nearby Hythe. After I'd turned down the Oscar, I had a ridiculous notion Nina would get in touch, not straight away, but I hoped the truth might allow some reconciliation between us. When I didn't hear anything, after months telling myself I would, I rented a car one day and drove down to see her. I sat in the shelter for four hours waiting for the Hythe Mermaids. Eventually, I saw them gathering on the beach, the ease between them, the laughs and life as they plunged into the cold water, reminded me how we'd all been at first at The Conservatoire, a merry band, bonded by a shared purpose, a quest to transcend. I went back to my car and drove twenty minutes down the coast, where I stayed.

For the first few months, I hoped we might bump into each other walking on the beach, but I found it exposing being out in the world with everyone knowing what I'd done. I never went into town, didn't go for coffee or to pubs in the neighbouring villages, so it never happened. I didn't want to upend her life again, being near her started to be enough for me. I swam a lot, walked, read books – never plays – my life became small and, unencumbered by the lie I'd had to live with, things in my head became calmer.

Then Vanessa rang to tell me Jonathan didn't have long to live. I went to the station as soon as we got off the phone. Within a couple of hours, I was standing at the door of his flat.

'Adam?' the community nurse who opened the door said to me.

'Did he know I was coming?'

'No, no,' she said, laughing. She was a statuesque woman in her fifties, a smile so genuine it felt like it should be on her CV. 'I've seen your films. Do come in.' The smell of mulch was gone, the cigarette smoke now ancient. 'He's a bit sleepy,' the nurse said, pointing me towards the kitchen. I walked in to see all the pots and pans, all the houseplants I remembered, gone. The sofa I'd woken up on in his house had been turned around and faced his beloved garden, which had become overgrown.

I walked to the foot of the sofa and my breath caught as I saw him propped against cushions, staring at the sky. He seemed shrunken, skin sucked into his bone, eyes narrowed to olive-pits at the back of his skull. But when he turned and fixed me with them, they'd lost none of their gorgon stare. He struggled to lift a hand, telling me to sit. I brought a footrest over and sat next to him. I found myself taking his fingers in mine. They felt like a bunch of dry twigs. I wanted to be able to hate him.

'Adam,' he said, the division bell gong of his voice now little more than a creaking hinge. 'I—' He tried to clear his throat, find moisture in his mouth.

I looked around and found a child's sippy-cup of water and put it to his lips.

He drank and nodded for me to take it away. 'You were always good.' He turned, huffed a strangled breath. 'But, I saw at your audition, how you looked when you talked about your mother. You didn't want to be happy. You didn't think you deserved it. Ingram said I was the same. He said it's why he chose me.' He coughed, blinked his eyes closed. 'You had to be great, Adam. You had to be. It didn't matter what happened to you, what happened to me.'

'To Patrick?'

'No,' he said, voice louder. 'No.' His hand slackened. It felt cold, lifeless in mine. 'You had to be great.'

'Was I?' I said. He closed his eyes, gave a slow shrug, which made me laugh. I watched his chest rising and falling in laboured breaths, the bones at the top of his ribcage like his steepled hands on the desk in his teaching room.

'You'll be remembered,' he said in a whisper.

'No, I won't,' I said.

One of his eyes opened, he shifted to listen.

'No one who matters will remember us.'

His jaw tensed beneath parchment-paper skin.

'When I die, I'll be a bunch of worthy tweets for twenty-four hours. In fifty years, I'll be a couple of movies, three if I'm lucky, watched by film students, wannabe actors and people boring their dates about their passion for cinema.'

He tried to pull his hand away from mine, but I held on.

'You won't even have that much. You killed The Conservatoire, destroyed Ingram's work, even if an actor did use some of your method now, he'd never dare tell anyone.' He stopped trying to pull his hand away, so I placed it gently on his chest. His breathing was ragged, reedy air fighting up his throat. The nurse heard him and arrived at the doorway. She made a face telling me to go. Jonathan's eyes were full of such terror I wanted to hold him, but I resisted.

'Last scene of all,' I said. 'That ends this strange eventful history, is second childishness and mere oblivion. Sans teeth, sans eyes, sans taste—' I leant into him, perhaps the nurse unsighted by the sofa thought I was planting a kiss on his forehead. I whispered into his ear. 'Sans everything.'

There was a memorial service three months later. Van came with me.

'Letting you go alone would be tantamount to criminal negligence,' she said when I told her she didn't have to accompany me.

It was held at The Church, which had been bought by a Turkish philanthropist and turned into a community art gallery. Room 1 had been transformed. The walls and pillars had been painted white, stage removed, the balcony too. In their place was a white-wall blank canvas. We took a seat at the back. There was no casket, no coffin. They'd burned his body the day after he died, as were his wishes.

Although there were thirty or forty people there, more than I'd expected, there was no family, no one I didn't recognise as having something to do with the theatre. Aggie was holding court. Although she and Jonathan were never more than colleagues, it seemed she'd organised everything. I'd find out later Jonathan left his estate, his flat in Hampstead, to The Conservatoire. As it was no longer operating, Aggie put the money into a trust in Ingram Dander's name. They asked me to be a trustee, but I suggested Emmy Reed. She's using the money to incorporate talking therapy sessions into the training at three of the top drama schools.

A humanist officiator talked about Jonathan's achievements, about Ingram and the lineage that went all the way back to 'the great Stanislavski.' He reeled off a list of The Conservatoire's illustrious students, the people we used to talk about like saints. She included my name. People turned round to look, some with barely concealed hatred for what I'd done to their mentor, some with pity, others amused.

Omar Fox-Daniels did a bit of *Cymbeline*, did it masterfully, but no tears were shed. The people there owed Jonathan so much but no one was sad he was gone. As Nina said that day by the sea, an idea can never love you back.

There was a table of warm white wine in the corridor where we used to change into our ballet jockstraps. I wanted to leave, but Van suggested we stay for a while. I discovered why when Emmy's agent, Benny, strode into The Church like the best man at a wedding. He made a beeline for us and gave Van a hug that told me she'd been expecting him. Van said she was going to 'leave the two of us to get acquainted'.

'You're an actor, Ad,' she said, giving me a kiss on my unshaven cheek. 'There really is nothing else you can do.' She left the building with the swagger of someone who was never coming back. Benny grabbed two wines and took me into what was Varda's studio which, despite the refurbishment, still smelt of feet.

Benny wanted to represent me and laid it on thick. He had an offer for the second series of a big streaming show, an ensemble piece, a chance to remind the world what I could do. I'd not seen the show, but it was universally adored, set around a group home for troubled teenagers. It was a show about good people trying to survive in near-impossible circumstances. As I stood there in the place it all started, I felt the yearning for the feel of a script in my hand, the lights, the camaraderie of the crew, the world shrink-wrapping around you when you're in the moment with another actor.

'Why are you doing this?' I asked him. 'Did Van put you up to it?'

'You make people feel something, Adam. We all need that.'

'Am I not too toxic?'

'People love a redemption story. You've probably never been in a stronger position.'

I nodded, wondering if I could throw myself into that headspace again, creating truth in a world where nothing is real. I looked at the corner I'd bashed my hip the evening Jonathan ghosted in and changed my life.

'I can't,' I said.

'Why not?'

'I just can't.'

Benny looked at the sprung floor. 'This was not what I was expecting,' he said. He drank down one of the glasses of wine, handed me the other, which sat in my hand warm and untouched. He pointed a finger into the air like he'd just had the idea. 'This is cheeky, but I have sounded out a few production companies that want to option your story, leading up to Oscar night—'

'Absolutely not,' I said, laughing.

'You could play yourself?'

'I respect the chutzpah, but the answer is no.'

Benny nodded and shook my hand. 'I'm going to try and wear you down.'

'You'd have to kill me first.'

Benny weighed it up before patting me on the shoulder, telling me we'd get lunch, and 'leaving me to grieve'. I stayed in the studio for a moment, thought about doing a bit of *Hamlet*, before shaking myself with a cringe at the pretention and leaving.

I walked down the steps, out the gates of The Church grounds. On the other side of the street, wrapped in an orange coat, stood Amber. I crossed the road to her.

'This doesn't feel right,' I said, after a few moments' silence.

'What doesn't?' A black cab turned the corner. I went into the street and waved it down. She looked well, freckles overlaid a golden tan. I opened the door for her, and she got in.

'Isn't that better?' I said, sitting opposite, closing the door.

'Where are we going?' the driver said.

'Where do you live?' I asked.

'Lisbon.'

'Not sure he'll take us there.'

'Pity. The Southbank, please,' she said. The cab pulled away from The Church. Amber watched the pillars receding behind us.

'You're a long way from home.'

'I'm here for work.'

'What's work?'

'Doing a masters. I want to do a doctorate.'

'In what?'

'Neuroscience. I'm getting help from the doctor we met in Essex.' The cab slowed as we crossed the bridge onto Camden High Street. She told me she and her mum had moved to Lisbon a few weeks after the Oscars. The press had found them in Edinburgh and wouldn't leave them alone, so they decided it would be good for both of them to make a fresh start somewhere warmer.

'Why did you come to The Church?' I said, as we moved through the converted factories of King's Cross. 'Make sure he was dead?'

'I wanted to see you. Check you were OK.'

'And?'

'You need a haircut, starting to look like the woodsman again.'

I felt the unruly tufts on the side of my head.

'But also,' she said, 'I want to scan you.'

'Scan me?'

'We're doing brain scans of actors, when they're in character, doing Shakespeare, when they've finished a challenging role. We're trying to work out what's going on in there.' She pointed to my head. 'I wanted to scan you.'

'I'm not an actor anymore.'

'Fuck's sake, you didn't say no to Benny?'

'What?'

'Do you know how long it took me to set that up? I didn't have Van's little black book anymore. Getting a message to Emmy Reed from Portugal was like cracking the Enigma code.'

'You did that?'

She smiled.

'Why?'

'I'm a fan,' she said, turning away to the window. 'And so was Pat. I wish you'd have stopped him that night, but, he did it, you were a kid. He stepped off the chair.'

'He was amazing. I used to watch him and . . . you fell in love with him.'

'He was easy to love. Such a waste, don't let yourself be another one.'

I put my hand out for her. She kept looking out the window but took it and squeezed.

'I can't do it,' I said. 'I can't act.'

'You don't need to do penance. People don't blame you. I don't blame you.'

'Thank you, really. But I can't go back. And now, I don't have to.'

She looked at me over her shoulder.

'You'll let me scan you though?' she said, breaking into a smile.

'Talk to my people.' She let my hand go. We broke into a laugh, I had tears in my eyes. The car took us down to Waterloo where I dropped Amber off. She had tickets to see a show at the Old Vic.

Just under a year later, I was sitting at the back of my train carriage looking out at a horizon of shingle. It was late autumn and a light rain pattered the pebbles in front of me. The sun was setting through strings of cloud over the sea, a view that, even having been there four years by that stage, I hadn't tired of.

I glanced at the crop of cacti I'd planted around the old rowing boat I'd got neighbours to help me drag into my garden, worrying the rain might make them rot. I'd been restoring the boat for the last few months. I'd stripped the paint off, so it was down to the wood, no sense of what I was going to do with it. It wasn't going out on the sea again. I thought I'd fill it with pots of flowering perennials. Keeping anything alive in Britain's only desert was an uphill battle, but I'd learnt to accept it. I didn't want immortality anymore.

I heard a sound in the distance. I turned down the record I'd had on, put down my mug of tea. The gentle screech of metal, an old bike, continued for some time, then stopped. I moved through the carriage to listen.

Steps on the pebbles outside. Most of the places here were second homes, rented to holidaymakers, so at this time of year there were very few other people here. The footsteps approached the house and I went to meet them, moving into the hallway. Whoever it was stepped onto the wooden pathway I'd built over the shingle leading to my door. A wedge of something poked through the letter box. A rolled-up newspaper. It dropped onto the hall floor with a thud and unfurled.

The local paper. On the front page there was a picture of the decrepit Manville Cinema, a crowd of smiling faces in front of its art-deco sign, lit up for the first time in thirty years. I knelt and opened the paper onto a double-page spread about the reopening of the two-screen old building up the way in Dymchurch. Someone had circled a paragraph in green biro that talked about how Oscar-nominated former actor and local resident Adam Sealey had made a major contribution to the cinema's reopening. I hadn't wanted to be mentioned but the organisers were very sweet and said it would be beneficial for the project.

There was a scrawled note, the same biro, in the top margin. *Local resident! Were you never going to tell me?* Followed by a mobile phone number.

I looked through the window into the black, but no one was there. I closed my eyes, stomach tight at the thought she was here. I dropped the paper back to the floor and turned, not knowing where to be.

Then I heard the squeak of a floorboard on the path outside. I grabbed the door open and there she was. Damp curls framing a heart-shaped face, illuminated by the lamps of my hallway like she'd been lit by a cinematographer: Nina.

Acknowledgments

I'm deeply humbled and grateful you've chosen to spend your time reading this book.

Firstly, I want to thank everyone at Penguin Michael Joseph. Like all great producers, Joel Richardson saw in my manuscript a story he wanted to share with the world and helped me craft and elevate it to a place I never would have been able to get to on my own. I'm hugely grateful to the inventiveness and graft of my PR supremo Olivia Thomas, to Jennifer Breslin for her marketing masterstrokes and everyone else at PMJ who have been a joy to work with from the off.

Moving on to my agent, Juliet Mushens, whose faith in the idea for this book, despite the many iterations and dead-ends we navigated together, was unwavering even when mine wasn't. For the record, Vanessa was not based on her, even though they do share a tigerish passion for their clients. With thanks also to Rachel Neely, Kiya Evans, Liza De Block and everyone else at Mushens Entertainment for their various reads, thoughts and support.

Huge thanks to Amber Trentham for her help both with plotting and moral support in the writing trenches, to Natalie Hadlow-Wood for helping me to see myself, to Sam H Freeman, Natalie Bray, James Kemp, Rory Murphy, Gommie, my drama school WhatsApp group and any other members of Group 46 who shared their war-stories and thoughts about our time training to be actors. To every actor I've worked with and actors everywhere, thank you for digging deep and 'going there', for entertaining us and moving us. It is a special kind of bravery.

I want to thank my brother and his family for their continued belief, my mum for being such a special and inspirational person, and Frankie my co-dependent dog for all the love.

I can feel the stage manager telling me to wind this up, but finally, boundless love, gratitude and respect to my wife Joanna who is my rock and does so much to support and encourage me in my work. And to Otis and Sadie to whom this book is dedicated. Every day you give me life.